THRESHOLD

Other Books by Bill Myers

The Face of God
Blood of Heaven
Fire of Heaven
The Bloodstone Chronicles
Threshold Audio Pages®
Eli
McGee and Me (children's book/video series)
The Incredible Worlds of Wally McDoogle
    (children's comedy series)
Secret Agent Dingledorf and His Trusty Dog, Splat
    (children's comedy series)
Blood Hounds Inc. (children's mystery series)
Faith Encounter (teen devotional)
Forbidden Doors (teen series)
The Dark Side of the Supernatural
Hot Topics, Tough Questions

Novellas
When the Last Leaf Falls

visit Bill's website at www.Billmyers.com

THRESHOLD

Are his supernatural gifts
the work of God ...
or Satan?

BILL
MYERS

ZONDERVAN™

GRAND RAPIDS, MICHIGAN 49530 USA

We want to hear from you. Please send your comments
about this book to us in care of the address below.
Thank you.

ZONDERVAN™

Threshold
Copyright © 1997 by Bill Myers

This title is also available as a Zondervan audio product. Visit
www.zondervan.com/audiopages for more information.

Requests for information should be addressed to:

Zondervan, *Grand Rapids, Michigan 49530*

ISBN: 0-310-25111-7

All rights reserved. No part of this publication may be reproduced,
stored in a retrieval system, or transmitted in any form or by any
means — electronic, mechanical, photocopy, recording, or any
other — except for brief quotations in printed reviews, without the
prior permission of the publisher.

All Scripture quotations, unless otherwise indicated, are taken from
the *Holy Bible: New International Version*®. NIV®. Copyright ©
1973, 1978, 1984 by International Bible Society. Used by permission of Zondervan. All rights reserved.

Published in association with the literary agency of Alive Commu-
nications, Inc., 7680 Goddard Street, Suite 200, Colorado Springs,
CO 80920.

Interior design by Tracey Moran

Printed in the United States of America

02 03 04 05 06 07 08 /❖ OP/ 10 9 8 7 6 5 4 3 2 1

Another one for Brenda . . .
who has stayed faithful for richer or poorer,
better or worse . . .
and everything in between.
Thanks for hanging in there with me.

I f I've learned anything in writing this book it's that truth can indeed be stranger than fiction. As with *Blood of Heaven* I've tried to make all of the science as accurate as possible—which includes the paranormal research being conducted to one degree or another in laboratories around the world. The same can be said regarding the various supernatural experiences. Except for the climax, which is more symbolic and allegorical in nature, most of the mentioned encounters have to one degree or another been experienced, documented, or verified by myself or others. When it comes to these two areas, science and the supernatural, I'm afraid what fiction I've added only pales by comparison.

My research began as early as 1976 when John Smalley, Keith Green, and I were involved in the deliverance of an influential West Coast psychic from intense demonic activity. It was then the story began to take shape. I wanted to show how crafty and deceptive the Adversary can be in comparison to the purity and power of Jesus Christ.

Other elements came from my trips around the world as a film director for various mission groups. The spiritual warfare some of these men and women are waging overseas is worth a book in itself.

Recently, I've spent hours in prison interviewing David Berkowitz, the serial killer once known as the Son of Sam—a man who had been deep into the occult and who was charged with shooting thirteen people, but who is now a dedicated brother in Christ.

There was also an extensive and gracious conversation with Dr. Edwin May, who for twenty years headed up a psychic research program for the CIA and who also provided the information on current Russian progress in this field. Dr. Richard S. Broughton was kind enough to speak with me and allow me to visit the Institute for Parapsychology, one of the top psychic research labs in the world.

There were also numerous conversations with pastors, physicists, medical researchers, and followers of Eastern religions.

Their stories and research were both encouraging and chilling. Encouraging in that their ongoing studies clearly demonstrate the presence of a supernatural world and the power of faith. Chilling in that sometimes many of these well-meaning men and women are entering into areas of the occult without even knowing it.

Grateful appreciation also goes to Dr. Schelbert, the Biochemical Engineering and Nuclear Medicine department at UCLA, Dr. Craig Cameron, David Carini, Angie Hunt, Al Janssen, Scott Kennedy, Jim Bass, Lynn Marzulli, Aggie Villanueva, Julie LaFata, Kenneth and Rebecca McCrocklin, Heinz and Maria Fussle, and to Thomas Gray for his "Elegy Written in a Country Churchyard." Special thanks also to Doug McIntosh, a talented writer who served as my research assistant, as well as to my agent and friend, Greg Johnson.

9

Writing a novel is one thing. Getting it ready out there for reading is another. And for that I want to thank the Zondervan team from sales, to marketing, to editorial. You folks are amazing.

And for their ongoing intercession I want to thank Greg Dix, Gary Gilmore, Robin Jones Gunn, Rebecca and Scott Janney, Lissa Halls Johnson, Larry LaFata, Lynn and Peggy Marzulli, Dorothy Moore, Bill Myers Sr., James Riordan, Carla Williams, as well as my extended family, John Tolle, Bill Burnett, Gary Smith, Tom Kositchek, Cathy Glass, Criz Hibdon, Mark Brown, and Dave Wray.

Finally and always, thanks to Brenda, Nick, and the Mack.

For our struggle is not against flesh and blood, but against the rulers, against the authorities, against the powers of this dark world and against the spiritual forces of evil in the heavenly realms.

EPHESIANS 6:12

PROLOGUE

The sand is hot. It sears the bottoms of her feet, raising welts wherever it touches, but she feels nothing. She never does.

The scorching wind makes her eyes water. It whips and tears at her faded housedress, but it carries no heat.

It never does.

Grains of sand bite into her face, chapping her cheeks. Talcum-fine grit works its way deep into her nappy hair, into the creases of her mottled black skin, beneath the elastic band of her dress. But it doesn't matter. None of it matters.

Gerty has stood in this desert, at this riverbank, a hundred times. A hundred times she has waited, and a hundred times she has been disappointed.

Once again she hears faint gurgling. She looks at the river—at a small patch of water. It is starting to boil. It always begins this way. Slowly. First one bubble. Then another. Then another and another and another, and faster and faster the bubbles rise until the small area in the river churns furiously.

Gerty struggles to hold back her excitement. She has come this far many times before.

She steps into the river. There is no sensation of warmth, or cold, or wet. Just the knowledge that once again she is in the river.

She sloshes toward the bubbles. Her dress wraps around her legs, binding her movement. She thinks of hiking it above her waist. But there is always the chance that this will be the time, and she would not dare stand half naked. Not on holy ground.

She arrives at the patch of boiling water. Steam rolls up and blows into her face. She blinks, squinting through it.

And then it happens . . .

A small dark form appears under the water. For a moment it looks like a fish, but as it surfaces it is obvious that this is no fish. It is a piece of metal. Iron. An ax head.

Maybe this will be the time.

The boiling comes to a stop. Now there is absolute silence as the last wisps of steam disappear. The ax head continues floating on the water as effortlessly as a newly fallen leaf.

This is the crucial part. She hopes, she prays that it will not disappear as it has so many times in the past. She takes a breath to steady herself, and finally she reaches for it. The tips of her fingers touch the cool surface.

Yes, cool. It is a sensation. A feeling. For the first time the ax head has substance. She can actually feel it!

Carefully she scoops it from the water, fearing that any minute it will dissolve and slip through her trembling fingers.

But it doesn't.

Tightness grows in her throat. Her eyes burn with tears of gratitude, but she blinks them back as she turns the ax head over and over in her hands.

This is the time.

Then she sees it. Senses it, really. The light. It hovers over the bank of the river. Brighter than the sun, so brilliant that it is difficult for her to distinguish any shape or detail, though for the briefest moment, she catches a glimpse of what could *be wheels . . . and eyes. The rest is light. Everywhere light. And sound, like a roaring waterfall. But there is no waterfall in this river. The sound comes from the light.*

Fear and awe grip Gerty; tears spill onto her cheeks. She hears the voice. It has been there all along—in the roar. It is the roar. It thunders all around her, yet resonates gently through her body. It is all-powerful and infinitely tender:

"HIS TIME HAS COME."

Gerty nods, the tears now flowing freely. Through her blurry vision she sees movement in front of her. A young man with long, dark hair is kneeling in the water. He wears a coarse, burlap robe. He is kneeling exactly where the water had been boiling. He looks up to her with gray, penetrating eyes. They are filled with fear and confusion. But, even more alarming, they are filled with a lack of hope. Gerty's heart swells with compassion. She has known of him since he was a child, has prayed and interceded for him these many years. She wants to comfort him, to encourage him, but he bows his head before she has a chance to speak.

She looks back up into the light, puzzled. But the light gives no answer. There is only the tender, thundering, consuming roar.

She feels the ax head move in her hands. She watches in alarm as it grows soft, starting to melt.

No. Please, dear God!

Has she come this far only to fail again?

And still it melts, becoming nothing but a puddle in her hands.

But only for a moment.

Immediately it reshapes itself. She watches in amazement as it grows, as its texture shifts from cool metal to rough,

*porous clay. Seconds later she is holding a squatty cylinder—
a flask. The ax head has become an ancient clay flask.*

*Joy floods through her. It radiates into her arms, her
hands, even her fingertips. This is what she has been waiting
for. This is what she has been hoping and praying for.*

*Instinctively, she removes the flask's stopper. Her hands
tremble in excitement. Without a word, she tilts the flask and
a thick, clear oil spills over its lip, falling in uneven spurts
onto the boy's head.*

*Her tears turn to quiet sobs. "Thank you . . . Thank you,
thank you . . ."*

*As the last of the oil drains, the light before her begins to
dim. The roar also fades. The boy, the river, everything
around her wavers like a mirage until, in a matter of
moments, they have all disappeared.*

Gerty Morrison opened her eyes. She was back
home, still kneeling before her bed. She kept her head
bowed, resting it on the thin, worn mattress that had
become soaked with her tears as she continued to pray,
"Thank you, dear Lord. Thank you, thank you . . ."

PART ONE

B randon hated it. How many years had they been pulling these stupid pranks? Three? Four? Ever since they were seniors in high school. Sure, it was fun back then, back when they were kids. But now it was getting old. Real old.

But not for Frank. Frank thrived on it.

Brandon stood alone, inside the giant trophy case. With a roll of gray duct tape in hand he carefully worked his way past the cups, plaques, signed bats, tournament balls, pennants, group photos, silver plates, silver bowls, and other awards on display. Bethel Lake Country Club prided itself on its members' athletic prowess. And if you couldn't tell it by their arrogance, you could see it in the new trophy room they were about to dedicate—a room complete with this enormous, dust-proof trophy case that covered nearly the entire front wall.

Frank was right about one thing. Pride and pretension like this couldn't go unrewarded. They owed it to their people. They owed it to the Townies.

Brandon tossed back his long, dark hair and knelt. He yanked off a sizable strip of duct tape and ran it along the seam, right where the clear Plexiglas wall of the trophy case met the floor. He carefully sealed it so no water would leak through.

Meanwhile, behind the back wall of the case, Del gave the Black and Decker drill the workout of its life as it moaned and groaned in his incapable hands.

"You're pushing too hard," Frank's voice whispered from behind the wall.

"No way," Del's voice answered.

Brandon glanced over his shoulder at the back of the case; the thick cherry wood bulged under Del's pressure. There was more moaning and groaning from the drill until the head of the bit popped through the wood, followed by the rest of the shank.

Then the drill stopped. Then started again. Then stopped. It was jammed.

Another start. Another stop.

Hoping to loosen it, Del began to wiggle the drill back and forth.

"Stop!" Frank's voice whispered. "You're going to break it, you're going to break the—"

SNAP!

Too late. The bit had broken off in the wall.

In the adjacent room, Tom Henderson, a twenty-one-year-old Aryan dream, complete with blonde hair and blue eyes, listened to a pompous master of ceremonies delivering another pompous speech. Tom stood with the forty or fifty other firm-bodied club members as the emcee continued his jibes at the locals:

"... can well remember when we first entered these events seven, eight years back. Why, no one ever gave a thought to Bethel Lake—unless, of course, they found themselves downwind of the hog farms."

Henderson and the crowd chuckled condescendingly. They always chuckled condescendingly when it came to Bethel Lake—at least the Bethel Lake that existed before they had moved in and started taking over. The old Bethel Lake of corn farmers and hog raisers, along with the usual variety of hicks and poor-as-dirt mobile-home owners who prided themselves on being called *Townies*.

But now things were changing. Henderson could see it every time he came back home from college. Cornfields were giving way to golf courses; three-quarter-ton pickups with gun racks were being replaced by four-wheeler yuppie mobiles. There was even talk of remodeling the bowling alley and turning it into a megabookstore with espresso bar.

In the past five years, the sleepy, Indiana farm community located just off Highway 30 between Fort Wayne and South Bend had come to life. And now it was growing faster than they could slap up townhouses and condos. Part of this was due to Orion Computech, a new computer manufacturer with a workforce of over eleven hundred and counting. Already the Chamber of Commerce was flirting with aspirations of becoming the Midwest's Silicon Valley. Besides Orion, there was the Diamond Cellular Corporation, Lasher Electronics—and, of course, Moran Research Institute.

Part think tank, part psychic research lab, the only thing more imaginative than the Institute's research were the rumors about that research. The latest had them housing extraterrestrials and breeding them with humans so we'd sweep the next Olympics. Henderson shook his head in amusement. The Townies may be ignorant, but you couldn't fault them for their lack of imagination. The truth was, no one really knew exactly what went on behind the Institute's low-lying, modernistic architecture, but the Townie rumor mills never lacked for grist.

The emcee continued to drone on as Henderson glanced at his watch. His father, a vice president at Orion, had moved here against Tom's wishes when the boy was a senior in high school. Now, home for the summer from Ball State, Henderson had to admit that the town was changing almost enough to make living in it bearable.

In the trophy case, Brandon heard Del asking from behind the wall, "What do I do now?"

"Tap it out," Frank's voice sighed. "Tap it out and get that hose in. We don't got much time."

Brandon heard the sound of something heavy, probably the drill itself, hitting the bit three, four, five times. Finally, it popped out of the hole and fell with a dull thud. He turned to see the bit rolling to a stop just a few feet from his knees.

"Bran," Frank called quietly, "aren't you finished yet?"

Brandon didn't bother answering. He smoothed the last of the tape against the Plexiglas and rose to his feet. As he crossed to the back of the case, he saw a garden hose being shoved through the newly drilled hole.

Things were right on schedule.

He stooped, opened the small door, and stepped out of the rear of the trophy case to join his partners. Frank, the leader of the three-man hit squad, was good-looking, volatile, and athletic enough to be a club member—if it hadn't been for his genealogy. He was a third-generation Townie. Del, on the other hand, wore Coke-bottle glasses and on a good day could almost stretch himself to a height of five-three.

Brandon turned to the trophy case door and ripped off one last strip of tape to seal it as Frank and Del quickly followed the hose down the hall toward the kitchen faucet.

Twenty more minutes passed before the emcee finally started winding down. Henderson sighed in relief. Earlier, he'd spotted a couple of beauties at the far end of the room, and he was hoping to introduce himself. But if the old duffer rambled on much longer, they might slip away without the pleasure of making his company.

"In short," the emcee concluded, "I can't think of a more fitting way to open the new trophy room than with the addition of the Beckman Memorial Tennis Cup."

He turned to the paneled doors behind him and, with a modest flair, slid them open.

The lights came up, and before the members stood their new trophy room. Dark cherry paneling, rich emerald carpet, paisley print chairs scattered around end tables that supported brass lamps with green china shades. And at the far wall stood the focal piece of the room: a massive Plexiglas trophy case—six feet high and eighteen feet long. Inside, near the top and center of the case, was a vacant space waiting to receive the most recent addition—a large silver trophy bowl that sat on the lectern in front of the case.

The emcee approached the lectern as the crowd moved in and settled down. "Peter? Reggie?" he called. "I think it's only proper that you two do the honors."

The group broke into polite applause as a couple of jocks, the winners of the trophy, broke from their dates and came forward. Henderson knew the guys. Even liked them. In fact, they'd spent more than one summer night cruising in his Firebird, putting down the brews. The applause increased as they arrived and held the bowl over their heads.

Meanwhile, the emcee turned to open the trophy case doors. At first they seemed stuck. Either his key wasn't working, or the doors were jammed, or . . .

Henderson was the first to spot it: the trail of tiny air bubbles rising to the surface of the case. For a moment he was confused. What on earth were air bubbles doing . . . ? Then the horror registered. He started to call out, to push his way through the crowd. But he was too late.

With one last tug, the emcee opened the doors.

Water roared out of the case, knocking him to the ground. Club members screamed and scrambled back as the water poured into the room. Some lost their balance, slipping and falling.

Across the room, through the oval window of the kitchen door, Frank and Del watched in delight. They were laughing so hard they could barely catch their breath—until Reggie, one of the fallen, rose to his feet, looked around, sputtering and coughing, and caught a glimpse of them. Frank and Del saw his eyes widen. They saw his trembling finger point. And they saw his mouth open as he cried out a single word:

"Townies!"

Frank and Del ducked from the window, but they were too late. The announcement had been made, their location spotted. Now club members slipped and sloshed toward them with a vengeance.

Brandon was standing farther back in the kitchen, checking out the contents of the stainless-steel freezers, when Frank and Del raced past and grabbed him, yelling, "Come on, come on!"

They flung open a hallway door and started down the corridor. When they rounded the first corner, they discovered most of the club members heading directly for them.

They doubled back.

Even now, running as fast as his little legs could carry him, Del couldn't resist firing off a few jabs. "'I know this place,' Frank says. 'Like the back of my hand,' he says."

"Hey," Frank shot back. "How'd I know they were going to remodel?"

They rounded another corner, then another. At last they spotted an unlikely looking door. "In here!" Frank shouted as he threw it open.

Brandon and Del followed. The door slammed behind them with a foreboding boom. Suddenly they found themselves in total darkness.

"Oh, Frank?" Del's voice echoed.

"Hold on . . ."

"Yo, Frank!"

"Relax, there's gotta be a light here somewh—"

Suddenly the overheads came on and the boys winced at the four brilliant white walls surrounding them.

Del squinted. "A racquetball court? You led us into a racquetball court!"

Before Frank could answer, the door opened and an attractive woman with amber, shoulder-length hair stood in the opening. She was a few years older than they were.

But Frank, who made it a policy to recognize any and all of the local beauties, stepped forward. "Hi," he ventured. "Uh, Sarah, isn't it?"

She simply looked at him.

He tried to smile.

So did Del.

It was a joint failure.

"Anybody in there?" a man's voice shouted from down the hall.

The woman stood silent. Still looking. Still deciding.

They fidgeted.

"Sarah?" the voice repeated.

Finally she turned and called back. "Nobody worth mentioning."

"Be careful," another voice warned as the group headed down the other hall.

Sarah didn't answer and waited for the footsteps to fade. Then, without a word, she opened the door wider and stepped back for them to exit.

Frank and Del exchanged glances, then quickly scurried past.

"Thanks, Sarah," Frank offered. Then, to further express his gratitude, he continued, "You're lookin' real good."

She ignored him and turned to Brandon.

For the briefest second their eyes locked. And for the briefest second Brandon couldn't look away. He sensed that she couldn't, either. There was a moment, a connection. He knew he should say something. Something cool, something witty. But he wasn't much good at talking to pretty women. Lately, he wasn't much good at talking to anybody. Instead, he gave a slight nod of thanks, moved past her, and headed down the hall.

The parking lot of Bethel Country Club was cut out of the side of a large hill. There was only one exit: along the bottom of the hill and down the private, tree-lined drive. Already several of the men, including Henderson and his buddies, along with a handful of women, had gathered along that drive. They stood just a few yards past the parking lot, forming a roadblock. Waiting. Watching.

"Just a matter of time," one of the men said.

"You phone the police?" a lithe blonde asked.

"Yeah, right," another scoffed. Others in the group voiced similar scorn. They knew the police didn't encourage these pranks. But they also knew they didn't *dis*courage them either. Like the kids, most of the police were Townies. Their attitude was simple: If these outsiders wanted to come barging into Bethel Lake uninvited, that was their business. But there were certain customs to be followed, certain dues to be paid—and if that included this type of occasional, low-grade harassment, then so be it. It was just normal social interaction.

A pair of headlights suddenly appeared as a half-ton pickup slid around the corner of the parking lot.

"There they are!"

It accelerated toward them.

"Hold your ground," the first man shouted. "They wouldn't dare try to—*look out!*"

Some leaped to the side of the road, others scrambled up the dirt embankment as the truck roared past.

Inside the cab of the pickup Frank yelled, "Eee-haaa!" as the last of the human roadblocks hit the bushes. "We did it, boys!" he shouted. "We did it!"

Del's voice was a little less sure as he glanced back for casualties. "This is insane!"

Brandon, who was driving, gave no response.

Meanwhile, Henderson, Peter, and Reggie scrambled to their feet and raced toward Henderson's '97 Firebird. Unfortunately, in his haste, Henderson had forgotten to turn off the alarm, and it began honking incessantly.

"Let's go, let's go!" Reggie shouted over the noise.

Henderson fumbled with the remote on his keys until he managed to shut off the alarm. They piled into his car, and he brought the 5.7-liter V–8 roaring to life. He dropped it into gear and hit the accelerator. Gravel spit in all directions as the car spun out and began pursuit.

In the pickup, Frank was exultant. "You see the look on their faces?" he cried as he popped a brew. It foamed, but he quickly slurped it up, careful not to let any get away. "I tell you, boys, I can die a happy man."

Looking over his shoulder, Del muttered, "You might get your chance."

Brandon glanced up at the mirror and saw the head-lights appear behind them. But he was unconcerned. They reached the end of the private drive, and the pickup bounced out onto the main highway.

"Who's the girl?" Brandon asked, shifting down and quickly accelerating.

"Sarah Weintraub," Frank answered through a loud belch. "Used to work at some fancy college out West."

Del watched through the back window as the pursu-ing lights bounced onto the road and continued after them. "Uh, guys?" But, as usual, the guys weren't paying him any attention.

"She started at the Institute a few months ago," Frank continued.

"She's a Techie, then?"

"Yeah."

"Too bad."

"Uh—Frank? Bran?" Del tried to keep his voice even as the approaching lights grew closer and began flashing their high beams at them.

Brandon glanced at the mirror. Then suddenly, without warning, he threw his truck into a hard left and hit the brakes.

"Brandon!" Del cried.

The truck slid sideways, its tires screaming. Del and Frank flew across the cab, but Brandon remained fixed at the wheel.

In the Firebird, Reggie shouted, "What's he doing?"

Henderson had no answer as he watched the pickup continue its spin and then bounce to a stop. It had done a complete 180 and was now facing them, headlights glaring.

Back in the cab, Frank shouted. "What's goin' on? What're you doing?"

Brandon gave no answer. He simply downshifted and stomped on the accelerator, leaving behind smoke and flying gravel as he sped toward the Firebird.

"Brandon!" Del repeated.

Brandon swerved the pickup into the Firebird's lane. *"Brandon!"*

Inside the Firebird, Henderson's mouth dropped open. The pickup was in his lane and heading directly for them.

"What's he doing?" Reggie cried.

In the pickup, Frank had the same question. "Bran— yo, Brandon?"

But Brandon didn't hear. He gripped the wheel tightly and concentrated on the lights of the Firebird.

A confused Henderson edged his car closer to the right shoulder, trying to get past.

Brandon countered by bringing his pickup just as close to the shoulder.

They were a hundred yards apart, speeding toward each other.

Reggie swore and shouted, "He's crazy! He's crazy!"

Henderson agreed. He swerved hard to the left, to the other side of the road.

Brandon followed suit. Concentrating, barely blinking.

"Brandon?" Del's voice cracked.

Brandon gave no answer.

Henderson squinted against the approaching lights of the pickup. He saw no shape, no detail, only lights—two bright beams below, and four orange running lights on top. Well, actually, three. The light over the driver's side of the cab was busted and glowed white. Desperately, Henderson whipped the Firebird back over to the far right.

The pickup duplicated his move exactly, once again heading toward him.

The vehicles were fifty yards apart now.

Back in the cab Frank began to laugh—it was the only way to hide his fear. "You're crazy, Brandon—crazy!"

Brandon's silence seemed to confirm it.

Panicking, Henderson searched for some way out, *any* way.

Thirty yards . . . twenty-five . . .

Henderson looked at the side of the road, hoping to veer off, but they were in a thick tunnel of trees.

Twenty yards.

With no other option, Henderson slammed on the brakes. Not that it would do any good. If the crazy in the pickup wanted to hit them, there was nothing Henderson could do to stop him. With tires squealing, he threw the Firebird into another left. It skidded and started to spin . . .

. . . just as Brandon swerved to *his* left, missing the Firebird by mere feet.

"*Wooooo!*" Frank screamed, enjoying the rush of his life.

Del would have shouted, too, but he was too busy trying to keep his pants dry.

The Firebird spun once, then half around again, before bouncing and sliding to a stop on the opposite side of the road, kicking up a huge cloud of dust that hovered above the car.

Brandon relaxed his grip on the wheel. He slowed the pickup, then made a careful U-turn to investigate the damage.

The Firebird's lights were on and its engine running, but there was no one at the wheel. Henderson had thrown open the driver's door and was racing to the back fender.

"You're certifiable, ol' buddy!" Frank laughed as they approached the Firebird. "Certifiable!"

"How'd you know?" Del mumbled, checking his pants for dampness.

Brandon pulled up to the Firebird and rolled down his window. Inside the Firebird, Reggie and his buddy were at various shades of white, coughing from the dirt and dust. Outside, Henderson was leaning over the rear fender, heaving his guts out.

Despite his feigned indifference, there was no missing a trace of concern in Brandon's voice. "Everybody all right?"

They gave no answer. Just more coughing, until, at last, Henderson raised his head. He managed a faint nod before being hit by another wave of nausea.

But for Frank the temptation was too great. He leaned past Brandon and, beer in hand, yelled, "How many times do I have to tell you Techies—'If you don't drink, don't drive!'" He let out a cackling laugh.

But no one in the Firebird responded. They'd had enough. They simply shook their heads, coughed, and waved Brandon on.

But Henderson would remember Brandon's face. More important, he would remember the broken running light on top of Brandon's cab. They would meet again; he'd see to it.

Brandon dropped the pickup into gear and pulled away as Frank let out another whoop—his infectious laughter lingering on the remote road.

"How'd you know?" Del asked again. "How'd you know—"

"How'd he know what?" Frank burped.

"That the guy was going to turn left."

Frank broke into more laughter. "He always knows that stuff." He reached past Del and gave Brandon a slap on the back. "Ain't that right, Bran? You always know."

Once again Brandon did not answer.

Dr. Helmut Reichner cursed softly as the 757 bounced and bucked on its final approach to Tribhuvan International Airport just outside of Katmandu. It wasn't the turbulence that bothered him, nor the fact that the Himalayas, which friends had predicted he would find so breathtaking, were completely shrouded in monsoon clouds. It was that every bump and jar reminded him of his last-minute inoculations for tetanus/diphtheria, hepatitis, typhoid, Japanese encephalitis, and of course, the ever-popular gamma globulin—three ccs in each buttock. And it was those buttocks that were suffering the greatest abuse during the bouncings and buckings.

True, he could have spread out the injections over a few days, resulting in less discomfort. But that would have meant delaying his flight—and the mysterious donor down there in the mountains of Nepal had wanted to see him immediately. If there was one thing Reichner knew about securing financial gifts, it was to make the people with the money think you were jumping whenever they said jump.

As executive director of the Moran Research Institute, Reichner was a pro at playing people to get what he wanted. Those from other parapsychology labs around the world described him in less generous terms: huckster, manipulator, shameless con artist. Let his peers say what they would. While they were busy scraping and fighting for the few funds available for paranormal research, he was enjoying a free ride from a single donor. It had been that way since the construction of the 2.8-million-dollar complex at Bethel Lake nearly three years ago. He had never understood why the donor had insisted that he build it in the backwoods community of northern Indiana, but that was a small price to pay for total and complete funding. Funding that would later include the purchase of expensive PET scan and MRI equipment. And funding that, if Reichner played his cards correctly, he would continue to enjoy for many years to come.

He didn't know who the guru down there was, where he got his money, or why he hid in the remote mountains of Nepal. Reichner had never actually met him; all their interaction had, until this point, been handled through the guru's intermediaries. There were rumors that he was a young man, perhaps even a boy, the result of a genetic experiment in the States that had gone awry. An experiment that had supposedly left him with incredible psychic powers—powers currently being groomed and guarded by some sort of international cartel. For what purposes, Reichner hadn't the foggiest. But the boy and the cartel had been sponsoring the Institute for three years now. And if Reichner handled this hastily called face-to-face correctly, it should not only answer some of his questions about his donor but ensure uninterrupted financial support for several years to come.

After all, using people and situations was what Reichner did best.

The plane lurched again. Reichner readjusted his meticulously kept six-foot frame, searching for some portion of his anatomy to take the final abuses. He was grateful to hear the dull whine of the landing gears as they opened and locked into place.

He glanced up; the flight attendant he'd been flirting with since New Delhi approached the bulkhead in front of him and folded down the flight seat. Her name was Gita. This was her first month on the job and she was still a little nervous. But the details didn't concern Dr. Reichner. The point was that she was slender, attractive, and very, very young—nearly thirty years his junior.

Just the way he liked them.

He'd been playing the powerful yet understanding father figure during the trip, and it had been working perfectly. Of course he'd made his occupation clear, and of course she found it incredibly intriguing. The younger ones always did. But now they were about to land and he'd have to work fast.

The plane gave another jolt and he winced.

"Are you okay?" she asked as she buckled in. "You look a little pale."

Reichner smiled. Adding a trace of vulnerability would only work to his advantage. "Just a little air sickness. I'm okay." He grinned, wincing just enough to make it clear that he was lying.

"We'll be on the ground in a few seconds," she said sympathetically. "Hang in there."

He smiled and nodded. She smiled back.

Good.

There was another jar as the wheels touched down and they began to taxi toward the terminal.

"So," he cleared his throat, "you've never met anyone involved in psychic research before?"

"No, never. It is most intriguing."

"Yes, well, we are a rare breed." He straightened his tropical wool slacks and folded his hands. "There are only fifty to sixty full-time parapsychologists in the entire world."

"Really?"

"Yes. With less than a dozen labs."

"That is all?"

He nodded. "Two in England and Russia, one in Beijing, Edinburgh, Bombay, the Netherlands, Brazil of course, and a small handful in the States. But that's all. As the leader in this field, I try to visit them often. But you can imagine how having no family and being on the road can make one lonely from time to time." He threw her a look.

She didn't get it. The kid was obviously too naive to appreciate his subtlety. They were approaching the terminal. He'd have to be more obvious.

"But the amazing thing is, I believe everybody on our planet has psychic abilities."

"Really?"

"Absolutely. In fact, right here, right now, I bet you could telepathically communicate to me what you're thinking."

She laughed. "You are not serious."

Reichner glanced out the window. The terminal was three hundred yards away. He'd have to work fast. "Of course I'm serious." He reached out to her. "Here, give me your hand, and I will tell you what you are thinking."

She hesitated.

"I'm serious. Simply focus your thoughts upon me and I will be able to tell."

She threw a nervous glance at the rest of the cabin, then leaned discreetly forward and held out her hand. Reichner took it. It was cool and smooth. So young, so firm.

He fixed his eyes onto hers and looked deeply into them. She faltered, glancing away, then looked back.

Good.

He dropped his voice into a soothing, controlled tone—the one he used on his subjects during their sessions at the Institute. "Just relax and concentrate . . . Concentrate." He noticed the terminal out of the corner of his eye. They were nearly there.

"Oh my, I am getting lots of thoughts." He smiled.

She fidgeted.

"First of all, you are feeling a bit lonely, too, are you not? In fact—hmm, you are wondering what you will be doing this evening." He could feel a slight dampness break out in her palm. Excellent. He tightened his grip so she couldn't easily pull away. Still staring at her, he continued. "You do not want to be cooped up in that hotel room . . ." His eyes widened, pretending surprise. "Well, now."

"What?" she smiled self-consciously.

"No, I—"

"Please, tell me."

"Well, somewhere in the back of your mind you are wondering . . . you are wondering if I will invite you to dinner."

Her smile wavered.

He'd gone too far. Immediately he went in for damage control. "It might be deep in your subconscious, of course, but—"

She pulled back her hand.

"I am sorry," he feigned embarrassment. "Sometimes our subconscious thinks things that we are not even aware—"

"Excuse me." She fumbled with her safety harness and unbuckled it. Without another word, she rose and entered the other cabin.

Reichner leaned back in his seat as the plane shuddered to a stop. He'd been clumsy, hadn't taken enough time. Too bad. In the proper environment he could talk anybody into anything. It was a gift he'd developed over the years. That's how he'd survived his childhood poverty in Austria. That's how he'd risen to his current level of success in his field.

He just hadn't taken enough time, that was all. But there were others. There were always others.

After retrieving his carry-on from the overhead and donning his Hickey-Freeman suit coat, he moved down the aisle. A moment later he passed the girl at the front exit. "It was very nice meeting you," he said, smiling.

She returned the smile and reached out to shake his hand. He was surprised, but he took her hand, once again enjoying the soft firmness of her touch. When he withdrew, he discovered a folded piece of paper in his palm. He waited until he'd stepped out of the plane to read it. Outside, the rain-soaked air was hot and humid, hitting him like a sauna. As he moved down the portable stairway toward the tarmac he unfolded the paper. It read:

Hotel Ganesh
312 Sukrapath Rd.

He smiled. Yes, he was good. He was very, very good.

"Mr. Reichner."

He glanced up to see two Westerners approaching the foot of the stairs. One was short and stocky, about five-five. The other was nearly Reichner's height and had a steel prosthesis for a left hand. Both wore suits almost as expensive as his.

They met him at the bottom of the steps and moved off to the side, out of the flow of traffic. "Are you Mr. Reichner?" the tall one asked.

"*Dr.* Reichner," Reichner corrected. "Who are you?"

"The Teacher has sent us."

Reichner frowned. They were obviously disciples of the boy guru. "We aren't scheduled to meet until tomorrow."

"The situation's gettin' a lot worse." Tall Suit's accent was lower British class. Reichner guessed Liverpool.

"Yes," Reichner cleared his throat. "Well, I have another appointment this evening, so I am afraid—"

He felt a hand lightly press against his back. "I'm sorry, but this can't wait." Not fond of being manhandled, Reichner held his ground. The taller man repeated, "The Teacher, he needs to see you. *Now.*"

Reichner considered his options. He could resist, but since these goons were connected to the money man it would be better to let them play their hand, at least for now. Later, he could complain, maybe even use their inhospitality to his advantage.

As if reading his mind, Tall Suit cranked up a feeble excuse for a smile. Reichner turned to the shorter man who was struggling to look equally as pleasant. The two seemed intent upon having their way, and judging by how they both filled out their suits, Reichner guessed that they were used to getting it. Well—best to play by the house rules. At least until he learned how to manipulate those rules to his advantage. And he would. That was his style. The secret to his success.

SLAUGHTER! KILL! DESTROY! MUTILATE!

The voices inside Lewis's head had been screaming for nearly three days. In calmer times they spoke in complete sentences. But when Lewis refused to obey, their demands grew louder, shriller. The rantings stirred other voices in him. Voices he didn't often hear but that he suspected were always there. Voices that joined in the screaming.

KILL! DECIMATE! ANNIHILATE!

He didn't always understand the words, but he knew what they wanted. They demanded destruction. They hungered for the hot, rusty smell of blood. They demanded the rush of power that came only from taking another life. Of course, Lewis wanted it, too. In fact, at times like this, he couldn't tell where their desires ended and his began. Not that he cared. At least not now. Now his appetite and their screamings had to be silenced—the throbbing, all-consuming hunger had to be fed.

"Which one?" a young teen with an acne-ravaged face whispered.

Lewis stood silently under the cover of trees near the pen. He stroked his red, ragged goatee and carefully surveyed the eight pigs. The moon made their lovely pale skins luminescent. They were beautiful animals. Any one would do.

"Let's go. Let's do it, let's do it." It was the other teen, a little older—the one with the long greasy hair and double-pierced eyebrow.

Lewis said nothing but watched in silence. The urgency of his companions caused him little concern. They were slackers. Hangers-on who were nominally attracted to his power. They were far more interested in witchcraft, Satanism, and the other childish games misfits like them needed to try to gain control of their lives. Neither boy fully appreciated Lewis's real powers—or what he would soon become.

The animals, aware of the strangers' presence, were growing uneasy.

"Come on," Pierced Eyebrow urged, casting a worried glance at the farmhouse. "Let's do it."

Lewis ran his hand over the red stubble atop his head. Yes, it was definitely time. He reached for his belt to check on the Buck hunting knife—one of the few things his daddy had given him before he'd killed himself.

KILL! DESTROY! RAVAGE!

Lewis's heart pounded as he surveyed the animals. Finally he focused on one to the far right. It seemed to be the youngest, the fairest, the most pure.

MUTILATE! DESECRATE!

This was always the best part. Just before the kill. The teasing. The building up of desire until it practically exploded inside him.

"Let's do it!" Acne Face whispered.

Lewis's breath came shorter now, in ragged pants of excitement. He had never killed an animal this large. Hamsters, yes. Stray cats, several. Even a neighbor's puppy. But never this.

Suddenly, he broke from cover and ran toward the fence. Five steps, up, over, and he was inside the pen. A moment later his partners joined him. The pigs squealed in panic, running in every direction. A chained dog began barking over at the house. But that was okay; they'd be done before the porch light came on.

"That one!" Lewis shouted. "That one, right there!"

They closed in on the young animal. It cut to the left, then to the right, then left again. In seconds they had it cornered. Pierced Eyebrow lunged; the others followed until they were all holding it. The thing kicked and jerked and squealed, but it was outnumbered.

"Hold him!" Acne Face yelled. He'd made the mistake of grabbing the haunches and was now suffering considerable abuse because of it. "Hold him!"

Pierced Eyebrow yanked up the animal's head, exposing its neck. Lewis reached for his knife, and then everything turned to slow motion. Ecstasy exploded in his chest, rushing through his veins, firing every nerve.

It was over in seconds. Lewis's legs buckled in euphoria, dropping him to his knees. Already the voices were subsiding. Of course, they would return. They always did. And each time their hunger and desire was greater than the time before. But that was okay. Lewis knew the reason. He was being prepared. There was a stirring in him. He'd felt it, known it, been told about it by the voices. He was about to enter his season. After years of patiently waiting, being ignored and humiliated, Lewis Thompson would shortly—very, very shortly—begin fulfilling the destiny for which he'd been born.

CHAPTER 2

Something was wrong at Moran Research Institute. Terribly wrong.

An exhausted Sarah Weintraub entered one of the two narrow labs and dimmed the lights. It had been a frustrating evening, and these rooms, with their subdued lighting and gray, ribbed panels of sound-absorbing material, always comforted her. She dropped into one of the two swivel chairs in front of a black console that contained a handful of controls, a couple of joysticks, some unwashed coffee mugs, a half-used legal pad, and a computer keyboard. Above this were two or three computers, some video monitors, a pair of speakers, and four red floodlights directed toward a plush leather recliner to the right. Behind her, almost within reaching distance, were waist-high racks of DATs, more computers, and other monitoring equipment. And finally, above that was the three-foot-high by seven-foot-long, one-way glass of the observation room, which housed even more state-of-the-art electronics and dirty coffee mugs.

Earlier that evening, she had made an obligatory public relations appearance at the country club—on the arm of some Neanderthal who had tried more moves on her than he had words in his vocabulary. That had been a mistake, but she had paid her penance by spending the rest of the evening and early morning hours here, at the Institute. Other twenty-eight-year-olds had their boyfriends, their husbands, their kids, but Sarah Weintraub had her work. And over the years it had become a demanding lover, one she seldom refused.

It hadn't always been that way. Granted, she was ambitious and even aggressive, more than most. As the only girl in a family with four brothers, she'd had to be. But at the appropriate time, she'd always been able to fit in and unwind with the best of them. Until her second year at grad school. That's when she'd gotten pregnant, and that's when the fights with Samuel had started. "Come on, Babe," he had insisted, "I want a kid as much as you. But not now. We've both got school to finish and careers to launch. After that, sure. The more the merrier. But not now."

Sarah hadn't wanted the abortion, but Samuel's persistence had worn her down. He understood her ambition perfectly, and he'd used it to get his way. At the end of her ninth week, she'd found herself on the table, legs in the stirrups, staring at a poster of a smiling Garfield up on the ceiling.

She knew the fetus was a boy, had sensed it from the beginning. She'd begged him to please understand, to please forgive her. But apparently he hadn't. There had been an accidental perforation of the uterus wall, followed by severe bleeding. By the end of the day, Sarah Weintraub had found herself the recipient of an emergency hysterectomy. Eight months later, she and Samuel had broken up. He'd never admitted it, but she suspected "damaged goods" to be a contributing factor on his part.

And for her, there had been the guilt and overbearing depression that she just couldn't seem to shake.

Fortunately, there had been her studies and later, her work. Not only had they kept her mind occupied and held back the depression, but they had also earned her the reputation as a diligent researcher and a go-getter—proving that she really was a good girl. Proving that her work really did count for something. Proving that maybe, after enough accomplishments in her field, that maybe, just maybe, the sacrifice of her son could someday be justified. Until then, all Sarah Weintraub needed were two to three dozen hours of overtime each week to keep the guilt and self-loathing at bay.

She leaned over the console and punched on the power. The board lit up, and one of the computers started to whir. She had spent the past several hours alone at the Institute, checking and rechecking last week's data. But no matter how carefully she scrutinized the procedural notes and reworked the probabilities, the results remained the same.

Something was wrong.

The red light on the board glowed, indicating that the random number generator, or RNG, was up and running. The original RNG had been developed nearly thirty years ago by a brilliant but bored Boeing employee out in Seattle. Today, its offspring are found in nearly every parapsychology lab in the world. Although it has many uses, it's particularly effective in measuring a person's psychokinesis, or PK—the ability to move physical objects through mental concentration.

In the old days, this meant trying to manipulate the outcome of tumbling dice or flipping coins. The process was slow and cumbersome, sometimes taking hundreds, even thousands of trials. But now, thanks to modern science, this and nearly every other area of paranormal research had turned high-tech.

Sarah never completely understood the electronics behind the RNG, but she knew it was designed to fire a random set of pluses or minuses over a given period of time. All the human subject had to do was hold down a button on the joystick and concentrate, trying to force the computer to fire more pluses or more minuses than would be normal for random chance.

Sarah had been working with a dozen volunteer subjects who came in weekly. Some demonstrated very strong PK. Others showed no giftedness in the area whatsoever.

But in the past seventy-two hours, all of that had changed.

Everything had gone haywire. Subjects with consistently high PK readings were flat lining. Those with no past history were going off the chart. Incredible. It was as if somebody was playing an elaborate hoax. That's why Sarah was here in these early morning hours. That's why she had reexamined every result, every figure, every procedural report.

But the outcome was exactly the same: Other than impossible PK scores, there was absolutely nothing unusual.

Sarah leaned back and sighed. Almost absentmindedly she reached to the console and snapped on a monitor. With the same lack of thought, she scooped up the joystick and started fiddling with the button in the handle. The speaker in front of her began to ping—high pings meant *plus* firings, low pings meant *minus* firings. On the monitor, a graph with a line appeared. It showed visually what she was hearing audibly. The more plus firings, the higher the line rose on the graph, the more minus firings, the lower it dropped.

Earlier that day a technician had run careful calibrations on all six of the Institute's RNGs. He'd found no problems. Not a one.

Having no energy to concentrate, Sarah lowered the volume. This wasn't an experiment, just something to do as she tried to relax. But she couldn't let her mind drift too far. After all, this was the first week of August—the week of bad dreams and deepest depression. The week of drinking just a little too much wine and working doubly hard to keep her mind occupied. The little whirlpools of memory were always present, but this week, the anniversary of her abortion, was always the worst. If she was careless, she could accidentally step into one of those memories and be pulled under—dragged into a spinning vortex that would take days, sometimes weeks, to pull out of. Over the past three years she'd grown to accept this period of time. She figured it was the price of admission. And, truth be told, she considered it mild punishment for her offense.

It had been about this time last year that Dr. Reichner had begun pursuing her. Having her Ph.D. in neuroscience and doing research for UCLA, Sarah initially had been repulsed at the thought of joining a parapsychology lab. There are few branches of science given less credit than parapsychology. But, like Samuel, Reichner knew how to get what he wanted. His offer had been nearly double what she had been making at the school and, gradually, his phone calls and persistent e-mail accomplished their purpose. She had agreed to move to this backwoods Indiana town and take a position as senior researcher for Moran Research Institute. New job, new part of the country, longer hours—maybe this would be what she needed to finally bury her grief and self-hatred.

She'd found research into the paranormal more credible than she had anticipated. In fact, she was surprised to observe the painstaking care and scientific objectivity with which studies in the paranormal were being undertaken throughout the world.

She was also surprised at some of the results.

Such as the PK research in Russia. A group of so-called psychics were brought in to focus disruptive thoughts upon preselected laboratory rats from a larger colony. They attempted to make the selected rats act more aggressively. Professional animal behaviorists observed the colony to determine which rats appeared to be most disruptive. Without knowing it, the behaviorists chose the identical rats that the psychics had been concentrating upon. To further verify the results, biologists were brought in to dissect all of the rats' brains, particularly studying the chemicals and regions that indicate aggression. Once again, this group selected the identical rats that both the psychics and animal behaviorists had chosen.

Of course, this was just one of dozens of PK experiments being conducted around the world. Others measured the human mind's effect on plants, atomic particles, even the human nervous system—often with impressive results. In fact, just recently the U.S. Department of Defense had admitted to pouring over twenty million dollars into their own special parapsychology studies. A waste of taxpayers' money? Perhaps. But if the human mind could maneuver the electrons necessary for firing the RNG, couldn't it do the same on an enemy's computer? If they could disturb a mouse's mind, couldn't they do the same with the thoughts of a military general?

Sarah's own thoughts were jarred by a faint, electronic whine. Earlier, she had turned down the RNG's volume, but now the soft shrillness caught her attention. She looked up at the monitor. The line on the graph was gone. It had completely shot up and off the screen.

Immediately, she released the button on the joystick. But the high-pitched whine continued.

That was impossible. She wasn't influencing the machine now. It should drop back down to the flat line of random chance.

But it didn't.

Instead the whine's pitch actually increased. Sarah rose to her feet, staring at the screen, wincing at the shrillness. It was a malfunction. Had to be. There was no other explanation.

She had to record this. Get the results on tape. She turned to the DAT machine behind her and punched up RECORD.

But just as the recorder came to life, the whine stopped.

Sarah looked back at the monitor. The line on the graph had gone flat. It had dropped back down to the acceptable level of probability.

And then she felt something. A chill. A damp, freezing sensation swept across the lab. From right to left. She gave an involuntary shiver as it brushed against her skin, then moved on toward the open door to the hallway.

Word of last night's Townie exploits rapidly spread through the plant of Bollenger's Printing and Lithograph. The fact that Brandon and Frank both worked there certainly helped. The fact that Frank loved retelling the story and thrived on all the attention didn't hurt, either. And since most of the employees were Townies like himself, they hung on his every word, vicariously reliving last night's escapade and sharing the victory. Even now, as Brandon drove his electric forklift past the giant printing press, he could see Frank recounting the story to Warner, the ponytailed operator.

Warner listened and laughed as he manipulated the reverse button of the press, inching the mammoth rollers backward with his left hand as the right deftly darted in between them with a cleaning rag.

Looking up and spotting Brandon, Frank shouted to him over the plant's noise. "Hey, there he is now. Hey, Mario—Mario Andretti!"

Both guys laughed and Brandon threw them a half-smile before turning his attention back to the forklift.

That's when he saw her . . .

His eight-year-old sister. She was wearing a white nightgown and looking even more lovely than he remembered. In her hand she held a pot, and in that pot was a small, ornamental tree.

Brandon slammed on the brakes.

The girl said nothing.

Quickly, he dropped the forklift into neutral and hopped off.

"Jenny?"

His heart began to pound. He felt a joy he hadn't experienced in months as he started toward her, anxious to hug her, to scoop her into his arms, to say how much he had missed her.

But she held out her hand, motioning for him to stop.

He slowed, confused. What did she mean?

She extended her finger and pointed. Brandon followed it to Frank and Warner. He looked back at her. He started to speak, to ask what she meant, but before the words came he was interrupted.

"Hey, Martus."

He turned to see Roger Putnam, the foreman of their shift, a lumbering mass of muscle and fat who was busy reading his clipboard as he rounded the forklift. He glanced up and spotted Jenny.

"How'd she get in?" he asked. "No one under eighteen on the floor, you know that."

Brandon looked at him in surprise. Was that all he had to say?

Tapping his clipboard, Putnam continued. "Listen, you're screwing up on the orders again. You know I can't keep covering for you."

As he spoke, Jenny again raised her hand and pointed.

"I mean, I've got my rear end to protect too, y'know."

Again, Brandon followed Jenny's gesture to Frank and Warner. What was she trying to say? They were just shooting the breeze. Just standing and talking—

Except for Warner's right hand, the one darting in and out of the rollers. He glanced at Jenny. Her face was filling with urgency. That was it.

He looked back at Warner, who was still laughing, paying little attention to his work.

"Now, you got another delivery over at the Institute today," Putnam was saying, "so try not to . . ."

But Brandon barely heard. He stared at Warner's hands as the man carelessly pushed the reverse button with his left, while darting the cleaning rag in and out of the rollers with his right. Suddenly, his left hand hit the reverse button too recklessly and slipped off, pressing the forward button instead.

Before Brandon could shout a warning, the rollers reversed. They grabbed the cleaning rag, yanking Warner's hand with it. The massive rollers crushed his fingers, then his hand. Warner opened his mouth, trying to scream, but no sound came—only Brandon's own anguished cry as he bolted up in bed, his face covered in sweat.

He glanced at the crimson glow of the radio alarm on his nightstand. It read 4:22 A.M.

"How long a drive do we have?" Dr. Reichner called from the backseat of the Peugeot. "Where exactly does your Teacher live?"

It had been twenty minutes since they'd met at the airport outside Katmandu. Now they had doubled back into the city and were making their way through the crowded, stone-paved streets. Both of his escorts sat up front—the shorter one on the passenger side, the taller one gripping a knob on the steering wheel with his steel prosthesis. The sunlight had started to fade, making the city look surreal—white plaster walls now orange from the sun, umber tiled roofs, holy shrines, strange statues covered in multicolored candle wax and flowers. And the people, everywhere people. Street vendors, barefoot children, emaciated holy men with painted faces and white, flowing hair.

"So," Reichner tried again. "How long before we get there?"

For the first time since they'd met, the shorter one spoke. Unlike his British partner, this man sounded Danish. "You have your degree in physics?"

Reichner didn't appreciate having the subject changed, but he decided to answer. "That is one of my doctorates. My first is in theology at Princeton Seminary. But when I couldn't find God in religion, I turned to physics." It was an old joke, but one that carried more truth for him than humor.

"So tell me," Short Suit continued, "don't you find the similarity between quantum physics and Eastern philosophy amazingly similar?"

Wonderful, Reichner thought, *a pseudo-intellectual. This guy will want to talk forever.* He glanced out the window and again wondered how long the ride to guru-land would take. "Yes," he answered almost mechanically. "There are interesting parallels."

Short Suit nodded. "I am reading about Schrödinger's cat. What an intriguing concept."

Reichner said nothing. It always surprised him how excited laypeople became when they first grasped quantum mechanics, as if it were something entirely new. The truth is, it had been around for three-quarters of a century. And in that time it had done some major damage. In fact, many would say that it had overthrown much of Isaac Newton's and Albert Einstein's thinking, causing Einstein himself to complain, "God does not play dice with the universe."

Well, guess again, Al.

Until the 1920s everything was clear-cut. Everyone knew that the movement and position of any object could be predicted. Just find its speed and direction, then do a little math. Of course this is still true with larger objects like cars or planes or planets, but when it comes down to particles the size of atoms or smaller, look out. At that level everything can turn topsy-turvy. The fact is, there's no telling where one of those particles could suddenly pop up, or in what direction they'll be heading—until we observe them.

Observation, that's the key that baffles everyone. Because somehow, someway, it's that very act of observation that determines where those objects will be. Until the observation is made, the particle is merely a ghost located in several places at the same time. It's only when we observe it that it materializes at the location in which it is observed.

At first the concept sounds absurd, unbelievable. So for beginners, Reichner usually explained it as if a subatomic particle were a magical car, one that is in St. Louis, New York, Seattle, Los Angeles, Dallas, and a hundred other locations all at the same time. It is only when we, the observers, go to St. Louis and see it there, that its ghostly appearances in all of the other locations disappear and it materializes in St. Louis. The same would have been true if we had first seen it in New York or Dallas. The car would have appeared in those cities instead. It was a crude comparison that left out more than a few details, but it helped Reichner make his point: Our act of observing has a profound impact upon subatomic objects. In truth, it actually determines where those objects will be or what direction they will be heading.

Astonishing? Yes.

True? Absolutely.

As a teen, Reichner used to think such theoretical double-talk belonged more to philosophers than to scientists—following such hypothetical questions as: "If a tree falls in the forest and nobody hears it, does it make a sound?" But quantum mechanics is far more than theory. It has been proven mathematically and through hundreds of lab experiments such as Thomas Young's two-slit system, or Alaine Aspect's work at the University of Paris as early as the 1970s.

Then, of course, there was Reichner's own work with Sarah Weintraub and their PK experiments back at the Moran Research Institute. The chain of logic was clear. If we can determine the location of a subatomic particle by observing it with our minds, can't we also *influence* that particle's behavior with those same minds? Isn't that really what PK is all about? When the Institute's subjects direct the firing of the random number generators to either pluses or minuses, are they not simply practicing everyday, run-of-the-mill, quantum mechanics?

But quantum mechanics is more than just some scientific laboratory's novelty. It is also responsible for such practical inventions as the transistor, electron microscope, superconductor, laser, and even nuclear power.

Unfortunately, Short Suit wasn't done talking. Not yet. "I am sure you and the Teacher will have many fascinating hours of conversation, particularly regarding the Buddhist and Hindu beliefs of the nonlocal mind."

Reichner rolled his eyes and looked back out the window. Once quantum mechanics had become accessible to the public, the Eastern religions had quickly jumped on the cosmic bandwagon. If subatomic particles don't really exist until we view them, couldn't the same thing be said about larger items, like the earth, the stars, the universe? And if the universe didn't really exist until we observed it, doesn't that make us its creators? And if we've created the universe, doesn't that make us all God, all part of a great single cosmic consciousness that has created itself?

It was an interesting theory, and one that had left the Western religions and philosophers in the dust.

Until now.

Now there were some new and powerful scientific theories on the block involving *superstrings* and the *eleven-dimension universe*. Theories that indicate higher dimensions, suggesting a reality beyond our perceived three-dimensional world—a reality that the less sophisticated could misconstrue as belonging to "God" or the "supernatural." Such theories didn't completely nullify quantum mechanics, but they thoroughly and quite effectively put Judeo-Christianity back into the system. Not that Reichner cared one way or the other. He just hoped he wouldn't have to be the one to break the bad news to his Eastern mystic sponsor. News like that might have a serious impact on his guru's check-writing ability.

"Here we go," Tall Suit said as he eased the car to the side of the road.

Reichner glanced around. They had reached the outskirts of the city. For the first time since they'd left the airport, they weren't surrounded by people. In fact, the place was nearly deserted. The nearest building was almost thirty yards away. "This is it?" he asked.

Without a word, both men opened their doors and stepped out. Reichner started to open his own door, then noticed that Short Suit was doing it for him. But instead of allowing Reichner to exit, Short Suit scooted in beside him.

"What is going on?" Reichner demanded.

"May I see your arm, please?"

"What?"

Short Suit produced a syringe and needle.

"What are you doing?"

Now the other door opened and Tall Suit moved in and sat next to Reichner on the other side. "The Teacher, he's very particular about revealing his location."

"I don't really see what—"

Short Suit took Reichner's right arm and shoved up his shirtsleeve as Tall Suit grabbed the other arm.

Reichner resisted, trying to push them away. "What are you doing? I don't want—what is that stuff?"

"Ativan," Short Suit explained as he wiped an alcohol-soaked swab across the arm. "It is a sedative."

Reichner continued struggling. "I know what Ativan is."

Tall Suit pushed him farther back into the seat as Short Suit continued. "It is four milligrams. You will be asleep before you know it."

Reichner struggled. "I will not be sedated!"

The two men were strong. Reichner twisted his body, kicking against the front seat, but they held his arms firm while keeping him pinned down.

Reichner felt a tiny burn in his right arm. He looked down. Short Suit had found the vein and was pumping the liquid into it.

"Just sit back," Tall Suit encouraged. "You'll be there before you know it, Mr. Reichner."

He could feel the drug rushing through his body. "It's *Dr.* Reichner." The chemical swept into his brain. "*Dr.* Reichner. I have a Ph.D. I have *two* Ph.D.'s."

"You certainly do, Dr. Reichner." The voice grew fainter, more distant.

Reichner fought the fogginess. He had to continue talking. "I have a degree from Princeton Seminary. I also ... I'm ..." He felt an irresistible urge to close his eyes, fought it, then obeyed, but only for a moment, just to gather his wits. "I also ... in physics ... I have two degrees. Princeton ... and in, one in ..."

That was the last Dr. Reichner remembered of Katmandu.

Brandon shuffled into Momma's kitchen wearing nothing but jeans and an old T-shirt. He'd have worn less than that if he thought he could get away with it. But Momma was from the South, and though she had been up here in Indiana for over twenty years, there were still certain customs, certain civilities she insisted upon from her family. And wearing a shirt to the breakfast table was one of them.

"Morning, darlin'," she called from the stove.

"Mornin'," he mumbled as he pulled out a chair and took his seat.

It wasn't seven in the morning and the kitchen was already sweltering. The weather had been hot like this most of the summer. But Momma didn't complain. It wasn't her way.

Sunlight blasted through the screen door, forcing Brandon to squint and turn his head. But the back door would remain open. That was where his father sat—every day, unmoving in his wheelchair, staring out at the world through the screen. The expensive, silver-and-turquoise wristwatch Brandon had given him six Father's Days ago glinted in the sun. Back then it had cost Brandon most of his savings, but it had seemed a small price to pay. Even now Momma made sure the man wore it every day. Not that it mattered. As a stroke victim, he couldn't look at it. Probably didn't even know he had it on. Even if he did, he could never show any appreciation. He was incapable of showing any emotion.

Brandon glanced down at the table. After all he'd put his father through, it was probably just as well.

"He sure loves that mornin' sun on his face, doesn't he?" Momma asked.

Brandon said nothing.

Momma continued, uncomfortable in any silence. "Looks like we're gonna have ourselves another blisterin' day." She scooped the pancakes from the griddle. "Weatherman says we're settin' ourselves some kinda record. Comin' up to thirty days without a speck o' rain. And none in sight."

She crossed to the table and set the plate of eggs and hotcakes before him. Brandon saw the sweat glistening off the hairs of her forearm, knew a thin dark stain was already working its way down the back of her housedress. He hated to see her working like this. He'd made it clear a hundred times that he didn't need breakfast. But she insisted. There were certain civilities expected from a family.

He picked up his fork and began to eat. She moved to the fridge. He could feel her standing there, pretending to busy herself by pouring a glass of milk but scrutinizing his every move.

"'Course, the farmers are complainin' to beat the band." She forced a chuckle. "Guess they need somethin' to complain about, though. If it's not too dry then it's too wet, or too cold, or too somethin'." She crossed to him and set the glass on the table, then nervously brushed the damp strands of hair behind her ear. "Still, I bet they could use a little help."

Brandon continued to eat in silence. He could feel her eyes still on him.

She turned back to the stove. Nearly half a minute passed before she finally turned and said what was on her mind, what he had suspected she wanted to say since he'd entered the room. "You had another dream, didn't you?"

He gave a half shrug.

"Jenny?" she asked.

There was no need to reply. She already knew the answer. She crossed back to the fridge and opened it, striving to be matter-of-fact. "You know, if you took that medicine like the doctor says, you wouldn't have to be puttin' up with those things. You slept real well when you took it before. Remember?"

He gave no answer.

"Oh, sugar." She had turned back to him and was now speaking from her heart. "Your sister's gone." She took a tentative step toward him. "She's gone and there's nothin' we can do about it."

More silence. Brandon continued to eat. She moved closer. "And you gotta stop blaming yourself. It was . . . her time. And the good Lord knew it. You just happened to be the one there, that's all."

"A tool in his hand—is that right, Momma?" The sarcasm came before he could stop it. "I just have to believe it was his will." They were hard words, stinging words, and he regretted saying them as he watched her retreat back to the stove.

Another minute passed before she spoke again, her cheeriness a little forced. "I'm dropping by the Wilson's this afternoon. Thought I'd pick us up some more of that cider your daddy likes so well."

Brandon looked toward the door. His father sat motionless, just as he always did.

"Remember—remember that jug we forgot and left in the cellar all winter?" She chuckled. "My, oh my, now that had some bite to it, remember? Wasn't too long 'fore we all got a little tipsy? Remember?" Her voice grew softer, drifting into memories. "What people would've said . . . the pastor's family gettin'—"

But Brandon had had enough. His chair scraped against the yellowed linoleum as he rose.

"Where you goin'?"

"The shop's got another deadline," he said as he turned and started for the door. "Putnam wants everybody there by 7:20."

"But you've barely touched your—"

"I'll grab something later."

"But—"

He squeezed past his father, careful not to look at him. He never looked at him, not if there was a chance of their eyes meeting. He headed out the door and down the porch steps. When he reached the bottom, Drool came lumbering after him. Normally, Brandon would have stooped to give the big old dog a scratch and rub, but he had to get away. He knew Momma was trying to help, but he also knew her suffocating ways and that he could literally drown in her chatter. He gave the dog a quick pat on the side and moved for his pickup.

He climbed inside and started up the engine. He dropped it into gear and started down the dusty, potholed lane that ran a hundred fifty yards to the highway. He knew she was standing at the screen, watching, and it took every ounce of willpower just to raise his hand and give her a wave.

He didn't know if she waved back. He didn't care.

He just had to get away.

Sarah stood in front of her bedroom closet, more asleep than awake. She'd spent less than four hours in bed. But four hours would have to do. Now it was time to put down the coffee and stumble out the door to work. But first, what to wear. Not that it mattered. Most of her wardrobe was the same: dark colors—grays, browns, greens, nearly all loose-fitting. Not that she'd planned it that way. It had just happened.

Friends scoffed at her. "You got a body most would die for. You can't keep hiding it. You've got to get back out there and ad-ver-tise."

But Sarah wasn't interested in advertising. Not anymore. In her high school and college days, oh yeah. Big time. It had been great fun, and she'd been good at it. But that was long ago and far away. Another life. Now there was her work and the lab and her research. Oh sure, she could still force the smiles, be charming, flirt and play the game. But that's all it was: a game.

And the truth was, she was no longer interested in playing the game, much less winning it.

She reached into the closet, pulled out a nondescript sack of a dress, and quickly slipped it on. It was important to hurry, today more so than ever. Because, although she was careful not to let the thought completely form, in the back of her mind she knew: This was the date, this was the third anniversary of her abortion.

Brandon slipped the hand dolly under a four-foot stack of pamphlets. He tilted them back, then turned and wheeled the pile across the floor of Bollenger's Printing and Lithograph. He'd started working for the plant part-time back in high school. After graduation, some friends headed off to college, but Brandon remained behind. What good would college do anyway? Just postpone the inevitable: searching for a halfway decent job. Besides, there were no guarantees, not for his generation. Skeptical, figuring America's best years lay behind, Brandon did what many of his so-called "Generation X" did. He found a safe place, then quietly and silently began giving up his dreams.

It hadn't always been that way. As a boy, he'd been everybody's favorite. Especially his father's. He had adored the man, and the man had adored him. They'd done everything together, and there wasn't the slightest doubt that he was destined to follow in his father's footsteps. It was believed by all who knew him that Brandon Martus would be a bright and shining light for his generation. Some thought he'd become a pastor like his father; others said a famous teacher or evangelist. Whatever the details, everyone knew that he was destined for greatness. Everyone told him so.

And Brandon had believed them. He had believed everything—until his father's stroke six years ago. After that, no amount of believing did any good. Not that he didn't try. At first he had tried everything, even insisting that Momma drive all the way to Chicago and later to Indianapolis to attend faith-healing crusades. But no matter how hard Brandon prayed, no matter how hard he believed, his father remained paralyzed.

That's when the doubts crept in. If God couldn't be trusted with a little thing like healing his father, how could he be trusted with bigger things? And if he couldn't be trusted with bigger things, then how could Brandon trust God with anything—including this supposed "call" that everyone said God had placed on his life?

The answer became crystal clear: He couldn't.

And that's when the downward spiral began—a spiral of doubt, anger, guilt, but most of all, self-hatred. A spiral that made it difficult to talk to his mother and impossible to look at his father. A spiral that had finally reached bottom just seven months ago when Brandon had sealed his fate by killing the only other thing that mattered in his life. That was the night he had accidentally killed Jenny, his little sister.

With the stack of pamphlets balanced on his hand dolly, Brandon crossed the plant, heading for the loading dock. As he approached the giant printing press, he could hear Frank laughing, no doubt reveling in last night's exploits at the country club. Word of their antics had spread quickly, due in no small measure to Frank's gift for gab.

Brandon rounded the corner of the press and saw Warner, the ponytailed operator, listening and laughing as he inched the press's big rollers forward, cleaning them with a rag. He spotted Brandon and shouted, "Hey, Martus—sounds like you boys done all right against them Techies!"

Brandon gave a nod as he moved past.

"I tell you, it was beautiful," Frank laughed. "And this guy"—he motioned toward Brandon—"this guy was insane, man. Thought he was Mario Andretti."

The familiarity of the phrase caught Brandon off guard. He glanced over his shoulder as Frank rattled on and Warner listened with admiration. Brandon's gaze shot to Warner's right hand.

It held the same rag as in the dream. It darted in and out of the same rollers.

He looked at the other hand.

It carelessly pressed the reverse button on and off, on and off, also as in the dream.

But before Brandon could react, he ran his dolly into Roger Putnam, the plant foreman. The stack of pamphlets tumbled to the floor, and Putnam grabbed his shin, swearing. "Come on, Martus!"

Brandon muttered an apology and quickly moved to restack the load—at the same time, keeping an eye on Frank and Warner.

With a groan, Putnam lowered his massive bulk to help him. "When you gonna start putting some mind into your work?"

Brandon gave no answer. Frank and Warner were still laughing.

"Listen," Putnam continued, "you're screwing up on the orders again."

The phrase chilled Brandon. Hadn't that also been in the dream? He shot another look at the press.

"I can't always be covering for you, man. I mean, I've got my rear end to protect too, y'know."

Incredulous, Brandon rose, staring first at Putnam, then at the press and at Warner's left hand pushing the reverse button.

"Now—you got another delivery over at the Institute this . . ."

Warner's right hand darted dangerously close to the rollers.

". . . so try not to—"

That was all Brandon could stand. He leaped to his feet, shouting: "Your hand!" He started toward them. "Look out, your hand, it's going to—"

Just as Warner hit the off button to shut down the press.

Brandon slowed and stopped as the big machine wound down. Frank and Warner turned to look at him. He could feel Putnam and other workers doing the same.

What had happened? He'd been so certain. It had been exactly like his dream.

Frank was the first to speak. "What's up, buddy?"

Brandon stared at the rollers of the machine, then over at Frank, then Warner.

"You okay?" Frank asked.

Slowly, Brandon nodded. "Yeah. I, uh—I'm fine." For another moment he stood, unsure what to do. Finally, he turned back to the dolly and finished restacking the pamphlets. He rose and quickly wheeled them off, more than a little grateful to be away from everyone's curious gaze.

CHAPTER 3

"I f he is in such a hurry to see me, why is he not here?"
Reichner paced back and forth on the bare, earthen
floor. The building was a single room, ten by twelve
feet, constructed of stone and plaster. At one end sat a
combination fireplace and open-hearth oven. At the other,
a roughly hewn wooden door and a single window that
looked out into the night rain. The furnishings consisted
of a spartan bed complete with microthin mattress, a
wooden chair and table, a chipped porcelain washbasin,
and a small thatched mat, probably used for meditation.

A tiny barefoot woman was replacing fruit in a bowl
at the table while a man in a yellow, long-sleeved robe
smiled politely. He was small and brown, like any of the
peasants Reichner had seen swarming the streets of Katmandu earlier that evening. But when he spoke, there was
no mistaking his university training. "Patience is a great
virtue, Dr. Reichner."

"I have been waiting nearly four hours!"

"I assure you, Teacher will arrive at the perfect time."

The woman completed her work and stood silently,
waiting to be dismissed. The man nodded and she opened
the door, exiting into the night.

"So you are holding me prisoner?" Reichner demanded.
"Is that it?"

"You may leave at any time you wish. Although I suspect it is as advantageous for you to see Teacher as it is for him to see you."

Reichner hesitated. For the second time that day, he'd heard that the guru wanted badly to see him. This was good. Valuable information to store for later use. "What about my laptop and my suitcases?"

"They will be returned to you in time."

Reichner ran his hand through his brown crewcut. He was getting nowhere fast. "Why won't you tell me where I am?"

"You are one-half kilometer from the main compound."

"And where exactly is that?"

"Now, Dr. Reichner, if Teacher had wanted you to know such things, we would not have given you the sedative."

"Yes, well, in the future it would not hurt to ask your guests' permission before you start pumping drugs into them."

"I hope the experience was not unpleasant."

"It was rude and frightening and entirely unwarranted."

"I am sorry. I suppose we could have thrown a gunnysack over your head and knocked you unconscious."

It was meant as a joke but Reichner didn't smile. The man nodded in understanding. He reached into his long, flowing sleeve, pulled out a small piece of paper, and handed it to Reichner.

"What's this?" Reichner asked.

"Teacher wishes you to have it."

Reichner looked down at the paper. One very long word was written upon it. The penmanship was sloppy, like a child's, and it was in language he didn't recognize.

"That is Sanskrit," the man explained. "An ancient Indic language."

"What does it say?"

"It is a special mantra the Teacher wishes for you to meditate upon."

"Mantra?"

"It is the God-name of Teacher. Just as our Hindu brothers recite 'om' to more fully connect with the universe, if you meditate upon this name, it will help cleanse your mind and allow you to more fully communicate with Teacher's spirit."

Reichner eyed the man, then glanced back at the words. He knew all about meditating. Back in his college days he'd practiced it. Even now at the Institute he used similar techniques to help relax his subjects before beginning their sessions. But he seldom practiced it himself, and never by chanting Eastern mantras.

"Please." The robed man motioned to the small woven mat on the floor. "You will find that meditating upon his name will facilitate both his arrival and your upcoming discussion."

Reichner's frustration rose. "What will facilitate his arrival is your telling him that I do not intend to stay here much longer." It was a bluff and they both knew it. "I have a busy schedule. I have many pressing engagements."

The robed man nodded and turned toward the door. "As you wish." He reached for the wooden handle and pulled it open. Rain and wind blew inside, whipping his clothes. He turned and motioned to the mat one final time. "I assure you, Dr. Reichner, Teacher will arrive much sooner if you simply prepare yourself for his visit."

Reichner stared at him coolly. The man forced a polite smile, then turned and stepped out into the rain. Reichner stood at the door watching as the deluge soaked the man's clothing, causing his robe to droop and cling to his body. But he barely noticed as he calmly plodded up the muddy road toward the compound.

Reichner slammed the door with an oath. It swung back open and he had to push it closed, then latch it. He wadded up the paper the man had given him and threw it across the room onto the bed. He wasn't about to be drawn into some sort of mystical hocus-pocus. "Prepare himself," indeed. More likely, relax and be lulled into a more susceptible mood so that his sponsor would have the upper hand in their discussion. Well, if anyone was going to have the upper hand, it would be Reichner. That was his specialty. "The Teacher" obviously had his own agenda, but Reichner would manipulate it to fit his.

Fifty minutes passed. Twice Reichner opened the door and thought of heading up the muddy road to the compound where the Peugeot would be, where he would insist on being taken back to Katmandu. But both times the wind, the rain—and most important, the guru's money—had persuaded him to exercise a bit more patience.

Having eaten the fruit from the bowl, and with absolutely nothing else to do, he eased himself onto the bed. The thin mattress and broken springs quickly reminded him of his recent inoculations. He spotted the crumpled piece of paper nearby and reached for it. He smoothed it out, then examined the name.

Other than the length, eight syllables, and the fact that it was in a foreign language, there seemed nothing unusual about it. He read it again, this time out loud. The soft consonants and gentle vowels rolled pleasantly enough off his tongue. He repeated them again. Interesting how gentle and comforting they sounded. But a "God-name"? Hardly.

Reichner sighed. He tilted back his head and stared up at the cracked, plastered ceiling. The things he put himself through to keep the Institute going. He turned toward the window and stared out into the wet blackness. He looked at the door, examining its rough, hand-hewn planks. Then to the table and chair, equally as crude, then to the fireplace, until he eventually found himself looking back down at the paper.

He repeated the syllables again. Slowly. Reichner knew it was no accident that they conveyed such warmth and peace. That was their purpose: to bring the meditator into a more relaxed alpha state, perhaps even increase his theta and delta brain waves as well. Sarah Weintraub was more familiar with these patterns than he was, but he did know that the lower frequencies often created the most peace while also making the mind more receptive to the paranormal.

Again, he repeated the syllables. He mused over how organic they sounded, how naturally they fit into the mouth. Without even trying, he'd already memorized them. He closed his eyes and recited them again. His warmth and sense of well-being increased. He could actually feel the tension in his body easing, the muscles along his shoulders and into his neck beginning to loosen. He'd be sure to keep the paper, perhaps run the syllables past Sarah when he returned home. Maybe even do a few tests.

Knowing the meditation routine, he decided to continue. What would it hurt? He focused on the sounds, gradually allowing his mind to empty, pushing aside extraneous thoughts, concentrating only upon the syllables. He spoke them again, softer. Then again. And again. Everything grew wonderfully still. Tranquil. And again. There were no other sounds, just the syllables, and the wind, and the rhythmic dripping of water from the roof, and . . .

What was that? Music? He strained to listen. Where was it coming from? Through the door? Down the road? No. It wasn't coming from outside the room. It was coming from inside. But from inside himself. Deep within. And soft—softer than the wind, as soft as a breeze brushing a feather. And he could hear harmonies, harmonies too beautiful to describe, too subtle to ever remember. They resonated through his mind, filling him with their beauty.

He listened, spellbound. He'd read of this type of thing in Eastern mysticism but had never experienced it. Then he noticed something else—an energy, a light. A tiny pulse began somewhere in his feet and gently rippled up through his legs, his stomach, into his chest, through his shoulders, and on into his head. When it was gone, another wave began, washing up through his body, a little brighter, a little faster. Then another, brighter, faster. And another. It was as if his entire body was beginning to breathe, to vibrate to this organic, euphoric rhythm of light. The sensation grew until he realized that he must either give himself over to it entirely or put an end to it. He hesitated a moment—then released control.

Immediately, he began to merge, to meld, to blend into all that was around him. He was no longer Dr. Reichner, owner of two Ph.D.s. He was no longer a single individual. He was part of something greater. Vaster. The vastness was him and he was the vastness . . . growing more and more into the vastness . . . growing into everything . . . everything growing into him . . . one with everything . . . one with the universe . . . becoming the universe . . . he was the universe . . . the universe was he and—

Excellent.

The voice didn't surprise him. It came naturally, as naturally as the music. As the light. As himself.

You do that very well, Doctor.

It was the voice of a child, a boy, maybe eleven or twelve years old. He used adult words and tried to sound grown up, but there was no mistaking his youth.

If you want, you may open your eyes.

Dr. Reichner's lids fluttered, then slowly opened. He was still in the room. Still on his bed. But coiled on the floor before him was a python, at least fifteen feet long. Its head was raised, and its pale golden eyes were locked directly onto his. But Reichner felt no fear. He was part of the python and the python was part of him.

Good evening, Dr. Reichner. Although the jaws did not move, it was obvious the voice came from the creature.

Reichner gathered his thoughts, preparing to speak, but he was surprised to hear his thinking broadcast before he opened his mouth. *Is this—a vision?*

You may call it that, the creature thought back. *I find it a more accurate form of communication.*

Are you— Reichner hesitated. *Are you the one they call . . . Teacher?*

I am called by many names. My mother of birth called me Eric.

Reichner was surprised. Eric was a Western name, certainly not Eastern. Then perhaps the rumors were true. Perhaps he did originally come from America. Perhaps there was some truth to the rumor of a genetic experiment gone haywire.

The python swayed its head silently, waiting for Reichner to complete his thought before it continued. *Others refer to me as Teacher. Some call me Shiva.*

Reichner recognized the name. Shiva was a major god in the Hindu pantheon. The god of destruction.

Still others call me Krishna, Buddha, Mohammed, the Christ.

Reichner nodded. The boy certainly had no lack of ego.

My appearance, does it frighten you?

Even now, amidst the experience, Reichner knew he'd have to be cautious. Provided that he was not going crazy, and provided that this was really the guru he was scheduled to meet, he knew he would have to play him very carefully. *You are a Nagas,* he answered. *In Eastern religions, deities often appear in the form of serpents.*

Very good . . . but of course you don't believe I'm a deity.

Reichner hesitated, already caught.

There was gentle amusement in the boy's voice. *Don't worry. What you believe is of little consequence to me.*

What is . . . of consequence?

This age is drawing to a close. And there's a stirring.

A stirring?

The one we've been waiting for has finally arrived.

Reichner scowled.

He's young, but his spirit has already been stunted. His narrow religious training has prevented his growth. We've decided he needs a tutor to help unlock his gifts.

We?

The cartel who first introduced me to my powers and ... The voice seemed to hesitate.

Reichner pressed in. *And?*

I also have a tutor. The one who guides me in all knowledge of good and evil, but he is not your concern.

Why are you telling me this?

Because we've chosen you to be the youth's instructor.

Reichner's suspicions rose. *Me?*

You understand these things more than most. We sponsored your institute because we knew that this day would come. We told you where to build, because we knew that Bethel Lake is where he would surface.

Reichner's frown deepened. He'd always wondered why they'd been so insistent he locate at Bethel Lake. In the three years he'd been there, he'd encountered only one person in the area who had shown any pronounced psychic ability—a kid, Lewis Thompson. That had been nearly eighteen months ago, and it had been a bust. True, the first few months had been remarkable; he and Lewis had made tremendous strides in developing the boy's paranormal abilities. But then Lewis had lost control, the voices had taken over, and he could no longer control his impulses. As far as Reichner knew, Lewis was still there in the vicinity, but the kid was far too unstable to work with.

You're not talking about the young man I experimented with last year? Reichner thought. *He's psychotic, far too risky to—*

Lewis Thompson was a mistake! the voice angrily interrupted. *Your mistake!*

The outburst surprised Reichner, and he grew quiet. It was time to wait and watch.

The voice regained control. *This one is far more gifted, Doctor. And you will instruct him in how to release and develop those gifts so that he may usher us all into the new paradigm.*

Reichner almost smiled. The boy was obviously trying to sound older than his years. And yet, at least for this meeting, he seemed to be the one calling the shots. Of course Reichner knew that there was a high probability that this was all a delusion, that the sedative probably wasn't the only drug they'd slipped him in the car. But if there was any element of truth to this hallucination, if this guru boy in the guise of a snake was actually communicating with him and making this request, the financial possibilities could be staggering. Who cared whether such a "stirring" actually existed, much less lived near the Institute. If Reichner played his cards right, he could ride this financial bandwagon for another year, maybe two. Who knew how long he could milk money out of—

I am not a fool, Dr. Reichner.

Reichner looked up, startled.

The voice continued. *If you won't find him and work with him, then we will utilize another. We will—*

No, wait. Reichner fumbled, flustered at having his thoughts read. *Who is this kid? Does he have a name? How will I know him?*

There is a dangerous road ahead for him, Doctor. Many enemies surround him. That is why he needs your help. That is why you have been chosen.

Before Reichner could respond, the python dropped its head to the floor. Then it silently slid over its coiled body toward the door.

That's all? Reichner silently called out. *You brought me all the way over here to tell me this?*

There was no answer.

Reichner threw his feet over the side of the bed and rose. *What if I make a mistake? What if the same thing happens to him that happened to Lewis? What if—*

He stopped and watched in amazement as the head passed through the door as effortlessly as if the wooden planks were mist.

You will make no mistakes, the voice spoke as the rest of the python's body vanished through the wood.

How can you be so sure? Reichner called.

The response was distant and faint but still clear enough to hear. *Because I will be with you, Dr. Reichner. Wherever you go, rest assured, I will always be with you.*

A moment later Reichner opened his eyes. He was surprised to see that he was still sitting on the bed. He looked about the room. The door remained closed, the rain still poured, and the python was nowhere to be seen.

Apparently, his meeting with the boy guru had been brought to a close.

Gerty's hand rested on the worn handle of the refrigerator. It had been three days since she'd last eaten. Three days since she'd had her vision of anointing the boy with the long black hair and piercing gray eyes in the river. She was weak and starting to grow light-headed. Common sense told her to eat, or at least to drink some juice. But sometimes common sense carried little weight in spiritual matters.

This kind can come forth by nothing but by prayer and fasting.

She'd read that verse many times during her seventy-eight years. And she'd practiced fasting more times than she could remember. In her younger days, a week-long fast, even two, hadn't been that unusual. But the older she got, the less tolerant her body became of the practice, and the longer it took to recover.

And still the impression stirred and rose within her:

This kind can come forth by nothing but by prayer and fasting.

It really wasn't a voice. Just a knowing. And it certainly wasn't a demand. Instead, it was a quiet request. If she refused, she knew it would go away. There would be no condemnation. After all, she'd been praying and fasting for the boy three days now. Surely, three days was long enough.

She pulled on the refrigerator door. The seal around the edges cracked and popped as it opened. Inside were the usual: bread, bologna, apple juice, tomatoes, a few vegetables. Not well-stocked, but enough, considering the size of her social security check.

For the past several minutes she'd been thinking of toast. A nice, gentle way to break the fast. Warm, soft, crunchy toast—maybe with some of that peanut butter she'd bought the other day. Already her mouth began to water.

She took out the loaf of bread, shut the refrigerator door, and shuffled over to the counter. She undid the plastic fastener, opened the wrapper, and pulled out two slices. But before she dropped them into the toaster, she held them to her nose and breathed in. What a marvelous smell.

This kind can come forth by nothing but by prayer and fasting.

It wasn't incessant, just a tender reminder making sure that this is what she really wanted to do.

She dropped the bread into the toaster and pressed the lever. As she waited, she thought of the words. They were the words of Christ, when he'd spoken to his disciples about casting out demons. But what did demons have to do with the boy? She'd known him when he was a baby, had watched him grow up from afar—had even drawn sketches of him and written letters she'd never mailed, hoping they'd all be of help to him someday. His gifts were pure, she knew that. They were God-given, God-ordained.

This kind can come forth by nothing but by prayer and fasting.

Unless . . .

Maybe those pure gifts were being threatened by something *im*pure, something demonic. Maybe *he* was being threatened. It had happened before, during other times in his childhood. That would explain why the verse kept coming to mind now, why she felt the need to continue interceding.

But it had been three days. *Three days* of not eating. Surely her Lord didn't expect more than that.

She opened the cupboard and pulled down the small jar of peanut butter, yet her mind was still on the boy. He was so young. And when he had looked up at her from the river, he'd seemed so lost, so frightened.

She removed the lid to the peanut butter and pulled off the aluminum foil. The aroma of peanuts filled her senses, almost making her dizzy. If she had been hungry before, she was ravenous now.

Of course, she knew that the boy's emergence would not be easy. She had always known that the forces of hell would do all they could to stop him.

But she was so hungry.

But he looked so frightened.

She opened the drawer and reached for a knife to spread the peanut butter.

This kind can come forth by nothing but by prayer and fasting.

Again, she saw his eyes, felt her own beginning to well up with moisture. She stared at the toaster, watching it blur as tears filled her vision. The boy needed her help. Her continued prayers.

The toast popped up. The combination of warm bread and fresh peanuts was more than she could stand.

But hell was preparing to destroy the boy and God was giving her the opportunity to help protect him—if she wanted.

Another moment passed. And then, ever so slowly, Gerty's veined and wrinkled hand reached for the lid of the peanut butter. She screwed it back on as tears spilled from her eyes. "Thank you," she whispered. "Thank you, dear Lord, thank you."

She turned and headed into the hallway, her slippers shuffling along the threadbare carpet. She entered her tiny room and crossed to the bed. Reaching out both hands, she eased herself down onto her bony knees.

And there, on her knees, Gerty resumed her prayers for the boy. Not because she had to, but because she wanted to. Because she understood the high calling. Because she counted it a privilege.

"Thank you, dear Lord. Thank you, thank you . . ."

CHAPTER 4

I t had been several hours since Brandon's little scene at the printing plant. Now he was in the company's delivery van, grinding the gears in an effort to find reverse. Once he'd found it, he eased the vehicle backward into the loading dock of Moran Research Institute. It was a low-lying building, mostly brick and tinted glass. On its roof were multiple rows of solar panels. Frank, who'd been there more times than Brandon, had always made a big deal about the cool futuristic equipment they had inside. Brandon had never taken the time to check it out, but he did know from experience that their employees' lounge had the best junk food in town.

He brought the van to a stop and rolled down both front windows to keep the insides from roasting. The outside air hit him like an oven. It was three o'clock in the afternoon and pushing a hundred and five. And with the Indiana humidity, forget the oven—it was more like a sauna.

From his side mirror he spotted a grizzled Afro-American approaching. It was Billy, the one-man shipping and receiving staff.

"You're late," the old man groused.

"C'mon, Billy," Brandon said as he popped open the door. "What's a week or two between friends?" He stepped out into the pounding sun. "Am I gonna have to unload this, or will your pet gorilla take care of it?"

Billy shouted over his shoulder. "Simpson! Simpson, get your sorry butt out here!"

A gangly teen suddenly appeared from the comforts of the air-conditioned building. He was summer help, an obvious favor somebody in management owed a friend. Unfortunately for the kid, Billy wasn't impressed by anybody in management.

"Let's move it, boy!"

The kid hopped off the loading dock and quickly moved to the back of the van.

"Come on, come on!" Billy hounded him. "Let's see if you can actually break a sweat today."

Brandon shook his head sympathetically and started for the building.

"Hey, Martus?"

He turned back to the old man.

"Heard what you guys pulled off at the Country Club last night."

Brandon nodded. Good news traveled fast. But before he turned toward the building, Billy hobbled closer. "You guys ever decide to pull off something like that again . . ." He lowered his voice and glanced over his shoulder to make sure he wasn't overheard. "You just count ol' Billy in, you hear?"

Brandon broke into a smile. "I'll keep that in mind." He turned and headed toward the building, as Billy resumed his favorite pastime of chewing up and spitting out his summer help.

Brandon entered the building. Inside, it was a good thirty degrees cooler. It took a moment for his eyes to adjust to the dim, recessed lighting as he started down the hall. The carpet was maroon with gray rectangular patterns, and the walls were paneled in thick oak. On both sides, running the entire length of the hall, hung modernistic pieces of art composed of torn paper and cardboard. He thought they were pretty stupid—and undoubtedly pretty expensive. Everything about this place was expensive.

It hadn't been a good day. Nor had it been a particularly good night. His dreams of Jenny were coming back again. The past three nights had been worse than ever—so real, so detailed. When they'd originally come, during those first few weeks after her death, they'd left him crying, sobbing her name, until Momma would wake him, until she would hold him and gently rock him as tears streamed down both of their faces.

And now they were returning, more vivid than ever.

The shrinks said it was just his guilt, a way of "achieving closure" and saying good-bye.

His Christian upbringing insisted that the dead never come back and appear to the living—no wandering souls dropping by séances to say hi, or spooky ghosts sticking around to haunt houses. "Absent from the body, present with the Lord," that's what the Bible taught. And those attempting to make contact with the departed, to try to cross the barrier were called sorcerers, practitioners of the occult—a crime so heinous that in the Old Testament those who practiced it were to be put to death.

But Jenny had seemed so real ...

And now his dreams of her had begun incorporating pieces of reality. Not accurately, not completely, but what had happened at the plant a few hours earlier was certainly no coincidence. Or was it? Part of him hoped so. But there was another part, the part that wanted so desperately to reach out to his little sister, to bury his face into her hair, to hold her and never, never let her go.

For a moment Brandon felt his eyes start to burn with moisture. He quickly blinked it back. Those first few months had been an embarrassment, breaking into tears at the most inconvenient of times. It had taken quite a while to get a handle on his emotions, and he wasn't about to let them start sneaking up on him again.

Up ahead was another hallway, but he ignored it because to his immediate right was the employee's lounge. The place was deserted. Just tables, chairs, and the twenty-seven-inch TV mounted up in the corner, currently featuring Oprah with her latest alien-abducted guest. Brandon wiped the sweat off his face with his T-shirt and headed over to check out the vending machines. With any luck there still might be some—ah, yes, there they were: barbecued sunflower seeds. There were still half a dozen packages left, about the same number as the last time he'd visited. Apparently, word of this delicacy had not yet spread. Their loss, his gain. It wasn't much, but drowning his anxiety in a couple bags of these culinary delights wouldn't hurt. He dropped in fifty cents, pushed D–15, and watched the first pack fall into the bin. He repeated the process for another.

After retrieving the bags, he tore one open and poured a few into his mouth. Excellent. Weird, but excellent. He walked back into the hallway. It was the end of the day and the place was deserted. And since he wasn't particularly excited about going back out into the heat, and since he could stand a little diversion, and since Frank had always made such a big deal about the equipment—now would be as good a time as any to do a little exploring.

"I think I can handle her from here, Dr. Weintraub," the stocky orderly said.

"Are you sure?" Sarah asked. She looked dubiously at the sedated patient between them as they walked her down one of the Institute's hallways. "Do you want me to call anybody at the hospital?" The three of them proceeded slowly down the hallway.

"No, I should get her back there and settled in with as little fuss as possible. If you know what I mean."

Sarah knew exactly what he meant. She'd had ethical questions about using patients from Vicksburg State Mental Hospital ever since she came on board. Unfortunately, Dr. Reichner hadn't. He was certain that some of the mentally ill had more highly developed paranormal abilities than others. And, thanks to his manipulative charm, along with the proper financial incentive discreetly slipped to the proper assistant manager, a carefully screened handful of patients participated in the tests. It was a dangerous game to play, but one that Reichner insisted was worth the risk.

Sarah slowed to a stop in front of Observation Room Two, where they'd been viewing this subject since early afternoon. She turned and spoke directly to the woman. "Thank you for your help today, Francine."

The woman turned her head, but the glazed look in her eyes made it unclear whether she'd heard. Her mouth hung open, and she gave no response. Sarah watched sympathetically. Earlier she had tried to convince the orderly that sedation wasn't necessary, that she could verbally talk the hysterical woman back down. But when Francine's agitation turned physical, the orderly insisted that it was better to be safe than sorry.

"Say 'You're welcome,'" the orderly said.

Francine moved her mouth, but no sound came. Just a small trickle of saliva.

Sarah pulled a tissue from her dress pocket and gently wiped the woman's chin. It wasn't exactly professional detachment, but Sarah could never feel detached, at least not with the physically or mentally impaired. She wasn't sure why, though she suspected that much of it had to do with little Carrie, her sweetheart of a niece who suffered from Down's Syndrome. Her brother and sister-in-law had known of Carrie's condition long before her birth, but they had decided to go through with the pregnancy anyway—a choice that pricked Sarah's own conscience. Maybe that's why Carrie held such a powerful place in Sarah's heart. And maybe that's why the Francines of the world, the weakest, the most vulnerable, always brought out the mother and nurturer in her.

Maybe. Then again, maybe it was her simple understanding that they were no different from her. That we are all cripples in some way. If not mentally or physically then, at least for some, as in her case, emotionally.

"Come on, girl," the orderly said as he eased Francine's arm forward and started her down the hall. "Let's get you home."

"Bye-bye," Sarah said.

Francine looked at her, gave what could have passed as a smile, then shuffled off toward the exit. Sarah stood, watching, until they rounded the corner and disappeared. Then, at last, she turned and took the three steps that led up into the observation room.

The back wall of the narrow room was full of racks of electronic equipment—recorders, computers, monitors. At the front was a console equipped with an intercom and a variety of complicated controls. Above the console was the one-way mirror, three feet by seven, that looked down into Lab Two, the very lab she'd worked in the night before—and the one housing the leather recliner where Francine had sat most of the afternoon.

Sarah reached to the console and snapped off the four red floodlights that were directed at the recliner. The lab grew dark, although the recliner was still clearly visible. On its seat lay a set of headphones, a pair of clear safety goggles, and two halves of a Ping-Pong ball. These had been used to help ease Francine into a deeper state of rest. Through the headphones, Dr. Reichner's prerecorded voice had taken Francine through the standard yoga relaxation exercises, tightening and releasing various muscle groups in her body. Meanwhile, the two halves of the Ping-Pong ball, with felt glued to their cut edges, had been placed over her eyes and held in position by the safety goggles. This was far more satisfactory than using a blindfold, which could press against the eyeball, creating distracting images. Meanwhile, the floodlights had filled Francine's vision with lovely, red nothingness.

The first hour had gone according to schedule. As soon as Francine had reached a relaxed state, another subject, in this case a retired Marine Corps officer who sat next to Sarah up in the Observation Room, stared at a randomly selected video image on a monitor. From here he had tried to mentally transmit to Francine what he had seen by sheer concentration. This was a common procedure, one Sarah had performed dozens of times. Everything had gone by the book—until, suddenly, for no explained reason, Francine had started growing agitated. They had tried to calm her, but nothing seemed to work. She had grown worse and worse until the orderly finally had sedated her and insisted that they stop the session.

Sarah plopped into the seat behind the console and sighed wearily. Like it or not, this day had become just as unpredictable as the last three. What *was* going on?

She punched up the DAT controls. Immediately, the speakers began to play back a voice. Francine's voice. The one they'd recorded just minutes before the outburst.

"And it makes my mouth all tingly inside. Everyone has it on their food and when they laugh I can see it on their tongues. It's all yellow and icky. I wonder if I have it on my tongue and I'm afraid to laugh in case they see it. I must be very—"

"Sounds like mustard."

The voice startled Sarah and she spun around to the open door. Silhouetted in it was a young man with long hair and impressive shoulders.

Her nerves already on edge, Sarah demanded, "What are you doing sneaking up on people like that?"

He gave no answer.

"Who are you?"

He entered the room. "I wanted to say thanks for last night."

Now she saw them. The eyes. The same piercing, steel-gray eyes she'd seen the evening before. "You're the boy from the Club."

He gave a half nod, holding her gaze. She sensed the power of his eyes again, the way they locked onto hers without letting go, making her a little unsteady inside. But she saw something else as well, something deeper, something very sensitive.

She forced herself to take a breath, then demanded, "How'd you get in here?"

He stepped toward the EMG monitor against the back wall and looked at it a moment. She could feel her senses sharpening, coming alive, aware of his every move. She tried to cover her uneasiness. "Excuse me?" she repeated. "How did you get in?"

"Deliveries."

Besides the power and sensitivity, there was an earthiness, a lack of pretension. From his worn Levi's to his T-shirt, what you saw was what you got. Still, she wasn't exactly wowed by his social skills. She tried again. Another tack, not quite as abrasive. "That was quite a stunt you boys pulled last night."

"You use all this stuff?"

"Pardon me?"

"All these monitors and stuff, you use them?"

"Yes. Well, most of them." She shifted. Along with his power and sensitivity came an unpredictability that both attracted and challenged her. "Lately, we've—uh, been experimenting with the Ganzfield Technique."

He looked at her.

Good, she had his attention, or at least part of it. "Ganzfield," she repeated.

His gaze was unwavering. She felt her face hike into a self-conscious smile, hoping for some response. There was none. She gave her hair a nervous push behind her ears and continued talking. "You see the lab down there?" She pointed through the one-way mirror to the room below.

He crossed for a better view. As he leaned past her, their bodies were less than a foot apart. She cleared her throat. It was important that she keep talking. "A volunteer is subjected to sensory deprivation—that's what the recliner and Ping-Pong balls are for."

He seemed unimpressed. She felt herself growing more flustered. "Once they're relaxed, they try to visualize an image another volunteer is viewing on this TV monitor here."

"ESP?" the kid asked as he turned and moved past her. The room was so narrow that he accidentally brushed against her hair. At least she thought it was an accident.

"Well, actually, we call it PSI."

Still not looking at her, he was examining more equipment.

"Excuse me." The edge had returned to her voice as she swiveled in her chair to more directly confront him. "Is there something specific you're interested in here, or did you just decide to take a personal tour?"

He didn't look at her. "Not really."

"Then would you mind telling me why you're here?"

Finally he turned to her. There were those eyes again. His lips moved slightly. Was that a flicker of a smile? Was he flirting with her? Or was it something else?

"What?" she asked.

His smile grew—and then he looked down to the ground and shook his head.

"No, please," she demanded, "I would appreciate your telling me what is so amusing."

"You Techies." He glanced up at her. Was that still a smile? "You come in here with all your money, all your fancy equipment." She strained to hear some teasing in his voice, some humor. "And all you're doing is hanging out playing fancy video games."

The phrase hit hard. That was it. Eyes or no eyes, the kid had definitely hit a nerve. Maybe he was kidding, maybe he wasn't. It didn't matter, not now. She swallowed, trying to keep her voice level despite the anger. "These *games,* as you call them—they may very well answer some of humankind's most basic questions."

The kid shook his head in amusement and moved past her toward the door.

The civility in Sarah's voice slipped a couple more notches. "Haven't you ever wondered who you are? Where you've come from, where you're going?"

He reached the door and turned to her. "Haven't lost much sleep over it."

"Maybe you should try it sometime."

It was meant as a slam, but he didn't seem to notice. "I doubt that some flake staring at a family picnic is going to help anybody."

Sarah swallowed again, though now her mouth was bone dry. "I think it's time you leave."

"You got that right." He turned and headed down the three steps into the hallway.

"Hold it—wait just a minute."

He turned back.

"The tape I was playing. How'd you know the subject was describing a picnic?"

"I heard it."

"No, you didn't." Sarah watched him carefully. "We never got that far, she never saw a picnic. The other subject was concentrating on it, but she never saw it."

The kid shrugged. "Guess it's just my PSI." With that he turned and was gone.

Sarah remained sitting, staring at the empty doorway. Frustrated, unnerved. And, although she hated to admit it, very, very intrigued.

"This is too weird. The board's never done anything like this before."

"Shut up," Lewis snapped.

Pierced Eyebrow stared at the plastic, triangular pointer under his and Lewis's fingertips. It continued moving as if under its own power, flying across the Ouija board, stopping at letters, spelling out words almost faster than Acne Face, the third member of the party, could write them down.

Lewis also watched the pointer but with far less interest. He no longer relied on such barbaric forms of communication. So crude, so juvenile. This was nothing but a children's board game that could be purchased at nearly every toy store in the country. "Communicate with the dead," its advertising proclaimed. "Contact spirits."

Yeah, right.

It was a kids' game, plain and simple. He'd even read that it was the most popular kids' board game in America. Hardly a tool for someone with his giftedness.

But the past twenty-four hours had again grown intolerable. The voices had resumed their screaming. One shrieking over another, over another. Too loud and numerous for him to discern any meaning, they were now a continuous cacophony of screaming rages and incessant urgings.

But urgings for what?

SLAUGHTER, BUTCHER, OBLITERATE, KILL!

Yes, but kill what? More animals? Not even the pig had satisfied them for long. He had to find some way to reduce the voices, to filter out the craziest screamings and understand what the others wanted.

They'd started seven years ago. The voices. Back in high school, back when Mr. Johnson, the philosophy teacher, had turned him on to Eastern mysticism, particularly Zen Buddhism. It was no big deal—just a cool way of relaxing and "connecting to the cosmic consciousness within." To heighten the effect, Lewis and a few friends started using pot, then later, hallucinogenics.

And then the whispering began. A gentle presence. Then another, and another. It seemed that the more he emptied his mind, the stronger and more numerous those presences became. Sometimes they whispered things to him, warned him, revealed information that no one could possibly have known. And the more he gave himself to them, the stronger they became.

That was when Dr. Reichner over at Moran Research Institute took him under his wings. He was one of the few who believed that Lewis wasn't crazy, that the voices really did exist. He began running tests on Lewis. And the more tests he ran, the more Reichner reassured Lewis that there truly was something remarkable about him, something "gifted." That was his exact word: *gifted.*

For a while everything had been great. Lewis had been Dr. Reichner's golden boy. But, as the tests went deeper and deeper, as he surrendered more and more of himself to the voices, they began to take more and more control. Eventually Lewis, growing frightened, tried to silence the voices, to demand that they leave.

That's when they became ugly.

That's when they grew terrifying, demanding. That's when they began disrupting the experiments, filling Lewis's head with shrieks and screams, causing him to explode in violence. And that's when Reichner turned traitor, insisting that it was just too dangerous to continue his experiments. Of course Lewis had pleaded with him, had begged him to understand. His giftedness was certainly worth the risk of a few outbursts. But Reichner disagreed and had said no to Lewis.

Unfortunately, it wasn't possible for Lewis to say no to the voices. They kept growing, in power and in number. And they kept increasing their demands. Usually there seemed to be one or two in charge, and Lewis could pick out their voices and understand what they wanted. But not when the others joined in. Not when they all began screaming and shrieking their demands for violence at the same time.

Yet, even now, he knew they didn't just want violence for its own sake. Even now, Lewis sensed a broader purpose. There was some sort of plan behind all of this, some logic. If he could just figure out what it was that they really wanted.

He looked down at the list of words Acne Face was writing from the letters that appeared on the board:

Slay

Execute

Kill

Exterminate

What did he need the board for? These were the same words he heard on his own. There must be some sort of pattern here. If the voices would just stop screaming long enough for him to—

"Is anybody else getting bored?" Acne Face asked as he stopped to rub the cramp out of his hand. "We've been doing this like for a couple hours, now."

Pierced Eyebrow glanced up. "Yeah, maybe we should give it a rest."

"Or start asking it other stuff," Acne Face said.

"Like what?" Pierced Eyebrow asked.

"I don't know. Hey, I got it. Let's ask it if I'm going to be rich."

Pierced Eyebrow frowned. Suddenly his face lit up. "No, I got it. Ask if—ask it if I'm going to get lucky with Julie Nelson."

Acne Face snickered.

"No, better yet, ask it if there's like some kinda spell I can cast on her—you know, words or something that will make her—"

Lewis leaped to his feet. He grabbed the board and threw it across the room. Then he turned his rage on the boys, swearing vehemently at them, using only a fraction of the words filling his head.

"Hey, take it easy," Acne Face protested as he rose to his feet.

Pierced Eyebrow did the same. "What'd we do?"

"Get out!" Lewis screamed. "Get out of my house!" He wasn't sure if it was he yelling or one of the voices. Maybe it was both. Didn't matter. He'd had enough of the two boys, of their childishness, of their need to be entertained. What was happening to Lewis was far more important than entertainment.

"Easy, man," they said. "Just take it easy."

Lewis swept the beer bottles and ashtray off the table. They exploded against the wall.

"Hey, come on," Pierced Eyebrow protested.

Lewis focused on him.

The boy took a half step back. "Take it easy, man, just—take it easy, okay?"

Spotting a half-empty bottle of Jack Daniels on the floor, Lewis scooped it up and smashed it on the table. Booze and glass sprayed in all directions. Before Pierced Eyebrow could move, Lewis lunged at him with the broken bottle. "Get out!"

Pierced Eyebrow stumbled back. "Hey!"

Lewis rounded the table and lunged again, this time catching the boy's arm, slicing through his shirtsleeve.

Pierced Eyebrow grabbed his arm. "You're crazy!"

Acne Face was already pulling his buddy back, trying to get him out of the room. "Let's go. Let's get outa here."

"Get out!" Lewis shrieked. "Get out! Get out!"

The boys turned and broke for the front door.

"Get out!"

"You're crazy, man! You're cra—"

"Get out!"

They threw open the door and raced into the night.

Lewis stood in the tiny living room, all alone, breathing hard, trying to get his bearings. Something was about to happen. Inside, he was about to explode. But he felt something else, too. A focusing. A focusing that would direct the explosion. And God help whoever it was that would receive the brunt of—

Hold it—*whoever?* That was the word he'd thought. "*Who*ever."

Then it *was* a person. The senseless animal slaughters had been only a harbinger, a preparation for the real thing. A real *person.*

But who?

Lewis stumbled back into the kitchen, kicking aside the empty pizza boxes and beer bottles. He yanked out a kitchen drawer, letting it and its contents spill to the floor. He dropped to his knees and in the dim light began searching through the clutter. A moment later he found it, wrapped in a cellophane bag. A joint. But not just any joint. He tore open the bag. This was a joint soaked in PCP, angel dust.

It had been partially smoked. That's how it was with this stuff. So powerful that he only took one or two tokes at a time. That's all he needed to make the connection, to feel the universe swelling up inside him, to open his mind to the infinite.

But not tonight.

He rummaged through the spilled debris on the floor until he spotted a book of matches. With trembling hands he placed the joint between his lips and struck a match. It flared, momentarily lighting the room and his face.

He took the first drag, inhaling deeply, letting it burn the back of his throat, his lungs. He held in the smoke as long as possible, making sure none of it was wasted. Then, a moment later, he felt it. The growing sense of perception, the strength surging through his body and mind. Normally, he would take one more toke and butt it out. But not tonight.

He exhaled and took another long drag. Perspiration popped out on his forehead. But it was only perspiration for a second. Soon it became beads of enlightenment. Rotating like colored prisms, vibrating in perfect synchronization, each connected to the consciousness of the universe, each pumping its power through the pores of his skin and into his brain, filling him with indescribable wisdom, overwhelming strength.

He exhaled and took a third toke. Then a fourth. He would continue until he had finished the joint. Then he would know exactly what he was to do. More important, he would have the unlimited power necessary to do it.

CHAPTER 5

"I'm telling you," Frank said, letting out a burp that swelled to a belch, "if we formed ourselves a band, we'd have to fight off the chicks."

Brandon said nothing as he inched the pickup along State Street. It was Friday night and summer. This meant that all four lanes of the main drag through Bethel Lake were packed with teens and young adults enjoying the ageless American tradition of cruising. Several shouted to one another from passing cars; others checked out the newest wheels or the added accessories to those wheels. Then, of course, there was all that guy-and-gal action.

Spotting an interesting prospect, Frank leaned past Del and shouted out Brandon's window. "Hey, Marty! Where'd you find the babe?"

A young man in a four-wheeler beside them flashed Frank a grin as his free arm tightened around the buxom blonde sitting beside him.

"Listen, sweetheart?" Frank shouted.

The girl turned toward him, all smiles.

"You stick with ol' Marty there. You got yourself a real nice boy."

She agreed, snuggling deeper into his arms.

"But when you want a man, you be sure to look me up, hear?"

The girl giggled and Marty pretended to laugh. But as they pulled away, his free hand was firing off a universal gesture of contempt.

Frank's laughter reverberated through the cab. No sooner had it faded than Del pointed at something up ahead and asked, "Say, guys?"

There, two lanes over, in the oncoming traffic, was Henderson in his Firebird. Beside him sat Reggie, the other kid from the Club. And crammed in the back were two passengers who could have passed as linebackers for any Superbowl team.

Frank was the first to speak. "You don't suppose . . . They're not looking for—"

The occupants of the Firebird spotted the pickup and immediately broke into a tirade of oaths and gestures.

"Lucky guess," Del replied.

Henderson began honking, trying to force the cars ahead of him to pull out of the way.

Brandon glanced up the street. The traffic in front of him was queuing up to stop at a traffic light. Luckily, he was in the outside lane, a good two lanes away from the approaching Firebird. But, judging by their anger, two lanes might not be enough.

As if proving his point, the doors to the Firebird flew open and the backseat passengers climbed out, rising to their full Herculean stature.

Frank cleared his throat. "Uh—Brandon?"

The hulks started across the lanes toward the pickup.

Immediately Del reached past Brandon and rolled up the driver's window. "I hope we're talking safety glass, here."

They closed in, less than twenty feet away. Other passengers in other cars turned to watch.

Fifteen feet.

"Yo, Bran."

Ten.

Suddenly Brandon yanked the steering wheel hard to the right and punched the gas. The pickup bounced up the curb and onto the sidewalk. Brandon hit the gas harder, causing the rear end to slide out—and the approaching hulks to leap out of the way.

"Alrighteeeee!" Frank shouted.

Pedestrians scattered as Brandon guided his pickup carefully down the sidewalk. Del turned pale and a wide-eyed Frank gulped his beer.

Brandon threw a look over his shoulder. The linebackers had already clambered back into Henderson's car. Copying Brandon's action, the Firebird bounced up on the opposite sidewalk and quickly backed up after him. Apparently, they had no intention of letting the pickup get away.

Brandon reached the end of the block and headed out into the intersection. Oncoming cars hit their brakes and horns blared as he made a hard right, tromped on the accelerator, and peeled out down the street.

The streams of water pelted Sarah's back, her neck, and the top of her head. But she didn't move. She remained on the floor of the shower, legs drawn in, head down, huddled into a tight ball as the water beat against her body. She was done crying now. At least she hoped so.

She had made a mistake. Maybe it was the lack of sleep, the second glass of wine, or just bad luck. Whatever the reason, she had momentarily lowered her defenses. It had taken only a moment. She'd started off by thinking about her day at work and the strange effect the boy from the Club had had upon her earlier that evening, which had led to memories of Samuel, which had led to memories of the baby . . . which led to . . .

. . . the grinning picture of Garfield up on the ceiling, and the shots of Novocain, and the soothing voice of the doctor, and the pain from the metal rods forcing open her cervix, and the assurance to herself that it was only a thing—a nine-week growth of her body, and then remembering that it had different DNA, which made it different from her body, and the grinning Garfield, and the doctor's soothing voice, and the digging and poking of the nozzle, and the sound of the suction machine with its clear vacuum cleaner canister, and the blood filling the tube, and the screams in her head begging the baby to forgive her, and the hope that he wouldn't feel pain, and the knowing that his pain receptor cells and neuro pathways were already forming, and the doctor's soothing voice, and the grinning cat, and the dizziness, and the doctor's concern over her loss of blood, and her demands to know what was wrong, and the panic, and the fighting for consciousness . . .

And waking up in a hospital room with a major portion of her reproductive system removed, followed by the helplessness, the outrage, the guilt, and the loss.

Back in the shower, Sarah's body convulsed in another sob. And then another. The crying had started again. "No!" she whispered harshly. "Stop it!" She forced herself to her feet. But another sob escaped and then another until she was leaning against the wall, her arms wrapped tight around herself.

For a moment, she thought of crumpling back to the floor. But experience told her she had to stop. *Now.* Not another sob, not another tear. This was nothing but self-pity, and self-pity served no purpose. It could undo no wrong; it could never bring him back. Now all she could do was make sure his sacrifice meant something. Now she had to be the best she could be, to work harder, to prove herself, to prove his death was not entirely in vain.

With a deep breath, Sarah stood upright and reached out to shut off the water. She stepped out of the shower and numbly reached for the towel. She was spent and exhausted, but she had to keep moving, to keep pushing. She was good at that. She could do that. She'd been doing that for years.

Five minutes later, Sarah Weintraub scooped the keys off her kitchen counter, passed the sink buried in two weeks' worth of dishes, and headed out the back door to her car. It was almost 11:00 P.M. Fortunately, she had keys to the Institute, which meant she could go to work anytime she wanted to.

Anytime she had to.

Things were coming to a head faster than Gerty had imagined possible. She was now conscious of the forces gathering, moving into position around the boy. Tonight there would be at least one assault. Maybe more. And others would follow, stronger, more frequent.

The hunger pangs were gone. They usually left during the third day. Now there was only the sense of urgency—and her prayers. There were no visions, no supernatural experiences, just prayer.

Over the years, she'd learned that although they were interesting, the supernatural experiences weren't usually necessary. More often than not, it was simple prayer that was the most effective . . . and the most powerful. Sometimes this merely involved singing, or directing quiet thoughts of adoration toward the Lord. Sometimes it was the slow, thoughtful reading of Scripture. Other times, she found herself confessing her failures, asking him to forgive her. And finally, like tonight, there were times of heartrending supplication and intercession.

"Please, dear God, protect him. Whatever he's goin' through, whatever he's about to meet, save him, protect him, dear Lord."

She had prayed for him frequently over the years. On more than one occasion, forces had tried to rise up and destroy him—but none like those coming at him now. Still, such attacks shouldn't surprise her. If he was to become such a formidable threat to evil, why shouldn't the forces of evil concentrate their attack upon him? It made perfect sense.

However, there was one thing that she had never understood: the boy's own weaknesses—his internal doubts, his external sins.

Why? Why did her Lord always choose to fight the impossible wars? Wasn't battling against the outside evil enough? Did he always have to choose as his champion someone who was wounded and weak on the inside as well? And what of the young man's sins? He was certainly no saint. How could her Lord use someone like him to accomplish such great purposes?

The thought had barely risen before Gerty broke into a quiet smile. Wouldn't she have said the same thing about other great men of God? Jacob the con artist, Moses the murderer, David the adulterer, Paul the persecutor?

Her eyes welled with moisture. It was true, his ways were not hers. And if one of his habits was to choose the weak to confound the wise, then so be it.

But this boy . . .

A picture came to mind. She'd sketched it years ago. It was a picture of the boy as a weak sapling, a tiny olive tree struggling to grow in a desert. At his roots were a thick, impenetrable mass of weeds that choked out the water and nourishment of the soil. Higher up, on the trunk, were dense parasitic vines that sucked out what little life he had managed to acquire. She sighed heavily. There were so many fronts on which to battle. The desert heat, the thick weeds, the attacking vines, his own internal weakness.

Should she pray against the vines, those demonic counterfeits trying to sap all of his strength? But what about the other outside forces—the heat, the weeds? And what of his internal struggles—his deep emotional scars, his obvious lack of faith?

She shook her head. No, a higher level of prayer was needed. Not a prayer of pleading and begging and groveling. But a prayer aligning itself with her Lord's will. A prayer thanking God in advance for accomplishing his purposes, whatever those purposes would be.

The smile returned to Gerty's lips. Thanking God in the midst of attack and confusion made absolutely no sense at all. Which was another reason she believed she was on the right track, that this was how she was supposed to pray for the boy.

She never understood why God didn't simply accomplish his will on his own—why he insisted upon his children joining him, why he allowed them to become the catalyst for releasing the will that he had already determined. But she always thanked him for the opportunity. What a privilege to work side by side with her Creator. What a privilege for the God of the universe to release his awesome will through her frail prayers . . .

Once again tears of gratitude sprang to Gerty's eyes as she remained on her knees, beginning to quietly and persistently pray in tandem with God's will—not fully knowing what it was but thanking him and worshiping him in advance as he began to accomplish it.

Brandon raced out of the city on old Highway 17. It twisted and turned, following Hudson Creek some thirty feet below.

"Whoooooeee!" Frank shouted, popping another brew. "Mario baby does it again!"

But there was little time to celebrate. Brandon had spotted headlights in his rearview mirror. They had just rounded the last bend and were quickly gaining on him. Suddenly, without warning, he cranked the wheel hard to the left and threw the truck into a screeching 180.

"Oh no," Del moaned, grabbing the dash for support.

"Déjà-vu!" Frank shouted.

Brandon straightened the pickup, hit the gas, and they shot back down the road, heading directly toward the other car.

Inside the Firebird, Henderson squinted as the glaring headlights approached. He steeled himself. He would not back down. Not this time. He'd been humiliated once, and once was more than enough. He just hoped that the driver of the pickup would be smart enough to know this.

Brandon pressed harder on the accelerator, and they picked up speed. Del desperately searched the seat beside him. "Where's my seat belt? I can't find my seat belt!"

The car and truck bore down upon one another.

Inside the Firebird no one said a word. They were somber and silent. Henderson flashed his lights on high. "Come on," he whispered to the driver of the pickup. "Don't be stupid, don't be stupid . . ."

The lights blinded Brandon as the Firebird approached, steady, veering neither to the left nor to the right. Brandon set his jaw.

They were seventy yards apart. Sixty. Fifty.

"Come on," Henderson whispered under his breath, "come on, come on . . ."

Forty. Thirty.

Suddenly, Brandon knew. He sensed, with complete conviction, that the Firebird would not budge—that if they were to survive, *he'd* have to back down.

Twenty yards.

He yanked the wheel hard, swerving to the right just as the Firebird roared past. Brandon fought the steering as they slid down the highway—until they ran out of asphalt, dropped six feet into a steep ditch, and bounced to a jarring stop.

A moment of silence passed before Frank observed, "They learn fast."

But Brandon wasn't finished. Not by a long shot. He threw the pickup into first and stomped on the accelerator. The bank was steep and the gravel was loose. The back tires spun, spitting stone and gravel, but the truck barely moved.

Brandon let up on the gas and wiped his face.

"Oh, well," Del offered hopefully.

Frank remained silent, waiting to see what Brandon would do next.

Again he pressed the accelerator, and again the tires spun. He pushed harder. The engine roared. The tires threw gravel and whined. Ever so slowly, the pickup began to move. They inched their way up the bank. The tires began to smoke, but Brandon would not let up. At last the tires caught the edge of the asphalt and squealed as they dug in and pushed off.

Brandon made another U-turn and they were on their way. But the Firebird was nowhere in sight.

"Where are they?" Del asked.

"Don't worry," Frank assured him, "we'll find 'em."

Del moaned and sank back into the seat.

A quarter mile up the road, Henderson had turned the Firebird around and eased it to a stop in the center of the road, directly behind a sharp, blind curve.

"What are you doing?" one of the hulks in the back-seat demanded.

Without answering, Henderson turned off the engine. He left his lights on and climbed out of the car.

"What!" Reggie asked. "Are you crazy?"

"They want to play hardball," Henderson said, "let 'em play hardball."

"Yeah, but—"

"Relax," Henderson said. "He'll see the lights in time. Barely, but he'll see them."

"This is crazy," Reggie protested.

But the driver had already pocketed his keys and was heading for the side of the road.

"Henderson? Henderson!"

Reggie glanced at the other passengers. It was obvious that they didn't approve, but it was also obvious that they weren't going to remain in the car for a debate. They quickly piled out and joined Henderson as he headed up the steep embankment for a better view.

Back in the pickup, Brandon was a study in concentration. Wherever the Firebird had gone, it couldn't be far. Up ahead was another curve. He picked up speed. Neither Frank nor Del said a word; their eyes remained fixed on the road.

Up on the embankment, Henderson and the guys heard the pickup approach. A couple of them fidgeted in concern, but no one spoke.

Brandon hit the curve. He'd barely started into it when his eyes widened in surprise: His headlights caught a white reflection directly in their path.

It was Jenny! She was wearing her white gown and holding a lantern.

He slammed on the brakes and steered hard to avoid her. Unfortunately he was too distracted to see the parked Firebird appear just around the bend.

"Look out!" Frank shouted. "Look out!"

Brandon spotted the car and threw the truck in the other direction. It made a three-quarter spin, barely missing the Firebird, and slid to a stop on the far side of the road, just inches from a steep drop-off overlooking Hudson Creek.

Suddenly everything grew very silent. A dog from a nearby farm began to bark.

At the top of the bank Henderson gloated. It had gone perfectly. Not only had he humiliated the driver, but he'd also impressed his buddies. He began to slide down the embankment, back to the road. "Come on," he called. "Nothing worth sticking around here for."

The others agreed and followed, laughing and scoffing—more as a release of tension than for humor's sake. They threw a few gibes and taunts at the distant pickup before finally arriving at the Firebird and piling in. Once inside, Henderson fired up the engine and, after his buddies shouted a couple more oaths for good measure, he took off. He glanced in the rearview mirror and caught a glimpse of the long-haired driver. The kid was already out of his truck. It would have been nice to stick around, rub his nose in it a bit, but justice had been served. And sticking around to bask in the victory would have definitely been uncool.

Outside, Brandon barely noticed the Firebird pulling away. He was too busy searching the road. "Jenny!" He raced to the bend where she had stood. "Jenny! Jenny!" He was breathing hard, trying to catch his breath. "Jenny!"

But nobody was there. He slowed. "Jenny . . ."

Peering through the darkness, he searched the bank above him. Nothing. He spun around, looking all directions, then dashed to the other side of the road, looking down toward the creek.

"Jenny!"

He blinked back the tears burning his eyes. He held his breath, straining to hear the slightest crack of a twig or rustle of brush. Nothing but crickets and the barking dog.

"Brandon! Yo, Brandon." Frank was approaching from the truck.

But Brandon barely heard as he continued searching the bank, the woods, the creek. *"Jenny!"*

"Hey, Bran." Frank slowed to a stop. "Jenny's not here, man."

Brandon turned to him.

Frank continued, softer. "She's dead, man. You know that. She's not out here. Nobody's out here."

The tears spilled onto Brandon's cheeks.

"You all right?"

Angrily, Brandon swiped at his eyes.

"Hey, don't worry 'bout it. We'll get 'em next time." Frank forced a grin. "I promise you, ol' buddy, it's our turn. We'll get 'em next."

Brandon stood in the road, searching the bank above them, the creek below. Finally, he turned and looked back down the deserted highway. Of course, Frank was right, there was nobody there. Nobody.

At least, not now.

It had taken nearly an hour for Sarah to lose herself in her work. But at last she'd been able to pull out of the relentless whirlpool of memories. The anniversary had nearly gotten her, but finally she had managed to pull out. And she'd do her best not to swim so close to those emotional waters again.

Over the past several minutes, she had begun to feel something else, another emotion. At first she'd thought it was the remains of her little pity party in the shower. But it wasn't. It was a strange, uneasy feeling, like she was being watched. But that was impossible. It was after 1:00 A.M. on a Saturday morning. No one had been in the Institute for hours. Just her. She'd parked her car in the front lot, entered through the lobby, and made sure the door locked behind her.

Still . . .

She took off her glasses and rubbed her eyes. It was probably exhaustion, or the anniversary, or her nerves—maybe all of the above.

She redirected her attention to her work. Sitting before the console in Lab One, she stared up at the figures on the monitor's screen. She sighed and put on her glasses. She was a neurobiologist, not a statistician. But, from the start, Dr. Reichner had made it clear that like all of the other parapsychology labs, they needed to include a "probability value"—the number that indicates the probability of an event happening simply by chance. This creates a standard that all tests can be compared to. For instance, take a test result with a probability value (p) of .05 or less. That simply means that the possibility of it happening by chance is less than five percent, or "$p < .05$." That's the normal cutoff point in PSI research. Anything higher than .05 is not taken seriously, but anything lower, such as "$p < .01$" (the chances of an event occurring as less than 1 in 100) is considered significant.

Sarah stared at her figures. She couldn't be sure, but her best estimate was that the probability value of this week's events in the lab was somewhere around $p < .0000000000001$.

No wonder her nerves were on edge. Maybe she was entitled to be a little paranoid. Something was very weird here.

For the second time in as many minutes Sarah stole a glance over her shoulder. There was nothing but the equipment and the three-by-seven, one-way mirror looking down on her from the observation room. Yet it was the mirror that caused her the uneasiness. Anybody could be up in that room spying down on her and she would never know it.

Or would she?

Like everybody else, hadn't she, at one time or another, known when someone was watching her? And wasn't that exactly the feeling she was experiencing now? Once again she tried to shove the thought out of her mind, only this time it wouldn't budge.

With a heavy sigh, she pushed herself back from the console. Something had to be done. Reluctantly, she rose, passed through the narrow room directly beside the one-way mirror, and out into the hallway.

Everything was perfectly still, perfectly normal, except—

How odd. Hadn't the door to the observation room been closed earlier? Maybe not. She couldn't be sure. But they always kept the doors closed overnight and through the weekend to help protect the equipment from dust.

With more than a little trepidation, she moved toward the observation room door. She thought of calling out, of asking if someone was there. But she was being ridiculous. She stepped up the three stairs leading into the room, then reached around the wall to the light switch and turned it on.

Light flooded the room. No one was there. Nothing but racks of equipment and the faint hum of the overhead

fluorescents. Of course, someone could be hiding behind
one of those racks or crouched under the console, or
maybe behind the—*Stop it,* she chided herself. *Stop it
right now.* She turned, hit the lights, and headed back
down the steps—but not before firmly closing the door
behind her. And locking it.

She shook her head. Definitely paranoia. Still, even
paranoïa had some scientific validity. She remembered one
of the Russian PSI studies where a subject was placed in a
room with a TV camera focused upon him. Galvanic skin
response sensors attached to his skin to measure any
increased anxiety he might feel. In the next room, another
subject sat before a TV monitor. Most of the time the second subject was only shown a test pattern. But at randomly chosen times, the first subject appeared on the
monitor and the second subject stared at him. When the
experiment was complete and the results analyzed, it was
discovered that the first subject's skin sensors recorded
increased anxiety at exactly the same times the viewer had
been looking at him on the TV monitor.

So maybe there was some validity to that uneasy feeling we've all had of being watched. What was the old
joke—just because you're paranoid doesn't mean that
they're not out to get you?

As she reentered the narrow lab and passed along the
one-way glass, she did her best to ignore it. She moved
back to the console and took her seat.

And then the room exploded.

She spun around to see a chair sailing through the
one-way mirror as pieces of glass flew in all directions. She
leaped back, barely dodging the chair as it smashed into

the console behind her. She bolted for the door, trying to get past the gaping hole in the mirror, but the room was too narrow—a hand reached through the hole and grabbed her arm. She cried out and twirled around to see a head emerge through the opening. He was a kid—eyes wild, ragged goatee, stubbly red hair.

"Where is he?" he screamed.

Adrenaline surged as Sarah pulled to get away. But the boy hung on—even as she began to drag him through the hole, even as the shards of glass tore into his upper arm.

"Where is he?"

"Let me go! Let me—"

"You are the one!" he screamed. *"You are the one, you are not the one!"*

She pulled with all of her might, dragging more of him through the jagged opening. He was bleeding now, but he didn't notice. *"You are the one, you are not the one!"*

He found a foothold and braced himself. Suddenly Sarah could pull no farther. In a panic, she searched the room for something, anything. There, over on the console. A coffee mug. She reached for it, stretching as far as she could.

"You are the one, you are not the one!"

At last her fingertips touched the handle. She scooted it, rotating it, until she was able to grab it.

"You are the one, you are not—"

She spun around and smashed the mug into his face. It shattered, cutting her hand and slicing into his forehead, but he didn't seem to notice. Blood streamed down his face, running across his brows, into his eyes, but he didn't react.

She stared, astonished.

His grip tightened on her arm. He began dragging himself through the opening—across the shards of glass, and toward her.

"You are the one, you are not the one! You are the one, you are not the one!"

Wild with fear, Sarah fought and pulled, doing anything to get away. She dragged the weight of his body through the opening until he finally tumbled out onto the floor. The fall broke his grip, and she lunged for the door. She nearly made it—until he grabbed her leg. For a terrifying moment he had her. She kicked two, three times until she managed to break free. She staggered out into the hallway, but she could hear him behind her, already struggling to get to his knees.

"You are the one, you are not the one!"

She ran down the hall, stumbling in fear until she entered the lobby. She could hear the distant popping and scraping of glass as he staggered out into the hall after her. She fumbled for the lock on the double doors and was surprised to see one already unlocked. She threw it open and raced toward her car. It was a beater, a ten-year-old Ford Escort, the only car in the parking lot.

She arrived at her door, gasping for breath, her sweaty hands fumbling with the key. She shoved it into the lock—just as the lobby door flew open.

She looked up. He'd spotted her and started toward the car.

She opened the door and threw herself inside.

"You are the one, you are not the one!"

She hit the door lock, then shoved the key into the ignition.

He was nearly there.

For weeks she'd had trouble with the carburetor, planned on getting it fixed, never found the time. She turned the key, hoping desperately that it would cooperate.

It didn't.

She looked up. He was ten feet away. Through the blood streaming down his face she could see the grin, mocking through crooked teeth.

She kept turning the key, pumping the gas. "Come on—please, please, please—"

He arrived and yanked at her door.

"Please!"

He banged the glass with his fist and she gave a start. He continued pounding it, again and again, leaving bloody hand marks.

She kept grinding the starter.

Through her peripheral vision she saw him step back several feet. He was searching the ground, looking for something to break in with.

"Come on, come on . . ."

He reappeared just as the engine kicked over with a roar. She glanced up; he was coming at the car with a giant rock in his hand.

She yanked the transmission out of park and stepped on the gas. It fishtailed, her hands so sweaty she could barely hang on to the wheel. There was a loud thud at the back. He'd thrown the rock. She glanced into the rearview mirror. He stood there, swearing at her. Swearing and shouting. Over and over again, shouting:

"You are the one, you are not the one!
"You are the one, you are not the one!
"You are the one, you are not the one!"

PART TWO

Brandon went to church for the same reason he wore a shirt to the breakfast table: Momma believed that civility required it. Every Sunday morning, the two of them sat in the front pew, just as they had when Dad was the preacher. Only now, Dad sat beside them, in the center aisle, unmoving in his wheelchair.

Brandon had learned, over the years, that it would do no good to protest coming. There were some things Momma would not be swayed from. So he consented to this Sunday routine while at the same time quietly and efficiently perfecting the fine art of zoning out.

"As you know, a week from this evening we will be holding our final service here in this building—a farewell celebration as we prepare to join our Unitarian brothers across town. Now I suppose some would consider the closing of this fine old church a defeat, but I assure you that the Higher Power in his infinite ..." The Reverend continued droning on through his justification for shutting down the church. But whatever his rationalization, the bottom line was simple: Attendance was so meager that there was no way they could afford to keep the doors open.

Brandon didn't mind. True, he'd spent his entire life going to this church; he'd been dedicated here as a baby, baptized here as a child. And he'd spent years listening to his father deliver sermons from that very pulpit. But maybe the change would do them good. It might even cool Momma's fanatical ardor for constant attendance—although that was doubtful. He guessed that whenever and wherever the Reverend decided to speak, she would always be there to listen. Yes, Momma and the Reverend had grown close—but there was nothing immoral about their friendship. After all, it had been six years since Dad's stroke, and Momma was entitled to a little male companionship.

Brandon stole a look at his father. Did he know what was going on—that they were about to tear down the church he had fought so hard to build? Who knew what was going on behind that slack, impassive face—except, of course, for the contempt Brandon always sensed lurking behind his silence. Contempt for him—for everything Brandon did, for everything he was and was not.

Brandon looked back up at the Reverend and pretended to listen as the man continued rattling off his bromides. It's not that Brandon hated church. He didn't even hate God. You have to care about something to hate it. And Brandon didn't care one way or the other. Not anymore. When he was a kid, sure. He'd followed the party line, wowed everyone with his zeal, even subbed as a Sunday school teacher for the little ones. But that was back when he'd thought life had guarantees, when he'd thought faith counted for something. Now, of course, he knew it didn't. Not after his father's stroke. And not after Jenny's death.

Brandon stared at the brass pipes of the organ mounted on the wall behind the pulpit, then at the white ash cross positioned immediately in front of them. The cross. What a perfect symbol of life's futility. Brandon shook his head at the irony: How Christians cherished and worshiped the very thing that proves that, no matter what you do, no matter how good you are, you die. Everything dies. He remembered hearing some comedian say that if Jesus came today, instead of crosses, Christians would be wearing electric chairs around their necks. What a joke. What a sad, hopeless joke. Yes, Brandon thought, if there was any symbol to capture the futility of life, it was the cross.

For the thousandth time, his mind drifted back to Friday night, to little Jenny standing in the road ... if it had been Jenny. Of course it had been Jenny. What else could it have been? And yet nobody else had seen her. Frank, Del—they hadn't seen a thing. Had it been a hallucination, something he'd just imagined? Brandon closed his eyes and pressed his fingers against his lids. If so, then he was *really* in bad shape.

It sounded like the Reverend was finally running out of steam. "At this time, we have some special music. Lori Beth, would you like to come forward now and share with us?"

Brandon watched as a fourteen-year-old blonde nervously walked down the aisle and took her position in front of the altar. Over the past year, Lori Beth had gotten quite a figure, and she was still painfully self-conscious about it—a little girl trapped in a woman's body. She took the mike from the Reverend and nodded to the soundman at the back of the church. A music track blared through the speakers until the volume was lowered. A few bars later, the girl started to sing. Her voice wasn't bad, though a little thin and tentative. That's how it always was with the new ones. A little nervous at first but gradually, as the song continued, their confidence increased.

Not so with Lori Beth. In fact it was just the opposite. With each line she sang, she seemed to grow less and less sure of herself, and more and more nervous. But it wasn't the congregation that unnerved her. It was something else, something toward the back. At first Brandon tried to ignore the problem, but by the second verse the girl was practically trembling.

Brandon stole a look over his shoulder. Mr. Gleason, the middle-school English teacher, a large man with thinning blonde hair, had risen from the back and was heading up the aisle toward her. Brandon remembered him as a friendly guy, always making jokes. But instead of his usual good-natured expression, his face was twisted into a leer.

Brandon turned back to Lori Beth. She still sang, but her eyes remained fixed on the approaching man, and her voice was beginning to quiver. Gleason passed Brandon. He was loosening his tie as he approached the girl. Lori Beth's voice grew more and more shaky. Finally the teacher stopped directly in front of her. He raised his big, meaty hands and placed them on her white, delicate shoulders.

And still she sang. Staring at him, terror-stricken, she continued to sing.

Brandon looked at Momma, then at other members of the congregation. Everyone was calm, some even smiling. Wasn't anybody concerned?

Suddenly the man pulled Lori Beth toward him. She gasped and tried to resist, but he was insistent. He grabbed the back of her head and pulled it toward his face—and then he kissed her. Hard. His mouth covered hers in consuming passion.

The Reverend smiled, nodding his head; the congregation sat complacently. Didn't they care?

After the kiss, Lori Beth took a shaky breath . . . and *still* she sang. But Gleason wasn't finished. He began kissing her neck, hungrily, demandingly.

No—no, Brandon had seen enough. Disgusted at Gleason, outraged at the congregation, he rose to his feet. "Stop it!" he shouted. "What do you think you're doing! Leave her alone!"

Gleason ignored him. He began pawing at Lori Beth's blouse, tearing at it, ripping off buttons. That's when Brandon moved to action. He leaped across the few feet separating them, grabbed Gleason's arm, and tried to pull him away. "What are you doing? Leave her alone!"

With little effort, the big man flung him aside. He turned back to the girl, kissing her, pulling at her clothes while, amazingly, she continued to sing!

Brandon lunged at him, grabbing his shoulders, using all of his strength to pull him away.

"Stop it! Let her—"

Then he felt a pair of hands on his own shoulders. He whirled around. It was the Reverend. But he wasn't helping to pull the teacher away. He was pulling *Brandon* away.

"Easy, son, take it easy."

"What are you doing?" Brandon shouted. "Look what he's doing to her!"

"Easy—everything's okay."

Surprised at the calming voice, Brandon looked first at Momma, then at the congregation. Their complacency was finally broken; now, everyone was staring in astonishment. But they weren't staring at Mr. Gleason; they were staring at *him*, at Brandon.

Confused and breathing hard, Brandon turned back to the teacher. He wasn't there. Only Lori Beth stood before the altar—her blouse neatly pressed, her hair and face showing no signs of the struggle. True, her eyes registered fear, but not fear of Mr. Gleason. It was fear of Brandon.

"It's okay, son." He could feel the Reverend's grip tighten as he gradually pulled him away. Brandon looked out over the congregation. There was Mr. Gleason at the back. Like Lori Beth's parents and several other members of the congregation, he had risen to his feet in apparent concern. But his tie was perfectly straight; there was no sign of a skirmish.

The Reverend eased Brandon away, toward Momma who was now standing. "It's okay, son," he kept repeating, "it's okay." Numb and confused, Brandon allowed himself to be guided to his mother, who helped him sit back in their pew. "It's okay. Just have a seat, son. Everything is all right. It's okay, everything is all right . . ."

Three hours later, Brandon was sprawled on the sofa in the living room. It was stifling. The fan drew air in through the front screen door, but that helped little, since the outside air was even hotter than the inside. Sweat trickled down his temples as he stared at the TV, pressing the remote, one channel after another after another, barely watching.

Drool, good old faithful Drool, had sensed Brandon's turmoil. Several minutes earlier, the massive, chocolate-colored mongrel had plopped down at the foot of the sofa with a heavy sigh. Over the months, the years, he had become Brandon's only confidant.

At one time, it had been Brandon and his father—Brandon and his father camping out, Brandon's father coaching Brandon's basketball team, Brandon and his father working on model cars when he was a child, then graduating to the real thing as Brandon grew older. Everyone who knew them envied their friendship. If ever there were two people who found joy and purpose in one another, it was these two.

But that was a long time ago.

Now there was only Drool. Brandon may no longer be able to talk to his father, he may not be able to stay in the same room with his mother, but there was always Drool. Quick to listen, slow to judge, and always faithful. Good old Drool. At the moment, the animal's devotion was being rewarded by Brandon's absentminded scratching behind his ears.

It had been seven months since Brandon had killed his little sister. Seven months of self-torment by day and agonizing dreams by night. Everyone had said that the dreams would go away, that he'd get better.

Well, everyone was wrong.

After the incident on the road last night, the fragments of conversation at the printing plant, and the weird whatever-that-was at church this morning, it was clear that not only were the dreams *not* going away—they were starting to plague him even when he was awake.

What had happened with Lori Beth this morning made no sense at all. But what he'd seen the other night out on the road, that was different. It had been Jenny. And that meant that the Bible was wrong—the dead *do* come back, at least in her case. But what did she want? What was she trying to say?

Brandon shook his head and let out a long, slow sigh as he surfed the channels.

Outside, on the porch, he could hear Momma talking to someone. Probably just another "concerned" neighbor or church member dropping by. Yes, sir, good news traveled fast in little Bethel Lake. He hit the mute button for a better listen.

"I'm sorry," Momma was saying, "but he needs his rest and I—"

"He's entering his season, Meg." It was an older woman's voice—thin and crackly. "You *knew* this day would come."

"It's been a very tiring morning for him—well, for all of us. Perhaps if you stopped by another time."

Bored, Brandon threw his feet over the side of the couch. He stepped over Drool and shuffled toward the screen door.

"If you'd just let me look in on the boy. Maybe offer a few words of encouragement. Let him know that . . ." The woman's voice trailed off as Brandon arrived at the screen. She was a frail old woman. Black skin, graying hair, dressed in her Sunday best, which wasn't much. Besides a print dress of tiny flowers, she wore slightly yellowed gloves and a small white hat. Brandon was sure he hadn't met her before, and by the way Momma stood on the porch, blocking the woman's approach, it was clear that things were going to stay that way.

As the woman stared at him, a look of wonder slowly spread across her face. Momma glanced over her shoulder at him. But before she could make the introductions, the old woman began to quietly quote: "'Behold, I will send you Elijah before the great and dreadful day of the Lord.'"

Brandon glanced quizzically to his mother, but she was already looking away.

The old woman continued: "'And he shall turn the hearts of the fathers to the children and the hearts of the children to their fathers.'" She stopped, then slowly smiled at him.

Momma glanced at him again and cleared her throat. "Uh, Sugar—this here is Gerty, Gerty Morrison. An old and dear friend of the family's. She used to attend your father's congregation. 'Course that was a long time ago, when you were just a baby."

"Eli." The woman's eyes filled with moisture. "Eli, we've been waitin'. Waitin' over twenty years for—"

"Brandon," he interrupted.

"'Scuse me?"

"The name is Brandon."

The woman glanced at Momma, then nodded. "Yes, of course." She continued: "The Lord would say much to you, Brandon."

"Now, Gerty," Momma warned her, "you promised."

"But he must be warned of the counterfeits." She turned back to him. "You do understand the difference? How to discern the spirits, and how to prepare for the battle you're about to—"

"Gerty, please!" Momma's outburst surprised them all, and she immediately struggled to recover her civility. "You promised, now. Remember? You promised."

Brandon continued to watch. He knew that most church circles had one or two well-meaning fruitcakes who insisted that they could hear God speaking. It came with the territory. At best, they were harmless—just folks looking for attention. At worst, they could be deluded, even dangerous. Brandon wasn't sure which category this old woman fell into.

"Yes." Gerty was nodding to Momma. "Yes, you are right, I did give you my word." She broke into another smile. "And I thank you for this opportunity, Megan. I thank you from the bottom of my heart."

Momma nodded, still keeping a wary eye on the woman.

Gerty turned back to Brandon. "It was a pleasure meetin' you, Brandon."

He nodded.

She nodded back. Then, in the silence, she turned and started down the porch steps. But, when she reached the bottom, she turned back to him, a look of concern filling her face. "Your shield," she asked. "You won't be forgettin' your shield of faith?"

"Gerty. . . ," Momma warned.

"No, ma'am," Brandon answered kindly. It was obvious this old-timer fell into the harmless category, so it wouldn't hurt to play along. "Got it right here in the house where it's good and safe."

Gerty nodded, though it was clear she was confused by his answer.

"Yes, ma'am," Brandon offered helpfully. "I never leave home without it."

Still confused, she smiled nonetheless. Then, slowly, she turned and hobbled toward her car.

Brandon watched, quietly amused and a little sad.

But not Momma. Even with her back to him, he could see the nervous tension in her body—a tension that remained even after the old woman was in her car and heading down the lane to the main road.

Dr. Reichner took another long sip of coffee—his third cup since he'd left the Fort Wayne airport ninety minutes ago.

"How long were the police here?" he asked.

Sarah Weintraub knelt beside the console in Lab One, examining a patch of blood-stained carpet. "About an hour."

"They have any idea who it was?"

Sarah shook her head. "If they did, they weren't saying."

Reichner fingered the jagged shards of glass still protruding from the one-way mirror that separated the lab from the Observation Room. He was exhausted, but he could not, would not sleep. It had been seventy-two hours since his encounter with the boy guru, or python, or whatever it was back in Nepal, and he was still a little shaken.

Initially, he had chalked up the experience to some sort of hallucination, an imagined mystical encounter. He had certainly been in the right place for it. That along with the drugs, the exotic location, and a person's normal susceptibility to suggestion—well, it was definitely a plausible explanation. Then there'd been that mantra and the Eastern meditation thing. Some medical studies he'd read hypothesized that the chanting of mantras and meditation was simply a way of depriving the brain of oxygen while increasing carbon dioxide. Since the temporal lobe of the brain is sensitive to the delicate balance of O and CO_2, altering that equilibrium can easily create a sense of well-being, the so-called Eastern mystical experiences, or even that tunnel sensation so many "near-death" participants babble about.

At least that's what the medical books said. But after his experience on the flight back home, he had begun to question the textbook explanation. It had only happened twice. During the New Delhi to O'Hare leg of his flight. But twice was enough. Reichner had closed his eyes, drifting into that in-between state of sleep and wakefulness, when he had suddenly seen the pale yellow eyes of the python floating before him. It had no doubt been some reaction to his dramatic earlier encounter with the guru. At least that's what he told himself. Yet it had seemed so real. Then, of course, there had been those parting words from the Nepal vision: "I will always be with you."

In any case, for the time being at least, he preferred to throw down a few more cups of coffee and stave off sleep just a little bit longer.

"Maybe we should get this typed," Sarah said, indicating the blood on the carpet.

Reichner stooped beside her for a better look. She smelled nice. Her hair was still damp from the shower she'd been taking when he'd called. He could smell the scented soap on her skin. Some sort of berry. Yes, very nice indeed.

Of course, he'd tried talking her into bed when she'd first joined the Institute. But she'd made it clear from the get-go that she was not interested in another relationship, especially with her employer. He knew that he could have manipulated her, worn her down (*nobody* said no to Reichner, unless he wanted her to), but she was already approaching thirty, which meant she really wasn't his type anymore. After all, he did have his standards.

Besides, she was an overachiever, a workaholic—the type who buried themselves in their job, looking to their work for all of their fulfillment and self-esteem. He had run a background check on her that hadn't been conclusive, although he assumed that her workaholism was a reaction to something unpleasant in her not-so-distant past. But the reason made little difference. The point was that someone like this could be exploited in far more profitable ways than for a little roll in the hay. And it was so easy. All he had to do was appear unsatisfied with her work and imply that she could do better. Or toss a brief compliment her way if she had nearly killed herself over a project. "Praise junkies," he called them. Like devoted dogs, they would kill themselves just to hear a kind word from their master. Everybody had an Achilles' heel, and by exploiting hers, Reichner was able to squeeze out twice the amount of work he would have gotten from a healthier employee.

Yes, he was a man who knew what he wanted, and he always knew how to get it.

"You said he had red hair?" he asked.

"And a goatee," Sarah added. "Looked like he was in his mid-twenties."

Dr. Reichner stood back up and took another sip of coffee. "What about his teeth?"

"Pardon me?"

"Were his teeth crooked?"

Sarah hesitated. "Well, yes. I'd forgotten but, yes, they were in terrible shape."

Reichner nodded.

"You know him?"

Reichner said nothing. He was rethinking his conversation back in the mountains of Nepal. At least that portion of it involving Lewis Thompson, the kid who had blown up on him some eighteen months earlier. How odd: They'd just spoken of him and now, suddenly, he was resurfacing. Reichner turned back to her. "Did he say anything else?"

"No," Sarah shook her head. "Just the same phrase over and over again—'You are the one, you're not the one.'"

Reichner nodded and glanced around the room. "Have you been working with any new subjects here? Anybody showing exceptionally high PSI?"

Sarah shook her head. "No. Just the usuals. Though as I told you, some pretty weird stuff's been happening here the past few days."

Again, Reichner said nothing. He continued rearranging the pieces, first one way, then the other, trying to fit them together.

"So are you going to have him arrested?"

Reichner looked at her and frowned. "No. If it's who I think it is, we have some history together. I should probably take care of this myself."

"You don't think he'll come back?"

"No."

Sarah glanced at the smashed mirror. "I don't understand. I mean, what was his purpose?"

Reichner shook his head. "He wants very badly to destroy something or someone."

"Why?"

"I'm not sure. Maybe . . ." A thought began to take shape. "Maybe it's jealousy."

"Jealousy?"

Reichner rifled through his thoughts, testing the theory. It seemed to hold. He nodded slightly.

"Of whom?"

He gave no answer.

After a moment, Sarah repeated, "You're sure he won't come back?"

Barely hearing, Reichner glanced at her. "What?"

"Here? You're sure he won't be coming back?"

He saw that she was worried and shook his head. "No, not here." He picked up a shrapnel of glass from the console and examined it. "Whoever he wanted is close, but he's not here."

"How do you know?"

"'You are the one, but you're not the one.'"

"Then *who?*" Sarah persisted.

Reichner shook his head. He fingered the jagged edge of glass in his hand. "I don't know. But whoever it is, it would be better if we found him first, before our friend does."

Late Monday afternoon, Brandon stood in the delivery bay, tossing one twelve-pound box of flyers after another into the back of the delivery van. Burton's Music and Video up on Lincoln Avenue was having a blow-out sale, and by the amount of print work they ordered, it looked like everyone in the county would know.

"Hey, Martus."

He looked up to see Putnam, the foreman, approaching.

"Think on your way home you could drop some boxes off at the Institute? They're still a couple short, so—"

Brandon cut him off. "Hey, I delivered exactly what you—"

"Easy, Cowboy. My mistake. I take full responsibility." He glanced up at Brandon. "At least this time."

Brandon nodded. He'd overreacted. With all that was happening, he was definitely on edge. But Putnam wasn't finished.

"Listen, uh . . ." He coughed slightly. "I heard what happened yesterday—you know, at the church and everything. Are you gonna be all right?"

Brandon reached for another box and tossed it in. "I'll be fine."

"'Cause if you're not, if you wanted like a little rest or something, you got some sick leave coming."

"I'm fine."

"You sure? 'Cause, I mean I've got my rear end to protect here, too, y'know."

Brandon hesitated. There was that phrase again. The same phrase he had heard in Thursday night's dream, the same one Putnam had used during the false alarm Friday. Brandon shook it off and continued.

"Well, all right then. I mean if you're sure."

Brandon nodded and continued loading.

"So, you'll catch the Institute this afternoon on your way—"

Suddenly a loud scream echoed through the plant. Putnam and Brandon spun around. Fifty feet across the floor, next to the press, Warner, the ponytailed operator, was on his knees, one hand holding another, both covered in blood.

"What the—" Putnam broke into a run. Brandon followed.

Frank was already there, quickly wrapping a rag around the screaming man's hand. Blood was everywhere. Other workers moved in as Putnam arrived. But Brandon slowed to a stop. Already he could feel himself growing cold, a tightness spreading through his chest.

"Call 911!" Putnam shouted. "Get an ambulance over here!"

A worker started for the phones. Both Frank and Putnam remained at Warner's side, trying to hold him down, trying to stop him from writhing.

An icy sweat broke out across Brandon's face. He had known. Down to the tiniest detail—Putnam's phrase, the press, Warner's hand—he had been warned.

"Is somebody calling an ambulance!"

Just as Jenny had saved him from the Firebird, just as she had tried to save Warner's hand, he had been warned. And, like it or not, his dreams, his visions, had started to come true.

CHAPTER 7

Two hours later, Brandon leaned against the vending machine in the employee's lounge of Moran Research Institute and opened another bag of sunflower seeds. As Putnam had requested, he'd swung by to drop off the remaining shipment on his way home. Although Billy and most of the Institute's staff had already gone, there were still a couple of cars left in the parking lot, so Brandon had entered through the loading dock and dropped off the boxes. Now, in the silence of the lounge, he closed his eyes and rested.

It had been another painful and confusing day.

Instead of waiting for the paramedics, Putnam and Frank had driven Warner to the hospital themselves. Word had it that the press operator would probably lose his hand. Brandon took a long, deep breath and slowly let it out. He had known. In the dream, Jenny had told him. Why hadn't he warned them? Why hadn't he been stronger, made a bigger deal about it way back last Friday? He popped a small handful of seeds into his mouth. Things were growing worse.

At the other end of the Institute Sarah Weintraub was fighting her own internal battles by doing what she did best: working hard and late. The one-way mirror had not been replaced between Lab One and the Observation Room, so she was using the other pair of rooms. Except for the carpeting and a different set of coffee stains, they were identical.

Sarah was testing two more patients from Vicksburg State Mental Hospital. The first one, Sheldon, was a wiry man in his mid-fifties. He sat calmly with Sarah in the Observation Room and stared at a video image on the monitor. It was a scene of a dairy farm, complete with barn, cows, and a tractor. Karen, a heavy woman with mousy brown hair, sat in the leather recliner down in the lab, on the other side of the glass. Attached to her body were numerous sensors: GSRs, EMGs, and EEGs. Her face was bathed by the four red floodlights, and she wore the Ganzfield goggles (complete with the Ping-Pong ball halves) over her eyes. The relaxation tape of Dr. Reichner's prerecorded voice played softly through the speakers.

"Tighten, tighten . . . and relax. Tighten, tighten . . . now relax. Good. Very good. Now your calves. Tight, tighter, tighter . . ."

The GSR showed the first anomaly. By measuring the amount of electricity her skin conducted, it indicated how nervous she was. And Karen was nervous. Very nervous. Instead of gradually relaxing during the test, her anxiety was actually increasing. Dramatically.

Sarah checked the EMG. The results were the same: a marked increase in Karen's muscle tension. The EEG followed suit, registering a rapid increase in beta waves, the brain waves present during stress and agitation.

Sarah reached for the intercom button. "Karen, are you all right? Sweetheart, just try to relax, okay?"

She glanced at the monitors. Karen's anxiety levels continued to rise. She looked back through the glass. Karen was scowling, starting to move her head.

"Karen? Karen, try to remain still. Just listen to Dr. Reichner's voice. Just listen to his voice and try to—"

She stopped, trying to locate the strange sound she'd just heard, something like a faint gurgle. She turned to Sheldon. He was still staring at the video picture, completely lost in it. She looked back into the lab. The sound was coming from Karen. Her head had begun to roll from side to side, and the sound grew louder. But it was no longer a gurgle. It was low and continuous, like a growl.

"Karen?"

No response. The growl increased.

"All right, Karen. Listen, sweetheart, we're going to end this session. Okay? You can come back up now, all right? Just open your eyes and join us."

The head rolled more violently.

Sarah pressed another button. She wasn't sure where the stocky orderly was, but she needed him. "William," her voice echoed through the Institute's PA, "William, please come to Lab Two, stat."

She turned back to the monitors. Some readings were beginning to spike, going off the screen. Karen's growls intensified into muffled cries as she began twisting and squirming.

Sarah rose to her feet. Sheldon was still oblivious to anything but the picture on the screen. She turned, raced down the steps into the hall—and was shocked to see the boy from the country club approaching. She started to say something, to demand an explanation for his presence, when suddenly an unearthly shriek came from the lab.

She threw open the lab door. Karen was writhing in the recliner. The big woman screamed again, and Sarah raced to her. "Karen! Karen, listen to me!" Sarah pulled off the woman's goggles.

Karen's eyes darted around the room in wild, animal-like panic.

"Karen—"

Karen's eyes froze on something. Over by the door. Suddenly she was scrambling, fighting to get out of the recliner.

"Karen!"

She struggled to her feet, breathing heavily. Then, pointing with a trembling finger, she growled, low and vehemently, "You."

Sarah followed her gaze to Brandon, who was standing at the door. "Get out!" she cried. "Can't you see you're scaring her? Get out!" She spun back to Karen and tried to calm her. "Karen, listen to me."

"No," the voice hissed.

Sarah grew more firm. "I want to speak to Karen."

"No!"

"Yes, I want to talk to—"

The woman shoved Sarah aside and ripped off more of the sensor wires.

"Karen—"

But Karen lurched toward Brandon.

When the woman headed toward him, Brandon had the good sense to back away. She was slightly smaller than he was—but there was no mistaking the look in her eyes:

She meant business. She panted heavily, her eyes glaring into his. *"You!"* she seethed.

He gave an involuntary shudder. It had been a long time since he'd seen such hatred—but this was more than hatred. There was something else: a reverberation, a unison of voices, as if more than one person was speaking.

"What have you to do with us?" The woman glowered in the doorway. *"Have you come to persecute us before our time?"*

"Karen." It was Sarah, approaching the woman from behind. "Karen, listen to me. I want to speak to Karen." She touched the woman's arm, trying to calm her. "I want to speak—"

"NO!" With an anguished shriek, the woman spun around, grabbed Sarah by the shoulders, and threw her into a rack of equipment. Brandon immediately moved to help Sarah, but the woman turned and lunged at him, screaming. She hit him hard, and they staggered to the ground. She landed on top, screaming, punching, scratching, clawing, mostly at his face and eyes. Her strength was incredible. He was able to hold his own, but barely. Off to the side, he spotted Sarah coming at them again.

So did the woman.

She twisted and punched Sarah hard in the stomach, sending her staggering. But Brandon took advantage of the woman's distraction and grabbed both of her wrists. They were sweaty and strong, already twisting, already breaking his hold, when suddenly another man appeared, a much bigger man. He came from behind and wrapped his arms around the woman's arms and shoulders, binding her movement, pulling her off Brandon.

"Come on, Karen," he ordered, holding her in what amounted to a fierce bear hug.

"Our name is not Karen!" she shrieked as she fought.

But the man was a pro. "Right, well, whoever you are, just calm down now. Calm down . . ."

Brandon pushed himself against the wall, wiping the sweat from his face, trying to catch his breath. In the background, he heard a recording of a man's voice with a slight German accent. "Tighter, tighter . . . and relax. Good, very good. And now your shoulders. Tighter, tighter . . . and relax. Excellent . . ."

"And that's legal, using crazies to experiment on? Ow!"

Sarah continued cleaning the young man's wounds, using the cotton balls and rubbing alcohol just a little too briskly. If he wanted to mouth off, that was fine with her, but he'd have to pay the price.

The rest of the staff was already gone. William, the hospital orderly, was on the road chauffeuring his two patients back to Vicksburg. Now it was just Sarah and the kid in the employee's lounge. His shirt was off, and she applied her limited first-aid training to the scratches on his neck and back with a definite lack of bedside manner. "Our work with the mentally ill isn't official. At least not yet. We're still clearing up some red tape." She hoped he wouldn't miss her meaning. "I'm sure you can appreciate the damage it would cause us if word of their involvement leaked prematurely."

He said nothing and she trusted he understood. She moved around to his back, grateful to be out of his line of vision. What was it about him that made her so self-conscious? He was just a kid, half a dozen years her junior, maybe more. And still she heard herself rattling on, sounding like some nervous schoolgirl. "Actually, the tests are harmless. Just some simple relaxation exercises—"

"And since it's for science and they're just loonies, it doesn't make any difference if—ow!"

She'd got him good that time. She continued, doing her best to keep an even tone. "These *loonies,* as you call them, are people just like you and me—except the chemistry of their brain is slightly different." It was time to move around to his front again, but she kept her eyes from his as she talked. "We have over fifty billion neurons in our brains. They fire ten million billion times per second. That's a lot of information. A healthy person's brain filters out much of that input before it reaches conscious level. We're interested in those people whose brains can't."

She waited for a response, some indication that he was listening. There was nothing. What was with him, anyway? And still she heard herself continue: "The theory is that there is paranormal activity all around us but that you and I filter it out. Some of the mentally disturbed may not be able to do that."

He cocked his head up at her and she glanced down. A mistake. Once again those intense gray eyes locked onto hers. And once again she felt herself growing the slightest bit weak inside.

"What about the voices?" he asked.

She looked back at the cuts on his neck and dabbed them with cotton. "What voices?"

"You know—how'd she make her voice sound like it was more than just one person talking?"

Sarah slowed to a stop and looked back down at him. "You heard voices?"

"Didn't you?"

She shook her head, this time holding his gaze. And it was then she saw it. A flicker of vulnerability. He was afraid. He was afraid and now, suddenly, he was the one who looked away.

She hesitated, then resumed dabbing the scratch along the top of his shoulder. When she spoke, she tried to sound casual. "How many voices did you hear?"

He said nothing.

Now his rudeness was beginning to make sense. He wasn't acting out some misguided machismo. He was just afraid. She could tell by his increased breathing rate, the rapid pulse in his neck. She dabbed the cotton along a nasty gouge near his left clavicle and saw him wince. This time his discomfort gave her no pleasure. "I'm just about finished," she offered.

He didn't speak. She tried to do the same. But curiosity, professional and otherwise, got the better of her. "So. You didn't answer my question. How many voices did you think you heard?"

He glanced up at her again—the strength of those eyes was now lost in his fear, and vulnerability. Once again she felt herself being drawn to him. He looked away and shrugged, but this time his feigned indifference was less convincing. "Three," he said, "maybe four."

The comment brought Sarah to a stop.

He looked back up. "Why? What's wrong?"

"Karen suffers from multiple personas."

"What's that?"

"She becomes different and distinct people at different times."

"So?"

Sarah began to treat his cuts again, more slowly this time. "So at last count Karen's number of personalities . . . came to four."

The boy sat motionless. Sarah saw his larynx rise and fall as he swallowed. Without warning, he reached for his shirt. "I gotta go."

"I'm almost done here, why don't you—"

But he was already on his feet, slipping on his shirt, buttoning it.

She quickly sealed up the alcohol and tossed the cotton balls toward the trash. He was heading out of the room. She couldn't let him get away, not yet. She grabbed her bag and moved into the hall after him. "You said you heard voices?" she persisted as she joined his side. "Three, maybe four?"

He didn't answer. Her mind raced. Wasn't this the same person who'd scored a direct hit with the Ganzfield test Friday? Coincidence? Maybe. But what about Karen's reaction? What about his "hearing" her personalities?

"Listen," she fumbled, "I'm sorry, I don't even know your name."

"Brandon."

"Listen, Brandon—what would you think about stopping by here again sometime? After work?"

"For what?"

They continued down the hall.

"I don't know. Maybe run a few tests. Get to know each other a little better."

It was a lame attempt at flirting, and his look told her he'd recognized it for what it was. She flinched and tried a more candid approach. "Remember your perception last Friday—about the hot dog and the picnic?"

No response.

"First that, then Karen's reaction to you—and now you say you heard voices, the same number as her personalities. Doesn't that strike you as all just a little bit odd?"

They'd nearly reached the door to the parking lot. He still refused to look at her, but at least he answered. "You never stop working, do you?"

The response caught her off guard. Was she that obvious? He barely knew her, and yet—well, no matter. She pressed on. "Something happened in that room. You know it and I know it. And it wasn't just with Karen. *You're* the one who heard the voices."

They had reached the door and he slowed, almost stopping. Then suddenly he pushed it open and headed outside. "I think I'll pass."

"Why?" She followed him, making sure the door locked shut before racing to catch up. Although it was early evening, the heat was intolerable. "Aren't you the least bit curious? Wouldn't you like to know if you're somehow . . . gifted? If there's a way you could use those gifts to help others?"

She was at his side again, and again he gave no answer.

"Why not?" she asked. "Why wouldn't you want to know?"

"Doesn't interest me, that's all."

She looked at him and felt her anger rising. So that was it. Vulnerable? Afraid? Hardly. That had been wishful thinking on her part. No, he was just like the others— jaded, self-centered, only looking out for himself—typical of so many men in her generation—younger, older, it made no difference. Her words came a bit sharper. "And if it doesn't interest you, then it's not important, is that it?"

"You got that right."

Sarah came to a stop and watched as he approached his pickup. It was time to take off the gloves. "And what does interest you?" she called.

No answer.

"No, I'm serious. Pulling those sophomoric pranks with your buddies at the country club? Is that what's important, is that what counts?"

He opened his door.

"Is it?" she persisted.

"Makes me smile."

"Well, I don't want this to come as too great a shock to you, but maybe there are more important things in this world than what makes you smile."

Brandon hesitated, giving it a moment's thought, then shrugged. "I doubt it." With that he climbed into the cab and fired up the truck.

Sarah stood steaming. Somehow, once again, he had managed to push all of her buttons. She turned and stormed toward her own car. She had barely arrived and was reaching for her keys when she heard him call, "So— when will I see you again?"

A half-dozen zingers ran through her head, but none of them befitting a lady. No, the best thing was to simply ignore him, to not let him know he'd gotten under her skin.

"How 'bout a pizza?" he called.

She couldn't tell if he was serious or trying to be funny.

"I'll even spring for an extra topping."

Well, at least she had her answer—and Robin Williams he was not. As she opened her car door she could sense him still sitting there in his pickup, watching her every move. This made her more self-conscious and awkward, which made her all the more angry.

Inside, her car reeked, probably the result of a half-eaten Whopper or one too many yogurts left all day in the broiling heat. She closed the door and reached for her seat belt. The smell was enough to gag her, but she wasn't about to roll down her window and risk more conversation.

She inserted the key and turned it. It ground away, but nothing happened. The carburetor. She stopped and tried again. "Come on," she muttered, "not now, not now . . ." But no amount of coaxing helped. She stopped and blew the hair out of her eyes. Then, deciding she would not be intimidated, and having this irrepressible urge to breathe, she finally rolled down her window.

She tried the car again. Still nothing.

She could feel him sitting over there, no doubt smirking away.

She tried again. This time, not letting up. With dogged determination she kept turning the engine over and over again as it ground slower and slower—the battery showing surer signs of giving up the ghost.

She stopped and waited.

He called out. "Need a lift?"

"I wouldn't want to put you out," she answered bitingly.

"No problem," he replied. "It might even make me smile."

Sarah ignored him and tried the car again until it finally ground to a halt. Wiping away the hair sticking to her face, she made one last attempt. But there was nothing left. Only a dull click followed by silence.

She could imagine him grinning, probably yucking it up. But she couldn't sit there forever. They were a half mile outside of town and at least that far from the nearest service station.

Okay, fine, maybe she'd lost this round, but it wasn't over. Keeping her cool, she removed the key, grabbed her bag, and climbed out. Then, summoning whatever dignity she had left, she started for the pickup.

Reichner pulled up behind the white, rust-streaked VW bug just as Lewis Thompson was opening its door to climb in. The young man looked terrible—dirty, barefoot, stained Grateful Dead T-shirt. And the sweat. Even through his windshield Reichner could see the sweat running down the boy's face.

Reichner turned off his Lexus, opened the car door, and stepped out into the intolerable heat. He'd always found this quarter-mile stretch of homes between Bloomfield and Second Avenue disgusting. Even when he had been working with Lewis, he'd made a point of avoiding this neighborhood, with its unpainted houses, sagging porches, and front yards sporting more abandoned cars than lawn. His distaste may have stemmed from memories of his own childhood poverty back in Linz, Austria, or simply from his contempt for people ignorant enough to live in such squalid conditions.

But none of that mattered. Right now he had to find out what Lewis was up to.

He slammed his car door, and the kid spun around, seeing him for the first time. Reichner walked to him, slow and deliberate. This was how he dealt with the kid— in exact contrast to the boy's own agitation and anxiety. It was a means of establishing power and superiority.

"Dr. Reichner." Lewis gave a nervous twitch that almost passed for a smile. He appeared distracted, torn between climbing into his car or staying outside to talk.

Reichner approached, keeping his voice low and stern. "Good evening, Lewis." It was a voice that Lewis had learned to obey during all those months of experiments, a voice he would want to please whenever he could. Reichner had made sure of it. "Where are you off to?"

"I, uh—church." Lewis was disoriented, looking at the horizon, the ground, anything but Reichner's eyes. "I'm going to church."

"We've not seen each other in some time."

"Yeah, uh . . ." Lewis ran his hand over his sweaty face, then over his red stubble of hair.

"Why church, Lewis?"

Lewis winced, still looking everywhere and nowhere. Reichner watched and waited. It was obvious that the kid was hearing the voices again—and equally obvious that he was doing drugs to heighten their intensity. Such a pity. Because the more hallucinogenics he took, the more demanding the voices became, insisting that he take even more drugs, which he would, which only increased their demands—and around and around he would go. A vicious cycle that would eventually destroy his sanity, stripping away any rational will, until he'd lost all control. Reichner had seen it happen before, and he shuddered to think what this pathetic young man would be like in seventy-two, even forty-eight hours from now.

The voices Lewis was hearing were no doubt the same ones he had heard before, the same ones that had been so helpful in the beginning but had later destroyed their experiments. What a waste. He had shown such potential, such promise. During that period they had made astonishing breakthroughs, more rapid than anyone in the field of paranormal research—until the kid blew up. Until he was no longer able to control the voices and they began turning on him, controlling him. Now Lewis was only a shell of what he had been, his powers completely unfocused, and by the looks of things once again losing control.

"Why church?" Reichner repeated.

"Because . . . I'm not—I'm not sure."

"Why church, Lewis?"

"I don't know!" The eruption was sudden. "I don't know, all right?"

Reichner said nothing, allowing his silence to play on the boy, making it clear that penance was due for the outburst. Lewis fumbled with his keys, repeating the words, mumbling them softer now, an obvious apology, "I don't know, I don't know . . ." He turned, then clumsily, haltingly, entered the car.

"You don't want to go, Lewis. Not yet."

Lewis hesitated. Reichner could tell that the kid wanted to shut the door, that something inside him was driving him to shut it. But he couldn't. The doctor smiled. Apparently all those months of hypnosis still gave him some control over the boy. He continued, keeping his voice low and even. "As a matter of fact, you would really prefer to step back out of the car for a moment."

Lewis's face showed the struggle. He had to obey his internal voices, but he just as desperately needed to please Reichner. Reichner watched and waited, curious to see how much power he could still exert over the boy. Finally, Lewis rose unsteadily from the car. He seemed more disoriented than ever.

Reichner was pleased.

"What do you want?" Lewis tried to sound angry, but he still could not look Reichner in the eyes.

"Why the church, Lewis?"

"I don't know, all right?" His breathing was heavy. Reichner guessed that his internal torture was overwhelming—needing to obey his internal voices, needing to obey Reichner's. Suddenly the boy began to pace, repeating the words. "I don't know, I don't know, I don't know."

Reichner knew he was telling the truth. Lewis seldom lied. He decided to change the subject. "I understand you paid us a little visit Saturday morning."

For the first time Lewis's eyes darted to Reichner's, then away. It was an admission of guilt. He resumed pacing.

"Talk to me, Lewis." Reichner waited. "Talk to me."

"He was there!" Lewis blurted. "He was there, but he wasn't!"

"Who was that, Lewis? Who was there?"

Lewis's eyes flashed at him, seething in anger. "You know who."

"Why don't you tell me, Lewis."

"The fake! The impostor!"

Reichner waited.

"The one you're trying to replace me with." Lewis stopped pacing and turned to confront him. "But I'm the one! I'm the one! I'll always be the one!"

"Of course you are, Lewis. You have always been the one."

Lewis's eyes seemed to soften. "And your favorite!" It was part declaration, part plea. "I will always be your favorite! I will always be the one!"

"Of course, Lewis, you will always be the one."

The words had their desired effect. Lewis began to relax, almost to wilt under the affirmation.

"But tell me about this impostor, Lewis. Is he here? Do you know who he is, where he lives?"

Lewis shook his head and resumed pacing, his internal distractions once again rising. "No, I, uh—church. I need to go to the church. I need to go."

"Okay, Lewis," Reichner spoke softly. "You may go to church. You may return to your car and enter it."

Lewis turned, quickly crossed to his VW, and climbed in.

"But Lewis."

He looked up at Reichner, blinking the sweat out of his eyes.

"No more uninvited visits to the Institute, all right?"

Lewis nodded and reached for the ignition. He turned on the engine, put it into gear, and released the brake. But, even now, he seemed to hesitate, unsure whether he had been given complete permission.

Reichner smiled and stepped back so that the boy could close the door. "It's all right, Lewis. You may leave now."

Gratefully, Lewis reached out and pulled the door shut. He inched from the curb and headed off. Reichner remained standing and watching while the car picked up speed, its chain whining, as it disappeared down the street.

The late afternoon attack on Brandon had not caught Gerty off guard. Though her physical condition was weakening from the fast, her spiritual perceptions had increased. She didn't know the details, only that the attack had come from a level low in the demonic hierarchy and that it was somehow associated with a patient from Vicksburg State.

Gerty was well aware of the dangers of associating mental illness with demonic activity. In her earlier, more zealous days she had seen the cruel treatment of such patients by well-meaning believers who insisted that every mental and emotional problem was demonic.

Even now, she wasn't sure where to draw the line. She knew all too well the verses where her Lord had cast out demons from an epileptic, and from another who was deaf and dumb. Did that mean that every epileptic was infested by demons? That every deaf and dumb person was possessed?

Of course not. And what about the patients diagnosed with multiple personalities? Were their symptoms always the result of demons, those rebellious angels who had been cast out of heaven with Satan?

Again, Gerty did not know. The adversary was clever. If he could inflict pain and suffering by having people underestimate his power, then he could do the same by having them overestimate it, by working believers into such a frenzy that they were casting demons out of every dark shadow and unexplained bump in the night.

And yet, demonic activity no longer lurked in the shadows. Not anymore. Scripture clearly warned that the Enemy, himself, could come disguised as "an angel of light." And as this age quickly drew to an end, such deceptions would become increasingly apparent. She was painfully aware of the growing acceptance of the counterfeit spirituality of New Age and Eastern spiritualism. She'd heard that over half of the world now believed in reincarnation. And it was nearly impossible to turn on the TV without hearing something about UFOs, the supernatural, the occult, or someone having some sort of mystical experience.

Yes, these were sobering times. Times, according to her Lord, in which "false christs and false prophets will rise and show great signs and wonders to deceive, if possible, even the elect."

No, Gerty did not have all of the answers. But she did have a gift. Something Scripture described as an ability to "discern spirits." She did not know all of its workings. She didn't have to. All she had to do was trust her Lord. Trust in his operation of the gift. A gift that increased as she devoted her time to prayer and fasting.

But at this particular moment, her concern was not the supernatural counterfeits coming at the boy. They would continue. Throughout the course of his ministry, they would continue, and he would learn to recognize them. No, it was his lack of faith that concerned Gerty now. It was his stubborn refusal to believe.

Because time was running out. A cold shudder had begun somewhere deep inside of her. It was coming. She was sure of it. Tonight. It was coming and he was not ready.

So far, the attacks and counterfeits—they had come only to confuse and wear him down.

But not now. Now, at last, it was here. It was approaching the city.

"Dear God—please, he's not ready, not yet. He doesn't have the faith, he doesn't have the tools." Her once serene prayers of praise and thanksgiving had suddenly given way to panic.

She had been lying on her bed. The lack of food and the earlier demonic assault on the boy had tired her, but she was ready to resume battle. She had to. For his sake.

It was coming and he was not prepared.

"Please, Lord," she murmured. She scooted across her bed and lowered herself back onto her knees. "Be merciful. He's not ready. He doesn't even believe. Without his shield he will be destroyed. Please, give him eyes to see. Protect him. Give him faith. Please, dear Jesus, give him your faith. Please, dear Lord. Holy Lord. Holy God. Holy. . . . Holy. . . . Holy. . . . "

The scratches on Brandon's face and neck burned. But that was nothing compared to the pain inside. The dreams, the plant accident, his little sister, the attack of the patient. In just four days everything had gone insane—and it was getting worse. If that wasn't bad enough, now he had a beautiful woman sitting in his truck, a woman to whom he was attracted. But one that he'd said incredibly stupid things to, and who now obviously hated his guts.

And how could he blame her? He'd been a first-class jerk. He knew how arrogant and uncaring he'd sounded back at the Institute. But what other defense did he have? There were too many things that she didn't know, that she shouldn't know. Add to that his natural inability to talk to any woman he found attractive and, well—there they were.

He glanced over at Sarah. She sat sullenly, as close to the passenger door as possible. Yes sir, he'd really outdone himself this time.

He looked back at the road. Twilight was settling over the fields. Off to the right, between the stands of trees, he noticed glimpses of a dark, billowing cloud. Grateful for a conversation starter, he motioned toward it. "Looks like we're gonna finally get ourselves some rain."

The woman glanced in that direction but said nothing. Brandon shifted his weight. This was going to be harder than he'd thought.

The road took a slow turn to the left. As he followed it, the cloud came more into view. There was a faint glow reflecting off the bottom. At first he thought it came from the setting sun, but the glow had movement. It seemed to shift and flicker.

The road continued to turn, and once again the cloud disappeared behind some trees. Brandon hesitated, then decided to keep it in view by slowing and turning off onto a side road.

"What are you doing?" Sarah asked, her voice still a few degrees below freezing.

"Looks like some sort of fire." He motioned toward the bottom of the cloud. "Check it out."

Sarah craned her head. "Where?"

"Right there, right in front of us."

She looked in the direction he pointed, then turned back to him, a puzzled expression on her face. He wasn't sure what her problem was, but this cloud was definitely weird, and worth investigating. As they approached, he realized that it was the only cloud in the sky. He estimated it to be a hundred feet wide and nearly three times that tall. It could have almost passed for a miniature thunderhead. And there was something else . . . it seemed to be drawing closer to the ground.

The road angled to the left and for several seconds a large stand of poplars completely blocked the cloud from sight. When it came back into view, it was off on Sarah's side. They were much closer now—so close that he could see a tremendous turbulence inside it as the cloud churned and boiled upon itself.

Another turn, this time to the right. And another stand of trees. When the cloud finally came back into view, it was dead ahead, less than two blocks away. And it was hovering directly over the church. *His* church. Brandon stared in unbelief as it slowly descended toward the structure—as if the building, itself, was somehow attracting it. Trees on both sides of the road started to toss and bend from the approaching wind. But there was something else, something even more astonishing.

The glow on the bottom of the cloud was not reflecting a sunset or a fire. It was reflecting light, yes, but a light that blazed through every window and opening of the church below it.

Urgency filled Brandon, and he quickly sped up.

"What's going on?" Sarah demanded.

"It's Monday night—they've got choir practice in there!"

Now they were a block away. Dust and debris flew all around the truck. And still the cloud descended, dropping closer and closer to the building until, finally, to Brandon's alarm, it enveloped the steeple.

He pushed harder on the accelerator.

He could hear the wind now. Like a roaring freight train, it grew louder and louder. And something else. Something inside the roar. A type of . . . groaning. Almost a wail. Voices, human voices. Dozens, perhaps hundreds of them.

The wind kicked up more dirt, making it nearly impossible to see the road. Brandon leaned over the wheel, peering through the windshield.

"What are you doing?" Sarah called, "Brandon, what's going on?" But he could barely hear her over the noise.

They were almost there. The trees writhed and twisted violently. The pickup shuddered, and Brandon had to grip the wheel just to keep it in the road. There was a loud snap, and suddenly the windshield exploded into a spiderweb of cracks as a tree limb smashed into it.

Brandon hit the brakes, and they skidded to a stop across the road from the church. He threw open the door and staggered into the wind. It pushed and pulled at him, throwing dirt and grit into his eyes. He squinted, covering his face with his arms, and continued forward.

"Brandon!" Sarah called from the other side of the pickup. "Brandon!"

He turned to her and shouted. "Get under the truck! Get under the truck!"

"Brandon, what are—"

"There are people in there!" He turned back into the wind. It bit into his face as he fought his way across the road. The howling voices grew to a deafening roar. He looked up at the steeple. It was completely engulfed by the cloud.

He was halfway across the street when he noticed another vehicle—a white VW bug approaching from the north. But no sooner had he seen it than he heard a thundering, rippling clatter. He spun back to the church just as the steeple ripped apart, flinging wood and rubble into the wind, creating a barrage of flying shrapnel. He ducked as pieces struck his legs, his back, his shoulders.

"Brandon!" He could barely hear Sarah's voice over the wind.

Another explosion. He turned to see a side window of the church blowing out. Then another. And another, and another, in rapid succession. But they didn't explode from wind rushing into the church; they exploded as its light rushed out—as shafts of blazing, piercing light burst through the openings.

Just as Brandon reached the sidewalk, he heard a loud crack. He looked up to see a giant cottonwood falling toward him. He leaped aside, but a branch caught him from the back and threw him hard onto the concrete. And then there was silence.

"Brandon . . ." Sarah's voice was far, far away. Another world. "Brandon . . ." He felt her shaking him by the shoulders. "Brandon . . ."

Dazed, regaining consciousness, he rolled onto his back. When his eyes focused, he saw her staring down at him, her face filled with concern, her hair flying in the wind.

And directly behind her—the cloud, much closer now. So close he could make out what appeared to be faces—swirling, contorting faces. Faces that were inside the—no, they weren't *inside* the cloud, they *were* the cloud. They were the source of the roaring winds, the deafening groans. It was these twisting, agonizing, tortured faces that made up the cloud.

"No!" Brandon shouted. "Stay away!"

But the faces continued their approach. As they came closer, they condensed, coming together, forming something new. A head. But not a human head. This was something more grotesque, more ferocious. It looked part leopard, part lion, part he wasn't sure. He could clearly see it, suspended in the air. There were the eyes, the mouth— and there were horns. But not two horns. No, there were several of them. He guessed at least ten.

"Stay away!" he shouted. "Stay back!"

The head drew closer. But it was no longer approaching the church. It was coming after them. Its mouth opened as it closed the distance. Brandon went cold with fear. But he was feeling something else as well. A stirring. Deep inside his chest. A swelling. There was a power he couldn't explain. A burning power that rapidly grew inside of him. It filled his chest then rose into his throat and his mouth. He gulped in air, but nothing would cool the searing heat. His lungs were on fire. The burning power had to escape. The approaching head had to be stopped. He took in another gulp of air; it did no good. The fire within him had to be released. He opened his mouth. A word came to mind; it formed in his throat, his mouth. Somehow it was part of the fire. And before he knew it, he had tilted back his head and shouted. *"GO!"*

The word roared from his mouth. But it was more than a word. It was also flame. Burning, leaping flames that shot high into the air. They struck the vaporous head, momentarily igniting, then completely evaporating one of the horns. The head howled in agony as it veered to the side, avoiding the rest of the fiery blast.

When the flames ceased, Brandon turned to Sarah. She looked back at him, terrified. He saw it again. Beyond her. The monstrous head. Only now where the horn had been destroyed, another had replaced it—a hideous thing, covered in eyes. He pulled Sarah to the ground. "Get down!" he shouted. "Get back under the truck!"

He struggled to his feet. Looking over his shoulder, he saw the thing coming directly at him. He raced to the church and ran up the steps, half staggering, half falling.

"Brandon!"

He yanked at the doors but they were locked. He banged on them, shouting, beating the glossy white wood with his fists. But the people inside were too frightened to help. Either that or they were already—

He shoved the thought out of his mind and looked back over his shoulder. The vaporous head appeared below the awning and quickly approached, once again opening its mouth. Brandon turned and slammed his shoulder into the door. It budged, but not enough. He tried again. Still nothing. The swirling head closed in. He leaned back and tried one last time.

The door broke open with such force that he stumbled, nearly fell, into the foyer. Inside, the room glowed with a brilliant, blinding light. So bright that he didn't see the three-tiered water fountain until he ran into it. He threw out his hands to catch himself and they splashed into the water. He'd never seen the fountain before and looked at it with astonishment. But even more amazing was the water he'd touched—it had suddenly turned blood red.

He pulled back with a gasp. Staggering, head reeling, he finally spotted the sanctuary doors. They were closed. On one side stood a strange olive tree, on the other, a giant lampstand holding lanterns identical to the one Jenny had held in the road. And directly over the doors was something else he had never seen before. A sign. But a sign whose words seemed vaguely familiar:

ENTER NOT WITHOUT THE SHIELD OF FAITH

With rising fear, he headed for the doors. He didn't want to go in, but knew he had to. He grabbed the handles, hesitated a moment to gather his courage, then threw them open. He staggered inside two or three steps before finally coming to a stop.

The sanctuary was absolutely calm. There was no storm. No howling wind. No blinding light. Only the sound of his gasping breath broke the silence.

Up at the front, below the organ pipes and towering cross, he saw the choir. Members he'd known since childhood—his mother, the Reverend, old man McPherson—they were all staring at him, their startled faces filled with concern.

Brandon closed his eyes, then opened them again. He looked back out the door behind him. There was no light.

No cloud. Only Sarah. She stood at the foyer doors, looking on with the same worry and concern as the choir. He reached out to the nearest pew for support. Unable to fight back the exhaustion and the flood of emotion pouring in, he slowly lowered himself into the seat. Tears sprang to his eyes. He leaned over and rested his head on the pew in front of him. The tears continued to form until one fell from his face. It splattered onto the worn oak flooring. Another followed. And then another. He tried fighting them back, but it did no good. They continued to fall, one after another, after another, and there was nothing he could do to stop them.

CHAPTER 8

Even at a quarter past nine, the living room was sweltering. Damp with perspiration, Sarah sat on a worn sofa, waiting for the next sweep of the electric fan. The meeting could have taken place out on Mrs. Martus's porch, but at this time of year and in this part of Indiana, unless they had an extra pint or two of blood for the mosquitoes, it was better to stay inside.

At the moment, Mrs. Martus was upstairs helping her son get into bed. Meanwhile, her husband, Brandon's father, sat in a wheelchair, staring out the screen door. He hadn't moved a muscle, hadn't even acknowledged Sarah's or the Reverend's presence since they'd arrived. She guessed that he was the victim of a severe stroke or some other brain injury.

She petted Drool, a huge dog who did not get his name by accident, as she carried on small talk with the Reverend. He was a handsome man in his late fifties—intelligent, well-read. Like everyone else in the community, they'd begun their conversation by discussing the drought—what it was doing to the crops, how it was affecting the farmers, the future impact upon corn and soybean prices. It wasn't long before the Reverend added, somewhat sardonically, "And in one more week we'll finally hit the forty-day mark."

"Is that significant?" Sarah asked.

The Reverend shook his head with a sigh. "Not to you or me. But you would be surprised at how folks, particularly in these more rural areas, still look to the weather as a sign of God's favor or disfavor."

"You're serious?"

"I'm afraid so. And, like it or not, forty days and nights of the heavens being sealed has a distinct biblical ring about it."

Sarah nodded, then look up just in time to see Mrs. Martus make her entrance from upstairs.

"Well, now." The woman was all smiles as she glided down the steps from Brandon's room. "I think he's going to be just fine. 'Course it took a bit of doing, but I finally convinced him to take his medication." She entered the room, full of poise and Southern grace. Still, there was a certain nervousness about her. An uneasy energy. "Gracious me, where are my manners. You've been sittin' here all this time without anything to drink?" She turned toward the kitchen. "Let me get us some iced tea. I'll only be a—"

The Reverend was immediately on his feet. "No, Meg." He smiled. "Please, let me get that for us."

"Nonsense. It's already made. The pitcher's in the—"

"Meg, please." He motioned toward the sofa.

She hesitated, seeming to waver. And for the first time since she'd arrived, Sarah caught a glimpse of the strain she was under.

"Please," the Reverend repeated, "you've had a very trying evening, Meg."

At last Mrs. Martus nodded and the Reverend headed for the kitchen. He'd no sooner left the room than she turned to Sarah with a smile. "Well, now, this is service, isn't it?"

Sarah smiled back as the woman sat beside her.

As if unable to endure any silence for long, Mrs. Martus continued, "So tell me, Dr. Weintraub—"

"Please, 'Sarah.'"

"All right, Sarah." Another smile. "How long have you known Brandon?"

"Actually, not very long."

"I didn't even know he had friends at the Institute." She pushed a damp tendril of hair to the side. "'Course gettin' any information from him these days is like squeezin' blood from a turnip—if you know what I mean." She chuckled quietly.

Sarah nodded. Now, at least, she understood his silence. If he was having such experiences as this, no wonder he was afraid to talk to anybody about them. "Mrs. Martus? How long has he been having these—attacks?"

"Oh, they're not attacks, dear. Sometimes—well, sometimes he just thinks he sees things that aren't there, that's all."

Sarah nodded. "How long?" she gently repeated.

"Dear me." The woman scrunched her eyebrows in thought. "As a boy, he always had himself a real vivid imagination. Tellin' stories that'd take your breath away." Once again she pushed her hair aside. "'Course his daddy, there"—she indicated her husband—"he'd always be encouragin' it. Thick as thieves those two; no separatin' them. But that was a long time ago."

Once again Sarah could sense the woman's weariness. "Mr. Martus—he's suffering from . . . ?"

"A stroke. Been almost six years now."

"And he has no use of his arms or legs?"

"Or speech," Mrs. Martus added. "Least that's what the doctors tell us."

Something about that last line led Sarah to believe there was more. "And you believe them?"

"Me?" Mrs. Martus chuckled. "Well, of course I do, honey. If the good Lord wants to send us a trial or two, then that's his business. Ours is to take what comes in life and make the best of it." She paused a moment, then glanced upstairs. "'Course, not everyone can accept that fact."

Watching her carefully, Sarah ventured a guess. "People like Brandon?"

Mrs. Martus nodded, almost imperceptibly. "Poor soul." She glanced at Sarah with a nervous smile.

Sarah waited, cocking her head inquisitively, making it clear she'd like to hear more.

The woman looked toward the wheelchair, then down at her lap. And then, after another pause, she started to talk. "The first few months he used to stay up, sometimes all night, praying at his daddy's side. He was so positive that if he prayed hard enough, if he just had enough faith, he could make his daddy walk." Her voice trailed off into sad memories.

Sarah looked back toward the wheelchair, touched by the woman's emotions but even more moved by this unseen, sensitive side to Brandon. She was about to ask her to continue when the Reverend entered carrying a tray with a pitcher of iced tea and three glasses. "Here we go."

Suddenly Mrs. Martus was all smiles and good cheer. "I do declare, Reverend, you are a man of many talents." He smiled as he set the tray before them and began filling the glasses. "Sarah was just askin' how long Brandon's been havin' these spells."

The Reverend nodded. "They really didn't get bad until after the accident, wouldn't you say?"

Mrs. Martus agreed. "At least that's when the dreams started."

"Excuse me?" Sarah interrupted. "Accident?"

"Oh, didn't you know?" Mrs. Martus asked. "We lost our little girl about seven months ago. An automobile accident. Brandon was driving."

Sarah's heart moved with compassion.

"'Course as Providence would have it, he barely had a scratch—but you can hurt a person deeper than in the physical, if you know what I mean."

Sarah glanced down. She knew exactly what the woman meant. That's why she had the lab, her work, the long hours. But what did Brandon have? She turned back to Mrs. Martus. "You mentioned dreams?"

The Reverend answered, "The doctors say Brandon is suffering from acute guilt—compounded by his inability to accept his sister's death."

"So he dreams about her?" Sarah asked.

"They say it's a release."

"But weird dreams," Mrs. Martus explained. "Not healthy at all."

The Reverend nodded.

Sarah continued a bit more tentatively. "Were they ever—the dreams—were they ever partially manifested?"

The Reverend frowned. "What do you mean?"

"Have they ever contained facts or bits of information that, later, seemed to come true?"

Mrs. Martus shifted slightly. Sarah couldn't be certain, but it seemed she'd grown more uneasy.

Once again the Reverend answered. "Why do you ask, Dr. Weintraub?"

"Well, the average person spends a total of six years of his life dreaming, and——"

"Usually emotional or psychological in nature," he interjected. "Unless, of course it's just plain fantasy."

"Not always," Sarah corrected. "PSI studies indicate that precognitive skills—the ability to perceive an event before it happens—most often occur when we're in the dream state."

Mrs. Martus and the Reverend exchanged a discreet glance. Sarah noted it, then continued. "What about premonitions? Feelings that he'd been someplace, seen something before the event actually occurred?"

"Dr. Weintraub." The Reverend quietly set down his drink. "We appreciate your interest, particularly given your area of expertise. But let me assure you, Brandon's experiences have nothing to do with what you folks refer to as 'the paranormal.'"

"How can you be so certain?"

"Brandon has suffered a severe emotional loss, and he holds himself responsible. To encourage him, to suggest that these experiences come from anything else, much less the supernatural—well, it would only do him more harm than good."

"But you do believe it is possible?"

He took a breath and folded his hands. "I believe the human mind is a remarkable instrument, capable of far more than we give it credit. But to think of these incidents in the context of the supernatural—well . . ." He gave a little smile. "I'd like to think we've all grown past those days of superstition, wouldn't you?"

Sarah looked at him, unsure whether to be offended. "Still," she insisted, "as a minister, as a man of faith, you're aware of these things. I mean, your own Bible talks about dreams, prophets—"

"The Bible was written a long time ago, Dr. Weintraub. Certainly, it contains great wisdom and insight into the human condition, not to mention its poetic grace and beauty. However, I'm sure you are aware of the problems created when people start taking it too literally, when they begin treating it as if it were infallible, the final word of authority in any type of social, historical, or even scientific issue."

"Certainly, but as a—"

"If that were the case, where would we stop?" he chuckled. "Would you also have us believing in a six-day creation, or handling snakes, or raising people from the dead?"

"All I'm suggesting is that, as a minister, you're certainly aware of—"

"As a minister, I'm aware that it is my responsibility to care for my flock." His voice grew more firm. "And if that means protecting them occasionally from half-baked theories or the latest fads in pseudoscience, then so be it."

Sarah felt her ears growing hot with anger. "Excuse me?"

"What I mean to say is that—"

"Gracious me," Mrs. Martus laughed, as she held out her hands, making it clear that the discussion was at an end. Sarah and the Reverend looked at her. She chuckled. "Yes, sir, there's nothing like a lively debate between friends." She reached over and poured more tea into

Sarah's glass. "I guess it's like my momma always said, if you want some spice in the conversation just add a little religion and politics."

The interruption gave Sarah a moment to cool down. She stole a glance at the Reverend. He was doing the same. She'd obviously hit a nerve. But what?

"Brandon will be fine," Mrs. Martus cranked up her smile a little higher. She patted Sarah's hand. "He just needs a little rest, that's all. Just a little rest and he'll be as good as new. Mark my words."

Mrs. Martus and the Reverend reached for their iced tea. The cubes in their glasses clinked, and Sarah watched as they raised the drinks to their mouths in almost perfect unison.

Dr. Reichner started awake. He blinked, once, twice, before finally getting his bearings. He sat up. His face was wet with perspiration and his heart hammered in his chest. He took several breaths, literally forcing himself to calm down and relax. It had been five years since his heart attack and he did not intend to have another.

It was only a dream, that's all. A flashback to his encounter with the python. He reached over and snapped on the light.

See, the room was empty. Only his Siamese cat lay at the foot of his luxurious, satin-sheeted bed. Nothing else. And definitely no python.

Still the words of the boy guru's voice had seemed so real, echoing in Reichner's head as clearly as the first time he'd heard them:

"We've chosen you to help him . . . to unlock his gifts . . ."

There had been no other communication from Nepal. Not by fax, nor e-mail, nor phone. But that's how it had always been. Besides the money that was wired every month into the Institute's account, there was virtually no other communication with the cartel. They definitely liked their privacy, and that was fine with him. The less interference the better.

Of course he was required to keep his financiers up-to-date on his research through semiannual reports and by copying them on all published articles, but that was about it. That's why the summons to Nepal and his conversation (if you could call it that) with the boy guru had been so significant. For three years the money had always been there when he needed it. And, except for their insistence that the Institute be built here in Indiana, they'd pretty much given him free rein.

Until now.

And yet it was a simple request. Find some young man with pronounced PSI abilities and run a few tests on him. No problem—virtually a carbon copy of what he'd done with Lewis. Although it would be fine with Reichner if they could forego the "voices" this time.

No, it wasn't the request that bothered him as much as it was the method in which it had been made.

More and more, he had begun to regard his initial vision in Nepal as legitimate. It was too vivid, too precise, to have been induced by drugs or the exotic environment. And he'd certainly read about such things happening—not only in Eastern mysticism but in the West as well, where shamans supposedly communicate with the spirits of animals. And there was at least one famous psychic in the States who claimed to receive her prophecies through a talking snake. The concept certainly wasn't new. In fact, it was as old as the Garden of Eden myth. But Reichner had never personally experienced anything like that, and it had definitely left him unnerved.

Then there was the other matter: this sudden urgency. The boy guru obviously believed something was going to happen. And judging by the pressure he was exerting, he believed it was going to happen very soon.

But all of that had little to do with tonight's experience. Tonight it had simply been a dream. Reichner had merely dreamed that the python was curled up on his silken sheets repeating the phrases. Phrases Reichner had obviously pulled from his memory. Phrases that his subconscious was using to urge him to begin the search. Of course it would have been easier to believe this if it hadn't been for that other phrase, the new one still ringing in his ears, the one that hadn't been used in his encounter in Nepal—the phrase that had finally awakened him.

"If you do not help," the voice had whispered, *"we will lose him. And if we lose him, you will pay."*

Reichner shook his head. It was only a dream. He glanced at the alarm on his bed stand: 12:11. He reached over to turn off the light, then hesitated. Maybe it wouldn't hurt to sleep with it on, just for tonight. Angry at the thought and at the weakness it betrayed, he snapped off the light and lay back down.

But sleep would not return.

Nor did sleep come for Brandon. It had been nearly three hours since Momma had helped him up to his room. The medication she'd given him hadn't even taken the edge off his torment. How could it? How could two little pills be expected to stop a living nightmare? The storm, the vaporous head with horns, the fountain of blood, the lampstand, the sign—they all seemed vaguely familiar, like pieces from forgotten dreams, or stories he'd heard as a child. But nothing made sense. His mind raced—to where, he wasn't certain. How to stop it, he hadn't a clue. The only things he could be sure of were the tears, his increasing confusion, and his ever-growing anger.

Sometime after midnight, he got up, dressed, headed out to his pickup, and quietly drove into town. Unsure where to go, he eventually found himself back at the church. He didn't expect to find any answers there, but he did expect to vent some rage.

The doors were unlocked. They always were. It was a policy his father had started way back when the church had first opened. And, over the years, it was a policy that potential thieves and vandals usually respected. Brandon stepped into the foyer. Everything was deathly still. This time, the sanctuary doors were open. There were no fountains, no olive trees, no lampstands, and definitely no hanging sign. Everything was real.

He entered the sanctuary and made his way down the slight incline of the aisle toward the altar. He didn't bother turning on the lights. He'd grown up here. The diffused glow from the outside streetlight provided what little illumination he needed.

He stopped just a few feet from the pew he'd sat in every Sunday for over twenty years. He glared up at the cross hanging on the wall, the same absurd symbol he'd seen each of those Sundays. The symbol of death and sacrifice and futility.

When he spoke, his voice quivered with rage. "What do you want from me?"

Silence.

Again he spoke, louder. *"What do you want?"*

But, of course, there was no answer. Just his own echo as it faded into the silence. A tightness grew in his throat. He tried to swallow it, but it wouldn't go away. Tears sprang to his eyes, but he fought them back. Not here. Not now.

He spoke again—a final, harsh whisper. "What do you want?"

"Maybe he just wants you to believe."

The sound spun Brandon around. He peered into the darkness, searching for its source. There. Almost at the back, near the center, a small sitting figure.

"Who's there?" he demanded.

With some difficulty the figure rose from the pew.

"Who are you?" he asked again. "What are you doing here?"

Slowly, the figure made its way toward the center aisle. "I'm here 'cause I knew you'd be here." It was a woman's voice—craggy and old. It sounded familiar.

"Who are you?" he repeated.

"I s'pose I could be askin' you the same question, Brandon Martus."

The figure stepped into the aisle. A faint pool of light spilled across her face. Now he recognized her. "You're the old woman. The one who stopped by the house yesterday."

Gerty started toward him, hobbling painfully down the aisle. "And you're the boy who refuses to believe."

Brandon watched in silence as she approached. She spoke again. "I'm sure gonna miss this place. Hear they're gonna be tearin' it down for a—what'd they say? Some sorta bank building?"

Brandon said nothing.

She continued, "Did you know that right there, right where you're standin' in front of that altar, your momma and poppa dedicated you to the Lord? You musta been only seven, maybe eight days old." She stopped halfway down the aisle to catch her breath.

Brandon said nothing.

"Believe you me, that was one special morning. 'Course we knew before that, before you were even born we knew that the Lord had his hand upon you." She chuckled softly. "Yes, sir, that was one special day. We were all standin' around singin' and believin' somethin' real special was gonna happen, right then and there. 'Course nothin' did. But still . . ."

Her voice trailed off and Brandon quietly answered. "A lot of things people believe don't happen."

At last she arrived and looked up at him. "But that don't mean you stop believin'."

Brandon carefully eyed her.

"Your belief, that's what makes it happen, Brandon Martus. All you need to do is the believin'. He'll take care of the rest. But you gotta believe. Do you hear me, son? You got to believe. Faith, that's your only shield."

"Well, then, I'll have to do without."

She looked at him.

He glanced away, then mumbled, "The only thing I know about faith is I don't have any."

The old woman watched him, saying nothing. Finally she looked past him to the cross on the front wall. "There are two types of faith, child. Earthly faith and heavenly. The earthly faith, that don't mean a thing. It's just man-made, just a way to try to make the good Lord do what you want him to." Her eyes fell back on him. "But there's another type. The type that surrenders to his will. Completely. And once it learns what that will is, it speaks it into existence. And that type of faith, anyone can have."

Brandon closed his eyes. He'd heard religious double-talk all his life. "Yeah," he said, preparing to move past her, "well, I'm fresh out of both."

"You're wrong."

Her comment angered him. "What?"

She said nothing, which only irritated him more.

"Look, I don't have any faith, okay? Not anymore." She remained silent. He continued, "Maybe once, when I was a kid, sure. But I've gotten a little older now. And smarter, if you know what I mean. I understand a lot more."

"You understand nothing."

His irritation grew. "I don't have faith, all right?"

The woman shook her head. "You're wrong, Brandon Martus."

He tossed his hair back in frustration. "What's with you, anyway?"

She held his look. "Anyone can believe who wants to believe. You just don't want to."

This was absurd. What was he doing arguing with a nutcase in the middle of the night? "I *can't* believe." His voice grew louder. "You got that? I *cannot believe.*"

"You *will* not believe."

He took a breath, holding back his anger.

"Your will is the key. If you'd turn that key, God would give you his faith. He is the author of faith, Brandon Martus, not you. You need only surrender to him."

Brandon shook his head. There was no reasoning with this type. He'd run into them before. It was best just to let them go on and live out their little delusions. "Look, I should have never stopped by here in the first place." He started to pass her. "Why don't you just—go back to whatever you were doing and—"

She grabbed his arm. Her grip was weak, but he let it stop him.

"Your will is the key, Brandon Martus. You just got to surrender."

He looked at her, then down at the hand on his arm. She released it and he started back up the aisle.

"Brandon Martus."

He kept walking.

"Beware of the seducers. Be keepin' your eyes open for the counterfeits."

He slowed to a stop.

"If you refuse the Lord's way, your adversary will be tryin' to seduce you down other roads." He turned to her and she continued. "There's only one path, Brandon Martus. His path. And it's narrow. Beware of the broader ways. Don't be reachin' for heaven with the arm of the flesh. Such ways lead to the occult, to destruction. All paths but the Lord's lead to destruction."

He held her look another moment before turning and continuing back up the aisle. Maybe it was good they were tearing down the place. Who knew what type of wackos were starting to show up.

He exited through the foyer and walked outside into the sultry night air. The moon was nearly full, but its edges were blurred by a faint haze. He headed down the steps and crossed the grass to his pickup. Then he heard footsteps behind him. Apparently the old gal could move a lot faster if she set her mind to it. He turned, ready to confront her one last time. "Look, I—"

That's when he was hit. Someone jumped him from behind and they both crashed into the side of his truck. Before Brandon could recover, his attacker was already landing punches. Brandon raised his arms to block the blows and staggered back, away from the truck.

He saw a young man with a shaved head, red goatee, and wild eyes. Crazed eyes, like an animal's.

"We knew you'd return!" the assailant screamed, spittle flying. *"We knew!"* But it wasn't a single voice. It was like the patient's at the Institute. Multiple voices. Dozens of voices. Dozens of voices all shouting and directing their anger at him.

"Look," Brandon said, catching his breath, bracing for another assault. "I don't know who you are, but I don't want any trouble, all right? So why don't—"

Once again the attacker leaped at him, and they tumbled to the ground. As they rolled, Brandon swung his fists, striking ribs, kidneys, gut, but nothing mattered. The assailant seemed oblivious to pain. They rolled one way, then the other, until the attacker wound up on top, and Brandon found himself pinned. He tried to buck him off, but the man seemed to have superhuman strength.

With Brandon's arms pinned by his assailant's knees, the man began landing punches squarely into his face.

Blow after blow, sharp and powerful. Brandon did his best to resist, trying to roll, trying to throw him off, but it did little good. Lights began dancing across his vision. A loud ringing filled his head.

With the attacker's blows came the swearing. Vile oaths, all directed at Brandon. But they were sounding farther away, fading . . . as was Brandon's pain. He was passing out. Any second now and he would—

"Get off him." It was the old woman's voice, faint and from another world. "Get off! In the name of Jesus Christ I command you to stop!"

The blows ceased instantly. At first Brandon thought he'd passed out, but no, he still heard her voice.

"By the power and authority of Jesus the Christ I order you to stop!"

Brandon felt the weight of the young man shift on his chest.

"Who are you?" the voices demanded.

"Who I am is of no importance." Her voice was clearer now. Brandon was coming back, regaining consciousness. "In the name of Jesus Christ, I order you to get up."

With a struggle, Brandon finally managed to open his eyes. His vision was blurred, but he saw the man on top of him and, beyond that, the old woman.

"Now," she ordered.

The attacker rose from Brandon and staggered to his feet. Brandon rolled to his side, coughing and spitting what he knew to be blood. When he looked back up, he saw the young man catching his breath and speaking. *"He must wage the war himself,"* the voices screamed.

"In time," the woman replied.

Slowly, unsteadily, Brandon struggled to his hands and knees, keeping his eyes on the confrontation. The woman had taken a step or two closer. She now stood face-to-face with the man, who towered over her by nearly a foot.

"He is ours!" the voices shouted.

The woman held her ground, unflinching. "Liar."

"He has chosen to—"

"You are the author of lies."

"He has turned. He has chosen to follow our—"

"You are the author of lies, and I order you to be silent."

Everything grew quiet. The woman and the young man remained glaring at one another, but the young man no longer spoke.

Brandon knew an attack was imminent. The man was about to grab her. The last thing in the world he wanted was to get back into the mix, but the old lady would definitely be needing his help. With painful effort he rose to his feet. His head throbbed and the ground still moved under his wobbly legs, but at least he was standing.

Yet, instead of attacking her, the man's head swiveled toward him—his eyes still wild and terrifying. *"You will not prevail,"* the voices seethed. *"Victory is ours."* The hatred sent a shudder through Brandon.

The young man turned back to the woman. Brandon prepared himself to leap to her defense.

But she showed no fear. "Go," she commanded.

The man glared at her, but she didn't yield. Her voice was not loud, but it was clear and spoken with unmistakable authority. "In the name of Jesus the Christ, I command you to leave."

Brandon watched. It was amazing. Instead of attacking her, the man's stature, his very countenance, seemed to wilt.

"Now," she ordered. "Go, now."

The young man hesitated, then momentarily looked around as if trying to get his bearings. When he spotted Brandon, he tried to maintain the bravado. "I am the one. It is *my* season. You are the impostor." But it was only one voice now—a hollow imitation of the power and hatred Brandon had felt moments earlier.

"Now," the old woman repeated. "In the name of Jesus Christ I order you to leave, now."

The man turned back to her. He shifted his weight, as if unsure what to do, where to go. Then, spotting a beat-up Volkswagen across the street, he turned and walked toward it. Brandon and the woman watched in silence as he approached the car, climbed in, and started it up. Not a word was spoken as he finally pulled away and headed down the street.

At last Brandon turned to the old woman. She was staring at him. He could feel his face already swelling from the blows, and he knew some of the cuts were still bleeding. But when she took a concerned step toward him, he backed away. Whatever was going on, whatever had happened, he wanted no more of it.

"Brandon . . ."

He raised his hands, motioning her to stay away. She ignored it and continued to approach. He turned, stumbled, then headed for his truck.

"Brandon Martus."

Keeping a hand on the truck bed to steady himself, he moved along it to the cab.

"You understand now," she called out. "Do you understand?"

He threw open the door and climbed inside.

"Eli."

He stole a look over his shoulder. She was still shuffling toward him. He reached into his jeans pocket for his keys. His right hand screamed in pain. It was either sprained or broken.

"Eli—you have the same authority, you have seen it work."

Gritting his teeth against the pain, he yanked out the keys and shoved them into the ignition.

"Child—"

He fired up the truck.

"You have the authority."

He dropped it into gear and released the brake.

"You need only surrender to his will. You need only believe."

He revved the engine and quickly pulled from the curb. She was still talking, but he no longer heard. He traveled nearly fifty yards before glancing up at the rearview mirror.

The old lady was still there, standing all alone in the road, watching after him.

Dr. Reichner sat in the passenger seat as Sarah drove. Her car was running, but barely. He'd been the one to suggest they take it—after all, she knew the way. But now he cursed himself for the idea. Besides worn-out shocks and the world's roughest-sounding engine, she had no air-conditioning. A serious oversight in this record-breaking heat.

The car gave a couple of extra shudders as she turned onto Highway 30 and accelerated. "I think it's a bad carburetor," she shouted over the roar of the open windows. "Last night it didn't want to start at all."

"Maybe you should have taken the hint," Reichner said, fingering a piece of window molding that disintegrated under his touch.

"All she needs is a little loving care," Sarah insisted. Then, throwing a gibe back in his direction, "That is, if her owner could ever get some time off to visit the garage."

Reichner smiled quietly. Sarah wouldn't take the time off, even if he gave it to her. And that was fine by him. As long as he could capitalize on her desperate need to achieve, she would always be of use.

This morning was a perfect example. Initially, she had balked when he suggested they drive out to visit the boy. She didn't want to exploit his trauma, to take advantage of his sister's death. Reichner pretended to understand—but all he had to do was remind Sarah that if this kid was for real, the potential breakthroughs in their field would be unparalleled. Minutes later they were in the car, heading out to pay him a little visit. Again Reichner smiled. It took so little to play this woman.

Earlier, when she'd first mentioned the boy, he had shown little interest. Somebody with a bad case of nightmares and hallucinations seemed a likelier candidate for Vicksburg State than for his studies. But when she had mentioned that he had also been at the lab, and that a patient had attacked him, and that he had been at a church the night before, Reichner had begun to wonder.

Hadn't the boy guru insisted that Reichner would find somebody in this area? Hadn't Lewis wanted to attack somebody else at the lab? And last night hadn't Lewis also spoken of visiting a church? Coincidence? Perhaps. But definitely reason enough to drop by and pay this kid a visit. Besides, it gave Reichner an opportunity to be alone with Sarah, and he liked that. He glanced at her legs. She was wearing a skirt today. Yes, he liked that very much.

"This must be the place," Sarah said, nodding toward a pickup parked along the shoulder of the road. They had just come from the boy's house, where his mother had reluctantly told them that he was probably down at the river. "He's taking the day off," she had explained. "That's where he likes to go and work things out."

Reichner had assured her that they wouldn't bother him, that they would only ask a question or two. It was a lie, but it made no difference to Reichner. After all, it was what she wanted to hear.

Sarah pulled the car to a stop behind the pickup, and they stepped out into the pounding sun.

"He may seem aloof at first," she said as they found the path and started down the steep bank into the woods. "But that's just a defense. Underneath, he's really quite sweet and sensitive."

Reichner arched an eyebrow. Was it his imagination, or did she have a thing for the kid? Throughout their drive, she'd spoken about him with concern—and now he was "sweet and sensitive"? He'd keep this in mind.

They were halfway down the path when they found him. Or at least when his dog found them. But instead of barking an alarm, the old animal lumbered to its feet and headed up the bank to greet them, all pants and slobbers. It recognized Sarah immediately, and she bent down to give it the appropriate pats and praises. Then it turned to Reichner, who for appearance's sake had to do likewise, petting and patronizing the beast while it drooled all over his two-hundred-fifty-dollar-a-pair Ballys.

Sarah called out, "Brandon."

The boy was stretched out on some rocks, shirt off, sunning himself. He was a good-looking kid, muscular build, and with long gorgeous hair that some of Reichner's women would have killed for.

"Brandon?"

He looked up, spotted them, then turned away.

They continued down the path, slipping slightly, as unruly blackberry vines snagged Reichner's slacks and sharp rocks assaulted his shoes.

Again Sarah called his name.

He finally turned back to them. "Come to see another show?" he shouted. "Sorry, the next performance isn't until—" He stopped when he saw Reichner. "You brought a friend. Maybe I should start charging admission."

They reached the bottom of the path and Reichner glanced at his shoes. They were scuffed and covered in drool. This kid had better be worth it.

"Your mother said you might be here," Sarah explained as they approached. "This is Dr. Reichner, my boss. He's head of the Institute."

The kid's eyes locked onto Reichner's. They were steel gray and riveting. Immediately Reichner knew that

Sarah had been right; there was a depth here, something that belied the boy's pretended indifference.

But Sarah had noticed something else. "Your face," she asked in sudden concern. "What happened to your face?" She was referring to the cuts and bruises around his eyes and on his cheeks.

Brandon looked away.

"Brandon?"

"I was at a late-night church service."

Sarah turned to Reichner with a concerned look. He frowned and motioned for her to continue.

"Listen." She shifted uneasily. "Do you mind if we talk to you for a few minutes?"

The boy turned back to her. Reichner watched and almost smiled. He'd guessed correctly. There was definitely something between them.

"Please," she asked, clearing her throat a little self-consciously. "I think it might be important."

The boy gave no answer. There was only the sound of the river and the groaning of the dog as it collapsed in some nearby shade.

Taking his lack of reply as an affirmative, Reichner searched for a seat. "Well . . ." He found a flat boulder nearby and eased carefully onto it, mindful of his slacks. "Dr. Weintraub tells me you've been having some pretty unusual experiences?"

The boy simply looked at him. But Reichner was unfazed. "So, tell me, Brennan—"

"Brandon," Sarah corrected.

"So tell me, Brandon, how long has this been going on?"

The boy glanced away.

Reichner waited.

Finally the kid responded. "Not long."

"And it started out as dreams, you say, that is before they became—" He chose to bypass the word *hallucinations*. "Visions." The boy made no response. Reichner pressed on. "Tell me, Brandon, I am curious: What do you know about quantum mechanics?"

The kid threw him a look.

Reichner chuckled. "Actually, it is not that complex a concept." He found a stick near his feet and picked it up. "It merely explains how solid objects, say this piece of wood here, can sometimes act more like waves of energy than as an actual physical object. That is, until we observe it. And then, for some reason, it collapses back into a lower state and becomes a solid object again."

Brandon looked at him. "They pay you money to think like that?"

Reichner forced another chuckle. Let the boy have his fun. At least he'd gotten Brandon's attention. Now he'd better move fast to keep it.

"What if I were to tell you that instead of a solid object, like this stick here, collapsing and appearing into our dimension—what if I were to say that I believe your experiences, your dreams and visions, are *you* actually stepping up into *its* dimension or into dimensions that are even higher?"

The boy looked skeptical but intrigued. Good. Now Reichner just had to wait for him to take the bait. He paused, letting the silence build. Finally, the boy spoke.

"You're talking like sci-fi movies—parallel universes and stuff."

Reichner shook his head. "Not exactly. Mathematically I have trouble with *parallel* universes. However, with existing mathematical formulas I can prove *perpendicular* universes."

"Perpendicular?"

Reichner nodded. It was a stretch, but if this preacher's kid still believed in a heaven and a hell—an 'up there' heaven, and a 'down there' hell—then this concept would work nicely. He continued, "Mathematically, thanks to Green, Schwartz, and dozens of other physicists, we have proof that our universe does not consist of three dimensions, as we once thought. Instead, it consists of at least eleven."

"Eleven?"

Reichner nodded. "That is correct. Eleven dimensions. It can be proved mathematically. Beyond question."

The boy shook his head—either in skepticism or wonder, Reichner couldn't be sure. He quickly moved on. "Now, of course, we can construct models like the tesseract to help us understand higher dimensions. But instead of bringing out the charts and diagrams, there is an easier way." Again he paused, making sure the kid was still on the line. He was, and he was waiting for more. Perfect.

With the stick still in his hands, Reichner rose to his feet. "Now, it is difficult for our three-dimensional minds to comprehend an eleven-dimensional world, so let us talk about two and three dimensions, instead." He stepped to a small pool near the edge of the river. It appeared to have once been a large eddy, but thanks to the drought, most of it had evaporated, leaving it only a few inches deep.

"Let us suppose that there were two-dimensional creatures living here on the surface of this water." He crouched and gently set the stick in the pool. "They would understand length—" He stretched his hands the length of the stick. "And they would understand width." He indicated its width. "But they would have no comprehension of height, of up and down, because they are only two-dimensional creatures. A third dimension, up here above the river, would be impossible for them to see or even comprehend, because they only live in their two-dimensional world."

The boy leaned forward. Good.

"But you and I, up here in the three-dimensional world, we could look down upon their entire world with a single glance." He motioned from one end of the stick to the other. "We could see their beginning, just as clearly as their end. And, even though we are all around, they would not see us at all—until, *poof*—" He poked his finger into the water. "We suddenly appeared in their dimension. Or *poof*—" He removed his finger. "We suddenly disappeared."

"We'd be like gods to them," Sarah explained. "We'd be omnipotent. Able to observe everything they do, being in all places at the same time."

"Now." Reichner reached into the water and lifted out the stick. "What if a two-dimensional creature were suddenly lifted up out of his world and into our three-dimensional world?"

"He'd freak," Brandon answered quietly.

Reichner nodded. "Precisely. He would see things that did not exist in his world, three-dimensional objects that his two-dimensional mind could not comprehend. And, as a defense, his mind would reduce those images into forms he *could* understand—most likely symbols from his existing world."

The boy shifted uneasily.

Reichner was obviously making his point. "You come from a religious background, correct?"

Brandon nodded.

"Think of all the great biblical visions and symbols: white horses, multiheaded beasts, slain lambs. These symbols all come from people trying to explain the inexplicable—using lower-dimensional terms to explain a higher-dimensional reality, a *superreality.*"

"And you're telling me all this because . . ."

"I want you to look upon science, at least our science, as just another facet of religion, just another way of trying to understand God."

Brandon repeated his question. "And you're telling me all this because . . ."

Reichner threw a look at Sarah. He'd done all he could. The fish had taken the bait, now it was up to her to bring him in.

She took her cue. "Because we need your help, Brandon."

The boy glanced at her, then looked away.

She gently persisted. "Let us run a few tests."

He shook his head and rose to his feet.

"In a controlled environment."

"No."

"You'd be in no danger. We'd be right beside—"

"No!" He turned back to her, obviously trying but unable to hide his agitation. "I'm not going to be some guinea pig in one of your laboratory experiments."

Sarah quietly rose to her feet. "That's not what—"

"I'm not one of those loony tunes you bring in from Vicksburg and hook up to a bunch of wires."

Reichner fired a glance to Sarah. How much did the kid know about their use of mental patients?

But Brandon wasn't finished. "It's just guilt, all right? The doctors say I'm getting better. It's just a matter of time and I'll be okay."

"But we're talking about more than just you." Sarah took a step toward him. "The implications of this research could affect the entire world, Brandon. We could be helping the human—"

"Well, *me* is all I got, all right?"

"Brandon, if you'd just stop and—"

"Not you, not the world—me!"

"And you is all that counts?" An edge had entered her voice.

The boy glanced away. "You got that right."

They were losing him. Reichner looked hard at Sarah, a signal for her to play the final card. She scowled, obviously reluctant to go into that area.

But Reichner nodded firmly, making it clear that she had no other choice.

And still she hesitated.

All right, then, if she wouldn't, he would. He turned to Brandon and asked a single question. "What about your little sister—what about Jenny?"

Brandon's eyes shot to him, then to Sarah. But Sarah was unable to look at him.

He turned back to Reichner. "She's dead. Or hadn't you heard."

"Perhaps." Reichner shrugged. "At least in this dimension."

He let the phrase hang, making sure the hook was back in the kid's mouth. Then he rose and began to brush off his slacks. "Well, I see that we have made a mistake. I thought perhaps you would want to help us. If not in the name of science, then at least for . . ." He pretended to hesitate, then shrugged. "Well, it really doesn't matter now. We are sorry to have wasted your time, Brandon." He turned to Sarah, who was unable to look at either of them. "Shall we go, Doctor?"

She nodded.

Without another word, they turned and started for the path.

"If I do that . . ."

The kid's voice stopped them. Reichner almost smiled. So predictable.

"If I go through with it, you're saying I might meet Jenny?"

Reichner said nothing.

Brandon repeated, louder, "If I go through with it, are you saying—"

"It's a possibility," Sarah gently interrupted. "But nothing's for sure."

Brandon persisted. "But there's a chance?"

Sarah paused, then nodded.

"And you'll be there?" he asked, keeping his eyes fixed on her.

"I'll be at your side the entire time."

Brandon stood a long moment. Then he looked toward the dog and gave a low whistle. The animal struggled to its feet and lumbered toward him. Finally he answered, "All right." With that, he turned and headed back toward the river.

Sarah hesitated, then called, "Brandon."

He started working his way upstream along the edge of the water. He didn't turn to her when he spoke. "I said all right, didn't I?"

To fully confirm it, Reichner called out, "Tomorrow afternoon. That will give us time to set up the equipment. Tomorrow afternoon, at two."

Brandon said nothing. Neither did Sarah as she stood watching.

Reichner turned and started back up the path. Several seconds passed before Sarah joined him. Reichner knew she felt guilty. Too bad. But using people, playing this type of hardball, was all part of the game. And she'd better get used to it if she planned to be a winner. Still, he wasn't worried. Because if there was one thing he knew about Sarah Weintraub, it's that she was driven to win.

CHAPTER 9

O kay, we're getting images." The Institute's biochemical engineer motioned for Sarah and Reichner to join him over at the computer terminal.

Across the room, Brandon lay on a hard, twelve-inch-
wide table that had been rolled inside the PET, or
positron-emission tomography scanner. It looked like a
giant white doughnut with an opening thirty-five inches
in diameter that ran forty-two inches deep. It completely
surrounded Brandon's head, which was held in place by
two leather straps fastened with Velcro strips. He wore no
gown, just jeans and his standard-issue T-shirt. His left
hand rested in a plexiglass pan of water heated to exactly
43.6 degrees Celsius. From this hand they would remove
multiple blood samples in order to monitor the radioac-
tivity they were injecting into his body through a syringe
in the other hand—a syringe surrounded by a silver cylinder designed to shield the technician from the very radiation he was injecting.

Outside the scanner, on a table near Brandon's
chest, a small cassette recorder played Reichner's relaxation tape.

Sarah knew that PET scans weren't always available
to parapsychology labs, partly because of the machine's

1.8-million-dollar price tag. She also knew that the Institute was preparing to order a second. A wonderful indulgence. But PET scans themselves were no luxury. Unlike SCATs or MRIs, which register the same condition of tissue—whether it's dead or alive—PET scans actually view and record the metabolic rate of a living organism.

Thirty minutes earlier, they had injected Brandon with three ccs of the radioactive isotope Fluoro Deoxyglucose, a sugar that enters the cells of the brain just like any other sugar molecule. But since it is radioactive, it gives off energy—which the special crystals inside the PET's plastic doughnut (over eighteen thousand of them) are able to record.

The purpose? To see which areas of Brandon's brain were the most active when he had his visions.

The process was relatively painless, except for the hard table Brandon now lay on. All he had to do was listen to Reichner's prerecorded voice and let it lead him into the lower-frequency brain waves—the brain waves present when the subject is most susceptible to paranormal activity.

Sarah joined Reichner at the computer screen to watch the first of the sixty-three sliced video images of Brandon's brain appear. To see pictures of the human brain actually working never ceased to amaze her. The organ is by far the most complex in the known universe, and to this day prompts more questions than science has been able to answer.

The brain had not always been held in such high esteem. Aristotle figured it to be nothing but an elaborate cooling system that was good for producing mucus (after all, look how close it was to the nose). But eventually, this relatively small, three-pound organ responsible for everything from a Shakespearean sonnet to the horrors of Hiroshima, received the credit it deserved.

The biochemical engineer sitting at the computer, a young man from Taiwan, whistled softly. "Take a look at that."

Sarah directed her attention back to the screen. Not only did the PET scan show what sections of the brain Brandon was using, but it also showed to what degree he was using them. The areas with the least amount of function were shown in the cooler colors of purple, blue, and green. The more moderate working areas appeared as yellow. And finally there was red—the "hot" areas, the areas where the radiation was most highly concentrated, where brain activity was the greatest.

"His entire right temporal lobe," Reichner whispered in awe, "it's on fire."

Sarah looked on with equal wonder. For ease in research, the brain was divided into regions by function. The frontal lobe controlled some motor activity but was also responsible for giving us our sociability. The occipital lobe was for vision. The parietal lobe received sensory information and helped in special orientation. But it was the right temporal section of the brain that held their attention now. When this area was stimulated during brain surgery, some patients experienced the so-called 'out-of-body experience,' or a feeling of déjà vu, or any number of paranormal sensations.

"Have you ever seen anything like it?" Reichner whispered.

"Not like this," Sarah said, shaking her head and staring. Brandon's entire right temporal lobe glowed a bright red.

"Amazing," the engineer whispered.

"Okay," Reichner nodded. "I have seen enough."

Surprised, Sarah turned toward him. "What?" she asked.

"Let's get him out of here and into the Ganzfield."

"But we're not done," the engineer argued.

"We only have him for a day. Get him unplugged and down to Lab Two."

Sarah frowned. "That wasn't the agreement. We asked him to participate in one experiment, and for only a couple of hours."

Reichner looked at her and scoffed. "We are not going to let an opportunity like this slip through our fingers, Doctor. Now, get him unhooked and moved."

"But . . ." Sarah glanced across the room at Brandon and lowered her voice. "What if he doesn't want to stay? Emotionally, we've put him through a lot already. What if he wants to go home?"

"He will stay."

"How can you be so sure?"

"How?" he asked.

She nodded.

"Because you, my dear, know how to convince him."

Gerty stood at the stove, savoring the smell of the chicken-and-rice soup. This was how she always broke her longer fasts. It was the gentlest way she knew of easing her digestive system back into operation.

She had finally finished her time of prayer and peti-
tion for the boy. It had not been as long as some of her
earlier fasts, but her Lord had said that it was enough. The
concentrated period of intercession was over. The boy
would still face counterfeits and challenges, and his
fiercest battles still lay ahead, but the Lord had made it
clear that her time of interceding was over. His perfect will
would be accomplished.

Of course she had no idea what that will would be.
And, after last night's talk with the young boy, she had
some very serious concerns. After all, despite the Lord's
power, he always respected an individual's will. It was
always up to the individual whether that person would
love the Lord, hate him, obey him, or even believe in him.

And it was that final choice, the choice of *un*belief,
that she feared most for the boy.

Of course she had asked her Lord. But in this area he
had remained silent. She knew that he wasn't being indifferent to her requests. He simply understood the com-
plexities far more than she did. So, at least for now, she
too would have to simply believe. Gerty smiled. Of course
she would believe. After all their years together, after all
those years of his love and tender mercies, how could she
do otherwise?

She reached over to the counter and picked up
another of the letters she'd been writing. Although the
Lord had said her time of intercession had drawn to a
close, he had promised that she could continue writing
her letters. How many more, she didn't know. Perhaps as
many as she had time for. Because he had promised her
one other thing: Before the week was over, he would take
her home.

Gerty picked up the letter from the counter and read what she'd written.

Dear Eli:

I know that you are confused and that you find your gifts frightening. At times you may even wonder if they are from God. It is good to be cautious. That is why he instructs us to "test the spirits." But let me assure you, dear child, as you turn to our Heavenly Father, those gifts will always be from above. Yes, there are counterfeits. Yes, if you strive for the gifts independent of his will, you will enter regions of the occult, a dangerous world where clever impostors promise good but seek to destroy.

The soup was steaming now, nearly boiling. Gerty turned off the stove, then reached up to open the cupboard. The door stuck slightly, squeaking when it finally gave way. She took down a small bowl, opened a drawer, and pulled out a ladle. The smell of the soup was intoxicating. With trembling hands, she dipped the ladle into the pan and slowly dished it up. It was Wednesday afternoon, the ninth day of her fast, and the soup smelled so good she could practically taste it.

When she had finished, she looked at the small formica-topped table, piled with sketches she had retrieved from the attic earlier that morning. Sketches she had been drawing for twenty-two years. She would drop them off at his house. Today, maybe tomorrow.

But not the letter. Like the other letters, this one was meant to be read later. After she was gone.

She took a spoon from the drawer and, holding the bowl in both hands, she shuffled past the counter toward the table.

She slowed as she passed the refrigerator. The Lord hadn't told her how she would die, or the exact day. But she had sensed, she had known, where it would be: right there, right between her old refrigerator and the kitchen table. Strangely enough, the insight hadn't frightened her. It simply helped prepare her.

She arrived at the table and pulled out one of the two chairs. Gently, she eased herself down. She pushed aside the letters and sketches to make more room. Then, after a quiet prayer of thanks, she picked up the spoon and dipped it into the soup. Her hand shook as she raised it to her lips.

It was warm and rich and full of flavor. She held the broth in her mouth, savoring it a moment, before finally swallowing. She dipped her spoon back into the bowl and took another sip. It was as good as the first. She wondered if she would miss this sort of thing in heaven. Then she smiled. How could she? Her Lord had promised a feast, a wedding banquet in her honor. How could there be a feast without food?

She took several more spoonfuls, feeling it warm her throat, her insides. She was less than halfway through when she placed the spoon in the bowl and pushed it aside. She would return to it shortly, but right now there were more important matters.

As she reached for her Bible, she felt a trace of sadness in her heart. She knew she would never see the boy again. Still, she would be allowed to minister to him. Through the sketches, as well as the letters and the verses in her old

Bible, she would still be able to help. The thought gave her some comfort as she opened the worn book and began turning its yellowed pages. At last she found the verses she was to give him. She would return to the soup in a moment, but right now it was more important that she clearly underline the verses for him to see.

"Like a leaf, floating upon the surface of a quiet pond . . ." Dr. Reichner sat in the Observation Room, speaking softly into the microphone. He glanced at the clock. They were twelve minutes into the session.

Down below, in Lab Two, Brandon rested comfortably in the leather recliner, bathed by the four red floodlights. His eyes were covered by the Ganzfield goggles.

Reichner continued speaking. "No cares, no worries, no thoughts. Just quiet, gentle floating . . ."

Sarah sat beside Reichner, still filled with guilt. She'd used Brandon, there was no doubt about it. At Reichner's insistence, she'd taken advantage of Brandon's trust in her and had convinced him to stay. It hadn't taken much; he was already so scared, so vulnerable.

And he had no one else but her to trust.

She winced. Once again, someone had manipulated her, someone had used her to exploit another. It was an all-too-familiar scenario, forcing her back to memories of the fights with Samuel, his arguments for the abortion, how having a child would hamper her career. Sarah closed her eyes. Once again, she was feeling cheap and used and very, very dirty. And, once again, to ease the pain, she focused on her work.

In front of her were the monitors registering Brandon's heart rate, respiration, GSR, EMG, and the all-important

EEG. During Sarah's childhood, her MD parents had often discussed the EEG craze. Back then, meditation and biofeedback were the talk of the town. Eventually interest died down, but not for the parapsychologist. In parapsychology, interest in the electroencephalograph and brain waves was still very high.

And for good reason. It was still an important gauge for measuring mental activity. The brain produces electrical current all the time, anywhere from .05 waves per second all the way up to forty. The frequencies of these waves indicate what type of consciousness we are experiencing. Generally, they fall into four categories:

The *beta* wave is the brain wave of highest frequency. When this wave dominates our mental activity, our minds are in high gear, concentrating, solving problems, having panic attacks. Next comes the *alpha* wave. It's strongest when we're in that daydreamy, half-awake state. Then comes the *theta* wave. It's strongest when our subconscious is functioning—when we're dreaming, or experiencing that inexpressible "nagging" feeling at the back of our mind, or suddenly solving a problem that we didn't even know we were thinking about. Finally, there is the *delta* wave. This is the slowest and most mysterious. It's been found to be strong in psychics, telepathics, and others who claim to be experiencing supernatural insight.

In her parents' day, when everybody was busy achieving "inner peace," alpha was the fad. But today, everyone from New Agers to Eastern mystics is focusing on theta and delta waves, the waves operating when the mind seems most susceptible to paranormal energy outside of the body.

Sarah stared at the EEG and frowned. Something wasn't right. She reached over and rapped the monitor.

"What's wrong?" Reichner asked.

"We have a malfunction." She motioned toward the screen. "Look how pronounced theta is. Something's over-modulating."

She reached behind the monitor, preparing to push the reset button, but Reichner shook his head. "No."

She looked at him.

"Let it go."

She pulled back, still looking at him. Did he actually think that Brandon could be generating that much theta, and in such a short period of time?

"That's very good," Reichner spoke into the mike with soft, velvety tones, "very, very good . . ."

Sarah glanced back at the screen. The theta started to shift, to decrease. She motioned to Reichner, who saw it and immediately spoke, "No, Brandon, don't listen to my voice, just feel it, make my voice a part of you. Let it guide you, help you keep your mind free, help you keep it nice and empty . . ."

Sarah watched. This part always made her nervous. She knew that a "free and empty mind" was essential in experiencing the paranormal. After all, the more empty your mind was of yourself, the more open it would be to other input from outside forces. Which was okay, she guessed, except—well, what assurance did they have that these outside forces were always good?

"Now, keeping your mind free and clear, I want you to tell me what you see, Brandon. Tell me what you feel."

Brandon's voice came back as a quiet whisper. "Peace."

"Good."

Sarah stared at the EEG. Now, the delta waves were starting to increase. This was remarkable.

"What type of peace, Brandon?"

"Waves . . . washing over me . . ."

"Any colors, sounds?"

"Wind—so quiet . . ."

Sarah leaned past the console to look at Brandon through the one-way mirror as Reichner quietly cooed, "Good . . . very good."

Brandon barely heard Reichner's voice. The waves of peace had completely enveloped him. He was deep inside them, floating, totally weightless. He was remotely aware that the wires and sensors were still attached to his head, arms, and chest, but he no longer felt them. He knew that he was still in the recliner back at the lab, but he was someplace else as well. Someplace beautiful and deep and crimson. The only sensation he felt was a soft breeze brushing against his face and a sound as gentle as wind stirring through pine trees.

At first he had been uneasy. Try as he might, he still couldn't shake the old woman's warning: *There is only one path. All others lead to the occult, to destruction.* Not easy words to forget, even if you didn't necessarily believe them. But in one sense he did. In one sense, he wondered: How different were all of these expensive machines and intellectual scientists from the crystal balls and sorcerers of old? Besides spending a few extra million dollars and investing a few dozen more years of schooling, weren't they in essence attempting to accomplish the same thing: contacting the spiritual world on their own terms?

The thought troubled him. But Sarah had promised that he would be safe. And there was the possibility of meeting Jenny again, of finding out what she was trying to tell him, of once again holding his little sister in his arms.

As Brandon floated, trying to push the fears aside and keep his mind free, he lost track of time. He didn't know whether he'd been there ten minutes or an hour. Then, finally, through the deep crimson, there was a glint of light. It came and went before he realized that he'd seen it.

There it was again. Piercing bright. A great distance away.

The wind picked up, blowing a little harder. With it, the sound also increased. But it wasn't really a sound. It was more like rapid, irregular puffs of air, like gentle whisperings. He had entered some sort of current. He could feel it pulling him—gently, yet persistently. And the more he gave himself over to it, the stronger it grew.

There was another glint of light, brilliant, and a little closer. Then another. And another, closer still. Yes, he was definitely moving. The current was drawing him toward the flashes. Directly in front of the light was a shadow, a silhouette. It looked human. He squinted, trying to protect his eyes from the blinding flashes, yet trying to see the form. He gave more of himself to the current and quickly picked up speed until, finally, he was close enough to make out that form.

It was a child. A girl in a white gown, her golden hair blowing in the wind. Although he was still some distance away, he immediately recognized her.

"Jenny . . ."

He watched as she reached into the folds of her gown and pulled out the lantern, the same one she had held out on the road. The same type that had been suspended by the lampstand in the foyer. This was the source of the light. It wasn't coming from behind her, but from inside her gown. Yet it was so bright that Brandon had to raise his hands to shield his eyes.

The current grew stronger and he moved faster. The sensation of speed began to frighten him. He wasn't sure why. After all, there was his sister, just ahead. He wanted desperately to reach her, to throw his arms around her, to hug her. But there was something holding him back. Maybe it was his fear of speed—or of giving up control.

Whatever the reason, he began to resist the current, turning his head, willing himself to slow. It proved to be harder than he had expected, but with great concentration he was able to retard his progress until he finally slowed to a tenuous stop. He turned toward her. She was a dozen feet away. He wanted so badly to touch her, to hold her—but he was afraid to give up control.

The current tugged and pulled, but he stood his ground. Part of him wanted to give in and be swept to her waiting arms. But he was simply too afraid.

As if understanding his fear, she raised her hand, the one holding the lantern. She held it out to him, offering to let him see it, to examine it.

Brandon looked on painfully. He wanted to trust her, he wanted to let go. But he couldn't.

The light grew brighter, the current stronger. But Brandon's panic only increased. He concentrated even harder to hold his ground. That's when he saw the hurt on her face. The pain of rejection. His eyes started to burn with tears. He wanted to call out, to explain that it wasn't her, that it was him, *his* fear, *his* cowardice. But no words would come.

Slowly, she withdrew the lantern.

Brandon's heart broke. He hoped she understood but feared she didn't. He watched as she lifted the lantern high above her head. Then, with great purpose, she released it. The lantern dropped, but it didn't shatter. Instead, when it hit the ground, it seemed to melt, to become a pool, a molten pool of light that began to churn and bubble upon itself.

Brandon and his sister stared as the light began to grow, horizontally as well as vertically. And the larger it grew, the more power it radiated. Now he understood. The light was the source of the current. As it increased in size and strength, so did the current. It pulled him even harder. He dug in, struggling to stand firm, to keep his balance.

The pool of light boiled, expanded—and the current continued to grow. Brandon fought harder. He looked back at Jenny, pleading for her to help, to make it stop.

She watched in quiet sympathy but did nothing.

The molten light was much bigger now, taking shape, forming a huge, growing rectangle that looked like some sort of doorway. A doorway that now towered high above him.

He turned away, trying to break free, to fight his way out of the current. His feet slipped once, twice. He was losing ground. He was being dragged toward the opening. He twisted and stretched, fighting with all of his will to break free of the current, until finally, with the greatest concentration—

Brandon's eyes exploded open. They darted about the room. He was back in the lab, back in the leather recliner. He was covered in sweat, trying to catch his breath, but he was back.

"If there was so much 'peace,' why did you resist?" Reichner demanded as he paced back and forth in the lunchroom. "Why did you pull away?"

Brandon sat at the table, staring down at his coffee, looking weary and shaken. Sarah stood nearby, feeling no better than Brandon looked.

"You said it was fear," Reichner said, crossing back to him. He leaned over the table. "Fear of what? Fear of the power? Of the intensity? Fear of what?"

Brandon remained silent. Finally he shrugged. "I was losing control. I don't like . . . losing control."

Reichner slammed his hand on the table and turned. Sarah was able to catch his eye and frown.

"He was there!" Reichner argued. "We were at Threshold. He even had his spirit guide."

Sarah nodded and looked down. Of course, the man was right. It was a shame to have gotten so close and not pressed on. But they'd already pushed Brandon so far.

In exasperation, Reichner turned, then stormed out of the room.

Sarah looked up in surprise. This was a first. Reichner never lost control. He always won his arguments and he never, *never* gave up until he got his way. But, at least for now, it appeared that he had failed on both accounts. She glanced at Brandon, impressed. This young man affected people in surprising ways.

Silence hung over the room. She wanted to say something, to let him know it wasn't his fault, that his fear was a natural response. She also wanted to let him know that if anybody was to blame, it was her. She shouldn't have pushed, she shouldn't have manipulated him to stay. She wanted to say all of this and more, but wasn't sure where to begin.

Fortunately, he saved her the trouble. Picking at the Styrofoam cup in his hands, he asked, "Has this sort of thing happened before?"

She nodded. "In other studies, yes. But never with us."

More silence.

She still wanted to apologize, to somehow make things better. "Listen, uh . . ." She cleared her throat. "It's getting late. Do you want to catch a bite to eat or something?"

He shrugged. "It wasn't that big of a deal." Then, pushing the cup aside, he started to rise.

"No," she said, "it was. A big deal, I mean." He looked at her and she held his gaze. "I'm sorry, Brandon. We had no business putting you through that, and I'm— well, I'm just very sorry."

She glanced down. She could feel him still looking at her. She hoped he could sense her sincerity. She swallowed and finally looked back up. "What do you think? How does—uh, do you like pizza?"

He kept looking at her.

She smiled nervously. "I might even spring for an extra topping."

Then, slowly, a trace of a smile began to spread across his face.

S
o with scholarship in hand, I left for Stanford vow-
ing never to set foot in Portland again, at least until
I was rich and famous."

"And you chose science," Brandon said, his eyes never
leaving hers.

She laughed self-consciously. "I wasn't sure whether I
wanted to find the cure for cancer or the purpose to man's
existence. But since I hate little white mice ..." She threw
him a grin. He nodded but didn't smile back. She took
another sip of Chianti. It was her third glass of the evening.
It had taken that many just to loosen up around him.

"I guess some people—well, some people would say
I might be overly ambitious," she heard herself confessing. "I don't know. Just because I plan on winning a
couple Nobel prizes before I'm thirty ..." She gave
another self-conscious chuckle. It wasn't the entire picture.
She could have talked about the baby, about her need to
keep pushing, to keep driving until his death counted for
something—but that was a part of her no one was allowed
to see. Ever.

She took another sip of wine and avoided Brandon's
eyes by glancing around Eddie's Pizzeria. It was dim and
smoke-filled—mostly Townies putting down the brews

after a hard day at the drill press or wherever they worked. She and Brandon had just finished off a medium Canadian bacon with pineapple (his choice) and, thanks to the Chianti, she was doing most of the talking. Still, she found herself being drawn to him.

She watched as he caught the waitress's attention and motioned for another Pepsi. Even that intrigued her. She'd figured him to be more of a drink-beer-until-you-drop kind of guy. And yet, here he was, ordering a soft drink. Such a paradox, so full of contradictions—like a man caught between two worlds, not completely fitting into either.

He looked back at her. She smiled. Maybe a bit more flirtatiously than she had intended. Still, it was her third glass.

"What about you?" she asked. "Didn't you ever want to be famous, make a name for yourself?"

Brandon shrugged. "I do all right."

"Terrorizing Techies?" She smiled at her barb.

He frowned, then understood and returned the smile. "It's a thankless job, but—"

"—somebody has to do it." They finished the phrase together and chuckled. It was the second time she had gotten him to smile, and she liked it—the way his face lit up, illuminating their corner of the room. They were starting to connect. At least she hoped so. But he still hadn't answered her question. Instead, he had looked away. This time he was the self-conscious one. And she liked that even better.

"Well?" she asked, waiting for a response.

He shrugged. But she didn't intend to give up until she got an answer.

Finally he cleared this throat. "As a kid, way back when I was little, I always wanted to be . . ." Again he looked away. "I always wanted to be kinda like a pastor."

Sarah nearly choked on her drink. Fortunately, the words were coming so hard for him that he barely noticed. "It just seemed like, you know, the right thing to do. I mean, my dad was a pastor, and his dad before him. It just seemed . . . it seemed good."

He looked back at her.

"What happened?" she asked, a little softer.

He took a breath and slowly let it out. Sarah listened intently.

"I'm not sure," he finally said, "but somewhere along the line I started to learn the truth. About Santa Claus, the Easter bunny—and God." He swallowed hard, looking everywhere but at her. "I tried. God knows how I tried. But there was . . . nothing. Nothing I could believe in anymore, nothing I could hang onto, nothing I could see . . ." His voice trailed off.

Sarah watched silently. There was deep water here, far deeper than she had guessed. She wanted to reach out and touch his arm, to tell him it was okay, that she understood. But she didn't trust herself, she didn't trust the wine. Instead she quietly offered, "Maybe—maybe that's what faith is all about. Believing in something, even when you don't see it." He looked at her, and she shrugged. "Not that our generation is terribly fond of believing in anything."

He nodded, musing.

They'd found another point of contact, and she pursued it. "What is it about us? Why are we always so afraid? I mean, half of my friends are still in graduate school because they're afraid to get out into the real world."

Brandon spoke slowly. "Maybe we've just been lied to by too many people."

Sarah nodded. He was right, of course. They were the ones raised by parents with broken vows, politicians with broken promises, and ads with impossible claims.

Another pause settled over their conversation.

Sarah resumed. "You know, you talk about faith. In a lot of ways, science and faith aren't that far apart. I mean, we're both asking the same questions: Why are we here? How did we get here? And most important, who or what is responsible?"

She glanced at him, but he was looking away again.

"I guess, in some ways, that makes me no different from your dad, or the local rabbi, or some Tibetan monk—we're all out there searching for some sort of God, some sort of Absolute."

He looked back at her, that penetrating look, the one that made her weak inside. She forced herself to continue. "Science doesn't have to be religion's enemy. In some ways it can actually be an ally in proving faith. I mean, look at the study they did at San Francisco General Hospital."

He stared.

"You've heard of it, right?"

Apparently he hadn't.

Her words came faster. After all, this was her work, this was where she felt safest and most secure. "The director of the coronary care unit agreed to put nearly four hundred patients on two lists—those who were to be prayed for and those who were not. A quarter of a mile away, a group of evangelical Christians prayed for the patients on the first list without either the patients or their doctors being aware of it. The study lasted ten months. During that time, the patients who were prayed for showed a significant decrease in congestive heart failure, fewer incidents of pneumonia, less need for antibiotics, and fewer cardiac arrests."

"This was an official study?" he asked.

She nodded. "Published back in '88."

He looked away, thinking.

But she wasn't finished. "Then there's the 1995 study at Dartmouth Medical School, where they discovered that the most religious of those who underwent heart surgery were three times more likely to recover than those who were not religious."

He looked skeptical.

"No, I'm serious," she insisted, "these were all legitimate studies. And there are plenty more, each and every one verifying the power of faith and prayer."

She took a sip of wine. She knew she'd become too chatty, but she didn't particularly care to stop.

"I'm not saying you have to believe in God. I mean, look at me. For me it's science. I've given everything I've got to science, poured my whole life into it. And I'm going to make a difference. You know why? Because I'm committed, because I believe. That's the whole point. You've got to believe in something, Brandon, otherwise your life will never have any—" She searched for the word. "I mean, everything will just keep on being so . . ."

"Pointless?" he asked.

"Exactly. Pointless. Otherwise your life will continue to be pointless, a waste with no meaning or purpose to—" She suddenly stopped. Even in her flushed state, she saw the pain cross Brandon's face. What had she said?

"Listen," she stammered, "I didn't mean to imply that your life doesn't have—you know, that it's a waste or anything like that."

But Brandon was already looking off and away. She'd hit a nerve and hit it hard. She reached out and touched his arm. "I didn't mean—"

"No, that's okay," he said, shrugging, pretending it didn't matter. "You probably have a point. I mean, I know you have a point."

She watched as he struggled to find the words. Why had she done that? They had been connecting so well, they had really been—

"Brandon! Hey, Brandon!"

She looked up to see two young men, the ones she had met with Brandon last week at the Club—a shorter kid with thick glasses and a taller, almost good-looking one. It was the taller one who had called out to them. "Well, well, well, what do we have here?" he asked as he sauntered over to the booth.

Brandon nodded. "'s up, Frank?"

"Not much. At least for me." Turning to Sarah, he smiled. "You're lookin' real good tonight, Sarah."

She nodded, trying unsuccessfully to cover her distaste.

"Hey, Bran." The shorter one in the glasses nodded. "Del."

"Haven't seen you at work," Frank said as he reached for the remainder of Brandon's drink. "Everything okay?"

Brandon nodded. "Couldn't be better."

"Yeah?" Frank raised the glass and chugged down the rest of the soda. Brandon threw an embarrassed glance at Sarah.

"Great," Frank said, finally coming up for air. "'Cause, if you recall, we've got ourselves a little vendetta to settle with the Techies." Turning to Sarah, he added, "No offense, of course."

She didn't respond. He turned back to Brandon. "It's been almost a week now, and people are startin' to talk. I figured since—"

"Not tonight, Frank."

"No, I don't mean tonight. But it oughta be soon. I mean, we got our reputation to keep up, right, ol' buddy?"

Brandon said nothing.

"So you just think up somethin' real good." Then turning to Sarah, he explained, "Brandon here, he's a genius at comin' up with ideas." He held out his index finger to Del, who took it and pulled while Frank released a giant belch.

Brandon lowered his eyes and stared at the table.

"You just let me know when," Frank said, preparing to leave, "and I'll grab us some brew and away we go." Turning to Sarah, he added, "You're welcome to come too, if you want."

"I think I'll pass." Her words carried an intentional chill.

"Suit yourself, but it's gonna be good times."

Neither Brandon nor Sarah responded.

"Well, all right then. You kids take care." Frank turned, gave Del a nudge, and the two of them headed for the door. "Have a good night," he called, "and don't do anything I wouldn't do." He let out a cackle of laughter and disappeared into the crowd.

An embarrassed silence fell over the table. When Sarah finally looked at Brandon, he was scowling hard at his glass.

Lewis stood on the back porch of the farmhouse, pressing himself against the wall. The kitchen window was directly beside him. It was open, and he could hear the woman washing dishes less than six feet away. She was humming to the radio—country gospel. His heart pounded. Hunger and desire throbbed all the way into his hands.

SLAUGHTER . . . KILL . . .

This was the place. The voices had told him. The impostor lived here. And, as soon as he was destroyed, Lewis could enter into his season.

SLAY . . . MUTILATE . . .

He'd parked his bug down at the end of the lane. This sort of thing wasn't new to him; he'd done it lots of times—sneaking up to people's homes and spying. Even climbing up on their roofs and watching when they thought no one could see. Like Mrs. Cavanaugh, the vice principal's wife. Or some of the girls from high school. He smiled to himself. If they had only known.

The lady began to sing. His smile twisted into a contemptuous sneer. So stupid and unsuspecting. Singing as her executioner lurked so near.

He turned and eased closer to the window until he could see through the screen and inside. He caught glimpses of her head as she moved back and forth. If she looked up at the right time, she would see him. What a delightful scare that would be.

He reached down to his belt and silently unsnapped the sheath to his hunting knife. He could break through the screen in a second. He inched closer, until she was in full view. If she would only look up. His fingers danced along the knife handle. If she would only look up, then scream in terror, and he would lunge through the screen and grab her, pulling her out, kicking and screaming and—

"NO!" the voices screamed. "*THE IMPOSTOR, THE IMPOSTOR . . . DECIMATE, MUTILATE, KILL! THE IMPOSTOR . . . THE IMPOSTOR!*"

But where? Where was this impostor? If he couldn't find the impostor, then taking out this lady would be next best. And it would help silence the voices, and it would—

"*THE IMPOSTOR . . . THE IMPOSTOR . . . THE IMPOSTOR . . . THE IMPOSTOR . . .*"

Reluctantly, Lewis removed his hand from his knife.

The back door was open, just ten feet away. He ducked below the window and silently crossed toward it. He was practically there when he noticed the shadow—a man's shadow. It was the impostor, he was certain of it. He was sitting just on the other side of the screen door.

ANNIHILATE . . . SHRED . . . TEAR . . .

Lewis's heart pounded harder. Barely able to contain his excitement, he inched along the wall.

SLICE . . . RIP . . . RAVAGE . . .

He was breathing heavily now—the exhilaration growing out of control as he reached the edge of the doorway.

SLAY . . . KILL . . . DESTROY . . .

He remembered, from their encounter at the church, that the impostor was strong. He would have to surprise him. But he could take him. With the help of the voices and the knife and the adrenaline, he could—

The woman spoke, but he couldn't hear her words. His voices were screaming, one on top of the other, writhing, shrieking, swearing. They were pulling him under, demanding complete control of his body. They could have it. In just a moment, they could have it all. Just let him taste the kill first, to experience the thrill, and then he would turn it over to them.

He reached for his knife and pulled it out.

He crouched beside the door, preparing himself, his heart pounding wildly. He took two gulps of air—and then he sprang.

He threw open the screen door and leaped inside. But he was wrong! It wasn't the impostor! It was some old-timer in a wheelchair. Lewis dug his feet in, aborting the attack. The screen door slammed behind him. The woman screamed. A dog upstairs started barking. He could take them out, he could take them all out. But between the shrieking voices, the screaming woman, the dog, the man, Lewis froze. Then the panic struck. He turned. He staggered back into the door, shoving it open, stumbling off the porch, and running into the night.

He ran until he reached his car. Then he was inside, firing it up and racing for home. The voices screamed louder than ever. Degrading, belittling, demanding, all-consuming. He had to stop them. He would stop them.

Someone had to die. It was the only way. And it had to be soon. Very, very soon.

Sarah glanced at her watch. It was nearly eleven when Brandon pulled up to her condo. Forty minutes had passed since she'd made the crack about his wasted life. Although he'd done his best to hide it, she could tell that she'd hurt him. And the visit by his two buddies hadn't helped any. He was distant now, aloof. Once again, he'd retreated into himself.

The car came to a stop and she turned to him. "Are you all right?"

He nodded.

She wanted to say something more, but she'd obviously done enough talking for one night. Then, to her surprise, he spoke.

"I was thinking. Maybe we should go ahead and continue that test. You know, see what's on the other side of that Threshold thing."

Sarah shook her head. "No, Brandon. We shouldn't have pushed you. That was my fault, I shouldn't have—"

"No, no. It's not you."

She looked at him.

"It's me. Maybe—maybe there is something I can do."

She watched him carefully, not sure what he meant.

"Maybe I can—you know, give you guys a hand with whatever you're trying to find out. I mean, if you really think it could be helpful to you . . . and to others." He forced a smile. "At least it would be a change from terrorizing Techies."

"Listen, Brandon, what I said back there, I didn't mean—"

"What about tomorrow?" he interrupted. "Is that—would that be too soon?"

"Tomorrow?"

He nodded. She searched his face. "Are you sure?" she asked. "I mean, is this something *you* want to do?"

"Tomorrow's okay, then?"

"We can make whatever arrangements you want, but I don't think—"

"Then I'll see you tomorrow."

She hesitated. "Brandon . . ."

For the first time since they'd stopped, he looked at her. There was that connection again. Deep, resonating. He smiled, a little sadder this time. Her heart swelled. When she wasn't intimidated or offended by him, she was moved by how vulnerable and sensitive he could be. The feelings were strong, stronger than anything she'd felt since Samuel. And since it was getting late, and since they were connecting so well . . .

"Listen," she said, "would you like to, you know, come in for a while?"

He looked at her, and immediately she knew she'd stepped over the line. He was a preacher's kid, for crying out loud. The same one who didn't drink, who went to church, who as far as she could tell didn't even swear. He may have lost his faith, but there was still something there, something innocent, almost naive. She glanced away, feeling a little embarrassed.

But his answer came without judgment. "Thanks, but I better get going."

She nodded. What had she been thinking of? Besides, he was just a kid and a lab subject, to boot. She knew better than to get personally involved with her work. "Of course," she said. "I understand." She reached for her door and opened it. "We'll see you tomorrow, then."

He said nothing as she climbed out. And then, just before she shut the door: "Sarah?"

She turned to him. He struggled for a moment, obviously trying to put his thoughts into words. But apparently they wouldn't come. Instead, he settled for a simple "Thanks."

She nodded, not entirely understanding. "Sure." And then she shut the door.

He dropped the truck into gear and pulled away as she pretended to head for the condo. But she'd gone only a few feet before she turned and watched the pickup head down the road. She stood there silently, not moving, until it disappeared into the night.

Brandon eased the truck into its usual spot between the house and the barn. It was eleven twenty-five when he turned off the ignition and stepped into the hot, night air. The heat wave hadn't let up. Thirty-six days without rain, and by the looks of things it would soon be thirty-seven. He quietly closed the cab door and paused to stare up at the night sky. Sarah had awakened something in him. He could feel it. Actually it was many things. But mostly it was a type of . . . hope. Was it possible? Could his life really have some sort of purpose? Could it really have meaning again?

He walked across the driveway toward the house. The grass and gravel were bathed in the blue-white light of the mercury vapor lamp mounted on the barn. He was emotionally exhausted, but his thoughts spun and tumbled and churned. Not only about Sarah and the hope she offered, but also about tomorrow's experiment—and about Jenny. After all, Jenny had been there, too, coaxing him, urging him forward, encouraging him to cross Threshold.

Then he was back to Sarah. How he envied her clarity, her sense of purpose. Not like Frank or Del. *Terrorizing Techies.* He shook his head. Truth be told, that really had been about his only reason for existence. Until now. Maybe he really could contribute something.

A moment later and he was back to Jenny. She had looked so loving and understanding. Of course, she'd always been sweet, everyone's favorite, but could it be that she'd actually forgiven him?

Other memories tumbled in, fragments he'd never be able to forget. His speeding car, her begging him to slow down, his laughter. The oncoming headlights. Her scream. The car sliding out of control. More screaming. Then the flipping and everything flying and her screaming and the car hitting the tree and the sickening explosion of glass and crunching metal—and the sudden end of her scream. Forever.

Brandon slowed as he moved up the porch steps. He'd had no idea how tired he really was. He was surprised to see the door closed. In this heat, they kept the windows and doors open all night. He opened the screen. A large manila envelope rested against the back door, his name scrawled across it in a large, unsteady script. He bent and picked it up. Studying the writing, he pushed on the door to find that it was locked. That was odd. They never locked the doors. He glanced at the car-port. The van was there; they were home. He reached into his pocket and pulled out his keys.

A moment later he was upstairs. After silently checking to make sure his folks were okay in bed, he entered his
room, peeled off his T-shirt and waded through the obsta-
cle course of dirty clothes, car magazines, and, of course,
Drool. For whatever reason, the old animal loved to sprawl
out directly in his line of traffic. Brandon collapsed onto
the bed, snapped on a light, and opened the envelope.

Inside there was a large pack of papers. He pulled
them out. On top was a letter written in the same hand-
writing as the envelope. It read:

> *Dear Eli:*
>
> *I drew these the week of your birth.*
> *I hope you find them helpful.*
>
> *Your servant,*
> *Gerty Morrison*

He recognized the name and fought back a wave of
uneasiness. The memory of the fight outside the church
two nights ago was still fresh in his mind. He hesitated,
too exhausted to continue, too curious to stop. He pulled
aside the letter to look at the first sketch.

The paper was yellowed and the pencil work
smudged. Portions were faded and worn away from age.
But there was no mistaking the subject. It was Brandon.
Exactly as he was today, complete with long hair, T-shirt,
and worn blue jeans. He glanced at the initials in the
lower right-hand corner. *GM*. Gerty Morrison. And
beside them was a date—it looked like 1976.

He hesitated. Was it possible? Had she really seen this
image of him, just as he was today, way back in '76? He

frowned and slowly pulled the paper away to look at the next. It was equally yellowed and aged. It was a sketch of a younger Brandon, on his sixteenth birthday. He was grinning and standing beside a used Toyota Celica, his first car, a gift from his father. It was also the car he had killed Jenny with. His eyes shot down to the corner to see the same initials and the same date: 1976.

He swallowed and pulled the sketch aside to reveal the next. In it he was thirteen years old and holding his newborn sister.

He closed his eyes. A dull ache spread through the back of his skull. He pulled the sketch away to look at the next. He was seven and holding another birthday gift: little puppy Drool.

Then the next. Age four.

Then age two.

Age one.

Until, finally, he was staring at a sketch of himself as a newborn. He was at the church, being held by his parents. They looked so young, so proud. And hovering over them, dominating the picture, was the cross. The very one that had tormented him for so many years. Brandon took a long breath and slowly let it out. His head pounded mercilessly.

He looked back down to his lap. There was one sketch left. It was different from the others, larger and folded in half. He reached for the edge of the paper and slowly pulled it back.

Near the left side of the drawing was the lantern, identical to the one Jenny had been holding, identical to the one he'd seen outside the sanctuary doors. He continued pulling, slowly revealing the picture bit by bit, until he saw an olive tree, also like the one at the doors. He faltered. For a moment he could go no further. Whatever was there, he didn't want to see. Whatever she had drawn, he didn't want to know.

Yet his hand continued to pull until the entire picture came into view.

It was of an older Brandon. Older than he was today. He stood in an ancient walled city. His head had been shaved, and he was wearing some sort of burlap robe.

Brandon looked at himself, nearly forgetting to breathe. The eyes were wild and intense, staring directly at the viewer. And the mouth—his mouth—it was opened in a primeval scream, so realistic that he could practically hear the sound. And out of it—out of his mouth roared flames of fire, *exactly* as they had in his vision outside the church.

Brandon sat paralyzed, unable to take his eyes from the sketch. The shaved head, the crazed eyes, the mouth, the flames—it was more than he could absorb. His head was ready to explode. He closed his eyes, forcing the moment to pass. But when he reopened them, everything was the same.

He needed help. He needed to talk to someone. With resolution, he threw his legs over the side of the bed. The sketches tumbled to the floor. He bent, scooped them up, and headed for the door.

A minute later, he was back in the pickup driving toward Sarah's. He wasn't sure what he was going to do when he got there, but he needed her, he needed her clarity of vision, he needed her understanding. He needed her presence.

He arrived in town and headed for Sarah's street. He approached the corner to her condo and rounded it. That was when he saw the jogger. A woman right in his path, too close to miss. He slammed on the brakes, swerving hard, but he was going too fast. Just before impact, she spun around and he saw her face.

It was Sarah.

She raised her arm and screamed as his left front bumper caught her leg and threw her up onto the hood. She rolled and slid across the metal, her expression frozen in horror as she hit the windshield—

Brandon bolted up in bed. His face was wet and he was breathing hard. The sketches lay scattered all around him. He wanted to curl into a ball, to make it all go away. But he knew it wouldn't. And he knew, more than ever, that he needed Sarah's help. He threw his feet over the side of the bed and slipped on his shirt.

Downstairs in the kitchen he flipped through the phone book until he found her name. Still shaken, he reached for the wall phone and dialed her number. Was the dream a premonition? Like the factory accident? Was something going to happen to her as well? He had to talk to her, she had to be warned.

The phone rang seven times before he hung up. Where was she? He hesitated, afraid to take the next step. But this was Sarah. If anything were to happen to her . . .

He stormed out of the kitchen and jumped into the pickup. It started noisily. He slipped it into gear and headed down the lane. He didn't understand the dream, didn't know whether it was like the one at the factory or like the others that made no sense. But he had to make sure she was all right.

He sped down the road, mind whirling, driving on autopilot. The roads were deserted and he made good time. When he arrived at the final corner, the one he'd dreamed of, he slowed down, just to be safe. Tense and nervous, he carefully negotiated the turn—and suddenly, out of the blue, a woman appeared. He slammed on his brakes, trying to avoid her, but they were too close. The bumper caught her leg, hurdling her onto the hood. She slid across it, and just before her head smashed into the windshield, she turned, and he saw Sarah's face—

Again Brandon woke up. Sweating, fighting to catch his breath. His eyes darted about the room, fearfully trying to get his bearings.

Unnerved and shaky, Brandon eased himself from the bed. Several of the sketches tumbled to the floor. He made it out to the hallway and used the handrail for support as he moved down the stairs and into the kitchen. He grabbed the phone book off the counter, found her number, and dialed. It rang twice before she answered.

"Hello?" a groggy voice mumbled.

Brandon hesitated. He wanted to say something.

"Hello?"

Then ever so slowly, he reached down and pressed the disconnect button.

He replaced the phone and eased himself into the nearest chair. He would sit there until dawn.

CHAPTER 11

B randon passed through the kitchen on his way to the truck. The room still smelled of the bacon, pancakes, and warmed maple syrup Momma had served earlier for breakfast. While he was eating, she had spoken of last night's intruder. Brandon had listened with concern, even insisted that she call the sheriff. Initially she had declined, saying that the young man wasn't as threatening as he was confused.

"In fact," she'd said, "when he ran off, he looked more frightened than *I* was!"

But Brandon had insisted, and reluctantly she had agreed.

That had been fifteen minutes ago; the sheriff was on his way. Now, Momma was upstairs making beds and Brandon was heading for the Institute. He didn't tell her where he was going; he knew she'd only be worried and scared. And the way he figured it, he was scared enough for both of them.

His father sat in the wheelchair, staring out the door, the early morning sun striking his face. Brandon started to squeeze past him, then hesitated. He paused a moment to look down. Finally, with great effort, he spoke.

"Pop . . ."

Of course there was no response. Brandon knelt. He glanced at the silver-and-turquoise watch he had given his father so many years earlier, the one Momma still insisted he wear, as if to prove he still loved his son. Once again Brandon hesitated. He knew the words would be difficult, but he also knew they needed to be said.

"It's been a long time, hasn't it?"

The man stared off into space.

Brandon swallowed. "You and me, we haven't done a lot of talking lately."

More silence.

"But you're always in my mind, somewhere—you're always there in the back of my mind. You, Momma, Jenny . . ." Brandon glanced away and swallowed again. This was harder than he'd thought. "I know—I know what a disappointment I am to you, Pop. And I don't blame you."

Before he knew it, emotion began to well up from somewhere deep inside. "Pop . . . Oh, Pop . . ." He tried to swallow it back, but it kept coming. "I'd give anything to bring her back. Anything."

His eyes burned. He blinked hard, but they continued to fill with moisture. Something had opened up inside of him, and he couldn't seem to close it. "I used to plead with God—when she was in the coma, I used to beg him, 'Take me! I'm the screwup, I'm the failure. Take me, not her.'"

Angrily, he swiped at the tears, but they continued to come. "I'm sorry," he whispered. "I'm so sorry."

And then, all alone in the kitchen with his father, Brandon did something he hadn't done since he was a little boy. He lowered his head and laid his face down upon his father's lap. "I'm sorry," he choked, his throat aching beyond belief, "I'm so sorry."

He lay there, for how long he didn't know. His father's hands were just inches from his face. He would give anything to feel them touch him, stroke his head, offer some sort of comfort.

But, of course, there was none. Not for him.

At last Brandon raised his head. Through blurry eyes he looked up at his father. "I'm not going to let you down," he whispered hoarsely, "not anymore. I'm going to make you proud of me, Pop. You, Jenny, Momma— I'm going to make you all proud."

His father did not reply.

Slowly, he rose to his feet, wiping his face with his sleeve. He started out the screen door. Then, hesitating, he turned back. "You don't have to love me, Pop." He swallowed. "But you won't have to be ashamed of me, either. Not anymore."

Once again there was no answer, and once again Brandon understood the condemning silence. Quietly, he shut the door behind him and headed for the pickup.

"Are you the woman who called?"

Gerty nodded and adjusted the large parcel she carried under her arm. The young man before her wore a dirty army shirt, worn jeans, and he sported a week-old stubble across his face. He opened the door wider; it creaked as Gerty stepped into the apartment.

The place was an electronics graveyard, Radio Shack thrown into a blender. Stacks of chassis lay here, gutted TVs there, pieces of stereos, cannibalized computers, circuit boards, transformers, half-empty spools of wire, monitors—all dumped and stacked throughout the dimly lit room. Gerty didn't recognize any of them, but she knew filth and squalor when she saw it. Empty pizza boxes, fast-food bags, half-crushed aluminum cans . . . along with the distinct aroma of spoiled food, body odor, and a cat box that definitely needed to be emptied. At least she hoped it was a cat box.

The man kicked a pile of junk mail out of his path and crossed toward the dining-room table, which was covered in more circuit boards and monitors. He didn't say a word. Nor did Gerty as she followed. She wasn't intimidated by him, nor by his environment. Knowing that she was soon going home to her Lord did a lot to keep things in perspective. She was here for a purpose. And, regardless of its appearance, this was where she had been sent to accomplish that purpose.

The young man sat down before three large computer monitors. Two of them were glowing. There was no chair for Gerty, and he didn't offer one. To his immediate right sat a pile of magazines with naked women on the cover. Gerty glanced away, embarrassed. But she felt neither revulsion nor disgust for the young man. Only pity. And compassion.

He sniffed loudly and wiped his nose with his hand. "Did you bring the data?"

"Data?" she asked.

"The information you wanted me to enter."

"Oh, yes." She pulled the two-inch stack of papers from her arms—the letters she'd been writing, some new, some decades old.

He took them in his thin white hands and plopped them next to the magazines. Again her eyes caught a cover photo, and again she felt embarrassed. For the briefest moment she wondered if she had heard wrong. How could her Lord possibly want her to work with someone like this? He had promised her that her letters would be used for holy purposes. But here? In this place? With this man? She looked at him and was once again filled with compassion. Not her compassion. This was deeper. It was the Lord's. He was not looking at the boy's crippledness. He was looking past the sickness to a heart, a heart that he longed to heal.

Gerty smiled quietly. In all the years she had known him, her Lord had never changed. He was still drawn to the dregs of society, to the outcast, to those who knew they were sick. Yes, sometimes it was difficult for her not to judge, but if he had chosen *her*, with all of her weakness, then he could and would use anybody. Even this boy.

She nodded in silent awe. Yes, her Lord was good.

The young man carelessly flipped through her stack of papers. Each page had a date on top, followed by a few Bible verses, and then some insight or practical observation on how to apply those verses.

"These dates here at the top." The man sniffed and wiped his nose again. "That's when you want him to get them?"

"Yes. He'll soon be havin' a computer and those are the dates I want him to be readin' these letters."

"Kind of a timed-release thing?"

"I'm sorry, I don't understand your—"

"You don't want him to have access to all of this stuff at once. Just on the date you've written here at the top."

Gerty nodded. "Yes. They're lessons from the Bible, each one needs to be buildin' upon the next."

The young man gave her a skeptical look. "The Bible?"

She nodded.

He smirked, then riffled through the pages. "Sure got a lot here."

She sensed his hesitation. "The price you quoted me over the phone, it was—"

"The price I quoted you was to scan this stuff into the computer, then design a program that would release it to your boy through e-mail at the right time. You didn't tell me it was all handwritten."

"Will that cause a problem?"

"Take more time, that's all. I have to manually type in all of this junk with the keyboard."

Now Gerty understood. "How much more do you want?"

She watched as he ran his hand through his greasy hair. "I don't know. We're talking quite a few man-hours here."

"How much?" Gerty persisted.

He looked at her, gauging. "I'd say—probably an extra hundred and fifty, maybe two hundred bucks."

Gerty held his eyes as she reached down and opened her purse. She pulled out a wad of bills. It was the last of her money, but that was okay. She wouldn't need it where she was going. "There's one hundred and eighty-five dollars here. It's all I have."

He reached for the money. "One hundred eighty-five will be just fine."

But she held it firmly in her grip until his eyes again met hers. "You'll be typin' it in yourself?" she asked.

"Yes, ma'am."

"No one else? Just you?"

"Every word."

She nodded and finally released the cash. He took the wad and stuffed it into his shirt pocket. "I'll start on it right away," he said as he turned back to the computer.

Gerty stood in silence, once again feeling a faint smile cross her face. This was why her Lord had chosen him. And this was why, over the years, regardless of how absurd his requests seemed, Gerty had always obeyed. Because, when she obeyed, he always amazed her. Now she understood. As this lost young man typed in the holy Scriptures she had written, he would be exposed to their life-changing truths. Truths that would give him the opportunity to be healed.

Gerty's smile broadened. Yes, her God was good. He was very, very good.

Brandon lay stretched out on the leather recliner. He was wearing the Ganzfield goggles, and his face was bathed in the glow of the red floodlights. Dozens of fine wires ran to the sensors taped to his temples, eyelids, face, arms, fingertips, chest, back, stomach, legs, and feet.

He was in Lab One. The instruments in Lab Two were being recalibrated; they wouldn't be up and running until the end of the day. Reichner had refused to wait, so they were once again using the first lab, the one Sarah had been attacked in. The pieces of shattered one-way mirror had long ago been cleaned up, but its replacement hadn't yet arrived, so clear window glass had been temporarily installed.

Up in the Observation Room, Sarah kept a careful eye on the monitors and readouts. The heart rate, respiration,

GSR, EMG, EEG, all were registering as before. Directly behind her, two DAT machines ran, one to record the multiple readings coming in, the other to serve as backup. This was too important to risk losing the records to a malfunction.

Reichner sat immediately to her left, speaking into the console's mike. As before, his voice was calm and soothing: "Like a leaf, Brandon. Like a leaf floating on the surface of a quiet pond."

"Yes." Brandon's answer was barely above a whisper.

"No thoughts . . . just quiet, gentle floating."

"He's reached level," Sarah said, motioning to the EEG. "Theta is up to where it was before."

Reichner looked at the monitor, surprised. They both glanced up at the digital timer. The readout glowed: 2:20.

Sarah blinked in surprise. He'd reached level in under three minutes—nearly four times faster than yesterday.

Reichner turned back to the mike. "Excellent. That's very, very good, Brandon. Now, Brandon, keeping your mind free and empty, I want you to search for that light again. I want you to find Jenny."

There was no response.

"Brandon? Brandon, stay with me."

Still, no answer.

"Brandon." Reichner's voice remained soothing but carried an edge of authority. "Brandon."

Sarah leaned forward to look through the glass. Down below Brandon's face registered the slightest frown.

"Brandon."

Finally he answered. "I don't see anything. I don't—"

"You're trying too hard," Reichner gently interrupted. "Relax. Let her come to you."

Sarah watched as Brandon took a deep breath and slowly exhaled. She knew he was trying to obey, to clear and release his mind. Again the thought made her just a little uneasy. And again she wished she could see and hear what he was experiencing . . .

Brandon floated in the deep, crimson void. There was no sensation, no up, no down, only the faint brushing of wind against his face and its gentle whispering in his ear. But it was more than wind. This time he recognized it to be something else, something tender, something encouraging, something—alive.

Then he saw the flicker. Like a welding spark. Just as bright as before, and just as brief. It happened again, but longer—a blinding shaft of light cutting through the emptiness. And with that light came the tug, the pulling of the current. He knew it was Jenny holding the light, and he knew if he gave himself over to the current, it would carry him toward her.

After a moment's hesitation he slowly began releasing his will. The wind increased; the current began moving him. There was another flash, a little closer. And then another as Brandon released more and more control to the current and began to pick up speed.

Another flash. Now he could see the light silhouetting a distant form. The form of his sister. His heart swelled as he drew closer. Soon he was able to see her features—her blonde hair blowing in the wind, her white gown—and, as he approached, the smile, that sweet, understanding, angelic smile.

As before, she reached into the folds of her garment and pulled out the lantern. Its brightness stabbed his eyes, forcing him to raise a hand and shield them. With the greater intensity of the light came increasing speed, and with the increasing speed his fear returned. Once again he began to resist the current, willing himself to slow. With all of his concentration and with great determination, he was able to decrease his speed until he came to a stop. The current continued to tug and pull, but he refused to go any further.

Jenny was a dozen yards away. Once again she held out the lantern to him. He knew she wanted him to approach and take it. But he couldn't. He hated himself for it, but he was still too afraid—afraid of coming any closer, afraid of giving in, of losing control.

She nodded, her eyes full of understanding. Then, as before, she raised the lantern high over her head and dropped it to the ground. It hit, and the light spilled out like liquid. As it spread into a large, molten pool, Brandon could feel the force of the current increasing, pulling him harder. The light churned and boiled upon itself, growing in width and height, until it formed the glowing rectangle that had towered over him the day before.

The current increased, and Brandon fought even harder to keep his footing. With rising panic, he struggled, exerting all of his will to resist being drawn in. Frightened, he looked up at the rectangle. It was solidifying, its liquid light turning into a doorway, the Threshold. The intense brightness dimmed slightly, as if the structure were cooling. Now he could see detail: intricate carvings on the pillars of the doorway, words and symbols he had never seen before.

And just inside the opening, waiting patiently, was little Jenny.

The gentle whisperings around him grew louder, clearer. They were voices, low and sustained, like singing.

And still the current increased, and still he resisted.

"Let it go, Brandon." He wasn't sure if it was Reichner's voice or the voices of the wind. "Let it go . . ."

He looked back at Jenny. So much love and compassion filled her eyes. This was where he had failed her before, where he had panicked, where he had shown his cowardice and stopped the experiment.

The wind and voices grew even stronger. He wanted to stop it; there was no need for him to cross through the Threshold. Let the Sarah Weintraubs of the world be the heroes, let them change civilization. Just let him continue to live his life of—he tried to block her words, but they came before he could stop them: *pointless.* That's what she had said about his life. *A pointless waste.*

She had been right. And yet . . .

Perspiration broke out across his forehead. He could still stop this, he *should* stop it. But what about Jenny? He looked up. She waited so patiently, so lovingly. And what about his father? And Sarah?

You've got to believe in something . . .

"Let it go, Brandon. Let it go . . ."

. . . a pointless waste, no meaning or purpose . . .

And his father. *"I'm going to make you proud,"* that's what he'd told him. *"I'm going to make you all proud."*

"Beware of the broader paths." Memories of the old woman's voice surprised him and did little to ease his fear. *"All paths but the Lord's lead to destruction."*

He closed his eyes, shaking his head. *"I have no faith,"* that's what he'd told her. *"I have no faith anymore."*

Pointless, a waste . . .

I'm going to make you proud of . . .

No meaning or purpose . . .

I'm going to make you all—

Other paths lead to destruction.

"Let it go, Brandon, let it go."

A waste.

"Let it go, Brandon . . ."

Beware of the broader—

You don't have to be ashamed . . . I'm going to make you—

Such ways lead to the occult. Beware of the—

No! Brandon's mind screamed. *No!* He turned his head, shutting off the old woman's voice, refusing to listen. With great purpose he forced himself to look back toward Jenny. It was time to end the cowardice. It was time to put aside his fears, to end the old way of believing. It was time to finally make something of himself. Slowly, with determination, Brandon raised his arms. There was one last moment of hesitation, of fear, and then Brandon Martus gave up his will.

The current immediately snatched him up, pulling him so quickly through the Threshold that, as he entered, Jenny leaped aside. She shouted as he passed, but he could not hear over the roaring wind.

Then, suddenly, instantly, it stopped—the current, the speed, the wind. Everything.

Now he was simply floating. In complete silence. Peaceful, serene silence. The towering doorway had vanished; so had its light. And as the quiet peace continued, his fear slowly began to ebb. It was then that he noticed the colors. Beautiful. Sparkling. As diverse as the rainbow, but many times more vivid. They were moving about him, gently brushing against his clothes, caressing his skin, his face, exactly as the wind had. In fact, they were the wind. Only now he could see them. And now he could clearly hear them—they were voices. Human. Human voices singing lovely, sustained chords.

He turned, searching for Jenny. At first he couldn't find her, and his panic began to return. Where was she? Had he left her behind? Had he—

And then he heard it. Gentle laughter. A little girl's giggle. Jenny's. He tilted back his head and saw her floating just above him, surrounded by the sparkling, dancing colors of light.

Brandon's heart leaped. He'd forgotten how much he loved the sound of that laughter. He smiled, reveling in it. What had he been so frightened of? Now, at last, after all these months, they were finally together.

As they floated, she motioned toward his stomach. He looked down and noticed a silver cord passing under his shirt. He pulled up the shirt to see that the cord was attached to his navel. How odd. It was like some sort of umbilical cord.

He looked back up at Jenny questioningly. She giggled and motioned for him to look for the other end, to see where it led. He obeyed and looked back down. To his surprise, he discovered that he was floating ten, maybe fifteen feet above the Observation Room at the Institute. Sarah and Reichner seemed completely unaware of his presence as they continued the session. The cord drifted above their heads, snaking this way and that until it dropped to the adjacent lab—the very lab where his body lay in the recliner.

Strangely enough, Brandon wasn't surprised at seeing himself. He'd watched this sort of stuff on TV, heard the stories of people leaving their bodies and hovering over themselves. Some thought it was a hallucination; others insisted it was their spiritual body looking down on their physical. It made little difference to Brandon. Not now. At last he saw the other end of the cord. It was attached to his *other* navel—the one in his physical body that rested on the recliner.

He looked up at Jenny. She had drifted several yards higher and seemed to be moving on, picking up speed. She motioned for him to follow. There was no fear now, and he nodded. By simply willing it, he started to move in her direction. But he had traveled only a few feet when he was suddenly brought up short. He looked back down to the cord. It had reached its limit and was stretched taut. Now it was acting as a tether, holding him back.

Jenny was moving farther away. She motioned for him to hurry. He noticed that the sparkling colors surrounding her were turning more golden in hue. The singing voices were growing louder, more pronounced. He had to do something. He hadn't come this far to be left behind. He reached for the cord, wondering if he could somehow disconnect it. He looked back up at Jenny. It was hard to tell from that distance, but it looked as if she was motioning for him to pull. Obeying, he placed both hands around the cord. Then he gave it a firm tug. There was no pain, no sensation of any kind, as it easily detached from him. He let it slip through his hands and watched as it fluttered back down toward the lab.

Sarah jumped at the sound of the alarm. Her eyes shot to the monitor. "Blood pressure is dropping!"

"What?" Reichner rolled his chair back to see for himself.

"Like a rock." Sarah scanned the other monitors. "So's his respiration, EMG. They're falling. Everything is falling!"

"That's impossible."

Sarah fought back the panic as she read, "Diastolic is 59 . . . 51 . . ."

Reichner spun back to the intercom button and hit it. "Brandon, Brandon, come back up."

"46 . . . 38 . . ."

Again Reichner spoke into the mike, less calm. "Brandon!"

Still no response.

Another alarm sounded. Sarah spun to the EEG. All of the brain waves were flattening.

Reichner leaped from his chair, sending it rolling backward. He headed for the door, took all three steps in one jump, and raced into the lab.

Brandon was free. Freer than he'd ever been in his life. But it wasn't just his body; it was his mind, his emotions, everything about him—clear, unbridled, free. He was picking up speed, moving faster toward his little sister. And, as his speed increased, so did the volume of the singing and the intensity of the lights surrounding him.

They sparkled brighter, gently caressing his body as they slowly changed from the beautiful ambers and golds to deeper, more vivid hues of orange and red.

Above him, Jenny slowed slightly, waiting for him to catch up.

Although he could see no trees or clouds or sky, Brandon knew they were now outside of the Lab. They were someplace in the cosmos, someplace vast and deep and wondrous. Jenny hovered less than twenty feet away. As Brandon closed the distance, he willed himself to slow so that they would not collide. Gradually, his speed decreased.

When they were ten feet apart, she stretched out her hands, waiting for him. He did the same. Seven feet. Four. Finally, at last, he arrived. They stared into each other's eyes, drinking in one another's love and affection. It had been so long. But now, at last, they were together. And for the first time since her death, Brandon no longer felt guilt or shame or failure. Here, everything was forgotten. Forgiven. For the first time in his life, he experienced only love and peace.

The voices grew louder. The beautiful oranges and reds dancing about him were darkening to even more dramatic scarlets. But he barely noticed. All he saw was Jenny, her image wavering from the tears in his eyes.

She smiled, blinking back her own tears.

Moved by her affection, he reached out his hand to her cheek, to brush away one of the tears. His finger touched the moisture, the smooth skin—

There was a tremendous searing, like lightning ripping through air, like gristle tearing from flesh. And with that sound came the transformation. Instantly Jenny's nose grew, turning into a long, doglike snout, its jaw open and panting. Her eyes shifted higher onto her face, then narrowed. Her skin erupted, suddenly bristling with gray and black fur as her lips pulled back, stretching, curling into a snarl that exposed large canine fangs.

It was a wolf! Not Jenny, but a wolf. She had become a wolf!

Before Brandon could pull back, the creature snapped at him. Its razor teeth tore into his arm, ripping and pulling away flesh. Brandon screamed. The animal showed no pleasure, no remorse—only hunger, only a ravenous desire to destroy as it shifted its weight, preparing for another attack.

Brandon lurched away. The force threw him backward, tumbling, spinning, head over heels.

"Jenny!"

But there was no answer.

As he spun, out of control, he saw other changes. He was no longer floating in some peaceful sky. He was falling. Falling into a fiery void that grew redder and redder every second. And the sparkling lights escorting and touching him now had shape and form.

They were humanoid and they were on fire. They were burning cadavers, clinging to him, wailing in agony. These were the voices he had heard. Not gentle whisperings, not beautiful sustained chords but burning corpses, screaming in anguished torture. And they were falling. Falling into a bottomless, burning inferno.

Back in the lab, Reichner grabbed Brandon, shaking him hard. "Brandon!"

Sarah watched as other alarms in the Observation Room began to sound.

"Come back up!" Reichner shouted. "Come back!"

There was no response.

She grabbed the phone.

Reichner dragged Brandon out of the recliner, ripping off a dozen sensors in the process. "Brandon!" He slapped him once, twice, but there was no response.

Sarah watched the scene through the glass as she quickly punched in 911.

Reichner spotted her and yelled, "What are you doing?"

"I'm calling 911!"

"Don't be a fool!"

She looked at him, confused.

"They'll close us down!"

She could only stare at him in disbelief. The phone on the other end began to ring.

"Records!" he yelled. "They'll go through everything. They'll find out about Vicksburg. They'll shut us down!"

Sarah understood, but she didn't move.

"Get in here!" he cried. "Give me a hand!"

The phone continued to ring.

"Dr. Weintraub, I need you, *here!*"

The voice on the phone answered, "Emergency, 911."

"Sarah!" Reichner's eyes flared in anger.

"911," the voice repeated. "Are you reporting an emergency?"

Suddenly a loud drone filled the room. Sarah spun around to the heart monitor.

"He's flatlining!" Reichner shouted. "Get down here, now!"

She looked at the phone, hesitating.

"Now!"

Another moment's hesitation.

"Sarah!"

And then slowly, but decisively, she hung up.

"Come on!"

She ran out of the room and into the lab, her hatred and self-loathing already rising to new heights. As she entered the lab, Reichner was ripping off the boy's shirt. Buttons and sensors flew in all directions. She dropped near Brandon's face, preparing to give him CPR as Reichner placed his hands on the boy's chest and began to pump and count.

Brandon was covered in flames. The burning corpses continued to cling, clawing, shrieking for relief. Pieces of their flesh dripped and fell onto his own body, burning whatever they touched, igniting his clothes, his own skin.

"Jenny!" he screamed. *"Jenny!"*

Through his own cries and the tormented wails of the bodies around him he heard laughter, but it wasn't Jenny's. It was deep, guttural, malicious. He craned his neck and spotted the wolf through the flames. It was heading directly for him, laughing, its mouth opened wide, ready for the attack.

"My God!" he screamed. "Help me! Please, somebody—my God, help me!"

The plea snapped the wolf's head around. His laughter faltered. He was only yards away, moving in for the kill, but now he seemed uncertain, tentative. He began to search, looking one way, then the other.

That's when Brandon heard it. Another, entirely different sound. It began to overpower the shrieks and wailings. Mighty, all-consuming. Like the roar of a waterfall, but a thousand times greater. It increased, booming, thundering, roaring. Not only did Brandon hear it, he could feel it. It vibrated through his entire body.

Then he spotted something high above him. It was another light, brighter than anything he had ever seen, many times brighter than the sun. Instinctively he knew that it was the source of the sound. The wolf and the burning cadavers tilted back their heads, looking up at it with fear and awe. As it approached, Brandon could see that its sides were moving, rotating like wheels. But they were more than wheels. They were alive. They were covered in eyes—hundreds, maybe thousands of eyes—all-searching, all-seeing, all-knowing.

Although its appearance was terrifying, Brandon somehow sensed that it was good. More than good—it was pure. But with that purity came a dread. Not the dread he had experienced with the wolf, or the horror of the burning corpses. This was different. Deeper. Yes, it was terrifying. But terrifying in its awesomeness, in its power—and its unwavering, absolute perfection.

He watched as it slowly came to a stop. Everything around Brandon seemed to be waiting, but the light moved no closer. It simply hovered a hundred yards above them. It offered Brandon no help, no promise of rescue. Just its presence. And yet, somehow, that presence was enough. It began to stir something inside of him. An expectation. Somewhere inside of him a quiet hope and assurance began to swell and grow.

Maybe it was this assurance, or maybe it was simply having a point of reference, an idea of up and down. Whatever the case, Brandon once again willed himself to move—only this time upward, toward the light, toward the wheels of eyes. Of course it frightened him, and of course he knew that its power and purity could kill him. But death by goodness seemed far preferable to destruction by evil.

As he rose, Brandon felt the clinging, burning cadavers start to lose their grip. First one, then another, they began slipping away, falling with horrific screams back into the flaming void below. And the more that fell away, the more swiftly he rose.

He looked up. Although he was traveling faster, he never seemed to draw any closer to the rotating light. It seemed that the more quickly he rose, the more quickly it rose. In fact, it had kept the exact same distance from him as when he'd first started his ascent. He wasn't sure why, but he sensed that this distance might be for his own protection—that if he drew too close, its terrifying purity could indeed destroy him. And as far as he could tell, it had not come to destroy.

Off in the distance, he saw the laboratory approaching. But it wasn't below him as before. Now it was above him—thirty or forty yards *above* him. It was as if he were looking up through a glass floor. There was the recliner, the console, Dr. Reichner and Sarah kneeling beside his body trying to revive him.

But there was something else around his body as well.

A group of creatures. Grotesque, hideous things. There were nearly a dozen, and yet Sarah and Reichner seemed oblivious to their presence. Some were small, some big, but all were equally repulsive. They reminded Brandon of gargoyles, of the trolls and monsters from childhood books and nightmares.

They spotted his approach and immediately snarled and screamed at him. Some shouted threats and obscenities. Others waved their claws and talons menacingly.

All but two. These two were several feet taller than the others. They were clothed in brilliant, shimmering light that made it impossible for Brandon to make out any detail of their features. One stood near the head of his body, the other at his feet. They said nothing and made no movement, but there was a presence about them. A strength.

The last of the burning corpses fell away, and Brandon realized that he was no longer fighting to rise. He found himself in another current—but this time, a current pulling him into his body instead of away from it.

The creatures moved to block his path. They continued waving their claws, gnashing their fangs, screaming their obscenities—some in English, others in languages he could not understand. They did everything they could to intimidate him, to scare him away. But, even if he'd wanted to, he could not have stopped his approach now; he was moving too fast.

He raced toward them with increasing speed. He was going to crash into them, and there was nothing he could do to stop it. He raised his arms to protect his face—

Then, just before impact, just before he felt their claws and fangs tear into him, the two taller figures extended their arms. Effortlessly, they knocked the smaller creatures aside, making a clear and direct path for Brandon to reenter his body.

Reichner sat back on his legs and wiped the perspiration from his face. He had finally restarted the boy's heart. Sarah leaned forward and felt for Brandon's breath. He was breathing. A moment later his eyes shifted under closed lids. They rolled once, twice, and then opened.

Time passed. Ten, maybe fifteen minutes later Brandon was on his feet, pacing the lab.

"Be reasonable," Sarah argued. "At least have a doctor examine you and see—"

"No." He cut her off as he continued buttoning his shirt, preparing to leave.

"But it's for your own good," she insisted.

"*My* good?" His voice trembled in rage. "You nearly killed me, and it's for *my* good?"

She had to look away. It was true. Once again she had caved in to her guilt and ambition, once again she had allowed herself to be manipulated—this time at the risk of nearly killing him. What was wrong with her? Why couldn't she stop? Would the past ever let her go?

"Listen, son." It was Reichner's turn. "I know you are upset. But what we are uncovering here may completely redefine paranormal research. And not only that branch of science."

Brandon said nothing.

"Everything may change. Physics, our understanding of the brain, the soul, even our most rudimentary—"

Brandon turned on him. "Shut up! Just—shut up."

Reichner appeared unfazed. "We are in the midst of a major scientific breakthrough. You, Dr. Weintraub, myself— we could advance science by logarithmic leaps, and—"

"Science?" Brandon was livid. "This isn't about science. This is about *you*." Reichner glanced away. Brandon spun toward Sarah. "It's so *you* can get your awards, your Nobel prizes. It's so *you* can prove whatever it is you think you've got to prove." His words cut deep. "That's it, isn't it? Isn't it?"

He waited, hovering just a few feet from her. She knew that he was waiting for an explanation, for her to defend herself. But when she looked up at him, there were no words. For a brief moment their eyes connected, looking into each other as before . . . until Brandon broke it off. He turned and headed for the door.

"I never said my purposes were selfless." Sarah was surprised at how calm her voice sounded.

Brandon came to a stop but did not turn to her.

"I never said they were pure." She took a breath, then continued. "They may have exploited you, even hurt you—and for that I'm truly sorry. But—"

Before she could finish, Reichner interrupted. "But at least she has one. At least she has a purpose."

She threw him an outraged look, but he ignored her. He'd already sniffed out the boy's weakness, and now he was going for the kill. "But tell me, son. If you walk out that door, what exactly do you have? Hmm? What purpose? What reason do you have for living?"

Sarah turned back to Brandon. He was looking down. Somehow he seemed a little smaller, a little more lost. He stood a long moment, his back to them. Then, without a word, he walked out the door, never to return.

PART THREE

CHAPTER 12

Sarah knew it was only a dream. Nothing weird or paranormal—just churning bits of emotions. It started with another shouting match with Samuel. Of course it was about the abortion. Only now he was no longer Samuel. Suddenly he had become Reichner— using that same smooth logic, the same manipulative reasoning. Only now she was no longer in her apartment but lying helplessly on a table as he stood beside her in a surgical gown, poking and prodding inside her with the vacuum nozzle, trying to calm her with his cool, relaxing voice, assuring her that everything was okay, that it was all in the name of science, only somehow the nozzle was now inside her brain, sucking something from her mind as the vacuum machine grew louder, screaming with sucking air until suddenly she looked up to the clear surgical tubing and saw that it was Brandon being sucked through it, his face distorted in a scream, but instead of his voice it was hers, crying hysterically, trying to move but somehow paralyzed by Reichner's soothing voice until she could stand no more, and then—

Sarah awoke. She was breathing hard, and her cotton nightshirt clung to her damply.

Four minutes later she stood in the shower. It was only 5:30 Sunday morning. But that was late enough. It was time to get to work. She tilted back her head and let the shower rinse the shampoo out of her hair.

She'd felt something with Brandon—something she hadn't felt in years. Something had come back alive, and she had hoped that it would offer a reprieve, an escape from her prison. But she'd only fooled herself. There was no way out for her. It was the same song—the same guilt and driving ambition—only in a different key. It would always be that way. Gradually, week by week, month by month, it would continue to destroy her.

And two days ago it had nearly destroyed Brandon.

The shower took longer than normal. She felt a need to lather up again. She wasn't sure why, but she just didn't feel clean enough.

And somewhere, in the back of her mind, Sarah Weintraub guessed that she never would.

"'What profit hath a man of all his labour which he taketh under the sun? One generation passeth away, and another generation cometh: but the earth abideth for ever.'"

Brandon thought it was odd for the Reverend to read from the Bible this Sunday. He seldom did. But, after urging everyone to attend the farewell service that evening, and reminding them that the top religious leaders of the community would be there to show their respect, he had opened up to Ecclesiastes and was again demonstrating his impressive oratory skills:

"'The sun also ariseth, and the sun goeth down, and hasteth to his place where he arose.'"

But it didn't matter to Brandon. He was already zoning out—back in his pickup, sitting with Sarah, remembering how he had enjoyed her company and how for a brief moment she had given him hope.

"'All the rivers run into the sea; yet the sea is not full; unto the place from whence the rivers come, thither they return again.'"

And what about Jenny? What had happened to her? Why had she become a wolf? Is that what death did to you? Or was that thing Jenny at all? "Beware of seducers." That's what that old lady had said. "Keep your eyes open for counterfeits." Was that what she'd meant? Was that what he'd experienced—not Jenny, but a counterfeit? Was that whole experiment just another way of entering that dangerous region she'd called the occult? And if so, if she'd been right about that, then what about—

A gentle breeze stirred through the church. It caught Brandon's attention and drew him back to the sanctuary. The candles on the altar were flickering.

"'The thing that hath been, it is that which shall be; and that which is done is that which shall be done: and there is no new thing under the sun.'"

Directly above the Reverend, at the apex of the sanctuary ceiling, there was some sort of movement. Brandon looked up and watched as a gray, swirling mist began to form.

Brandon closed his eyes. But when he reopened them, the mist had grown larger and was taking a shape—slowly whirling into faces that twisted and melded into one another. The same swirling faces he had seen in the storm outside the church with Sarah.

"'There is no remembrance of former things; neither shall there be any remembrance of things that are to . . .'"

Again Brandon closed his eyes, this time clenching them tight, concentrating, trying to make the image disappear. When he reopened them he saw that he had at least stopped the thing's growth. Encouraged, he stared at it, trying by sheer concentration to make it go away. He scowled hard until, slowly, stubbornly, the cloud began to recede.

It was exhausting, but he would not stop. This was *his* life, and he didn't have to put up with this. He would deny these illusions, these intrusions. He would make them leave for good. Out of the corner of his eye he saw his mother turn toward him, cautiously watching. She took his hand, but he would not look at her, he could not look at her. Not until he forced the thing away.

"'And I gave my heart to seek and search out by wisdom concerning all things that are done under heaven . . .'"

The cloud continued to recede. So did the faces—until they were only a thinning mist, growing fainter by the second. A moment later, the wind slowed to a stop, and the mist was completely gone.

Brandon closed his eyes. He took a long, deep breath and let it out. He had won. It had taken every ounce of his will, but he had won. He turned to his mother; she gave him a questioning smile. He returned it, then directed his attention back to the Reverend.

"'I have seen all the works that are done under the sun; and, behold, all is vanity and vexation of spirit . . .'"

Reichner settled himself comfortably behind the expensive mahogany desk and turned on his home computer. It had been a good morning. Earlier he'd met a girl at Kroger's supermarket. Some pre-med college student.

She looked barely twenty and came with all the accessories—good legs, a pert body, and long, gorgeous hair. Just the way he liked them.

Of course she'd heard of the Institute, and of course she was flattered by his attention—particularly when he commented on her strong ESP potential. She had declined his offer for dinner, but his persistent charm had eventually paid off. By the time they'd reached the parking lot, she'd agreed to stop by the townhouse with a friend, later that evening.

Things were getting back to normal.

Reichner logged on to his Internet server and opened his e-mail box. There was the usual correspondence: a handful of fellow researchers, a film producer who wanted to do a documentary, and some loony tune in Great Britain who needed his CD player exorcised. Reichner saved the letter from Nepal for last. He popped it onto the screen and started to read.

Doctor:

You have failed. He will no longer listen to you.

There was more, but Reichner had to pause. Not only was this a reference to the past encounter he'd had with the boy guru or python or whatever. But now the kid was speaking of events he couldn't possibly have known about. Not yet.

A lucky guess? Perhaps, but Reichner had his doubts. There really had been a young man in this area who really had proven to be exceptionally gifted. And now, just as the e-mail pointed out, Reichner had let him slip through his fingers.

If this was *remote viewing* that the boy guru was practicing, then Reichner had never seen anything quite so accurate. Granted, the U.S. military had trained and used remote viewers for decades. But they had only been able to observe physical sights like military installations, or specific events such as missile launches. They'd seldom if ever observed a situation involving relationships.

The letter continued:

> *Perhaps he'll listen to one of his own. She could do more harm than good, but time is running out. Visit Gerty Morrison. Convince her to reason with him. Your window of opportunity is nearly closed, Doctor. If we lose him, you will pay.*
>
> *Eric*

Reichner had no idea who this Gerty Morrison was but figured he could track her down easily enough, especially if she was local. But it was the last phrase that caught his attention. *"If we lose him, you will pay."* It seemed familiar, but he couldn't place it. Obviously, it was a reminder that if he failed, the Institute would suffer financially. But why did it seem so familiar? What about it—

And then he remembered. It was from his dream. The one with the python on his bed. Those were the identical words the thing had used as it had departed, just before Reichner had awakened with his heart beating like a jackhammer.

"But the important thing is, you were able to resist it," the Reverend insisted. "You were able to fight it off. And the next time it will be easier, and the time after that, easier still."

Brandon poked at the green beans on his plate. It was Sunday afternoon and, as happened at least once a month, the Reverend was over for Sunday supper.

Momma sat across from Brandon, lifting another spoonful of potatoes to her husband's mouth. "And with that determination," she said, "along with the help from your medicine, we'll finally be able to close this awful chapter once and for all."

Brandon watched as she slipped the spoon into his father's mouth and encouraged him to chew. Then he turned to the Reverend. "I have a question."

"Certainly."

"Weren't visions and dreams—didn't prophets, like in the Bible and stuff—didn't they have them?" He didn't miss the look between Momma and the Reverend before the Reverend cleared his throat and answered.

"The prophets were a long time ago, Brandon. And even if they did exist, we have no way of verifying whether they actually had such insights or whether their 'future predictions' were simply written *after* the fact."

Brandon glanced at his mother. Was it his imagination or was she doing her best not to look at the Reverend?

The man continued. "To believe in the miraculous or the supernatural today, in this age of scientific reasoning, well, I'm afraid those days of superstition and folklore have long passed. Yes, I know that doesn't agree with the latest trends and TV talk shows, but the supernatural has never been proven, Brandon—whether it's good or evil, it's never been proven."

"So what is there?" Brandon asked. "I mean if you don't believe in—"

"I believe in man. And his choices. What we choose to make of ourselves. Anything more than that is simply wishful thinking, striving after wind." The Reverend reached for a biscuit and broke it apart. "Now it's true there are many people who would take issue with that. Good, sincere people, like your father there."

Brandon looked at his father, who continued to chew and stare off into space.

"He was quite a believer in those early days, wasn't he, Meg?"

Momma nodded and turned to Brandon. "When you were first born, things got a little crazy around the church there for a while."

Brandon frowned, not understanding.

She continued. "Truth be told, we all got a little carried away. Some of us were even sayin' things like the world was gonna come to an end."

Brandon stared at her. "The world coming to an end?"

Obviously embarrassed, she reached for the green beans and began to dish up seconds. "It was all anyone talked about back then—how we were all supposed to be taken up to heaven, how the Antichrist was supposed to be comin', and how some end-time prophets were gonna rise up and fight him."

Drool, who had been asleep near the back door, suddenly lifted his head. The movement attracted Brandon's attention. The poor animal was so deaf he could barely hear, but now he was staring up at the ceiling. Brandon ventured a look and was grateful not to see anything. He turned back to his mother. "You said this all happened when I was born?"

Momma nodded. "Thereabouts. People thought they were havin' all sorts of visions, and prophesyin'. Some even believed there would be a major showdown right there inside our own church." She gave a nervous chuckle. "I'm afraid we definitely got a little carried away."

Brandon scowled. "Why didn't somebody—why didn't you ever mention it?"

Momma shrugged as she brought another spoonful of potatoes to her husband's mouth. "It's not really somethin' we're proud of, Sugar. Fortunately, it only lasted a few months. When nothin' happened, things finally settled down. 'Course your daddy here, he was always hopin' some of it was true."

Brandon looked at his father.

"And that's certainly no reflection on him," the Reverend interjected. "It's not every man who can start a congregation from scratch. But without the proper education, the proper checks and balances—well, something like this can spread through a church like wildfire."

Brandon turned back to the Reverend. "But visions and stuff, I mean, they could happen, couldn't they? I mean, what about all this talk about angels and the Devil—"

"Brandon," the Reverend gently interrupted. His voice was quiet, and he spoke earnestly from his heart. "You must believe me, son, these things just don't happen—not to the

educated, not to the rational. And not to the . . ." He hesitated. "Not to the healthy."

Brandon searched his face. The man was sincere,
there was no doubt of that. But before Brandon could
continue, Drool suddenly broke into a fit of barking. All
three gave a start as the animal lumbered to its feet.

"Drool," Momma scolded.

But the animal continued barking as it hobbled out
of the kitchen toward the living room.

"Drool, come back here."

They exchanged looks, and Brandon rose to investigate. "Hey, fella," he called as he headed out of the room.
He found the dog standing at the foot of the stairs looking up, barking.

"What's wrong, boy?"

More barking.

"What's the problem?" Momma asked, as she and the
Reverend entered.

Brandon shook his head, then started up the stairs to
see for himself.

"Could be a squirrel," she offered hopefully. "You
know how they're always playin' on the roof outside our
windows."

The dog continued to bark but remained at the foot
of the steps, refusing to follow his master.

Brandon arrived at the top of the stairs and headed
down the hall. Before him was the bathroom, his bedroom, his parents' room—and finally Jenny's. For some
time now, Momma had been promising to clean out
Jenny's room, to save a few mementos, maybe store the
bed and furniture up in the barn. There had even been

talk of turning it into a guest room. But Brandon knew that would never happen. She didn't have the heart. There were still those times, late at night, when he heard her slip into her little girl's room and have a quiet cry. It had been seven months since her death, and so far the only change had been that they kept her door closed.

Until now. Now it was open. Not by much. Just a few inches. But a few inches was enough. Brandon slowed his pace. He approached, carefully avoiding the floorboards that he knew would creak.

Downstairs, Drool continued his incessant barking.

"Brandon," Momma called. "Brandon."

But he didn't answer. He'd heard something. A tiny tinkling—breezy, far away. And the closer he approached, the louder it grew. It was music. One of Jenny's music boxes had been opened, and it was now playing a song.

He continued down the hall until portions of her room came into view—a canopy bed, her vanity. The afternoon sun struck the pulled window shade and bathed everything in a dim, ivory-yellow glow. As the melody grew louder, he began to recognize it. Something from one of those Disney movies she loved so much.

He caught a glimpse of her bookshelf, then the corner of the dresser. At last he arrived. He nudged the door open a bit further. There on the dresser sat the music box—glass with gold trim and a red rose etched upon the open lid. Other than the music, everything was completely still.

Against his better judgment, Brandon heard himself quietly whisper, "Jenny?"

There was no answer. Only the music.

He pushed the door farther until he saw the entire room—the stuffed animals on her bed, the ballerina poster, the dolphin mobile hanging from the ceiling.

He took a tentative step inside.

"Jenny."

And then another.

"Jen—"

It lunged at him from behind the door. He fell hard, crashing to the floor. Somebody was on top of him. In the dim light he saw the glint of steel—a knife coming toward his chest. He raised both hands and barely caught the wrist in time.

"Impostor!" a chorus of voices screamed.

Adrenaline surged through Brandon as he struggled to push the knife away. Now he saw the face behind it. Short red hair, goatee. The young man who had attacked him at the church.

Brandon squirmed, throwing his body hard to the left, then to the right. The kid toppled off, and for a brief moment the knife disappeared. Brandon struggled until he was on top. But only for a second. He was thrown off, flying through the air until his shoulder slammed hard into the dresser. He heard the popping and shattering of china dolls as they fell to the floor around him.

The attacker lunged again. Brandon rolled to the side, momentarily dodging him. He scrambled to his feet but was broadsided. They fell and rolled—Brandon on top, then underneath. The knife reappeared. Coming down hard, this time toward his face. Brandon jerked his head to the right and heard the blade thud into the wood an inch from his ear.

The voices swore and grunted as the attacker pinned Brandon's arms with his knees and yanked the knife from the floor. Suddenly the blade was high overhead, once again glimmering in the light. Below it Brandon could see the kid's crooked teeth, his leering grin. The knife plunged toward him. With his arms pinned, there was nothing he could do. Nothing but watch the blade and brace himself—until suddenly, the hand and knife were swept aside. Fur and fangs filled his vision as his attacker was knocked off.

Brandon kicked himself backward scooting out of the way as Drool tore into the man's hand, biting it, savagely shaking it.

The multiple voices screamed curses. The knife reappeared in the other hand. Drool continued growling and tearing into the first. He did not see the blade preparing to strike.

"No!" Brandon shouted. "Stop!"

The order startled the attacker, carrying more weight than any punch Brandon had landed. But it lasted only a second before the young man focused back on the dog. He raised the knife high into the air, and this time he brought it down hard.

The dog yelped in pain but continued to fight.

"No!" Brandon shouted again. "Stop it! Stop!"

Again the assailant turned to him, this time with confusion and fear. That's when Brandon understood. That's when he remembered what the old lady had said about his power. His authority.

"I command you—" He took in a gulp of air. "I command you to stop this!"

"You have no authority!" the attacker shouted.

Brandon searched his memory, trying to remember what the old woman had said, the phrase she had used. He had it. "In the name of Jesus—"

"You have no authority!"

"In the name of Jesus Christ I command you—"

"You have no authority! You don't believe! You don't believe!"

The accusation hit hard. Brandon faltered for a second, and a second was all it took. With a mocking grin, the attacker raised his knife high over the animal and drove it down again.

"No!"

Brandon's cry was lost in a thundering roar that filled his left ear; plaster exploded from the wall behind him. He spun around to see his mother standing at the door, holding a smoldering shotgun. Before either could speak the attacker leaped into the window. Glass shattered and the shade ripped away as he hit the roof, rolling and scrambling out of sight.

Glaring sunlight flooded the room. Out in the hall Brandon could hear the Reverend shouting, running down the stairs after the intruder. A moment's silence passed before Momma finally spoke, her voice shaking. "You all right?"

But Brandon barely heard. Drool lay less than a yard away, whimpering and panting.

"Brandon."

He pulled himself through the broken plaster and pieces of glass to the animal. Drool looked up at him, unable to move, eyes begging him to make the pain go away.

"Sweetheart, are you all right?"

But they were deep wounds. One in the chest, the other in the gut.

"Brandon? Sweetheart, are you okay?"

The boy dropped closer to the dog and wrapped his arms around him. There was nothing he could do. He thought his heart would burst as the big animal whimpered again, this time more faintly. With great effort and a slight groan it turned its head toward him. Then, finding Brandon's face, the dog began licking him. It was more than Brandon could stand. He lowered his head and buried his face in the animal's fur. He would not leave. He would stay with him until the end.

CHAPTER 13

Taking a break to walk down the hallway for a cup of coffee, Sarah was surprised to notice that the sun had just set. She'd been in Lab One all afternoon, carefully going over the data and results on Brandon Martus. The whole Martus affair may have been over, but a tremendous amount of ground had been broken, and it was important that someone transcribe and evaluate the information—if not for now, at least for future reference. Then, of course, there was the other matter, the one of her heart.

So far, today's work had revealed nothing new—just a review of the rapid drop of vital signs as Brandon had crossed Threshold, and of the sketchy accounts he had provided after their first session. Earlier she had brought up the PET scans and studied them on the monitor. Again, nothing new—just the pronounced stimulation of the right temporal lobe that they had originally observed.

She reached for her notebook and flipped through its pages. These were sporadic notations she'd taken from their conversations—information on Jenny's death, Brandon's vision outside the church, his dreams, the reaction of the multiple personality patient, and his mention of the old black woman who kept wanting to help him. Sarah paused at her name for just a moment, then reached for the envelope of her sketches that Brandon had brought in.

They were drawings of him in various stages of childhood, nothing unusual—except that the woman had supposedly drawn them all during the first week of his life. Then there was the last sketch, in which he stood in an ancient city wearing burlap and breathing fire from his mouth. Sarah studied the picture. If this woman had legitimate PSI, and if she had accurately seen into the future with this sketch as she had with the earlier ones . . .

Sarah flipped over the envelope to look at the front. It was old and previously used. The name and address of Gerty Morrison had been crossed out but was still legible. She grabbed her notepad and copied it down.

She looked over the other notes, the ones mentioning the factory accident and Brandon's precognitive dream four days before it had happened. Then there was his hallucination involving the young singer at church.

Again she stopped. Brandon's account of the teenage soloist at church had been shaky at best. But it was interesting that this teen and the factory worker were the only two people outside his family to appear in his visions. And if the accident at the factory had come true, then what about this girl?

Sarah hesitated. She didn't particularly want to call up Brandon. She wasn't even sure he would speak to her. But she had to try. Partly to satisfy her scientific curiosity—and partly because, if his vision was accurate, this girl could be in trouble.

Brandon stood in the doorway of his pickup, looking over the top of the cab. He carefully scanned the countryside for signs of danger as Frank and Del continued their shoveling in the back.

"We missed you, ol' buddy," Frank said. He was breathing hard, and for good reason. They'd been shoveling for over ten minutes; the bed of the pickup was nearly full. "Sure glad you're back in the saddle again."

Del, who was breathing even harder, leaned against his shovel a moment to catch his breath. "You've had some pretty classy ideas in the past, Bran, but this is definitely *Guinness Book of World Records* time."

Brandon nodded and continued to search the driving range and the parameter road for any signs of activity. "Just keep shovelin', boys," he said, "just keep shovelin'."

Sarah picked up the phone, dialed, and waited nervously as the phone rang on the other end.

"Hello?"

"Hello, Mrs. Martus? This is Sarah Weintraub. Is Brandon in?"

"No, he's, uh, he's out for the evening."

Sarah hesitated, unsure if she was hearing the truth. "Well, maybe you could help me. Do you remember that girl who sang the solo in your church last Sunday—you know, when Brandon had one of his 'spells'?" There was no response, and Sarah fumbled with her notebook to get the name. "A Lori Beth? Lori Beth Phillips?"

Again, no response.

"Mrs. Martus?"

"Yes."

"Would you happen to have her phone number—maybe an address?"

"Sarah . . ." The woman cleared her throat. "Please understand, I appreciate your tryin' to help. But Brandon is much better now, and that's a part of his past I think we'd all do better to forget."

"I can understand that, but if you would just tell me—"

"I'm sorry, dear, but we've got the farewell service at the church tonight, and I'm already runnin' late."

"What about Gerty, the old black woman who—"

"I've got to go now, darlin', but thank you for your concern."

"Mrs. Martus, if you—"

There was a click on the other end, and for a moment, Sarah sat, puzzled at the woman's abruptness. Then she rose and walked to the shelf against the back wall. After some searching, she found the local phone directory and began flipping through the pages.

Hills are few and far between in northern Indiana. Fortunately for Brandon and the boys, Bethel Lake had a couple. Even more fortunately, one of them rose directly behind the Bethel Lake Country Club. It wasn't a huge hill, no more than a hundred, maybe a hundred and twenty feet at best. But in making room for their parking lot, the Club owners had cut away a good third of it, leaving an impressive fifty-foot ridge that dropped sharply toward the lot.

After taking the back way around a gate or two, Brandon had managed to drive the pickup to the top of that ridge. Now he maneuvered it backward until the rear tailgate was aligned over the parking lot below. He remained behind the wheel, keeping the motor idling, as Frank and Del piled outside.

"You sure they're there?" Del asked as he hoisted himself up and climbed onto the load.

"That's his car, ain't it?" Frank asked, climbing up to join him.

Del pushed up his glasses, took another look down into the parking lot, and nodded.

"Then they're there." Without another word, Frank reached down to the tailgate and unbolted his side. Del unbolted the other.

"We're ready!" Frank shouted back to the cab. "Hit it!"

Brandon punched the accelerator. The rear wheels spun out as Frank gave the tailgate a good kick. It flew open, and twenty-three hundred golf balls began to tumble out. Frank and Del tried to help push them, but they were unable to keep their balance as they slipped and fell and flopped around in the back.

"Yee-haaa!" Frank yelled, laughing, having the time of his life—as all twenty-three hundred golf balls bounced down the steep ridge directly toward Bethel Lake Country Club.

The score was 30-Love in the second set. Tom Henderson and Beverly, a new lovely he'd been strutting for all evening, were two games short of winning the match against Reggie and his babe of the month. Henderson delivered a powerful serve that hit the baseline before zipping past Reggie's racket.

That's when they heard the first explosion. It sounded like a small firecracker. It was immediately followed by another, and then another, and more and more in rapid succession.

Reggie called to Henderson. "Is that hail?"

Henderson wasn't sure, and they both crossed the court, heading for the lobby to investigate. By now the entire structure was thundering. Jogging into the lobby, Henderson saw movement through the front glass door. Giant, white somethings were bouncing into the glass and pounding against the aluminum wall.

The girls arrived, and everyone edged closer for a better look. It was then that Henderson recognized the little white somethings.

"Golf balls!" he shouted over the roar. "They're golf balls!"

Golf balls pounded everywhere—against the door, the front wall, ricocheting around the walk, raining down on the parking lot. He approached the door, cupped his hands against the glass, and searched the cars. His beloved Firebird sat directly in the center of the downpour, its carefully waxed finish slowly but quite surely breaking out in a severe case of acne.

Reggie pushed past him, shoving open the door, attempting to brave the onslaught. But the pounding balls forced him back in.

Not Henderson. That was his Firebird out there, his pride and joy. He raced outside and was instantly hit by a stinging ball against his shoulder. Then his thigh. Then his head. They hurt. So did the other dozen that hit. He raised his arms to protect his face as he fought his way forward, staggering toward his car. He'd made it only ten feet from the building when, over the din, he heard a distinct and unforgettable cackle of laughter. He looked up to the ridge and caught a glimpse of a pickup—the one with the broken running light on the cab—just before it bounced and disappeared out of sight. And then he opened his mouth and shouted.

"Townies-s-s . . ."

Sarah's car was acting up again, but she managed to coax it out of the Institute's parking lot and up Brower Avenue to Third. Then it was just a short jaunt over to Lambert, then left to Klaussen. That was the address the phone book had for Herb and Margaret Phillips: 339 Klaussen.

It was an older ranch home, mostly brick. The porch light was off, but Sarah could see lights on inside. As she stepped out of the car and approached the house, she heard the TV blaring. Some mindless sitcom. She headed up the porch steps, pushed the doorbell, and waited.

There was no answer. She tried again. Still nothing. She opened the aluminum screen door and knocked. A moment later the porch light glared on. A worn woman in her late thirties opened the door.

"Mrs. Phillips?" Sarah asked.

The woman squinted. "No, I'm . . ." She glanced past Sarah to make sure no one else was there. "I'm her sister."

"My name is Sarah Weintraub. Is Lori Beth in?"

"Are you a friend?"

"Well, not exactly." Sarah heard a car slowly pull up to the curb behind her. "I tried to call earlier, but—"

"I don't believe it," the woman muttered half under her breath. But she was no longer listening or even looking at Sarah; she was staring past her. Sarah threw a glance over her shoulder to see that a white Taurus had pulled up to the curb. The driver's side opened, and a large man with thinning blonde hair stepped out.

The woman turned and called into the house. "Jim? Jimmy, he's here!"

The front door of the house opened wider, and a burly mountain of flesh appeared. At first his eyes glared at Sarah. They were angry and bloodshot. Then they moved past her to the man on the curb.

The man at the curb came to a stop and called to him. "Hello, Jim."

The burly man answered, low and intense. "You've got a lot of nerve coming here. Go. Now."

"I just, uh . . ." The man at the curb coughed slightly and took half a step closer. "The parents, how are they doing?"

Jim seethed. "What do you care?"

The man at the curb continued his approach. "Listen, I, uh—"

"Get out of here!" The response was so venomous that it brought the man at the curb to a stop. "You take another step, and I'll come out there and kill you myself."

"I need to talk to the parents, Jim. I need to explain. It's not as it appears—"

"Get off their property!"

The man hesitated.

"Get out of here!"

The standoff lasted another moment before the man at the curb lowered his head, turned, then slowly headed back to his car.

But Jim wasn't finished. "Filth! Pervert!" He stepped out onto the porch, pushing past Sarah. "We're going to get you locked up!" he yelled. "They'll lock you up and throw away the key! Do you hear me? Your life is over! It's over!"

The other man said nothing as he approached his car, opened the door, and entered.

Suddenly Jim turned on Sarah. "What do you want?" he glowered.

"She's a friend of Lori Beth's," the woman beside him explained.

"Lori Beth is dead. She killed herself this morning." He watched as the car slowly pulled from the curb. "More like she was murdered."

Sarah stood in stunned silence. She was unsure how to respond. The man gave her little opportunity. He turned and headed back into the house.

Finally Sarah found her voice. "Wait a minute. I don't understand. What happened?"

The woman at the door hesitated, then spoke. "You mustn't hold it against her, honey. The note said that that monster"—she motioned toward the departed car—"that her teacher there had been . . ." She searched for the word. "You know—'hurting her.' Poor thing, she just didn't know how to tell anyone, how to make him stop."

Sarah's head reeled. It was true then, what Brandon had seen. The teacher had been assaulting the girl. Maybe not right there, right in the church, but behind school doors. Once again Brandon had seen the truth, had seen what really was happening. She was so lost in thought that she barely heard the woman conclude, "I'm sorry." By the time she looked back up, the door had closed in her face.

Gerty sat at the kitchen table, writing another letter. She suspected that it would never get to Brandon. Not that it mattered. All the important notes were already over at the computer hacker's house, being entered for future retrieval. These notes were simply loose thoughts, rambling odds and ends. Still, if she could save Brandon even a little suffering on his treacherous road ahead, it would be worth the effort.

Earlier she had arranged the table so that nothing would be missed. She had carefully laid out the remaining sketches she had not yet given him. She'd also opened her worn Bible to the underlined passages. She hated parting with that Bible; it had been her companion for over thirty years. But now he would need it far more than she.

Her pen had barely begun the second paragraph of the letter when she heard the creaking. It came from the back porch. She stopped writing and held her breath.

There it was again, the groaning of old wood. Somebody was outside, making his way toward the screen door. She tried to remember if she had locked it but couldn't recall. Not that it mattered. If he wanted in, he could easily rip out the little hook and eyelet.

She continued to listen. Another creak, more groans. She forced herself to take a breath. It came out shaky. She had known that this moment was coming, had sensed it for days, but still she was frightened. It's not that she didn't trust her Lord. She trusted him completely. And she was anxious to finally see his face, to fall into his arms.

But still she was frightened.

There was a knock. "Hello?" The voice was young. It attempted to be friendly, but she could hear the pain and torment underneath. "Hello, is anybody home?"

She took another breath to steady herself before answering. "Who is it?"

"I'm Lewis," the voice said, "Lewis Thompson. My car ran out of gas in front of your house, and I was wondering if I could use your telephone."

Gerty paused a moment before slowly rising to her feet. She pushed the chair back, and it squeaked against the worn floor.

"Ma'am?" the voice persisted.

"I'll be right there." She started toward the door. As she approached she felt a peace settling over her. A peace that was beyond any understanding. It was a quiet confidence. A resolve that filled her entire body.

The boy's face came into view through the screen. She immediately recognized the short, nearly shaved hair, the red goatee, and the crooked teeth. This was the child at the church, the one who had attacked Brandon, the one she had sent racing off. She couldn't tell whether he recognized her; he seemed too agitated to recognize anything. He pulled at the door, but the tiny hook and eyelet kept it closed. She could refuse him entrance, but he would only rip the door open and there was really no need to ruin it. She took the remaining steps to the screen door and flipped up the hook.

He pulled it open. He was nervous and sweaty, but he managed to speak. "Yeah, run outa gas right here in front of your house."

His right hand was wrapped in gauze. He saw her staring at it and twitched a nervous grin. "Got attacked by a dog this afternoon," he said, holding up his hand so she could get a better look. The gauze had dark spots where the blood had soaked through.

Gerty nodded, and they stood facing one another in silent confrontation. He was sweating, agitated, ready to explode. She could still stop this. She could still exercise her authority and send him running. But to do that would mean disobedience. It would mean using her powers outside of God's will. The temptation wasn't a surprise. She remembered how the Lord himself had been tempted to turn stone into bread, to oppose his Father's will in the garden, to call down legions of angels as he hung on the cross. She thought of Stephen, or the thousands of other martyrs who had gone before her. God could have delivered any one of them—if it had been his will.

With steely determination, she took her eyes off the boy. She turned and headed toward the refrigerator. "Phone's over on the wall," she said. "Can I get you somethin' to drink?"

He gave no answer. She could hear him waiting, preparing to attack.

"Still mighty hot," she continued. "Never seen nothin' like it in all my days." She arrived at the refrigerator, opened it, and reached for the beige Tupperware pitcher of iced tea. She could hear the brush of his clothing as he moved toward her. Without looking, she closed the refrigerator door and crossed to the cupboard for a glass. She'd washed the dishes earlier that afternoon. No sense having others clean up after her. She pulled down a glass, the one with the little sunflowers on the side. She'd had it for years. Won it at the County Fair dime toss.

The boy moved closer. She could hear him breathing now. Short, labored gasps.

She no longer felt fear. Only compassion and pity. Compassion for the boy and pity over what he would have to live with in the years to come. Unless . . .

Maybe she could still help him. Maybe there was still a way to prevent his pain. She poured the iced tea. "So tell me, you ever go to church?" she asked.

No answer.

"Sunday school?" She turned and was startled to see how close he was. His face was wet and his eyes were wide and wild. She thought she saw him nod but wasn't sure. She held out the glass. He looked down at it, confused. Finally he took it.

She moved past him and headed back to put away the pitcher. "Remember how they was always talkin' 'bout Jesus? How he suffered and died on the cross? How he shed his blood for the forgiveness of our sins—for everything you and I ever done wrong?"

Her back was to him again and she heard movement, a shifting of weight. The topic obviously made him uncomfortable. Either him or the multitude that she knew lived inside of him.

"I just want you to know, son, that there's nothing you can do that's too bad for him to forgive. You just remember that. It's never too late to ask his forgiveness, and to let him come in and be your Lord."

She opened the refrigerator door, placed the pitcher back on the top shelf, and closed it. Now she headed toward the table. "'Cause he loves you, son. Don't you ever be forgettin' that. No matter what happens, remember he loves you."

She could hear him approaching, his breath faster, heavier.

"All you got to do is ask."

There was a snapping sound, something being unfastened. Then the sound of steel sliding from leather.

"And I forgive you, too. Remember that. I forgive you, too."

He stood behind her, so close she could feel his ragged breath against her neck. She looked at the ground. She was there. Right where it would happen, right between the refrigerator and table. And she was ready. She had told him the truth, the only truth that mattered, and now she was ready.

She heard the rustle of clothing as he raised his arm and then a faint grunt as his hand flew toward her. She cried out, but not in agony. It was in anticipation. The pain would only be a moment. The joy would be eternal.

"Did you hear him shout?" Frank asked as he leaned over the table toward his two buddies. He scrunched up his face and gave a mournful howl. *"Townies-s-s . . ."*

Del chuckled and Frank broke into his infectious laughter, stopping just long enough to finish off another beer. He turned to the locals who were listening. "It was beautiful, man. A work of art. Ol' Brandon here, this time, he really outdid himself."

Del pushed up his Coke-bottle glasses and nodded as Brandon shook his head in modesty. But Frank was right; it had been a great idea, and they had pulled it off beautifully. Only twenty minutes ago the country club had undergone an attack that would go down in the history books.

Unfortunately, the celebration was short-lived.

"Looks like you've got company," Del said.

Brandon glanced up to see him staring out of the window into the parking lot. Sarah had pulled her Escort alongside his pickup and was climbing out. Part of him leaped at seeing her again. But an equal part was cautious.

His eyes followed her as she crossed to the doors of the pizzeria, threw one open, and entered. He made no effort to get her attention. He figured she would find him soon enough. He was right.

She headed toward his table with obvious determination. By the looks of things, she'd been working all evening, and even though she was disheveled, he still found her very, very attractive.

"Hey, Sarah." Frank raised his glass as she approached.

She ignored him and focused directly upon Brandon. "May I speak to you? Alone."

"They're my friends."

She hesitated, then dragged up a chair to join him. "Okay, have it your way. I just came back from Lori Beth's house."

He didn't like the urgency in her voice and braced himself for more. "So?"

"So, she's dead."

"What?"

"Lori Beth Phillips?" Frank asked in equal surprise.

"She committed suicide. Her teacher had been sexually assaulting her—just like you saw. She couldn't find any way out."

Brandon stared, still trying to digest it.

Sarah continued, just as determined but a little softer. "They're coming true. Lori Beth, the guy at your plant."

"No." He began shaking his head. "It's not—look, I'm finally getting better, all right?"

"Better?" She looked around. "You call hanging around these slackers better?"

Frank, who was definitely feeling the beers, allowed his anger to surface. "Listen, sweetheart, I don't know who you think you are, or what your problem is—"

She ignored him, speaking only to Brandon. "What about Jenny?"

The question hit Brandon almost as hard as the news about Lori Beth.

She persisted. "What about Jenny?"

He finally looked back at her. "That thing wasn't Jenny. It never was." He fought to keep his voice even. "I don't know where she is, I'm sure someplace good. But that thing—that thing was evil."

"Out on the road, didn't it try to save you?"

"Or get me killed."

Sarah leaned forward. That dogged persistence that so infuriated him and that he found so attractive focused directly upon him. "What about Lori Beth? What about your friend's hand? You could have saved them both. You could have—"

"I was in hell!" The outburst surprised them both.

The room grew quiet. He tried to pull back his anger but didn't quite succeed. "I saw the fire, all right? I saw the burning bodies. How can you tell me that's not evil?"

His anger only fueled Sarah's intensity. "But if there's a hell, then there's a heaven. Don't you see? 'Perpendicular Universe,' remember? If there's a below then there's got to be an above. An evil, then a good. If there's a counterfeit, then there's got to be the real thing."

"What about the church?" he insisted. "I've seen that—that thing two different times now. It's just as real, and it's scarier than all of the others combined. And nothing, *nothing's* ever happened there."

Her eyes darted up to him. She took a breath, obviously trying to keep her voice even and in control. "Then I'd say it's just about time, wouldn't you?"

They held each other's gaze. A sinking sensation filled his stomach. She was right. Something was going to happen at the church. Something awful and powerful . . .

He noticed a new look coming over her face. A realization. "Your mother." She spoke more urgently. "Your mother said that the last service in the church—it was tonight. Right? Is that what she said?"

Brandon lowered his eyes.

"Is that right?"

He looked away, somewhere, anywhere but at her. He could hear the wheels turning, knew her next thought.

"Brandon—"

"No."

"But—"

"There's nothing I can do." He turned back to her. "Even if it's true, there's nothing I can do."

"What about that black woman? Gerty? The one with the sketches?"

"No."

"I've got her address, maybe we could go—"

"No."

"Maybe she could help, tell you how—"

"No!"

"We're talking innocent people!"

"Leave me alone! Why can't you just . . ." He turned directly to her now, but already he could feel his anger dissipating. "Why can't you just leave it alone?"

She held his gaze until he had to look away, down at the glass in his hand.

"Brandon, I'm not talking about the experiment now. I don't give a rip about the work. I'm talking about—"

Suddenly Frank had her arm. "All right, sweetheart, you heard the man. I think it's time—"

She wrenched herself free, spilling his beer onto the table. The restaurant grew quiet. She rose to her feet, still speaking to Brandon, who was still staring at his glass.

"You may have been to hell, Brandon. But there's another kind of hell." She paused, waiting. When he didn't respond, she continued. "We've both, you and I, we've both lived there."

He looked up at her, knowing exactly what she was talking about. The hell of his purposelessness. The hell of her driving ambition. Both trapped in the never-ending loop of guilt, and self, and pain.

"I just thought . . ." She took a deep breath. "I was just hoping that you might have wanted out."

He tried to think of something cool to say, something flippant. But there was nothing. She waited one more moment before finally turning and heading for the door.

Her words burned in his ears. Frank was saying something, but Brandon didn't hear. He watched as she walked outside, climbed into her car, and tried to start it. But it wouldn't kick over. He could hear it grind and grind but with no success. She grabbed the papers from the front seat and threw open her door.

He lowered his head, preparing for another onslaught. But she didn't come back in. Instead, he suddenly heard his own truck roar to life. He looked up just in time to see the headlights blaze on.

"Hey!" Del shouted. "She's got your truck!"

She found reverse and pulled out.

"She's got your truck!" Del repeated as he leaped to his feet and started for the door. "She's got your truck!"

Brandon rose as Sarah threw his pickup into gear, stomped on the accelerator, and fishtailed onto the main road.

CHAPTER 14

Sarah clung to the pickup's steering wheel with one hand while trying to unfold the map with the other. She knew Gerty Morrison lived on Sycamore. The address suggested that it was a mile or so outside of town, probably past the gravel pit. But she needed to check the map to be sure.

Blinding lights suddenly appeared around the bend, letting her know that she had drifted into the wrong lane. She grabbed the wheel with both hands and swerved back as the passing car blasted its horn in anger.

Sarah blew the hair out of her eyes and again reached for the map. If Brandon's precognitive skills were as accurate as they had been in the past, then something was about to happen at the church. Something dramatic, terrible—and, since this was the final service in the church, it would probably be tonight. There was nothing Sarah could do to stop it, but if this Gerty had had a similar premonition, if she had some sense of what was about to occur . . .

Sarah glanced at the speedometer. She was doing nearly seventy. She let up some, but not much.

The curfew tolls the knell of parting day,
The lowing herd wind slowly o'er the lea,
The plowman homeward plods his weary way,
And leaves the world to darkness and to me.

Momma sat in the front pew, keeping her eyes fixed on the Reverend as he recited another one of his favorite poems. The farewell service was more difficult for her than she had anticipated. But it would be her final act as the church's cofounder, and then it would be over.

Now fades the glimmering landscape on the sight,
And all the air a solemn stillness holds,
Save where the beetle wheels his droning flight,
And drowsy tinklings lull the distant folds.

She turned to steal a glance back at the rest of the church. She was pleased to see so many folks. This was the end of nearly twenty-five years of hard work and tradition, and it brought out some of the dearest and best. Leaders of the religious community, like Reverend Jacobsen over there from the Lutheran church, Father Penney, Pastor Burnett, Pastor Smith, even Rabbi Cohen—none of them to gloat over another church's failure but to bid it a fond farewell.

There were only a handful from this church. That's all that ever attended now. In its heyday, before her husband's stroke, they'd had nearly four hundred members. They'd even had to go to two services. But that had been a long, long time ago.

Save that from yonder ivy-mantled tower
The moping owl does to the moon complain
Of such as, wand'ring near her secret bower,
Molest her ancient solitary reign.

Momma turned back to face the front, but not before glancing at her husband. She was grateful that he couldn't comprehend what was happening, that he didn't understand what had become of all their hard work, of the promises and prayers that had never been fulfilled.

> Beneath those rugged elms, that yew tree's shade,
> Where heaves the turf in many a mold'ring heap,
> Each in his narrow cell forever laid,
> The rude forefathers of the hamlet sleep.

Henderson turned the Firebird onto SR 15 and headed north. He and Reggie had started out searching the major roads, but if they had to, they would work their way down to the smaller streets and avenues. The guy had to be out there somewhere. The half ton with the broken running light was out there, and they would find it. If they had to travel every highway and back road in Kosciusko County, they would find it.

It was more cottage than house, and even at night Sarah could tell that it hadn't seen a paintbrush in years. A faint light shone from somewhere deep inside, nearly obscured by the drawn shades, dirty windows, and overgrown shrubs.

Sarah stepped out of the pickup and into the warm night air. She was struck by the sudden silence. She figured much of it was due to the surrounding woods and thick vegetation. Even the perpetual hum of Highway 30 was dulled and absorbed by the jungle of maples, mulberries, and sprawling junipers. At one time it must have all been very picturesque and parklike; now it was a jungle that seemed on the verge of swallowing up the entire house.

She waded through the knee-high grass along what she thought to be a walkway. At the front porch, she carefully made her way up the stairs and knocked loudly on the blistered door.

There was no answer.

She tried again. "Hello," she called. "Gerty? Gerty Morrison?"

Strange. There was a light on inside and two cars parked in the driveway.

She knocked again. "Hello?"

She pushed at the door. It was locked. She moved to the nearest window and tried to peek inside. The pulled shade blocked her view, but she could tell the light was coming from somewhere in the back. She turned, made her way down the porch, and walked around the house. For a second she thought she caught movement inside, the flicker of a shadow. But it was gone before she could be sure.

From the rear of the house, the light was clearly visible. It came from the kitchen. The back door was open, and the light spilled from the kitchen through the screen door and onto the porch.

Not wanting to scare the old lady, Sarah called from the yard. "Hello? Mrs. Morrison?"

She walked up the weathered steps to the screen door. "Hello." Through the screen she could see the kitchen counter. Off to the right was a table cluttered with papers. She reached out and knocked on the door. It bounced and clattered, apparently unlatched. Her instincts told her to stop, that something wasn't right. Still, she had come this far.

She pulled on the door. It opened with a low squeak. "Hello, Mrs. Morrison? Anybody home?"

She took a tentative step inside and let the door close against her back.

The table was stacked with papers, but the rest of the kitchen was as neat as a pin—except for a recent spill on the floor between the refrigerator and the table. It still glistened with moisture and was a little smeared, as if someone had hastily tried to wipe it up. She knelt for a better look. The best she could figure in the poor light, it was some sort of juice, probably grape. She felt no inclination to touch it.

She rose to her feet and looked around. Now that she was nearer to the table, the clutter appeared more organized. She stepped closer. In the very center lay an open Bible. On either side, carefully arranged, were stacks of papers. On the left side were handwritten letters; on the other were sketches like the ones Brandon had given her. She moved closer. The sketches were not of Brandon as a child. They were of the older Brandon—the one in the burlap robe who stood inside some ancient walled city.

Sarah picked up the pile and examined the top one. In many ways it was identical to what she had seen at the Institute. But instead of fire coming from his mouth, this sketch showed Brandon looking toward the heavens with an expression of fear and apprehension.

She pulled it aside to look at the next. It was at the same location, but now Brandon had a companion, dressed in a similar coarse robe. Although the companion's back was to her, Sarah guessed him to be a boy because of his slighter build and shortly cropped hair. He had one arm outstretched as if confronting some unseen force. In the other hand he held a lamp, exactly like the one in the sketch at the Institute—exactly like the one Brandon had described from his dreams and visions.

She turned to the next drawing. Same city, but this time the horizon was filled with a vaporous, monstrous head covered in horns and peering down upon Brandon and his companion. Now Brandon was the one holding the lamp, and now—

Suddenly Sarah went cold.

In this sketch Brandon's companion had turned to look directly at the viewer. The face was drawn in careful detail. Sarah bit her lip and closed her eyes. But when she reopened them, nothing had changed. She felt her head growing light and leaned against the table for support. It wasn't a boy standing beside Brandon. It was a woman. A woman with a jagged scar across her forehead that ran down her cheek. Other than the short cropped hair and the jagged scar, the woman looked exactly like her. Exactly like Sarah Weintraub.

Sarah took a deep breath to steady herself, but it did no good. What type of hoax was this? She looked back at the table, at the pile of letters, then at the Bible. It was opened, and a large portion of one page was underlined. Like the sketches and letters, it seemed to be carefully laid out, on display, as if waiting for someone to find it.

She picked up the book and noticed her hands were trembling. She began to read. Her lips moved inaudibly. Color slowly drained from her face as her mind began to whirl. These words, what they were saying . . . but it was impossible . . . And yet, there they were, clearly written and making perfect sense.

She read them a second time. Her trembling grew worse as unfathomable thoughts rose and surfaced. When she had finished, she slowly lowered the book. That's when she saw him.

He'd been standing in the shadows of the living room. For how long, she didn't know. Realizing that he'd been spotted, he moved into the light. She recognized him immediately. He was the attacker from the lab—same short hair, same ragged goatee, same wild look in his eyes.

She recalled that it was always best to talk to an assailant, to make human contact. They were less likely to attack if they made a personal connection. "Where—" Her voice was shaky. She stopped, took a breath, and tried again. "Where is she?"

He gave no answer.

"Gerty Morrison? Is she here?"

He leaned forward, squinting, as if trying to hear what she was saying.

She spoke louder. "Where is the woman who lives here?"

He looked at her, still not comprehending. His mouth had begun to quiver, then twitch. Finally it exploded with the words she had heard before:

"You're the one, you're not the one!"

She took a half step back, bumping into the table.

"You're the one, you're not the one!"

His eyes darted to the pile of drawings. She followed his gaze. He was staring at the one of Brandon and her as they stood inside the walled city.

"You're the one, you're not the one!"

Her head reeled. "I don't under—do you know what any of this means?"

He frowned, but not at her question; it was at something else, something in his head. His face twisted, contorted. Suddenly he leaned over and gasped in pain.

"Are you all right?"

He groaned, almost mournfully. "You *are* the one."

He ran a shaky hand over his face to wipe off the sweat, and then righted himself. That's when she saw the reflected light in the other hand. It was a large hunting knife.

He saw her eye it and raised the knife into view, grinning, relishing the look of fear it brought to her face.

Still feeling the table against her back, Sarah began to inch her way along its edge. He was going to attack, she was certain. And if she got just a little closer to the back door she might be able to run for it.

He wiped his face again. His eyes darting in all directions, growing wilder.

She had to stall him, to keep him occupied, at least until she got closer to the door. "How did you know?" she asked.

He scowled.

"That I'm the one."

He cocked his head again, as if preoccupied, as if listening to something else.

Then Sarah made a mistake—she glanced at the door. He saw it. Swearing, he lunged for her. She tried to get away, but she didn't have a chance. He was too fast. She saw the knife coming at her, toward her chest. Instinctively, she brought up her hand to defend herself, expecting to feel the burning pain of the blade. But instead to her surprise the knife hit the Bible she'd been holding.

She dropped the book and tried to run, but he grabbed her arm. She swung it hard and tore free, stumbling toward the door, but he threw himself at her, catching her at the waist and bringing them both down to the floor. She was all fists and knees and feet, flailing and kicking, but blindly, barely landing a blow. She finally brought her knee into him, hard enough to make him gasp, allowing her to break free. She scrambled for the door on her hands and knees, but he caught her leg. She screamed and tried to kick free, but he hung on.

"You are the one," he gasped, "you are not the one."

She squirmed and kicked, but he hung on, moving up her legs, fighting to grab her swinging arms.

"You are the one."

She landed a powerful blow to his face, and for a second it looked as if some sanity had returned to him. But only for a second. Instantly it was replaced by the sneering grin. She fought and kicked, but he climbed to her chest now, pinning her shoulders to the ground. That's when the knife reappeared.

Sarah fought and squirmed for all she was worth, but there was no way to move. He was breathing so hard he could barely speak. Sweat fell from his face and splattered onto her neck.

With one hand he grabbed the back of her hair, pulling her head to the ground, exposing more of her throat. With the other, he shoved the blade against her jugular. Sarah looked at him, wide-eyed.

His mouth was open, gasping for air, preparing for another explosion of violence, when suddenly—

"Hello, Lewis."

His head jerked up.

Unable to move, Sarah strained to see Reichner standing at the screen door.

"She's the one," Lewis panted. Sarah felt the blade press harder against her neck. "She's the one, but she's not the one!"

Reichner's voice remained calm and controlled. "I don't think so, Lewis." It was the same voice he used with his subjects during the lab sessions.

"The pictures," Lewis gasped, motioning toward the table.

Reichner opened the door and strolled toward them, slow and deliberate. "She is not the one, Lewis. You know that."

Lewis looked down at her. More sweat fell from his nose and chin. He adjusted his weight but kept the knife firmly against her throat.

"But . . . she's the one, she's—"

"Lewis, Lewis, Lewis." Reichner shook his head. "*You* are the one, you know that. You have always been the one."

She felt the kid catch his breath. Again he adjusted his weight, then looked down at her and frowned in confusion. "But the pictures, the—"

Reichner stood four feet from them now. "It is you, Lewis. Listen to the voices."

Sarah felt the pressure of the knife lessen slightly.

"You are the one, you have always been the one."

Pain crossed the boy's face. "Yes . . . no. Me, I'm the—"

"Where is the old woman, Lewis?"

A scowl crossed the boy's face as if he was trying to remember.

"The one who lives here. Where is she, Lewis?"

"The back. Hall closet. I put her in the—"

"Did you kill her, Lewis?"

The blade left Sarah's throat and he sat up, his weight still heavy on her chest. She wanted to roll him off, to slide away, but Reichner was playing the kid now and it was important that she didn't interfere.

"Did you kill her, Lewis?"

"I . . . I don't—"

"Do not lie to me, Lewis. You know that I know. I always know, don't I?"

Lewis stared at him, transfixed. Reichner's voice was smooth and calm. "You killed someone, didn't you? You killed someone and not the one."

Sarah felt Lewis's body shudder.

"And the one—that is whom you are supposed to kill. That is the one the voices want, isn't it?"

Lewis slowly nodded.

"Not some old woman, not some beautiful girl."

The kid fidgeted—confused, distracted. Part of him seemed to be listening to Reichner, another part hearing something deep in his own head.

"That is what you want, Lewis. To kill the one. That is what your voices really want."

Lewis winced, trying to hear, trying to clear his mind. Reichner took a half-step closer, then quietly knelt down to his level.

"Listen to your voices, Lewis. Listen very carefully."

The anguish on the boy's face increased.

"They want to kill the one."

"But . . ." Lewis's voice was weaker.

"And that is you, Lewis."

Sarah's eyes darted to Reichner. What was he saying?

"You are the one. They want to kill the one, Lewis, and you are the one. Listen to your voices, Lewis. Let them have their way."

The kid continued to stare, mesmerized, almost nodding in agreement, until suddenly he shook his head. "No!"

Reichner's voice continued, softly. "Yes, Lewis, listen to your voices. You are the one. You have known it all along. You are the one. And the one is whom you must kill."

"Doctor," Sarah whispered, but he paid no attention.

"Close your eyes, Lewis."

The kid hesitated. "It's okay, just close your eyes for a moment. They are so heavy, just close your eyes and listen, listen to your voices. Just for a moment . . ."

The boy's lids fluttered, then lowered.

"That is good, Lewis. Very good."

Sarah watched in fear and awe.

Reichner dropped his voice to an intimate whisper. "You are the one, Lewis. You have always been the one. You are the one who must be killed. You are the one the voices must kill."

"Doctor," Sarah protested. But Reichner stared so intently at the boy that she doubted he heard her. "Just have him drop the knife," she whispered.

"You must obey the voices," Reichner continued.

Eyes still shut, Lewis began to nod.

"Dr. Reichner, you can't—"

"Do it, Lewis. Obey the voices."

"Doc—"

"Now, Lewis." His voice became more insistent. "Obey the voices, now."

"Dr. Reichner!" But neither Reichner nor Lewis heard.

"You are the one who must be destroyed. Do it. Do it now, Lewis!"

The boy rose to his knees. Taking advantage of the movement, Sarah immediately slid out from under him and scrambled to her hands and knees. The boy remained transfixed, continuing to nod his head, his entire body beginning to rock under the movement. Silently, he turned the knife around, until the blade was facing himself.

"Dr. Reichner!" Sarah shouted.

"Do it, Lewis, do it now. Obey your voices."

The boy placed it against his chest, directly over his heart.

"Stop it," Sarah protested. "He's going to—"

"That is right, Lewis. Now."

"Stop it! Stop—"

"Now, Lewis!"

Sarah reached out and grabbed Reichner's arm. "Stop it!"

"Now!"

The boy drove the knife hard between his ribs.

Sarah screamed.

Lewis's eyes exploded with pain and realization.

"You're crazy!" Sarah yelled. "Look what you've done, look what you've done!"

But Reichner was too immersed in the victory to hear. "That is good, Lewis. You did well. Very well."

The boy slowly looked at him.

"The voices are proud of you, Lewis. They will be leaving you now, and you will never have to hear them again. Never again."

Sarah moved to try and help the boy, but Reichner's arm shot out and pushed her away. She turned to him, stunned, then to the boy who was looking down at the wound in his chest, the spreading blood on his shirt, his hands. Reichner reached out his hand and set it on top of the boy's head—a blessing, a benediction. "Good, Lewis. You have always been good."

Lewis looked up at him.

"And you will always be the one. Always."

A smile spread across the boy's face. The expression slowly froze, and then he toppled to the floor.

CHAPTER 15

Y ou . . ." Sarah's voice was hoarse, just above a whisper. "You killed him."

Without looking at her, Reichner rose calmly to his feet. "It was necessary to save your life."

She could only stare at him. "Not like that. He didn't have to kill himself. Not like that."

Reichner said nothing. He turned his back to her and moved toward the kitchen table.

Sarah looked down at the boy. "You killed him. You didn't have to, but you . . ."

Reichner picked up the sketches on the table and casually flipped through them. "He killed once. How did we know he would not do it again?"

Sarah slowly turned to him.

Reichner shrugged. "It was a murder/suicide. That's what it was, and that's what we will tell the police."

Sarah rose unsteadily to her feet. "But it's—it's not true."

"It is true enough for our purposes."

Revulsion stirred deep inside her. "*Our* purposes?"

He ignored her, pointing to the first sketch. "Interesting likeness."

"It's true enough *for our purposes?*" she repeated

"The boy was trying to kill you, Dr. Weintraub. And when he was through with you, he would have gone after your boyfriend here."

Sarah glanced at the sketch in his hand, angry, confused. "What?"

"'You're the one, you're not the one.'"

"Does that makes sense to you?"

He brought the sketch closer to his face for examination. "Not entirely. But if this artist's precognitive skills are anywhere near Brandon's, it appears that you may very well be assisting him in the years to come." He glanced up at her with half a grin. "That is to say, *we* will be assisting him."

Sarah stared at him.

"He is 'the one,' whatever that means—no doubt somebody of great psychic ability. And you and I, we will be by his side, we will be there observing his every experience, recording his every encounter." He looked back at the sketch, the slightest trace of wonder filling his voice. "Imagine the possibilities, the discoveries waiting to be made."

Sarah's revulsion grew. How could he be so callous? She looked back down at Lewis's body. The corpse of the boy he had killed wasn't even cold, and he was already making plans for the future. What type of creature was this?

"Don't look so shocked, Doctor."

Her eyes shot back to him.

"I was merely protecting our interests. If I did not stop Lewis now, he would have been an obstruction, perhaps even trying to destroy our work."

Sarah stared, trying to grasp all he was saying, sickened at what she understood. She spotted the Bible on the floor and moved to pick it up. There was a deep gash on the front cover where it had saved her from the knife.

Reichner continued examining the sketches. "We are on our way, my friend. What is the saying about the goose who laid the golden egg? We have found that goose, Dr. Weintraub, and now we must be very careful to protect him. At any cost."

She looked back at Reichner, her anger growing.

Reichner smiled at her and tapped the picture. "He is 'the one.'"

"How dare you." Her voice was low and trembling.

Reichner chuckled. "Dr. Weintraub—"

"You killed this poor boy just so—"

"He killed himself."

"—just so you can continue your experiments?"

"*Our* experiments, Doctor. And, as I have pointed out, he would have no doubt tried to destroy your young man."

"How can you be so cold-blooded, so—"

"We are on the verge of a major breakthrough, Doctor. Your boy has crossed Threshold and has returned. He can do it again—anytime he wills, I suspect. You saw the findings, the PET scan, the Ganzfield. And that is only the beginning. With his powers, and our tutelage, there may be no end to the progress we—"

He looked at her and came to a stop. She knew her face showed her disgust, but she no longer cared.

He smiled. "Come, come, Doctor. Don't play pious with me."

She stared at him.

"We are cut from the same cloth, you and I. This we both know."

Instinctively she pulled the Bible into herself, bracing for more.

"We are people of ambition. That is how we are wired. Your ambition is no less than mine. Nor should it be. You are young, with many years ahead of you. And if this sketch is true, if indeed, this boy is 'the one,' there may be no end to our discoveries and advancements."

The words sounded strangely familiar, but she couldn't place them. Her head was starting to hurt. She glanced back down at Lewis. She was numb and sickened. And yet she continued to listen.

"You could be the next Newton, Galileo—think of it. You, a Salk, an Einstein. That is heady company, Sarah Weintraub."

"Please." Her voice was thin. "Stop it."

"A Nobel prize *would* be nice. Not to mention the world acclaim. Think of the—"

"Stop."

"Greatness is nothing to be ashamed of."

Sarah took half a step back. She knew what he was doing. His words both excited and disgusted her. And still he continued. And still she listened.

"Think of the millions, of the billions you will be able to help. Your name will be synonymous with hope and encouragement, with the most important break-throughs of our generation. You will be—"

"Stop it," she demanded. "Stop it now!"

He took a step toward her.

"Sarah." He smiled again. "It is true. We are cut from the same cloth."

She tried to look away but could not.

"Any mistakes of the past will be forgotten. You have your whole future ahead of you."

Now at last she recognized the words. They were Samuel's. And that boy—she looked down at the body. That could just as well have been her baby, or Brandon, or—

"You're disgusting," she seethed, but she knew her words were spoken more out of desperation than conviction.

Reichner's smile increased. "As are you, my dear. That is the price we must pay for our greatness."

Again he held her eyes, and again she could not look away.

"There is nothing wrong with ambition, Sarah. Not if it means changing the world. Not if it means exonerating us from past mistakes, absolving us from—"

"Leave me alone!" She was slipping, and they both knew it.

"That is the glory of greatness."

Her eyes shot around the room.

"To be remembered only for our good."

She had to make him quit. The door. She had to get away.

"Everything else will be forgotten. Only our—"

She broke for the door, threw it open, and bolted down the porch stairs, running for the pickup. Reichner's heavy footsteps followed. She didn't look back.

"We are cut from the same cloth!" the voice called. "You and I, we are one and the same!"

Sarah flung open the pickup's door, threw the Bible onto the seat, and crawled inside. Quickly, she fired up the engine. She could no longer hear Reichner's words, but their truth, or her fear of their truth, echoed inside her head. She had to get away. She had made it this far, she had to keep going.

"And I still remember those early years when Pastor Martus and I rolled up our sleeves and worked together to create the Kosciusko County Food Co-op."

318

Rabbi Cohen, a short bald man with a stately presence, stood at the front of the church, near Momma and her husband. Like the clergy before him, he was paying special tribute to both the church and its founders.

"We put some long hours in, my friend." Then with a twinkle, he grinned. "Not always in agreement, mind you. But the fruit of our labors has been well worth it." He smiled at Momma and momentarily rested his hand on her husband's shoulder. "And for that I count it a privilege both to have known you and to have served with you." He gave the man a pat on the shoulder and turned to head back to his seat.

Momma stole another look at her husband. During the past several minutes, as leader after leader shared their memories and spoke their praise, it had taken all of her Southern steel to hold back the tears. Still, as grateful as she was for their kindness, part of her resented how their praise was beginning to sound less and less like a tribute and more and more like a eulogy.

The Firebird slid around a corner and headed up Center Street. Inside, the CD throbbed with another raw and angry group that kept Henderson's adrenaline pumping. It had been ninety minutes since the attack on his car. They'd been down a dozen roads and still hadn't seen a sign of the pickup.

Now they were heading back into town by way of Eddie's Pizzeria. It was a favorite hangout of the Townies. In fact, Reggie was certain that he'd seen the pickup there before. Henderson slowed as they passed the parking strip in front. It held a couple of vans, a beater Mustang, a rusted-out Land Cruiser, and an old blue Escort. No sign of the pickup.

Henderson gunned it and they sped down the road into town. He reached for the CD and cranked it up.

They'd find him. If it took all night, they'd find him.

Inside the pizzeria, Frank called to Brandon. "Come on, ol' buddy, loosen up. This is a celebration, remember?"

Brandon forced a grin and raised his glass. With all the trouble the guys were going to, to cheer him up, the least he could do was pretend to have fun.

But his uneasiness continued. Sarah's words kept haunting him, as did his thoughts about the church. Something wasn't right. And the more time passed, the more un-right it became.

Sarah raced through town, heading back to the pizzeria. She had to tell Brandon what had happened, what was going on. She had to make him see that the stakes were far higher than either of them had thought. She glanced at the Bible on the front seat. It was no longer possible for Brandon Martus to be a passive observer.

The Firebird had just crested a small knoll when Reggie pointed through the windshield. "There he is!"

Henderson peered ahead. Sure enough, above the headlights of the approaching vehicle he could see the telltale broken running light. He pressed down on the accelerator and popped on his high beams.

Back inside the pickup, Sarah squinted at the brightness. It took a moment to find the high beams and give the approaching car a courtesy flash.

Brandon looked up. What was that sound? Where was it coming from? He glanced at the others at his table. Frank, Del—no one seemed to notice. But it was growing louder. Some sort of roar. A car. More than one. And music. Loud and driving. Nothing like the country-western coming from the nearby jukebox.

Sarah flashed her high beams again. But the oncoming car didn't respond. She flashed them a third time.

From the passenger seat of the Firebird, Reggie yelled, "What's he doing?"

"I don't know," Henderson shouted, "but it's not going to work."

Brandon gave a start when Frank slapped him on the back. He turned to see him talking—something about picking up girls, but he couldn't make out the words. Frank's mouth moved and he was speaking, but from another world—his voice was no longer discernible above the roar of engines and the pounding music.

The high beams were blinding, and Sarah had to keep her eyes low and to the right side of the road.

Henderson's grin broadened. Any second now, they would begin the game. Both he and the pickup knew the rules; they'd been clearly established. And he would play them perfectly. Only this time he would not back down. Maybe parking the car in the middle of the road the other night had been a little underhanded. Maybe he had deserved the equally cowardly attack of golf balls. But not this time. This time, he would win fair and square.

Sarah raised her left hand, shielding her eyes from the blinding brightness.

Henderson drummed his thumbs on the wheel to the beat of the music. It was time. He swerved the Firebird into the pickup's lane.

Brandon's eyes shot around the restaurant. Everyone was having a good time. Del was laughing, Frank was flirting with a couple of girls. But Brandon heard only the roar of engines and the swelling, pounding music. He took another gulp of his drink, trying to relax, to force the sounds away.

They only grew louder.

Sarah's heart pounded. The car was in her lane, coming directly at her, high beams blazing. She swerved to the left.

So did the car. *What was he doing?*

Back in the Firebird, Henderson clenched his jaw. It was up to the pickup to make the move, to back down. Not Henderson—the pickup. And he'd better make it now.

Sarah panicked, unsure what to do. Left? Right? Which way would this car turn?

Back in the Firebird, Henderson's eyes suddenly widened in surprise. For a split second his lights lit up the pickup's cab. Those weren't Townies inside but a woman. He swerved back into the other lane . . .

Just as Sarah made a similar move.

Their fenders caught. Red fiberglass collapsed into rusted steel—hoods crumpled, frames twisted. And glass. Everywhere there was flying glass. The air bags in the boys' car exploded open and their seat belts locked into place.

Sarah wasn't so lucky. She flew forward, screaming . . .

Brandon heard the explosion of metal and shattering glass. For the briefest second he saw Sarah's face—exactly as he had seen it in his dream—her terrified expression as she flew into his windshield. Her mouth opened in a scream, but a scream she would never finish.

Brandon leaped to his feet crying, "Sarah!"

Hark! a thrilling voice is sounding:
"Christ is nigh," it seems to say;
"Cast away the works of darkness,
O ye children of the day."

It was an old hymn. Momma knew that the Reverend had chosen it especially for her—because of the memories. It was one they'd sung in the old days, when the church was first starting out, when they were so full of hope and expectation.

So when next he comes with glory,
And the world is wrapped in fear,
May he with his mercy shield us,
And with words of love draw near.

Sarah!
Momma froze at the sound of her son's cry. She turned and scanned the sanctuary, but he wasn't there. All she saw were the townsfolk standing and singing. Some looked back at her, smiling, but no one had heard what she had heard.

Yet that had been her son crying out. She was certain of it.

She looked back up at the Reverend, who smiled down warmly upon her. She hesitated, then closed her hymnal and stepped past her husband into the aisle. Trying to draw as little attention as possible, she quietly headed up the aisle toward the exit.

Brandon threw open the doors to the pizzeria. He heard Frank shouting something, but didn't stop to listen. He sprinted toward town. He had no idea where he was going or what had happened. He knew only that Sarah needed him, and she needed him now.

Momma reached the church steps. Outside, a slight wind had picked up. She felt compelled to turn to the right. She followed the instinct, heading down the steps, and turning onto the sidewalk.

Brandon continued to sprint. He didn't have the endurance to keep up this pace forever, but he'd go as far as he could.

Momma had traveled barely a block when she heard the neighborhood dogs start to howl—and moments later the sound of an approaching siren.

Brandon's lungs began to burn. And still he pushed himself. He had sprinted nearly half a mile, and he was definitely feeling it. His throat was on fire and his legs were growing weak. Up ahead rose a small hill. He started the ascent and was about to slow his pace when he caught a glimpse of red and orange lights flashing against the upper-story windows.

"Sarah!"

He pushed harder, the rushing air cutting a groove into his throat, his legs slowly turning to rubber.

He crested the knoll. At the bottom was an EMS vehicle and a small crowd. Behind them, illuminated by the flashing lights, were two other vehicles, both crushed and twisted. He flew down the hill, barely able to control his legs, trying to convince himself that neither of those vehicles was his pickup.

As he approached the EMS truck he could see Henderson was being eased down onto the curb by a paramedic. He looked shaken, but other than some cuts and an injury to his right arm, he appeared okay.

Brandon arrived, gasping for breath. "Where—where is she?"

Henderson looked up, startled. He tried to rise to face Brandon, but the paramedic forced him to stay down.

"Where is she?" Brandon demanded.

"I didn't know it was her." Henderson's eyes were red, his cheeks still wet from crying. "I swear to God, I thought you were driving. I thought you were—"

Brandon turned from him and headed toward the crowd, toward the center of activity. He pushed his way through the onlookers until he saw another paramedic. The man was huddled over a body on the street. Heart pounding, fearing the worst, Brandon approached. At first the body's face was blocked from his view. Then the paramedic shifted and Brandon saw her. The blood and open wound made it difficult to recognize her, but he knew it was Sarah.

Brandon's throat tightened. He hurried the last steps as the paramedic pressed a blood-soaked gauze against a gash that ran across Sarah's forehead and down her cheek. Brandon knelt. "Sarah." His voice was swollen with emotion. "I didn't . . ." He searched for the words. "I'm sorry . . ."

Through his tears, he could see the lid of her good eye start to move. Finally it opened. It took a moment to focus. When she spotted him, she tried to smile, but with little success. Ever so slowly, her lips parted, then closed, then parted again. She was attempting to speak.

A gurney rattled beside them as the other paramedic arrived and quickly lowered it.

She continued moving her lips. Brandon leaned forward, concentrating until he finally made out the broken, raspy words: "It's . . . you . . ."

He nodded, fighting back the ache in his chest. "Yes, I'm here. I won't leave."

She frowned and tried to shake her head.

"Please," one of the paramedics ordered, "give us some room here."

Brandon pulled back as the first paramedic called to his partner. "On my count. One, two, three." In one swift move they transferred Sarah from the ground to the gurney. They elevated the gurney to waist level and prepared to wheel it toward the EMS vehicle. Brandon saw that Sarah was still trying to speak. Again he leaned forward.

"Revelation eleven," she whispered hoarsely. "It's . . . you."

"Please step back." The warning was severe as the paramedics pushed past Brandon and rolled Sarah toward the ambulance. He stayed as close to her side as possible until they arrived at the back and lifted her in. For the briefest second her eyes found his. Then they slid her inside, closed the door, and she was gone.

Brandon stood motionless in the flashing lights. His mind raced in every direction, but he understood nothing. The wind was much stronger as it whipped at his shirt and blew his hair, but he barely noticed. The vehicle pulled from the curb and started its siren. Brandon watched as it headed down the street and disappeared from sight.

Unsure what to do or where to go, he turned toward his pickup. It lay twenty feet away, a crumpled piece of steel and broken glass. Slowly, numbly, he started toward it. People continued to mill about, but he paid no attention. He arrived and stood silently at what had been the right front fender. It was peeled up and back—much of it shoved into the front seat. It was amazing that Sarah had not been killed instantly.

He walked beside the wreck, slowly running his hand over the twisted metal, hearing the broken glass pop and crunch under his feet. At the passenger's door, he looked inside. More glass, as well as crushed dashboard and torn upholstery. He glanced to the portion of floorboard still visible. There in plain view lay a Bible.

He frowned. He reached inside, careful to avoid the sharp and ragged metal. He took hold of the book and cautiously fished it out. His heart had started to pound again, and he was breathing a little more heavily. "Revelation eleven." That's what she'd said. But it had made no sense. He knew, of course, that there was a Revelation in the Bible, the last book. Could that have been what she meant? No, it was an absurd thought. And yet . . . what was she doing with a Bible in his truck? No, it was too crazy.

So why was he afraid to open it and see?

He held the book in his hands, working up his courage, before finally opening the cover. The wind flipped and snapped at the pages.

"Revelation eleven." He turned to the back of the book and noticed his hands shaking. The wind blew harder against the pages, but he kept them open with his hand as he ran down the verses—two, three, four . . .

He stopped cold. He moved back to the third verse, then began to read out loud, his voice low, barely above a whisper.

"And I will grant authority to my two witnesses, and they will prophesy for 1,260 days clothed in sackcloth."

He gulped air in and continued reading.

"These are the two olive trees and the two lampstands that stand before the Lord of the earth."

His head grew light. *Lampstands? Olive trees?* He was beginning to feel cold. Still he continued.

"If anyone desires to hurt them, fire proceeds out of their mouth and devours their enemies."

He closed his eyes, trying to understand, remembering all too well the fire that had escaped from his mouth during the encounter outside the church. He reopened his eyes.

"These have the power to shut up the sky in order that rain may not fall during the days of their prophesying; and they have power over the waters to turn them into blood . . ."

Images of the drought and the three-tiered water fountain came to mind. He was hyperventilating now, breathing hard but still unable to get enough air. He lowered the book. He could read no further. He now understood what Sarah had meant, and he was very cold and very frightened.

Then, from behind, he heard his mother's voice, as she continued to softly quote:

"And when they have finished their testimony, the beast that comes out of the abyss will make war with them and overcome them and kill them."

Brandon spun around. The wind blew her hair as she continued to recite the Scripture from memory.

"And those who dwell on the earth will rejoice over their dead bodies and make merry; and they will send gifts to one another, because these two prophets tormented those who dwell on the earth."

Brandon swallowed. When he finally found his voice, it was afraid and angry. "Why—why didn't you tell me?"

"I wasn't . . ." He could barely hear her over the wind. "I wasn't sure."

He took a step back from her. He had to get out of there. But where? He stepped toward her again, then turned away. He began to pace, struggling, trying to make it make sense.

"Brandon," Momma shouted over the wind. He heard her but would not look at her. "It doesn't have to be you. Someone else will be chosen. You can refuse it."

He spun back to her, staring. What was she saying?

"It doesn't have to be you," she repeated. "You don't have to be the one!"

He opened his mouth but could find no words.

"It's true," she shouted. "You don't have to be the one. You don't have to be anything, if you don't want. We always have a choice. You don't have to be anything at all. Nothing at all."

The phrase struck him to the heart. Had she any idea what she'd just said? Did she know that this was the very issue he'd been battling with? He took another step away from her, and then another. But she continued to plead, driving the stake in deeper.

"We can live like we've always lived. You don't have to be the one, you don't have to be anybody. I can take care of you, it can be just like it's always—"

Brandon grabbed his head, trying to make her stop, trying to make it all stop.

She moved closer. "Sweetheart, you don't have to get involved. We can go somewhere else. We can—"

Suddenly she quit talking. A low rumbling had filled the air. It rattled the windows behind them, shook the ground at their feet. But it wasn't an earthquake. It was an eerie resonance, a deep moaning that rapidly grew in intensity. Brandon turned, searching, making sure it wasn't his imagination. But other people had noticed it, too. Some pointed, others stared. He followed their gaze up the street and to the left. There, eight, maybe nine blocks away, hovering in the sky, a dark, swirling cloud was forming—a cloud exactly like he'd seen in his visions. As it condensed, it slowly approached the earth. And, although he couldn't see the source, he saw that its bottom surface was reflecting light that could only be from—

"The church!" He turned back to his mother and shouted. "It's the church!"

"Brandon!"

He turned and started down the street, first at a trot, then at a run.

"Brandon!" Momma called. "It doesn't have to be you. Brandon! Don't leave. You're all I have left! You're all I have! Brandon, don't leave me. Don't leave me!"

CHAPTER 16

The gurney wheels chattered as the paramedics hustled the unconscious Sarah down the emergency hallway of St. John's Hospital. They were already running an IV of Lactated Ringers into her right arm. Sterile gauze was pressed firmly against the cut on her face.

A nearby elevator rattled open and the on-call surgeon, a Dr. Hibdon, joined them as they continued down the hall. He was an older man, tall and lean, with unruly puffs of gray hair sticking out from both temples. "What do we have?" he asked.

"Compound and depressed skull fractures, fracture of the right clavicle, severe facial laceration." The first paramedic ran down the list. "BP increasing, pulse and respiration depressed."

The doctor pulled a penlight from his shirt pocket and, as they continued moving down the hall, opened her left eye. "Left pupil mid-position and unresponsive." He glanced up at a nurse who had just entered through the swinging doors. "Start eighty milligrams of Manatol. I want a CT scan and then I want her prepped. Stat."

The nurse nodded as the doctor peeled off from the gurney to enter the scrub room.

Explosions pounded the air, one after another. Brandon watched as he ran, but the bottom of the cloud was now obscured by tossing and blowing trees. He bore down harder until he rounded the final corner—just in time to see the last of the church windows blow out. Glass flew in all directions, and piercing light blazed from each of the openings. The wind was gale force, whipping and bending the trees, throwing all manner of dirt and debris into the air. Directly above the church, the black cloud's swirling vortex drew closer and closer to the steeple. By now even the bravest of onlookers was backing away, starting to run. Brandon doubted that they could see all that he saw, but whatever they'd experienced was obviously enough.

"Brandon!" He looked across the street to see old man McPherson yelling, his thin gray hair blowing wildly. "Your father!" he shouted. "When the storm hit—I'm not sure, he still might be in there!"

The steeple exploded. Brandon turned just in time to see the cloud envelop it, spewing pieces of wood in all directions. He held out his hands to protect his face. The exposed skin of his arms and hands stung with flying splinters and rubble. He looked back at McPherson, but the old man was already gone. Lowering his head into the wind, Brandon struggled forward.

From the steeple, the cloud's vortex snaked its way across the roof toward the back of the building, where it tore out another hole and entered the church.

Brandon fought his way across the street as the trees blew wildly. Limbs snapped and cracked. A power line suddenly dropped in front of him, leaping and sparking a crazy dance on the asphalt. He veered to the right, giving it a wide berth. A minute later, he reached the church steps.

By now he had recognized something else in the howling wind. Voices. Human voices. Agonizing voices from his previous visions—crying, screaming, tormented voices—wailing voices.

He started up the steps. The wind was so strong that he had to cling to the railing. A ripping *crack* was followed by a *whoosh-thud* as a giant cottonwood crashed to the porch, missing him by mere feet. He arrived at the double doors and struggled to open them. The right one gave way. As he pulled it open, he was struck by a light so bright that it practically blinded him. Covering his eyes, he inched his way through the door and into the foyer. He could not find the source of the light, but as his eyes adjusted to the brightness he saw the same water fountain he'd seen before. It was in the center of the foyer and already bubbling red liquid. The sanctuary doors lay directly ahead. On each side there stood an olive tree and a lampstand.

Dreading to look up, but knowing he had to, Brandon raised his eyes. Above the entrance, just as he expected, hung the sign:

ENTER NOT WITHOUT THE SHIELD OF FAITH

He hesitated. He knew the warning and the implication. Worse yet, he knew that he did not qualify. But he also knew that his father was in there. Cautiously, Brandon took hold of the doors. He paused one last moment to gather his courage, and then he threw them open—

The wind inside had virtually stopped. The light was nearly normal. But at the front of the sanctuary, spiraling in through the hole in the roof, hovered the swirling cloud of contorted faces. And not six feet above the altar, these misty apparitions had tightened and condensed until they formed a distinct image—the same image Brandon had seen in his earlier vision: a giant, multihorned head.

Brandon gasped.

And there, sitting in his wheelchair, halfway down the aisle, where he had no doubt been left in the panic, sat his father. Brandon knew that if the poor man could see even a fraction of what he, Brandon, saw, he must be terrified.

He started down the aisle toward his father when, off to the right, he noticed movement. Another man. The Reverend. He rose from a place of protection behind the pews and started to approach the altar. He looked up at the hole in the roof but seemed totally oblivious to the cloud swirling through it, and to the monstrous head hovering just above the altar.

"Reverend!" Brandon called. "Reverend, look out!"

The Reverend turned to him, then looked back up at the roof. "I've never witnessed anything like it. The twister came, ripped off the steeple, then tore open this hole, and—"

"That was no twister!" Brandon shouted.

The Reverend shook his head. "And at this time of year, too. A single cloud with no other storm activity. I'm sure there is a natural explanation for the phenomena, but . . ."

As the Reverend talked and approached the altar, the beast's head slowly opened its mouth.

"Reverend." Brandon could barely find his voice. "Look out."

The Reverend followed Brandon's gaze to the altar but saw nothing. He was six feet away now, looking directly at the head, but he seemed totally unaware. "I'm sorry, what did you—"

Suddenly, a dense, pencil-thin mist shot from the beast's mouth. It entered the Reverend's own mouth with such force that he staggered backward, his eyes bulging in surprise. He coughed and choked, trying to catch his breath. When he finally looked at Brandon, it was with bewilderment. His hands began to shake. Then his arms. He looked down at them, confused, staring at them as if they were foreign objects. The shaking grew more violent. He looked back at Brandon, his confusion turning to fear. "What's . . . going on?"

Brandon could only stare as the man's entire body began to bounce, then to shimmy and gyrate. Now the Reverend's fear turned to horror. "Help me!" he cried to Brandon. "Please, help—"

Suddenly his head flew back, and mocking laughter echoed through the room. Brandon spun around, looking everywhere for its source—until he turned back to the Reverend and realized that the laughter was coming from the man's open mouth.

Reichner had eased his tall frame into the calfskin armchair of his living room. With some difficulty, he tucked his stocking feet under until he was sitting crosslegged. He was not pleased with what he was about to do, but he saw no alternative. The e-mail waiting for him when he had returned from Gerty's house was quite explicit:

We must talk at once. Use my God-name.

It had been forty-five minutes since his encounter with Lewis and the good Dr. Weintraub. He knew Sarah was upset over what had happened, but he also knew it wouldn't last. She was his—if not personally, then at least professionally. She belonged to the Institute; she belonged to her work. In a day or two she'd be fine, and then they would resume their pursuit of Brandon Martus.

He looked up at the computer monitor. The message still glowed:

We must talk at once. Use my God-name.

He could try answering by phone or return e-mail. But the instructions were specific. Very specific. Reluctantly, he reached up to the brushed aluminum lamp that arched over his head and dimmed it to low. He had half an hour before the pre-med from the supermarket was to show up. That should give him enough time.

He stared at the piece of paper, the one from Nepal with the so-called God-name written on it. It had worked before. At least something had happened up there in the Himalayas. But here, in Indiana, the environment was considerably different. And, to be honest, Reichner wasn't particularly thrilled about subjecting himself to the python experience again.

Still, the initial reciting of the mantra had proved relaxing. And with the current level of stress he'd been under, as well as his weak heart, it might not hurt to start practicing a little meditation from time to time. Then, of course, there was the other matter—the fiscal survival of his Institute.

He read the eight syllables of the God-name quietly, barely above a whisper. Then he read them again. They were as smooth and calming as he remembered. He closed his eyes and repeated the sounds two, four, half a dozen times, letting the syllables roll from his tongue. He shifted, trying to relax, to empty his mind of the week's events.

He repeated the syllables over and over again until, ever so softly, he heard the breeze, the delicate wind. As gentle as a baby's breath. The sensation was pleasant and relaxing, allowing him to release even more of himself to it.

As he did, the sound grew louder, melding, merging into those lovely sustained chords, the same wondrous music he had heard back in Nepal. It surrounded him, gently lifting him, welling up inside and washing over his mind, his body, his very being. Once again the light pulsed in his feet, then rippled up through his chest and into his head. Wave after gentle wave followed, until his entire body was again breathing and resonating in this lovely, euphoric rhythm. Until he was again becoming one—one with the music, one with the wind, the light. One with something far greater and vaster than he could ever imagine.

The Reverend danced, legs and arms flying in all directions like some out-of-control marionette. His laughter echoed through the room, tying an icy knot deep in Brandon's stomach.

Brandon ran the remaining steps down the aisle to join his father. Whoever had abandoned him there had at least locked the wheels so that he wouldn't roll down the gentle incline to the front. Brandon faced him, momentarily turning his back on the Reverend and the head. "It's okay, Pop, I'm here now. I'm here. Let's just hurry and get you out—"

Sensing movement, he spun around to see the Reverend's body propelled rapidly up the aisle toward him. He braced himself, preparing for impact, but the Reverend suddenly came to an abrupt halt. The man stood less than six feet away. His eyes were rolled back into his head, and his arms and legs continued their wild dance.

"I HAVE WAITED A LONG TIME FOR THIS."

The voices were multiple—just like the kid who had attacked him, just like the woman at the lab. They came from the Reverend's mouth, which opened and closed as if he were speaking, but they did not belong to him.

Brandon stiffened, recalling his past confrontations with the multiple voices—particularly the one with the kid outside the church, and later in Jenny's bedroom. He remembered the authority with which Gerty had controlled the red-headed kid that night—the same authority she kept insisting he had. The same authority he'd tried back in Jenny's room but with little success.

Unsure what to do, but left with no alternative, Brandon cleared his throat. He would try it again. "Leave him!" he shouted. "I command you to leave him, now!"

The Reverend's head shot back as more laughter filled the sanctuary. Then he spoke. *"HE DOESN'T EVEN BELIEVE I EXIST!"*

Brandon swallowed and tried again. "I command you to leave him!"

"AND YOU BELIEVE IN NOTHING." More laughter.

Brandon steadied himself, remembering all too well how his bluff had been called back in Jenny's room. "I— I do believe." He centered his voice, trying to give it more authority. "I believe and I command you to leave. Do you hear me? I command you to leave. Leave him now!"

This time there was no response. No words. No laughter. Brandon held his breath and waited.

Gradually the macabre dancing slowed, then stopped altogether. Brandon watched, saying nothing.

At last, the Reverend's eyes rolled down. He blinked and looked about, confused and disoriented. When he saw Brandon, he frowned. "What . . ." It was a single voice now. The Reverend's voice. "What happened?"

Brandon stepped toward him. "Are you all right?" The Reverend nodded but wobbled slightly. Brandon reached out to steady him. "It was that head." He motioned back toward the altar. "It—"

Without warning, the Reverend's body twirled. His arms flew out; his right hand smashed into Brandon's face. Brandon staggered backward as more unearthly laughter filled the sanctuary.

Holding his cheek, angered at the deception, Brandon took a step forward and braced himself. "Leave him!" he shouted. "Leave him! Now!"

More laughter.

"I said, leave hi—"

Suddenly, the Reverend's body was picked up, dragged between the pews, and violently hurled against the left wall. Brandon started toward him but stopped when he noticed the beast's head leaving the altar. Its vaporous faces swirled faster as it moved up the aisle toward him. Trembling, Brandon forced himself to step back into the aisle, taking a stand between it and his father.

"Stay away!" he shouted. "Stay back!"

The head slowed to a stop. It hovered at eye level less than a dozen feet away. Brandon could see the horns clearly now. There were ten, counting the new one that had grown back—the hideous-looking one covered in moving eyes. The head did not open its mouth, yet it spoke with the same voices that had spoken through the Reverend.

"YOU HAVE NO AUTHORITY."

Brandon's heart hammered in his chest. He had tried everything he had known, everything he had seen the old woman do. And nothing had worked.

As if reading his thoughts, the head resumed its advance.

"Stay back!" Brandon ordered. "I command you to stay back!"

The voices repeated themselves. *"YOU DO NOT BELIEVE."*

"I do."

"LIAR."

Brandon pulled back a step. Then another. The creature was right.

"YOU DON'T EVEN KNOW WHO YOU ARE," the voices hissed. *"NOT THAT IT MATTERS. LOOK WHERE SUCH BELIEF BROUGHT YOUR FATHER."*

Brandon couldn't resist looking back at his father in the wheelchair. Once again the thing was right. His father had been a strong believer, and look where it got him. But as Brandon stared, something caught his attention. Was it his imagination, or were his father's vacant eyes actually registering emotion? Was it fear? Pain? He couldn't tell, but something was definitely going on inside of him.

"Brandon!"

It was his mother's voice. He spun around to see her entering from the back of the sanctuary. But before he could respond, the beast shot another stream of mist, this time to the wall opposite the Reverend. From it the human wolf of the lab experiment suddenly materialized. It crouched low, baring its teeth and snarling.

Apparently Momma saw it, too. But not the wolf. She saw something entirely different. "Jenny!" Her hand went to her mouth in astonishment; her face filled with joy. "Jenny!" She ran toward the wolf.

"Momma, no!" Brandon cried. "Momma, it's a trick!"

But she gave no sign of hearing as she raised her arms and raced toward what she thought to be her little girl.

Brandon ran along the pew toward the wall to cut her off. "It's not Jenny! Momma!"

He was barely aware of the head. Taking advantage of his distraction, it quickly moved in, rotating to his left. For a moment he couldn't see it.

And then it screamed. An unearthly roar. Agonizing voices. Blaspheming voices. A chorus of cries and shrieks so powerful that they hit Brandon's body with physical force. He fell against the pew as the beast appeared at his left. The voices pushed him, forcing him to stumble, to stagger along the pew until he fell back into the center aisle just a few feet from his father's chair.

The assault had begun.

The head continued rotating until it was behind him. Brandon struggled to his feet but the voices were too loud, their hatred too strong. They blasted him with an even greater barrage of screams and obscenities. The impact threw him off balance, sending him staggering down the aisle. The beast pursued, pushing and driving him toward the front of the church. Brandon turned to confront it, but another blast threw him backward, stumbling, falling, until the back of his head struck the hard ashwood altar with a sickening thud.

This time he did not rise.

When he opened his eyes, he saw through a blurry haze. The beast's head hovered fifteen feet away, in the center of the aisle, staring directly at him. Off to the left stood his mother, apparently torn between running to help him or running toward her daughter . . . until the head rotated, opened its mouth, and shot another stream of vapor toward the wolf. Suddenly a wall of flames ignited and surrounded the animal.

"Momma!" the wolf screamed in Jenny's voice. "Help me, Momma! Help me!"

"Jenny!" Momma ran toward the animal. But the wall of fire was too tall and too thick. Brandon understood. It was merely a decoy—something to keep his mother occupied, to keep her from interfering during the real showdown.

Now the head turned its full attention to Brandon. Slowly, menacingly, it started its approach. Brandon tried to clear his vision, to move his body, but nothing would cooperate.

The thing was ten feet away when something caught Brandon's attention—a glint, a moving reflection, behind the vaporous head. He squinted, trying to clear his vision. Then he saw it. It was his father's silver-and-turquoise wristwatch. The one he'd given him so many years before. But why was it—and then he had his answer. The watch was moving. To be more precise, his father's hand was moving, just enough to catch and reflect the light. Was it possible? Was his father actually moving his hand?

"YOU ARE MINE."

Brandon focused back on the approaching beast. It was eight feet away, its mouth opening wider. And now, for the first time, Brandon could see into its throat. To his astonishment, it was not a throat but a swirling, glowing pit. A spinning whirlpool of fire that stretched as far as the eye could see. A whirlpool that created a tremendous wind, a vacuum so strong that it began sucking in all of the surrounding air. Hissing, howling wind rushed into the creature's mouth. Brandon could feel his hair, his clothes being drawn toward it.

And still the beast approached. The wind pulled harder until Brandon felt his body starting to move. Just as in the experiment at the Institute, the current was attempting to drag him toward it. Toward the mouth. Into the throat.

He struggled to get to his feet, but his unsteadiness coupled with the powerful wind made it impossible. He was sliding toward it faster now. He had to stop himself, he had to grab something. But there was nothing except the altar behind him. Twisting around, he grabbed the nearest corner. It was smooth and slick. His grip wouldn't last long, but it was all he had.

The beast closed in. Brandon tried not to look over his shoulder into its throat, but he couldn't help himself. The swirling fire went on forever. And now he saw faces. Human faces. The same tortured, burning faces that had surrounded him when he was tumbling in the experiment, when he was falling into the fiery void. The same terrifying, burning, screaming faces.

Once again he caught a glimpse of a reflection. Behind the head. The moving reflection of his father's watch. His father's hand was trembling and shaking as it continued to inch its way forward.

The operating lights illuminated Sarah's shaved head in an unearthly glow. Dr. Hibdon could have waited for the neurosurgery team to come in from South Bend, or they could have evacuated her to Fort Wayne. But the CT scan had confirmed his suspicion of an acute subdural hematoma. They'd already run the Glasgow Coma on her. She'd not scored well. It was a judgment call, but Hibdon was a competent surgeon and seconds counted.

He picked up the stainless steel scalpel from the tray. "All right, let's see what we can do for her," he said as he reached down to the marked incision site on her skull.

That was when the EKG went off.

The doctor's eyes shot up.

"She's arrested!" a voice called from the right.

Hibdon leaned past a nurse to see for himself. The green line on the oscilloscope had dropped. There was no tracing. It was smooth and flat.

"Check her leads," he said.

"Leads okay," the voice replied.

"Give her a milligram of Epi," he ordered. "Bring in the paddles."

The team moved into action.

"Give me two hundred joules."

The creature's mouth opened wider. The swirling abyss of fire and faces pulled harder; the tug on Brandon's feet and legs was relentless. He clung to the edge of the altar, but his handhold was too weak. He was already beginning to slip.

And then he saw the wheelchair. It had started down the incline. Somehow, his father had moved his hand far enough to release the brake. Now he was rolling down the aisle directly toward them.

"YOU ARE MINE," the voices in the throat shrieked.

The chair rolled toward them. It was heading straight for the back of the beast's head! So that's what his father was up to. He was trying to stop it!

Brandon's grip on the altar was nearly gone.

"YOU ARE—"

And then the wheelchair struck. But instead of slamming into the head, it passed through the vaporous back and entered it!

The creature roared in surprise. It shrieked and screamed. It pitched its head back and forth, but Brandon's father and the chair remained inside. For an instant Brandon saw the man's eyes. They were wild with fear. But they showed no more fear than the eyes of the beast. It was clear that his father's presence was inflicting pain—but not just his presence. Brandon guessed that it also had something to do with his faith. A faith that had been trapped inside a lifeless body for six years, but a faith that was finally being released—and doing some extensive damage in the process.

As the creature writhed, his father was thrown from side to side. The beast's screams grew to a shrieking resonance that vibrated the entire church. Above, the light fixtures began to crack; some shattered into a rain of glass. On the front wall, behind the cross, the organ pipes began to explode. One after another—fiery, popping explosions. And still the shriek continued. The supports holding the cross vibrated until they shook loose and the entire structure broke from the wall. With a groan, it toppled forward. Spotting it, Brandon rolled out of the way just as it crashed to the floor, missing him by inches.

Thanks to his father's attack, the wind had momentarily lessened, giving Brandon the time he needed to struggle to his feet. But he'd barely risen before he heard:

"YOU ARE MY DEEPEST DISAPPOINTMENT."

He looked up to see his father standing, floating inside the beast's head just a few feet away. The chair had already been flung to the ground, and the man hovered before his son.

"YOU HAVE ALWAYS BEEN A DISAPPOINTMENT."

The words hit Brandon hard. Part of him knew that they were coming from the creature—that his father had put up a gallant fight but had been overcome. Still, the other part of him knew that the man standing before him was his father, that he was finally speaking to him after so many years of condemning silence. And that the words he spoke were the very words Brandon had known he would say, had feared his father had been thinking for all of these years.

Brandon's response was faint and trembling. "Pop—"

"YOU ARE NOT MY SON."

The indictment brought instant tightness to Brandon's throat. It was nearly impossible to speak. "Pop, please. Please don't say—"

"MY SON WAS TO BE A LEADER. TO EMBODY MY FAITH."

"I do. I have faith. I—"

"LIAR!"

The accusation made Brandon's legs weak. He took half a step back, trying to regain his balance as tears sprang to his eyes.

"FAITH DOES NOT DESTROY."

"Poppa, I swear to you. I believe!"

"YOU ARE DESTRUCTION. YOU HAVE DESTROYED JENNY, SARAH—ALL THAT YOU TOUCH!"

The words hit with such force that Brandon gasped. He tried to catch his breath, but couldn't. "Please. I—"

"YOU ARE DESTRUCTION. ALL THAT YOU TOUCH, YOU DESTROY."

The ache in Brandon's throat was agonizing, his breathing impossible. Everything his father said was true. And that truth was relentless, powerful, devastating. Slowly, he dropped to his knees. He was no longer able to stand.

And still the onslaught continued.

"YOU ARE NOT FAITH. YOU ARE DESTRUC-TION."

"I . . ." He could no longer look up. "I belie—"

"YOU BELIEVE NOTHING!"

"I do." Brandon's voice was barely a whisper. "I . . ." He felt his body shudder. It was an escaping sob.

"YOU BELIEVE NOTHING. YOU HAVE NO PURPOSE. YOU ARE NOTHING."

Brandon choked, trying to talk. "I . . ." But he could not. There was another sob. Then another. Deep, gut-wrenching. His father was right. He *was* a failure, he *was* nothing. Whatever fraction of faith he might have had before his father's words, was gone. It was all gone.

"I'm . . . sorry."

"YOU BELIEVE NOTHING!"

Brandon lowered his head, silently weeping, nodding in agreement. He was remotely aware of his father's body being tossed to the floor like a rag doll. He knew that it had served its purpose. The beast had used it to break him . . . and it had succeeded.

Brandon remained on his knees. He did not look up. He sensed the beast approaching. He could feel the wind increasing, pulling harder. But he no longer cared. What was the point. This was his fate; this was what he deserved.

The wind grew, pulling with greater and greater force. Brandon was moving now, being drawn toward the open mouth, toward the swirling flames of the throat. But it did not matter. He no longer cared.

CHAPTER 17

Sarah's body lurched under the electrical paddles. The doctor looked at the monitor. The line remained flat.

"All right, give me 370."

The male nurse manning the crash cart nodded and reset the calibrations. He was new—tall and gangly with a steel prosthesis for a left hand. He had spoken only a few words, but Dr. Hibdon recognized them as British. Lower middle class.

An intern placed the paddles back on Sarah's chest, one near the sternum, the other just past the nipple. "Clear," he called.

The body leaped.

The alarm continued to sound.

The open mouth filled Brandon's vision, the swirling abyss of flames and faces were all he could see. Still on his knees, he instinctively leaned back. It was more reflex than resistance and it did little good, except to free his feet and legs. They were the first to be sucked into the mouth. He watched in terror as the howling wind pulled them into the throat. The heat and flames ignited his pants with a pain so excruciating that all he could do was scream . . . and scream. He spun onto his stomach and tried to crawl away, but the wind was too great. He clutched at the carpet in a vain attempt to slow himself, but there was nothing for his fingers to grip; their tips burned raw dragging across the coarse fabric.

To his left he saw a pew, the very one he and his mother had sat in for so many years. He lunged toward it, grabbing the base, and hung on fiercely. The pain in his burning legs hardened his grip to iron. But it made no difference. For the pew itself began to move. He was dragging the pew right along with him into the mouth.

"No!" he screamed, searching for another handhold. Something heavier. Anything. There was only the fallen cross. It had wedged itself against the altar with the crossbeam jutting out toward him. It was close enough for Brandon to grab, but he had no assurance that it would be any more stable than the pew.

The burning pain exploded around his waist, igniting his shirt, the flames eating into his back and belly. Over half of his body was in the throat now. He grew lightheaded; his consciousness started to shut down. Pain was everywhere and nowhere. It would be easier to just—

"Brandon!"

His senses sharpened. It was Sarah's voice. It was softer than the tormented screams surrounding him, softer than the screams coming from his own mouth, but somehow it was closer, clearer.

"Help me," she whispered, *"Brandon . . ."*

"Sarah?" he groaned.

"You must believe."

"Sarah!"

"Believe."

The plea was unmistakable but confusing. Believe what? Believe in himself? He'd already proven the futility of that. Gerty had been wrong. He had no authority. He had no power. He had—

"Believe!"

"What!" he cried. "Believe in what?"

Desperately, he turned his head in every direction. There was nothing he could believe in, nothing to hold on to. Nothing but the flames dancing around the edges of his vision. Nothing but the pew that served no purpose, and the cross wedged behind the—

"Believe!"

No. She couldn't possibly mean the cross. Yes, he could reach out and grab it, he could take hold of the horizontal beam stretching toward him. But there was no promise it would hold.

"Believe."

Was that what she meant? To grab the cross and believe that it would hold? Even now, the irony wasn't lost on him. Once again, that foolish symbol of death was offering help. The very icon that had mocked him since childhood, the perfect representation of all that was hopeless and foolish and futile was again before him—testing him, taunting him, offering its meaningless help.

"Believe."

"I can't!" he shouted—and then screamed as fire enveloped his shoulders, lapping around his neck. He closed his eyes. He wanted to pass out, to put an end to it. But he couldn't. He looked back at the cross one last time—and, despite the pain and the difficulty in breathing, he gasped. For there, on the beam of the cross, was a hand. A human hand lashed to the wood. It hadn't been there a second ago. It had never been there.

And it was alive.

The hand was covered in blood, but its fingers were moving—stretching, reaching out. Stretching toward him!

Of course. What did he expect? This would be his final hallucination. The perfect, mocking end to all of his suffering.

But it looked so real.

No! And even if it was true, even if it was real, even if he did reach out to it, he would have to let go of the pew. And the wind was too strong, the power too intense. He would be sucked away before he ever made contact.

"Believe . . ."

The hand stretched, reaching. Urging. Brandon was no fool. He knew whose hand it was supposed to be. But he also knew how he'd rejected it in the past. How he'd scoffed at it—and worst yet, how he had remained indifferent to it. Even if it was *the* hand, it wouldn't accept him. Not now, after all he'd done. Not after all that he'd become.

And then he saw something else. Through the blood on the hand he saw the open wound. The gaping hole in the center of the palm. It *was* the hand. The hand with the hole. The hand with the perpetual wound. The hand that received its scar because . . .

Sunday school verses rushed in. Songs and sermons and prayers. Memories of why that hand had been wounded. Not because of Brandon's faith or success. It had been wounded because of his doubts and failures. Wounded for his defeats, not his victories. And now it was reaching out to him.

"Believe . . ."

But if he let go of the pew, if he let go of his only security and grabbed the hand, how did he know that *it* would take hold of *him?* It had every reason to ignore him, to reject him, to let him perish. That was, after all, what he deserved.

But there was the open wound—and its promise of forgiveness.

"Believe . . ."

The fire had burned through his skin, igniting flesh and muscle, organs and bones. He had to decide, and he had to decide now.

But he couldn't.

And that, he suddenly realized, was in itself a decision. If he refused to reach out, wasn't that his decision? The skin of his face ignited in the intense heat, searing his mouth, obliterating his vision.

"Believe . . ."

Finally, with a scream from the depths of his doubt and agony, Brandon let go of the pew and lunged for the hand.

But it did no good.

Just as he'd feared, the hand failed him. He was sucked into the throat. He screamed one last time as the fire roared into his mouth, down his own throat, burning his lungs, every inch of his body consumed in flame, everything but his outstretched hand—when suddenly, something gripped that hand. Brandon couldn't grip back—he didn't have the strength. But something was holding on to him firmly, around his wrist.

And it was pulling.

Rapidly. Steadily.

The fire disappeared around his face. He didn't have the courage to open his eyes, but he felt the flames recede from his lungs, his throat, his mouth. He gulped in cooler, soothing air. His head and neck were out, followed by his shoulders and chest, then his stomach. He still didn't have the strength to hang on, but he didn't have to. He knew the hand was holding him. Its grip was firm, and it would not let go.

The cool air hit his waist, then his legs as he continued to emerge. Finally he opened his eyes, looking down just in time to see his feet exiting the mouth. And still the pulling continued. He tilted back his head to look at the cross. It was several feet closer to the front wall than he remembered. But that wasn't the only surprise. Because now it was empty. There was no hand. There was only the cross.

Then the pulling stopped. Brandon lay on the carpet, gasping for breath. The screams and the howling wind behind him slowly subsided. He twisted around to see. The horned beast had closed its mouth and had pulled away several yards.

Brandon looked back at the cross. There was only the wood and his own hand reaching out. And yet, even though he didn't see it and didn't feel it, he knew that it was still there. He knew that the hand was still there, and he knew that it would not let him go. It would never let him go.

Maybe this sense of knowing was faith, maybe it was something else. He wasn't sure. All he was sure of was that the knowing didn't come from him. It wasn't something he'd imagined or worked up.

"*He* is the author of faith," Gerty had told him. "Not you. You need only surrender."

Is that what he'd done? Simply given in, simply stopped trying and given up? Could it really be that easy?

There was no time for reflection. Another sound had replaced the wind. It had started off softly enough, then quickly grew in intensity. Brandon turned, looking back around the church, but he saw nothing except the beast's head—and his mother. She still stood to the left, but there was no longer any sign of her daughter or the wolf or the flames. The illusion had abruptly disappeared, leaving her confused and disoriented. But only for a moment. Suddenly her attention was drawn up toward the ceiling.

On the other side of the church, Brandon saw the Reverend slowly rising to his feet. He was also looking up, staring toward the roof.

Brandon followed their gaze. There, at the apex of the ceiling, a brilliant light was emerging through the rafters. It didn't damage the structure; it simply passed through it. And as it approached, the roar grew louder. But instead of wind, it sounded like water. Like a giant waterfall, pounding, thundering, filling the entire church with its presence.

The beast's head quickly turned inside itself, inverting, until it faced the opposite direction—away from Brandon and toward the blinding brightness. But the brightness really wasn't a light. It was something more. A quality. A purity. A purity so intense that it generated the brightness.

Brandon had seen this same purity before. Back in the lab, during the experiment. This is what had saved him, what had guided him back through the floor of the lab and into his body. He shaded his eyes and squinted into the brilliance. Yes, there were the four spinning wheels he had seen earlier, and the thousands of all-searching, all-knowing eyes. But he saw something else this time. Amidst the brightness he caught glimpses of what looked like faces. Four of them—some human, some animal. Between the four spinning wheels were blinding flashes, a lightning that arced back and forth between the wheels and between the faces. And, at the very center, between these wheels, was a form so excruciatingly bright that it was absolutely impossible to look at.

A voice sounded. It didn't speak; rather, it resonated through every object in the room, as if the molecules themselves vibrated with its power.

"DEPART."

It took several seconds for the sound to fade. When it had, the beast raised its head and spoke to the light—though its mouth never moved. *"HE IS MINE."*

The room responded:

"DEPART. HIS TIME HAS NOT YET COME."

The head did not answer. It could not. The command had been given, and it had no choice but to obey. Slowly, purposefully, the brilliant purity rose back through the roof. It took several seconds for it to disappear, and even after it was gone its presence seemed to linger. The roar took even longer to recede as everyone, including the beast, looked up in awe.

Finally, the head moved. Brandon tensed as he watched it turn and invert upon itself to once again face him.

"OUR BUSINESS IS NOT YET FINISHED."

Brandon swallowed. He was too frightened to speak, and wasn't sure what he'd say if he could. He looked at Momma, then at the Reverend. They had both started toward him. Apparently neither could see the creature, though it was directly in front of them. He began to call out, to warn them, but stopped. Something was happening to the head. It had started to dissipate. The mouth, the horns, everything was growing less distinct. Details faded, dissolved, until the entire creature had become a nebulous cloud.

"Brandon," Momma called. "Sweetheart, are you all right?"

The closer the two approached, the less defined the cloud became until it was nothing but a mist that wisped and swirled, then disappeared altogether as Momma and the Reverend passed through it in their rush to him.

Something wasn't right. Dr. Hibdon had ordered that they increase the wattage from 200 to 370. But the patient's body had convulsed exactly as it had the first time. There was no difference. A less experienced surgeon might not have noticed, but Hibdon did.

"You gave her 370?" he called over the sound of the alarm.

The male nurse checked the cart. "Yes, sir."

A small trickle of sweat started down the doctor's temple. Over the years he'd seen dozens, perhaps hundreds of hearts resuscitated. The reaction of the body varied slightly, but never like this. This was not how a body responded to 370 watt-seconds of electricity surging through it.

"You're sure it's set at 370?" he repeated.

Without looking at him, the nurse shifted slightly. "Yes, sir, 370."

Hibdon frowned and glanced at the intern holding the paddles. He gave him a motion to check. The intern nodded and leaned past the nurse to see for himself. He did not answer immediately.

"Doctor?" Hibdon asked irritably.

"It's set at 150," the intern answered.

Hibdon scowled and the male nurse with the steel prosthesis immediately protested. "That's impossible. I—"

"See for yourself," the intern pointed.

"Set it to 370!" Hibdon barked. "We have a woman in asystole here!"

"It *is* set at 370," the nurse protested. "The calibrations on this machine are wrong. I've made the correct compensation—"

"Nurse! Set it at—"

"But—"

"Set it at 370 and leave the room."

The team froze.

The alarm continued and the nurse blinked. "Excuse me?"

"You heard me," the doctor ordered. "I don't know who you are or what you're pulling, but you're out of here."

The nurse held his gaze a fraction too long. There was no missing his animosity. Hibdon looked at the intern. "Set it at 370 and call security."

There was a shuffle of feet, a commotion as the nurse turned and stormed out of the room. Hibdon wasn't sure what had happened, and he had no time to think about it. Later, he'd find out where the nurse came from and how such incompetence wound up on staff, but not now. He glanced down at his patient.

"370?" the intern called to verify.

"Does everybody have a hearing problem?" Hibdon demanded.

"No, sir—370 joules."

Hibdon watched as the paddles were again placed on the woman's chest.

"Clear."

There was a quiet thud and the body convulsed—this time far more violently, as every muscle contracted, arching the body grotesquely while the electricity surged through it.

The alarm stopped.

"She's back," the intern called. "We've got a rhythm."

Hibdon nodded, then refocused his attention on the brightly lit skull.

CHAPTER 18

The music had swelled, completely enveloping Dr. Reichner. It had lifted him and filled him with indescribable peace. He was floating, now, in a deep, beautiful crimson. For how long, he didn't know. But with each passing moment, he became more of the music, more of the crimson, more of the peace. They had truly become one. Inseparable. Everything had become him and he had become everything.

Finally, from within the center of the music, from within the center of himself, he heard the voice:

Good evening, Dr. Reichner.

He recognized it instantly—the juvenile timbre, the attempt at speaking with a maturity beyond its years.

Slowly, Reichner opened his eyes. To his surprise, he was not in his living room. Nor was he in Nepal. Instead, he was perched on the tallest structure of Bethel Lake, the water tower in the park. He looked around. He was still sitting cross-legged, but at the very top of the tower. Leaning one way or the other would send him toppling down the side of the steel and aluminum sphere. But he felt no anxiety. Peace still permeated him, filling everything—the trees, the distant buildings, the moon, the passing clouds. They were all one, created from the same atoms, the same stardust. He was them and they were him. Everything was one . . . including the python curled up at his feet.

You have failed us.

Immediately Reichner's peace began to drain. The boy guru sounded cold, angry.

You have all failed us.

Reichner watched as the python raised its head, beginning to weave and bob. It flicked its tongue in and out, again and again. He thought of ending the encounter, of forcing himself to wake. But there had been so much peace. And he wasn't about to be intimidated, not by some kid—and not when it came to the financial support of his beloved Institute.

It is not over yet, Reichner answered, doing his best to sound in control.

You are wrong.

There was a finality about the statement, a detachment that made Reichner even more uneasy. Maybe he *should* end it—but on his terms, when it was clear he was in charge.

The python drew closer. The boy guru's voice became more agitated. *He has entered his season.*

The python touched Reichner's left stocking-covered foot. Instinctively, the man pulled it back. But not too far—after all, he was balanced high on the pinnacle of the water tower. He felt his heart starting to pound. He resented the rising fear. After all, he could play anybody, especially a child. He swallowed, trying to sound calm and poised. *Then we will try another approach.*

The python's tongue darted in and out even more quickly. It stretched its head out farther until it actually rested on Reichner's foot. It took all of Reichner's willpower to hold back a shudder. But he would not back down; he would not show his fear.

As if reading his resolution, the snake's head moved across his ankle. It drew up the rest of its body as it slithered across his leg and up toward his lap.

His body rigid with fear, Reichner could only watch, swallowing back his revulsion. It was time to end the encounter.

The head arrived in Reichner's lap and began coiling in the rest of its body to join it. Child or no child, money or no money, it was definitely time to end this encounter. Reichner clenched his eyes shut and then, with a jolt, forced them to open.

But he was still on the water tower. And the python was still drawing its body onto his lap. Its tongue darted and flickered even more quickly. Reichner was breathing harder now. His heart pounded faster.

You have failed us, the boy guru repeated. *You have all failed us, and now we must start again.*

Reichner tried to swallow, but his mouth was desert-dry as the python finished pulling its fifteen-foot body onto his lap. The weight was enormous, far more than he had imagined.

Once again he tried to end the vision. Once again he clenched his eyes, tightened his entire body, and forced himself to jerk awake.

Once again he failed.

We have lost him and you will pay.

There it was—the phrase from his dream, from his e-mail. His heart raced. He wondered whether the creature could feel the pulse throbbing through the arteries in his lap. Perhaps its acute hearing could detect the pounding in Reichner's own ears—a pounding that had grown so rapid that it was nearly impossible to distinguish the individual beats.

Again he tried to take the offense. *I'm afraid you are jumping to conclusions.* But his voice was thin, no longer able to mask his fear. His heart pounded so hard and fast that it was growing difficult to breath. He reached his hands to the roof behind him and tried to scoot out from under the creature.

But the snake was far too heavy. He was pinned, unable to move, which only increased his panic.

We have lost him and you will pay.

The thing slowly raised its body. Reichner watched in fear as it rose until its head was level to his chest. It came no farther, staring at the center of his chest as if concentrating. All the time its tongue flicked faster and faster, almost in rhythm to his—wait a minute. Was it possible? Those flickings, those rapid dartings of the tongue, in and out—they were in perfect synchronization to his heart. Of course, they were still one. He was the moon, the trees, the boy, the python, and they were him. And yet . . . no. The thing wasn't matching his heart rate. That wasn't it at all. It was *controlling* his heart rate. The faster the tongue flicked, the faster his heart pounded.

Reichner broke into a sweat. He realized the boy would know about his heart condition. There were records, his hospitalization, the weakened muscle. And if he knew all that, and if he could control his pulse—

Reichner was finding it more and more difficult to breathe. He was beginning to pant, fighting for air.

At last the creature quit staring at his chest. Now it rose up, passing his throat, his chin, its tongue flicking faster and faster. In a moment they were eye to eye. Face-to-face. Just inches apart. Reichner's panic turned to terror. His chest began to cramp. The pain spread into his shoulder.

But the yellow, black-slit eyes would not move. They remained staring coldly into his own. The tongue, a blur of movement, faster and faster and faster. *We have lost him, and you will pay.*

Reichner's pantings became short, ragged gasps. The pain spread, searing into his neck, cramping his left arm. He was sweating profusely. Gasping and aching and sweating.

Again he tried to force himself awake. Again he failed.

He leaned away, as far back as possible.

The python drew closer until, unbelievably, its whirring tongue began to lightly brush Reichner's lips.

The man stared, wide-eyed, his chest exploding in pain. If he could just get away, pull back. If he could just—

The python lunged. But not toward Reichner. Rather, it lunged away from him, off him, purposefully removing its weight from his lap. The movement startled Reichner, making him pull harder.

And that was his mistake.

With the weight gone, Reichner was off balance. Before he could catch himself, he tumbled backwards onto the steep decline. He tried to turn, to stop himself, but only succeeded in twisting sideways as he began to roll.

His heart thundered in his ears as he rolled three, four, five times before running out of roof.

And then he fell.

If he managed to scream, he didn't hear it. Not over the roar of his heart. And the pain, the unrelenting, excruciating, exploding pain. Now there was only the pain and the roaring and the eternal falling. The falling . . . falling . . . falling . . .

Momma threw her arms around Brandon and began to weep. Even though he was exhausted he held her, feeling her body shudder as she clung to him. He caught sight of the Reverend. The man was kneeling beside his father, who lay on the ground where he'd been tossed. Gently, Brandon freed himself from Momma, took her hand, and crossed with her to join him.

"Poppa?" Brandon called softly as he knelt. "Poppa." He reached out and picked up the man's hand. He pressed it to his face. "Oh, Poppa . . ."

Then, to Brandon's amazement, he felt movement—the hand was beginning to tremble, struggling to move. He looked down into his father's face. The old man's eyes had opened. Now they were staring at his hand, using every ounce of willpower to move it.

"Poppa?"

Brandon loosened his grip and watched as the hand slowly opened. He glanced at his mother, who knelt on the other side. She was looking on with equal astonishment.

The hand opened now, stretching its fingers. To him. Much like the hand on the cross. Brandon pressed it to his lips and kissed it. He closed his eyes against the tears spilling onto his face. When he reopened them, he saw moisture in his father's own eyes. And the lips—his father's lips were starting to quiver.

At first Brandon didn't understand. Then he realized his father was trying to speak. He leaned over and listened. There was nothing but a faint wheezing crackle. Then he heard it. It was dry and raspy, not even a whisper, but it was a word.

"Son."

The tears came faster. It was true, then. He was his father's son. Even when he had failed. Even in the disappointment. He was still his son.

Brandon wiped his face as he sat back up and looked lovingly down at his father, at the faint smile on the man's lips. But there was no longer an expression in his father's eyes. Now they stared off and away. Frozen, vacant.

"Robert!" Momma cried. "Robert, don't go!" She leaned forward, shaking his shoulders. "Robert! Robert, come back!" She began to sob. Brandon looked on sadly as she threw herself onto his chest, crying. He'd had no idea how fiercely she still loved him.

They stayed that way, for how long Brandon didn't know. But when he finally looked up, he saw people—firemen, paramedics, members of the congregation—cautiously entering the building. Another moment passed before he slowly rose to his feet. He looked down one last time at his father, at the faint smile on his lips. Then at his mother, still crying. He exchanged looks with the Reverend, who nodded and gently took Momma's shoulders, helping her to her feet. A moment later she was in his arms, sobbing.

As the paramedics moved in, Brandon turned to survey the church. Everything was a mess. Broken glass, strewn debris. Behind him, the cross lay on the ground exactly where it had fallen. Exactly where it had saved his life. How much of it had actually happened and how much of it had been a vision, he didn't know. But he did know that it was real. All of it. A "superreality," that's what Reichner had called it, and that's what he had experienced.

Dazed and weak, Brandon started up the aisle. More people were entering, many of them heading to the front. Some spoke, most simply stared. He'd nearly reached the back doors when Frank and Del appeared. Not far behind them trailed a silent and very meek Henderson, his right arm in a sling, his wrist bandaged.

Brandon slowed to a stop. Frank was the first to break the silence. "You all right, buddy?"

Brandon looked at him. Even though Frank sounded concerned, Brandon saw something else—sensed it, really. In Frank's eyes, in his voice, he sensed an anger. A hurt and an anger. How odd. They'd been friends all of these years, and Brandon had never seen it before. Not like this. Until that moment, he'd had no idea the kind of rage Frank held inside.

"Bran?"

Brandon blinked, then slowly nodded to the question. The three of them stood another moment. But no other words could be found. Somehow things had changed. Things had changed, and Brandon suspected that this would be their last conversation for a very long while.

He turned and started back up the aisle toward the doors. Henderson stepped aside to let him pass, but Brandon hesitated. Henderson shifted uneasily under his gaze. Brandon sensed his shame, but he sensed something else as well. There was a goodness here. He knew that there was nothing he could do to take away the pain of Henderson's guilt. But, just as he had sensed Frank's rage, he now sensed there was something he could do for Henderson. For the physical pain, for the pain in his arm.

It was an odd impulse, but slowly, tentatively, Brandon stretched out his hand toward the arm. Henderson watched, shifting uncomfortably, throwing a nervous look at Frank and Del.

When Brandon's hand finally touched the arm, Henderson flinched. Not in pain, but in uncertainty. He looked up at Brandon but didn't move. Slowly, Brandon felt a heat spread through his fingers and into his palm. Henderson must have felt it, too, for he watched in amazement. The heat lasted only a few seconds. When it faded, Brandon removed his hand. He looked up at Henderson, who reached over with his good hand to rub his injured arm, then squeeze it. Carefully, he pulled it from the sling, holding it up in amazement, wiggling his fingers, checking for pain. There was none. He looked back at Brandon, speechless.

Brandon gave a reassuring smile. He knew that it had been healed.

And with that knowledge came yet another insight. Somebody else, another person, needed his help. Without a word, Brandon turned and made his way through the crowd and toward the exit.

Melinda Hauser knocked on the townhouse door a second time. She saw lights on inside, but there was no answer.

"You sure you got the right address?" Robin asked.

Melinda glanced down at the business card in her hand. The back read "1223 Ramona Drive." The doctor had written it down earlier that morning while they had stood in line at the grocery store. And that was the address they now stood in front of. As a pre-med student visiting her aunt for the summer, Melinda had heard plenty about Moran Research Institute, and she was more than a little interested. But she knew that this Reichner fellow wasn't only intrigued by her ESP. His wandering eyes had told her that he was also fascinated by other, more obvious attributes. That's why she'd invited her friend Robin. It would be fun to listen to the man, to ask questions, to hear him tell about paranormal studies . . . and Robin's company would ensure that that was all he did.

"Try the door."

Melinda hesitated.

"Go ahead."

Melinda turned the handle. It was unlocked. She pushed it open. The entryway floor was green marble. A chandelier hung above them, and a beveled mirror faced them from the opposite wall.

"Dr. Reichner?"

No answer. They stepped inside. Melinda cleared her throat and tried again. "Doctor?"

Beyond the entryway a dim light glowed.

"Hello? Is anybody home?"

She glanced at Robin, who motioned her forward.

"Hello . . ." They eased through the entry hall and around the corner to see the living room. "Dr. Reich—"

She stopped. By the armchair, a body was sprawled out on the floor.

"Dr. Reichner!" She raced toward it. Even in the dim light, she could see that his eyes were open and frozen. The skin was ashen white. But it was the expression on his face that made her skin crawl. The mouth was open as if caught in mid-scream. And the eyes—she couldn't recall ever seeing such horror in someone's eyes.

She stooped and touched his neck. She could find no pulse, and the body was already cold.

Robin leaned past her. "Should we call 911?"

For a moment Melinda didn't respond. She was still unable to take her eyes off the tortured expression.

"Mel?" Robin repeated.

Melinda glanced up, then shook her head. "No," she said, looking back down. "No need to bother them. Not now."

As soon as Brandon joined the crowd outside, he felt something cold and wet strike his face. Then again. And again.

"It's raining," someone shouted. "Look, it's raining!"

Brandon tilted back his head. More drops splashed onto his face. He could hear excitement sweep through the crowd as the drops came down harder and faster. At last, the long, hot weeks of drought had come to an end.

Brandon lowered his head and surveyed the crowd. They were all looking up at the sky, blinking as the drops splattered on their faces. Old man McPherson had removed his hat. Some of the children started to cheer. The adults were smiling, talking; some were beginning to laugh.

"Brandon?"

He turned to see the Reverend moving down the church steps to join him. "Brandon . . ." The rain came harder now. Both were getting soaked, but neither moved to find shelter. "In there—I don't understand. What happened?"

Brandon saw something in the Reverend's eyes he had never noticed before. Fear. A fragile vulnerability. These insights, this seeing into people was growing stronger. Once again, Brandon was moved with compassion. He wished he could do something to ease the man's fear, to remove his pain as he had Henderson's. But healing an arm seemed far easier than healing a man's soul.

"I'm sure it all has a logical explanation," the Reverend continued. "But that voice from the roof. And Henderson's arm. I saw what you did to his arm."

Brandon shook his head. "I don't understand it all—but I've got some ideas."

The Reverend looked at him, waiting for more. Once again, Brandon was struck by the man's eyes, by his searching, his loneliness. Such need.

"Where are you going?" the Reverend asked.

Brandon looked over the crowd, then up the road. "To the hospital."

"The hospital?"

Brandon nodded. "I've got a friend there who needs help."

The Reverend continued to stare. Brandon offered no explanation but turned to leave.

"Brandon?"

He looked back.

"Be careful. God knows what you've gotten yourself into."

Brandon nodded slowly. "Then I guess . . . I guess I'll leave it to him to get me out."

They stood silently in the rain. There was much more to be said. Brandon could feel it. But he could also feel a sense of urgency from the hospital. Sarah was in deeper danger than he had thought. Without a word he turned, took a deep breath, and started walking. The battle was over, he knew that. But the war had barely begun. There would be other confrontations on other fronts, far more sinister and far more deadly than what he'd faced in the church. "Our business is not yet finished," that's what the beast had said.

But Brandon would be ready.

Not because he was smarter, or stronger, and not because he'd worked up some sort of synthetic, man-made faith. No, Brandon Martus would be ready simply because he now knew how to trust. It would be just as it had been on the floor in front of the altar. In all of his helplessness and ignorance and failure, he would simply reach out to the pierced hand and put his trust in it.

That was his only hope, the pierced hand. And as he continued walking into the downpour, making his way up the darkened street, Brandon knew that was all he would need.

NOTES REGARDING
REVELATION 11

I realize some of the issues in this novel are controversial. That's probably why I chose them. Like Christ's parables, good storytelling should stir up the audience, wake us from our complacency, and get us to think.

One area of disagreement may involve the two witnesses mentioned in Revelation. There are numerous interpretations of this prophecy. Some believe the two are Elijah and Moses, or Enoch and Elijah, or others. Some scholars don't even believe that the witnesses are people at all but that they are symbols of the law and the church, or the Jewish people and the church. No one is certain.

And while we're speaking of uncertainty, I've checked with Greek experts about the gender of the two prophets. According to the original language, if the witnesses are indeed individuals, one of them needs to be male. However, there is nothing in the Greek preventing the other from being female.

All in all, I hope these portions of the story will make for interesting thought and discussion. That's the excitement of finite minds trying to understand an infinite God and his inerrant Word . . . we seldom get the details of prophecy figured out until after they happen. If you disagree with the book's interpretation, that's fine. I'll probably agree with your disagreement. Again, my purpose, while staying within the boundaries of Scripture, was to stir up our thought, not dictate it. I hope it worked.

Blessings,
Bill

Now
Available

THE FACE OF GOD

BILL MYERS

Best-Selling Author of *Eli* and *Fire of Heaven* Trilogy

Softcover 0-310-22755-0

CHAPTER ONE

"Jill ..."

She gave him a brief nod, indicating that she'd heard.

"Come on," he urged, "the rest of the group is waiting."

Her brief nod was followed by a brief smile, indicating that she'd heard but was in no particular rush to do anything about it.

"Jill ..."

Another nod, another smile.

He shook his head, frustrated and amused. After twenty-three years of marriage he knew the futility of trying to hurry his wife when she wasn't interested in being hurried. He sighed and glanced around the tiny shop, one of a hundred stalls squeezed next to each other inside Istanbul's Spice Bazaar. Every inch of floor space was covered and every shelf was filled with spilling bags and open barrels of nuts, candies, fruit, seeds, pods, stems, leaves — some fresh, some dried; some ground, some whole — more spices and herbs than he'd ever seen or smelled in his life.

The aromas were dizzying, as were the bazaar's sounds and colors. A menagerie of vendors beckoning the passing crowd to "come, see my jewelry ... perfume for your lady friend ... a souvenir for your children ... beautiful key chain to ward off evil eye ... finest gold in all Turkey ... natural *pirinc*, good for much romance ... Visa, Mastercard accepted ... come, just to talk, we have some tea, my friend, just to talk."

It was that last phrase that did them in yesterday. They'd barely left the hotel lobby before a merchant was escorting them into one of the city's thousands of oriental rug shops. They'd made it clear they were not buying. The rugs were beautiful but there was no

15

room in their house nor their budget. The owner nodded in sympathetic understanding. But after two hours of chitchat, pictures of a brother who lived in America, and more than one glass of hot tea, they found themselves viewing his wares and feeling obligated to at least purchase something — which they did.

Seven hundred and fifty dollars' worth of something!

But today was another day — he hoped.

"Jill . . ."

She nodded. She smiled. And she continued talking to the leather-faced shopkeeper. The bartering was good-natured. Jill had purchased a quarter kilo of *halvah* — a deadly rich concoction of ground sesame seed and honey. She'd already paid for it, but before passing the bag to her, the old-timer tried to persuade her to buy more.

"I'm afraid it will make me even fatter," she said, pretending to pat an imaginary belly.

"A woman of your beauty, she could eat a hundred kilo and it would make no difference."

Jill laughed and the man threw Daniel a wink with his good eye, making it clear the flirting was all in fun.

Daniel smiled back. It was obvious the fellow liked Jill. Then again, everyone liked Jill. The reason was simple. Everyone liked Jill because she liked everyone. From the crankiest congregation member to the most obnoxious telemarketer, his wife always found something to like. And it wasn't a put-on. The sparkle in her eyes and delight in her voice was always genuine. Unlike Daniel, who had to work harder at his smiles and often thought his social skills were clunky, Jill was blessed with a spontaneous joy. And that joy was the light of his life. A day didn't go by that he didn't thank God for it — even as high school sweethearts, she a cheerleader, he a tall, gangly second-stringer for the basketball team. He could never figure out what she saw in him, then . . . or now. But he never stopped being grateful that she did.

As the years of marriage deepened their love, she had moved from someone who always touched his heart to someone who had become his heart. In many ways she had become his center, a constant point around which much of his life revolved. He cherished this woman. And though he seldom said it, her heart and love for others was a quiet challenge and model that he never ceased striving to emulate.

16

Yes, her love for people was a great gift — except when they were on a tight schedule, as they were now, as they always seemed to be. Because no matter how friendly you are, it takes more than a sincere smile to keep a forty-five-hundred-member church afloat.

"Jill . . ." He motioned to his watch, a Rolex. It had been presented to him by the elders for twenty years of faithful service. Twenty hard-fought years of sweating and building the church out of nothing. Originally he'd hated the watch. Felt it was too flashy for a pastor. But because of the politics involved, he'd forced himself to wear it. You don't keep a forty-five-hundred-member church afloat without understanding politics.

"This I do for you," the shopkeeper was saying. His good eye briefly darted to someone or something behind them. "I sell you one-quarter kilo and give you an extra quarter for free."

"No, no, no . . ." Jill laughed, suspecting another ploy. "Just one-quarter kilogram, that's all we need."

"No." The man's voice grew firm. "I have made up my mind."

"But we only have enough to buy one-quarter."

"This I have heard." The shopkeeper spoke faster. He turned his back to them, momentarily blocking their view. "But for you, I give a most special gift." When he turned to them, he was already wrapping it in the same slick, brown paper he had used before.

"Please," Jill said, laughing, "you don't understand."

Again the man's eye flickered to somewhere behind them. "I understand everything," he said, forcing a chuckle. "It is free. I make no joke." He dropped the item into the bag and handed it to her.

"But I can't. I mean, that is very generous, but I can't accept — "

"You must," he said, smiling. "It is the Turkish way." He glanced behind them and spoke even faster. "It is an old Islamic custom."

Jill frowned. "An old Islamic cust — "

He cut her off with growing impatience. "It is good for your soul. It will help you hear the voice of God. Go now." He waved his hands at her. "Leave my shop now. Go."

Jill glanced at Daniel, unsure what to do.

He hadn't a clue.

She turned back to the shopkeeper, making one last attempt. "Listen, I don't think you understand. We are only paying for — "

17

"Leave my shop now!" His impatience had turned to anger. "Do you not hear? Leave! Leave or I shall call the authorities!"

Jill frowned. Had she inadvertently offended him? Had she —

"Leave! *Allah Issalmak*. God keep you safe!" He turned his back on them and set to work organizing a nearby barrel of pistachios.

Again the couple exchanged glances, when suddenly two uniformed men jostled past them. In one swift move they grabbed the shopkeeper by the arms. He looked up, startled. He shouted at them but they gave no answer. He squirmed to get free but it did no good.

"Excuse me!" Jill reached toward them. "Excuse — "

Daniel grabbed her arm. "No ..."

She turned to him. "What?"

Although he wanted to help, he shook his head.

"Dan — "

"We don't know him. We don't know what he's done."

The shopkeeper shouted louder. He pleaded to the crowd but no one moved to help. The two men dragged him from the stall and out into the cobblestone street, where his shouts turned to panicked screams as he kicked and squirmed, trying desperately to escape.

Again Jill started toward him, and Daniel squeezed her arm more firmly. She came to a stop, not liking it but understanding. Off to the side someone caught Daniel's attention. He was a tall man dressed in a dark suit and a brown sweater vest. But it wasn't the clothing that attracted Daniel's attention. It was the man's focus. Instead of watching the shopkeeper, like the rest of the crowd, he was scrutinizing the two of them.

The look unnerved Daniel but he held the gaze — not challenging it but not backing down, either. The man gave a slight nod of greeting. Daniel hesitated, then returned it until his line of sight was broken by more uniformed men rushing in. They shouted at the crowd, forcing the people to step back as they began scouring the premises, rifling through the bags and barrels, tipping them over, spilling them to the ground.

When Daniel glanced back to the man in the suit, he was gone. But Daniel had an uncanny sense that they were still being watched. He leaned toward Jill and half whispered, "We need to go."

"What are they doing?" she demanded.

"I don't know but we shouldn't be here." He wrapped a protective arm about her shoulder, easing her forward.

"What are they doing?" she repeated. "What's going on?"

"I don't know." He guided her through the crowd.

"Where are they taking him?"

Daniel did not answer. Instead he continued moving them forward. He didn't look back for the man in the suit. He didn't have to. He knew he was still there. And he knew he was still watching.

*

"But, Ibrahim, with the greatest respect, the Qur'an calls for only 2.5 percent of our profit to go to the poor."

"That is correct. And now I wish for us to double that."

A palpable silence stole over the *Shura,* the council of ten men, most of whom were under the age of thirty-five. They came from various countries — Egypt, Iraq, Libya, Afghanistan, Syria, Jordan, Lebanon, Azerbaijan, and of course right there in Sudan. Each was well trained; many held degrees from universities in the West. Each was responsible for a specific operation within the organization. And now as Ibrahim el-Magd spoke, he knew each was quietly calculating the financial impact his imposed charity would have upon each of their divisions.

Abdullah Muhammad Fadi, in charge of the organization's European and American businesses, continued speaking as he reached for his laptop computer. "So by doubling it, we are changing it to . . ."

Ibrahim el-Magd already knew the figure. "Five percent of 1.8 billion increases our *zakat,* our charitable gifts, to ninety million dollars."

The silence grew heavier. Only the rhythmic beating of the overhead fan could be heard. With quiet resolve Ibrahim surveyed the *mujihadeen* sitting about the table, his dark, penetrating eyes peering into each of their souls. They were good men, devoted to Allah with all of their hearts and minds. Despite their devotion to family, they had left behind wives and children for this greatest and most holy of wars. They had given up all for this, the most final *jihad* that Muhammad himself, may his name be praised, spoke of.

19

Across the table, young Mustafa Muhammad Dahab cleared his throat. "May I ask ... may I ask why this sudden increase in charity?"

Ibrahim turned to the youngest member of the group. Mustafa was a handsome fellow who had not yet taken a wife and who, according to sources, was still a virgin, Allah be praised. He would make a great father, a great husband. More importantly, he was becoming a mighty man of God. At the moment he was in charge of managing and laundering drug money for the Russian Mafia — a one-billion-dollar operation for which their organization received twelve percent. Ibrahim did not begrudge the boy his question. He knew he merely asked what the others were thinking.

For the briefest moment he thought of sharing his vision of the night — the dream that had returned to him on three separate occasions. The dream of a face. A terrifying, blood-covered face. A face twisted with rage and fury. A face so covered in its opponent's blood that it was nearly unrecognizable. Nearly, but not quite. Because Ibrahim knew whose face it represented; he sensed it, felt it to the depth of his soul. It represented the face of God — the face of Allah as he poured out his great and final wrath upon all humankind.

Ibrahim stole a glance at Sheikh Salad Habib, his chief holy adviser. Although every man in the room had memorized the Qur'an as a boy, it was Sheikh Habib who helped interpret it in terms of the jihad. Knowing Ibrahim's thoughts, the old man closed his eyes and shook his head almost imperceptibly. Such truth as the dream was too holy to share; it would be considered blasphemy, at least for now.

Ibrahim understood and quietly raised his hand toward the table. "It is no small honor to be chosen as Allah's great and final winnowing fork. And for such honor we must all increase our devotion and our commitment. Time and time again the Western infidels have proved how power and money corrupt." He leaned forward, growing more intense. "This shall not, it *must not*, happen to us." He looked about the table. "This small gesture — what is it but merely a reminder that it is Allah and Allah alone whom we serve. Not ourselves. And if necessary, if we need another reminder, I shall raise the percentage again, to ten percent or forty percent or, if Allah wills, to one hundred percent." He lowered his voice until it was barely above a whisper. "This is the time, my friends, above all other in history. This is the time to purify ourselves. For our families. Our world. This is the time to take charge of every thought and deed, to remove every unclean desire — ensuring that all we say and think and do is of the absolute and highest holiness."

Ibrahim looked back to Mustafa. The young man nodded slowly in agreement. So did the others. He knew they would understand.

After a suitable pause Yussuf Fazil, his brother-in-law, coughed slightly. Ibrahim turned to him. They had been best friends since childhood. They had grown up together in a tiny village on the Nile. Together they had studied the Qur'an, attended Al-Azhar University in Cairo. And though Yussuf had chosen Ibrahim's sister for his younger, second wife, it did little to bring them closer — for they were already family, brothers in the deepest sense of the word.

"What about the remaining stones?" Yussuf asked. "What progress is being made?"

Ibrahim was careful to hide his irritation. His insistence that they wait until the stones were retrieved had created a schism within the council, an ever widening impatience lead by Yussuf Fazil himself. Yet despite the group's frustration, Ibrahim remained adamant. They already had four stones. They would not begin the Day of Wrath until the remaining eight were found and consulted. He turned to the group and gave his answer. "Another has been sighted in Turkey."

"Only one?" Yussuf asked.

Refusing to be dragged into yet another discussion on the issue, Ibrahim glanced at Sheikh Habib. The old man took his cue. His voice was thin and reedy from lack of use, from his many days of silent study and prayer. "It is our belief — " He cleared his throat. "It is our belief that the remaining stones will surface very, very quickly."

Ibrahim watched the group. He knew many considered this action superstitious, even silly. And because of Yussuf, he knew that number was increasing. But he also knew the absolute importance of consulting with Allah before unleashing his greatest and most final fury. Still, how long could he hold them off? Plans for the Day of Wrath had been under way for nearly four years. And now as the day finally approached, they were supposed to stop and wait? How long could he hold them at bay? A few weeks? A month? Every aspect of the plan was on schedule. They were nearly ready to begin . . .

Except for the stones.

Sensing the unrest, Sheikh Habib resumed. "There have been several rumored sightings, all of which we are pursuing. Europe, Palestine, here in Africa. It should not be long."

Mustafa Muhammad Dahab asked respectfully, "And we are certain they will enable us to hear his voice?"

The sheikh nodded. "According to the Holy Scriptures, just as they had for Moses, the twelve stones, with the two, will enable the inquirer to hear and understand Allah's most holy commands."

"And yet the additional two stones you speak of, are they not — "

The rising wail of an air-raid siren began. Tension swept across the table. Some of the Shura leaped to their feet, collecting papers; others moved less urgently. But all had the same goal — to reach the underground shelter as quickly as possible.

The compound, like many others of Ibrahim el-Magd's, was well protected by armored vehicles, tanks, antiaircraft guns. At this particular base in northern Sudan there were even Stinger missiles. Since the vowed retaliation for the World Trade Center, such precautions were necessary for any organization such as theirs.

Ibrahim rose to his feet and gathered his robes. Although he was anxious to join his wife, Sarah, and his little Muhammad in the shelter, he was careful to watch each of the Shura as they exited. He owned a half dozen camps scattered throughout the Middle East. Less than twenty people knew this was the compound where they would be meeting. In fact, to increase security, the location had been changed twenty-four hours earlier. The odds of the enemy choosing this particular time and this particular location to launch a strike were improbably high — unless there was an informant. And by watching each of the men's behavior, Ibrahim hoped to discover if any was the betrayer.

The first explosion rocked the ground, knocking out power and causing the white plaster ceiling to crack and give way. Pieces fell, shattering onto the table before him.

"Ibrahim!" Yussuf Fazil stood at the doorway, motioning in the darkness. "Hur —"

The second explosion knocked them to the ground. Dust belched and poured into the room.

"Hurry!" Yussuf staggered to his feet, coughing. He raced to Ibrahim, then used his own body as a shield to cover him as they rose. Supporting one another, they picked their way across the cluttered floor. The explosions came more rapidly as they stumbled into the dark hallway, as they joined office personnel racing toward the tunnel with its open steel door ten meters ahead. Ibrahim could see the people's mouths opening in shouts and screams, but he could not hear them over the thundering explosions.

He arrived at the tunnel and started down the steep concrete steps. The reinforced shelter lay twenty-five meters below — a shelter that security assured him could never be penetrated, even by the West's powerful Daisy Cutter bomb. The earthshaking explosions grew closer, throwing Ibrahim against one side of the tunnel, then the other. They continued mercilessly, lasting nearly a minute before they finally stopped.

Now there was only silence — and the cries of people down in the shelter. Ibrahim emerged from the stairway and joined them just as the emergency generator kicked on. Nearly forty faces stared at him, their fear and concern illuminated by the flickering blue-green fluorescents. Two tunnels entered the shelter — one from the living quarters, one from the office area. His wife and little boy had no doubt entered through the living quarters.

"Sarah!" he shouted. "Muhammad!"

He scanned the group but did not see them.

"Sarah!"

Still no answer. People started to stir, looking about.

"They were outside," a voice coughed.

Ibrahim turned to see a secretary. Her veil had fallen, revealing black hair covered in plaster dust, and a face streaked with tears. "They were outside playing when the ..." She swallowed. "They were outside playing."

Ibrahim shoved past her. He began searching the group, holding in his panic in check. "Sarah!" The people parted for him to pass. "Muhammad!"

There was still no answer. He turned and started toward the office tunnel.

"Ibrahim!" It was Yussuf's voice. "Don't go up! Not yet! It is not safe!"

He paid no attention as he arrived at the tunnel and started up the steps two at a time. Bare lightbulbs in wire cages lit his way.

"Ibrahim!"

His heart began pounding. Up above he could see the dull, hazy glow of daylight.

"Ibrahim!" The shouting persisted but he did not answer.

The higher he climbed, the thicker the dust grew. But it was not the dust of his beloved desert. No. This dust tasted of plaster and concrete and destruction. He arrived at the top of the steps and saw the steel door half twisted off its hinges. He stepped through the opening, crawling over a jagged piece of concrete as he entered the hallway. It was illuminated by dust-choked shafts of sunlight. He looked up and saw that much of the roof was missing.

"Sarah!" The dust burned his throat. He coughed violently and staggered forward. To his left was the collapsed wall of the communication center. And beyond that more daylight. He choked and gagged as he climbed over another concrete slab, slipping in the debris, splitting his shin on the broken cement. "Muhammad!" He entered the room, side-stepping fallen desks and shattered computers until he reached the gaping hole where a wall had been. "Sarah!" More coughing. He could barely breathe.

He climbed through the opening and jumped to the ground, hitting so hard that he heard his ankle snap. But he barely noticed as he continued forward, coughing, choking, limping. "Muhammad!"

Everything was eerily still except for the desert wind and ... He strained to listen. Was that a voice? "Sarah?" he called.

There it was again. A woman. Crying.

He started toward it. "Sarah ..." Limping, squinting through the dust, he continued forward until ... There! Thirty meters ahead. The color of dirt. The form of a woman kneeling with her back to him.

"Sarah?" He limped toward her.

She was weeping.

"Sarah?"

24

At last she raised her head and looked over her shoulder. His heart sank. It was just as he feared. Though the face was coated in blood and dust, he instantly recognized her. "Sarah!"

He hobbled toward her.

She held something in her arms. A form — much smaller, covered with the same blood, coated in the same dust. Then he saw the face. It was not crying. And though its eyes were open, it did not move.

The anguish leaped from Ibrahim's heart before he could stop it. *"Muhammad..."*

*

"These caves, were they not excavated first in ... what was it?" The stooped old man from the Israeli Department of Antiquities and Museums turned to his two colleagues — one a heavyset middle-ager, the other a frail thirtysomethinger.

Before either man could answer, Helen Zimmerman spoke up. She didn't mean to interrupt, but it had always been difficult for her to remain silent amid ineptness and ignorance — both apparent strong suits among these three. "It was in 1885," she answered. "And later, in the 1970s, the area was surveyed by Barkay and Kloner for Tel Aviv University's Institute of Archaeology."

The old man eyed her suspiciously. "No ... I believe the later date was 1968."

Of course he was wrong, dead wrong; it couldn't have possibly been 1968. But Helen knew she had to play the game. Though it killed her, she managed to choke out the words, "Yes, 1968 ... I believe you are right."

The old duffer nodded, pleased with his superiority.

Helen led the officials behind the altar of the Church of St. Etienne, just a stone's throw from Jerusalem's Garden Tomb and only two blocks from Damascus Gate. As she moved down the worn limestone steps into the cave's musty, cooler temperatures, she could feel their eyes watching her. At least that's what she'd anticipated. That's why she'd worn the tailor-fitted slacks and snug-fitting shirt — neither immodest enough to offend their Orthodox sensibilities but definitely enough to hold their interest. All part of the game.

They arrived at the cave's entrance hall, a fifteen-by-twenty-foot room surrounded by six burial chambers — two in the north wall, two in the east, and two in the west. She removed her baseball cap and shook back her hair, allowing the thick auburn curls to fall suggestively to her shoulders.

"And you think ..." The middle-ager coughed. It could have been from the sudden change in temperature or out of self-consciousness. Helen hoped the latter. "And you think your group can find more artifacts here?"

"I know we can," she said with a smile, holding his eyes a moment — not long enough to be flirtatious but long enough to fluster and cause him to look away.

Good, she had him. One down and two to go.

"And why exactly is that, Dr. Zimmerman?"

She turned to the old-timer. "Our resistivity meters, as well as ground-penetrating radar, indicate there are at least three more hollow spaces underneath this floor, perhaps four."

"Burial vaults?" Thirtysomethinger asked.

"Perhaps ..." She reached to the scented handkerchief about her throat, slowly working it loose. At least that was her intention. Unfortunately, she'd tied the knot just a little too tight. She pulled harder. Still nothing. *Great*, she thought. *Just great*. But that's okay, she'd improvise. She'd simply dab the perspiration at the nape of her bare neck with her long, slender fingers.

Thirtysomethinger swallowed, causing his Adam's apple to bob up and down.

She continued, pretending not to notice. "But regardless of what it may or may not be, the chances of it belonging to the First Temple Era are high — and each of us knows the rarity of such finds." She lowered her fingers to the top of her open blouse, gently wiping away the dampness. "Do we not?"

Again Thirtysomethinger swallowed.

The old-timer cleared his throat. "We can appreciate your interest in this area, Dr. Zimmerman, and your expertise. But the committee's decision to grant permission to dig here — well, it would be much easier if you ... that is to say ..."

"If I were to embrace your literal interpretations of the Scriptures?"

The old man shrugged. "There are many groups interested in the First Temple Era, and if word of your theory were to spread ..."

Helen had been expecting this move and knew it was time for the speech. The one she'd given a dozen times in a dozen such situations. "Gentlemen, as a child of Orthodox parents, I can appreciate your devotion to the Holy Word. But as I have proved in my research of Mizpah as well as my assistance at Megiddo as well as numerous other locations, there is no archaeologist more qualified, none more committed to finding truth, than myself. I am a woman of science, gentlemen, of cold, hard facts."

She gave a dramatic pause before driving in the stake.

"I have no bias. I have no agenda to prove or disprove. I am only interested in truth. That is why my work is so frequently published and why you have agreed to meet with me today. If the Scriptures are truth, then you having nothing to fear. My care and exactness will only validate their authenticity."

That was it, short and sweet. She had finished — well, except for holding the eyes of Thirtysomethinger a bit longer than necessary to make her point. Well, a bit longer than necessary to make *that* particular point. He swallowed again, giving his Adam's apple the workout of its life, then glanced away.

Two down.

Again she reached to her handkerchief, giving the knot another tug. And then another, somewhat harder — until it finally gave way, but with such force that her elbow shot out and nailed Thirtysomethinger directly below the left eye.

"Augh!" he yelled, doubling over and grabbing his face.

"I'm sorry!" she cried. "Are you all right? I'm terribly sorry. Here, let me see."

He shook his head.

"No, please. I'm so sorry. That's . . . Really, I'm so sorry." And she was. More than they could imagine. Because it always happened. Whenever the stakes were raised, whenever she got nervous, she'd inevitably come down with a severe case of . . . well, there was no other word to describe it but clumsiness. Severe, incredible clumsiness.

Of course Thirtysomethinger assured her that everything was fine. But when he was finally persuaded to remove his hand, she saw the large red mark on his cheek. She could only imagine what stories would be flying around the office about how he had acquired his shiner. It was an unfortunate setback but not the end of the world. She'd just have to work doubly hard to reestablish the mood. She had to. Because once she mended fences with Thirtysomethinger, there was still the old-timer to work on.

She stole a look over at him. The old codger would take a bit longer but that was okay. She had been playing the game for nearly a decade, ever since grad school. She knew the rules. She knew what men were like. And she knew the disadvantages of being a woman in their world. But she also knew how to use those disadvantages to her favor — even if it meant utilizing these somewhat demeaning tactics.

Now they would move deeper into the cave. In its intimacy she would share with the old-timer her deep respect for the Scriptures — and eventually confess how she looked forward to someday embracing their inerrancy as he did. Yet for now, as a scientist, she must force herself to simply look at the facts. It was all true. She never lied ... unless she had to. But it would take time. Still, the old guy would eventually join his colleagues in supporting her proposal. That's how it worked. Dr. Helen Zimmerman, University of Washington professor of archaeology, sighed wearily, almost audibly. Like it or not, that's how it always worked.

✳

Daniel Lawson sat in the tour bus parked outside their hotel and endured another verbal barrage from Linda Grossman. Boy, could that gal talk. Nine times out of ten it involved issues she thought the church needed to address. And what made it even worse was that nine times out of ten she was usually right. She was definitely a woman on a mission, which explained her going back to college for her master's degree in education. It would also explain why on two separate occasions she had applied to be their director of Christian education. Unfortunately, she was a woman, and though the position didn't involve the actual teaching of men, as the Scriptures prohibit — well, she was still a woman.

At the moment she had attached herself to one of the elderly ladies, Darlene Matthews, and was sitting with her behind him, doing her best to increase the old woman's self-esteem.

"You should see the lovely scarf she purchased, Pastor. And at such a low price. She's become quite the bargain hunter on this trip. Haven't you, Darlene?"

Darlene shrugged, the crinkled skin of her face glowing from the attention.

"Don't be so modest. Tell Pastor what the shopkeeper started off asking."

"Really, Linda," the old lady murmured, too embarrassed to speak.

But not Linda. "One and a half million lira. Can you imagine that, Pastor? They wanted one and a half million lira for one little scarf."

Daniel shook his head. "That seems a little steep." As he spoke, he noticed movement through the bus window behind them. One, then two, blue-and-white cars with *"Polis"* written across their doors slid to a stop in front of the hotel.

Linda rattled on. "That's what she thought. So she—well, go ahead, Darlene, tell Pastor what you did."

Darlene looked up nervously.

He smiled. "Please, tell me what happened."

She took a timid breath, then finally began sharing the trials and triumphs of buying a scarf in downtown Istanbul. Daniel continued to smile and tried his best to stay interested, particularly after Jill's criticism of him earlier that morning. *Not loving his congregation?* What was she talking about? After all he'd done? After all he'd sacrificed?

Still, even now as he listened to Linda and Darlene, he caught himself dropping into autopilot, uh-huhing and you-don't-saying whenever appropriate. Of course he rebuked himself. After all, he was their pastor; these details should be interesting to him. They certainly were to Darlene. And as a pastor, wasn't it his responsibility to "rejoice with those who rejoice" and "mourn with those who mourn"? Even if it was over a scarf? So why during the past few years had it become so difficult? When the congregation was one or two hundred members, his interest and compassion had come easily. But now—now that they were up to forty-five hundred, now that he had in essence moved from senior pastor to CEO—it had become next to impossible. Yet impossible or not, it was still a requirement, a command. And despite the difficulty, despite his failure, he would strive to obey it. That was Daniel Lawson's trademark. Regardless of the cost, he always obeyed.

"So I told him that the scarf was far too expensive and then I turned and I started walking away, and then he called back to me and said he would make an exception and sell it to me for only one million lira, and I said . . ."

Daniel glanced at his watch, then out the window. What was taking Jill so long? Again he tried to focus.

". . . it was still too expensive and that I really meant it. Then he said . . ."

And again he failed.

Initially Jill had been opposed to going back into the hotel. This morning the group was only going to visit the palace museum, Topkapi Sarayi. Why did she need to cover her shoulders for a museum? But Daniel was gently insistent and explained, as he often had to, that a pastor's wife needed to go out of her way to appear modest. As usual, Jill didn't see his logic and had dug in — good-naturedly, but dug in nonetheless. And it wasn't until he offered to go back to the room himself that she told him to stay put and headed off the bus to the hotel.

But that had been — he glanced at his watch — twelve minutes ago.

". . . and then he dropped the price once again to eight hundred thousand lira. Can you believe that, Pastor — eight hundred thousand lira?"

Daniel gave another nod of interest and glanced about the bus. There were forty-two of them on this year's tour. The same tour he and Jill led church members on every year — six days in Israel, one in Ephesus, yesterday and today in Istanbul, tomorrow Athens, then Rome. It was always the same, and though he knew he should be enthusiastic, though he tried to be enthusiastic, he had grown bone weary of the routine. But not Jill. No sir, she thrived on mixing with the people and getting to know them as they traveled together. She always had a great time on these things. Until last night . . .

Until the incident with the shopkeeper. Until they arrived in their hotel room, unwrapped the halvah, and discovered it wasn't exactly an extra piece of candy that he'd slipped into their bag. Instead it was a strange, rectangular-shaped stone. It was about the size of one of those complimentary bars of soap they give you in hotels. Yet it was anything but soap. By its green color, Daniel guessed that it was some type of emerald. It appeared very old and was worn smooth — so smooth that the written inscription on the front, which looked Arabic or Hebrew, had nearly disappeared.

"... and so I told him it was still too expensive and that I really didn't want to waste any more of his time, and then he said to me ..."

Daniel nodded as he reached for the stone in his pocket. Silently he ran his fingers over its smooth edges. It was obviously stolen. The cagey old merchant had simply passed it on to them to get rid of the evidence. Both he and Jill had agreed to turn it over to the authorities first thing that morning, once they got the group up and going through the museum. But the fact that it was illegal didn't bother them as much as did the dream. Jill's dream. The one that had led to her criticism about his lack of love for the congregation. The one that had caused her to cry out in her sleep, waking both of them earlier that morning ...

"It's nothing," she had said somewhat sheepishly as they lay together in the small hotel bed.

But her voice betrayed her and he persisted. "Please, tell me ..."

"It's just the excitement from that stone and the old man's arrest, that's all."

There it was again, the uneasiness. He reached over and snapped on the bedside lamp. "What was it, Hon? Tell me, what's wrong?"

She shook her head.

"Tell me," he softly persisted. "What is it?" He waited. Finally she turned to face him. That's when he saw the tears. And that's when he reached out and took her hand. Was it his imagination or was she trembling? Gently he repeated, "What's wrong ..."

She took an uneven breath. He said nothing but waited until she was ready, until she finally spoke. "It was about you."

"Me?"

She tried to smile but didn't quite succeed. "You were all decked out in some sort of holy man's garb — you know, with the robes and everything."

"Like a priest, a Catholic priest?"

"No ... fancier than that. Like one of those paintings from the Old Testament. You know, the high priest with all those robes and a turban and that vest thing in the front. And there was the stone, our stone, right near the center of the vest."

"And that was scary?"

She shook her head.

"What, then?"

She took another breath. "You were weeping. It was the weirdest thing. You couldn't stop crying. And when I asked you why, you tried to answer but couldn't. You were too overcome."

"With what?"

She wiped her face and looked at him. "With love. God's love. You were overwhelmed with his love for your congregation. It was incredible. I've never seen anything like it ... especially from you."

The last phrase surprised him. "Especially from me?"

She said nothing but glanced away. He could see that he'd stumbled upon something, and tried again. "I'm not sure what you mean. Are you saying I don't love the congregation?"

She looked down at his hand.

"What is it?" he asked.

She shook her head.

"No ... please, tell me."

She sighed, then with quiet resolve answered. "You used to love them like that, Danny ... but that was a long time ago."

"What?" He tried to hide his incredulity. "What does that mean?"

"I think ..." She paused, constructing her thoughts. "I think you love *serving* God ... and I think you love serving his people. But I don't think you really love either of them, sweetheart ... not like you used to."

The words were a shock. If he didn't love God and his people, why was he killing himself serving them all these years?

"But it's okay," she said, reaching up to his face and gently pushing the hair out of his eyes. "Because you'll get that love back, Danny Boy. He told me."

"Who?"

She smiled.

"Who, Jill?"

"The face."

"Face?"

"Of God."

Daniel blinked. "I thought you were dreaming about me as a high priest."

"I was. You were a high priest and you were wearing that stone and then it started to glow. And the brighter it glowed, the more your face ..." — she swallowed — "the more your face started to

32

twist up and contort, like you were being tortured or something. And then suddenly . . ." — she took another breath — "suddenly it was covered in blood . . . so much blood that I couldn't even recognize you, until at that instant I somehow knew. I was no longer looking at your face, but at . . . at the face of . . ."

"God?" Daniel asked.

She nodded, then answered hoarsely, "Yes. I've never seen such pain and passion. But it had also become yours — your pain and your passion. And then he spoke. And then you spoke. It was you but it wasn't you. It was like the two of you were the same . . . sharing the same face . . . the same passion. And then you spoke . . ."

Daniel hesitated, almost afraid to ask. "What did I say?"

"You said . . . you said, 'I hear his voice, Jill. I finally hear his voice.'"

"And then?"

She swallowed again. "And then I woke up."

The conversation had been nearly six hours ago, yet it continued to haunt him. The images were so strange and eerie. And the accusation. Of all she had said, it was the accusation that ate at him the most. Not love God? Not love his congregation? How could she possibly mean that?

He ran his fingers over the stone again. *"It will help you hear the voice of God,"* the old man had said. Yeah, right. More likely to give you spooky dreams and send you to a Turkish prison for possession of stolen goods. He sighed. Yes sir, the sooner they got it into the hands of the authorities —

"Pastor Lawson!"

Daniel glanced up to the front of the bus. The hotel's young desk clerk stood at the door. "Pastor Lawson . . ."

Darlene stopped her story.

"You must come!" the desk clerk shouted. "Come at once!"

Daniel rose to his feet. "What is it? What's wrong?"

"Your wife."

A cold knot gripped his stomach. "Jill?"

"Come!"

Daniel raced up the aisle to the bus door, then down the steps. "What's wrong?" he demanded. They started running along the sidewalk to the hotel. "Tell me what's wrong!"

The young man did not answer. He didn't have to — it was written all over his face. They entered the hotel and rushed through the carpeted lobby, jostling more than one patron, until they reached the brass doors of the elevator. But Daniel didn't stop. He headed straight for the stairway, throwing the door open so hard that he nearly shattered its glass window. Trim and still athletic, he took the worn marble steps two at a time. He flew around the second-floor landing, grabbing the iron railing to make the turn, and sailed up to the third floor. He burst through the door, barely winded — until he saw the other door, the open one at the end of the hall. *Their* door. Her clothes were strewn across the carpeted floor inside the room. Two or three police stood about. Suddenly it felt as if someone had punched him in the gut.

He sprinted down the hall. As he arrived, a roly-poly official with a mustache turned to block his entrance, but Daniel easily pushed past him and into the room. That's when he saw her — sprawled on the carpet between the doorway and the bed, her chest heaving, her white blouse soaked in blood.

"Jill!"

He shoved through two more officials and dropped to his knees at her side. He wanted desperately to pick her up, to hold her, but knew better.

She heard his voice and opened her eyes. They twinkled slightly in recognition.

"Get a doctor!" Daniel turned to the police. "Someone get a doctor!"

"He is on his way," the mustached man answered.

"Danny Boy ..." Her voice was a faint whisper.

"Shh. Don't move. They'll be here. They're getting some help. Don't move. You'll be okay."

She tried to shake her head but broke out coughing, wincing in pain.

"Don't move, don't move." He reached down to her belly, to the soaked, slashed shirt. A wave of nausea swept over him when he saw her stomach. He looked back to her face and forced out the words. "You'll be ..." His voice constricted. "Hang on, you'll be okay." Turning, he shouted over his shoulder, "Where's the doctor? How long's she been this way? Get a doctor!"

The men shuffled, trading glances, examining the tops of their shoes.

"I see him," she whispered.

Daniel looked back to her. "What?"

"His face." She was looking directly at him. "That awful, passion-filled face."

"Shh," he croaked. "Don't talk. Will someone get a doctor!"

"I'm going to leave now, Danny Boy." Her voice grew fainter.

He lowered his face closer. Hot tears sprang to his eyes. "No," he fiercely whispered. "You can't . . ."

"It's going to be okay."

"You can't!"

"I have to." Her voice was mostly breath now. "It's the only way."

"No. We're supposed to grow old together, remember? We're supposed to laugh at each other's wrinkles. That's the deal, remember?" He angrily swiped at his tears. "You can't leave . . . not now, not like this."

"He loves you, Danny." The words were nothing but air.

"No!" Tears splattered from his face onto hers. He tried wiping them away but only smeared the blood from his hands across her cheek.

"And you'll love him . . ."

"Stop . . . be quiet. You need your strength. Be quiet now."

"He promised. You'll hear his voice and you'll love him."

"No . . . You can't go. You're all . . . You're all I have."

"You'll have him . . ." — the words were barely audible — "soon . . ."

"No, you can't . . . You can't go . . ."

She gave him the faintest trace of a smile, part sad, part understanding.

"Listen to me . . . Listen!"

She did not respond.

"No, you can't . . . Listen to me. Listen to me!"

But she no longer looked at him. She no longer looked at anything.

"No! No . . ."

He felt hands taking his shoulders. They tried pulling him away.

He fought them. "She'll be okay. She's just . . . She'll be all right . . ."

The hands continued to pull.

"She's okay." He looked up at them, images blurred by tears. "She's just . . . Where's the doctor! Somebody get a doctor!" He turned back to her. "Jill!" And still they pulled, beginning to drag him away. *"Jill . . ."*